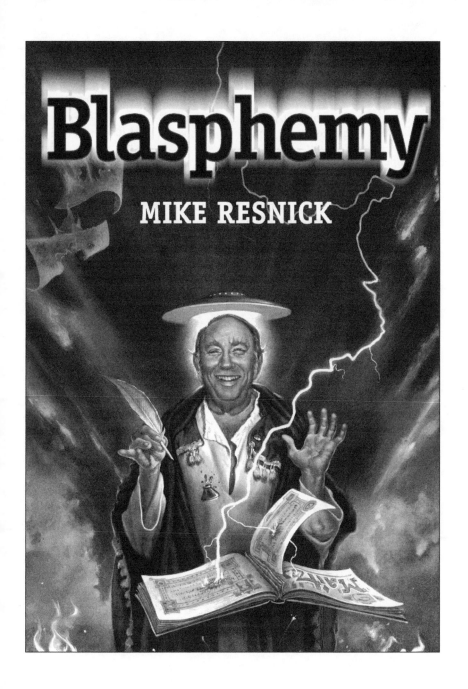

Blasphemy

MIKE RESNICK

GOLDEN GRYPHON PRESS • 2010

Foreword, Copyright © 2010 by Jack McDevitt.

"Genesis: The Rejected Canon," first published in *Dark Regions*, V3 #1 1995.

Walpurgis III, first published by NAL/Signet, 1982.

"God and Mr. Slatterman," first published in *Unauthorized Autobiographies and Other Curiosities*, Misfit Press, 1984.

"The Pale Thin God," first published in *Xanadu*, ed. Jane Yolen & Martin H. Greenberg, Tor, 1993.

"How I Wrote the New Testament, Ushered in the Renaissance, and Birded the 17th Hole at Pebble Beach," first published in *Aboriginal SF*, Jul/Aug 1990.

The Branch, first published by NAL/Signet, 1984.

"Interview With the Almighty," first published in *Quantum Speculative Fiction* #1, 1999.

"A Few Blasphemous Words," Copyright © 2010 by Lezli Robyn.

LIBRARY OF CONGRESS CATALOGING–IN–PUBLICATION DATA

Resnick, Michael D.
   Blasphemy / Mike Resnick. — 1st ed.
     p.   cm.
   ISBN-13: 978-1-930846-64-7 (hardcover : alk. paper)
   ISBN-10: 1-930846-64-9) hardcover : alk. paper)
1. Science fiction, American.   2. Fantasy fiction, American.
I. Title.
PS3568.E698   B63   2010
813'.54—dc22   2010007900

First Edition.

Contents

To Carol, as always,
And to Gary Turner

Foreword

IT'S PROBABLY TIME TO REVEAL THE TRUTH ABOUT Mike Resnick. Anyone who looks at what he has accomplished, several hundred novels, fourteen collections (not counting this one), forty-three anthologies, more than two hundred fifty stories, and a prodigious number of essays and reviews, would be justified in asking: How does one man do it?

It might be possible if one were to visualize somebody who does little else. Who doesn't stop to eat, doesn't sleep, and would never take time to go bowling. But Resnick, it seems, has also enjoyed a substantial second career. He's edited newspapers, magazines, and performed as a columnist, written about horses, collies, and a wide assortment of other topics. Most recently, with Barry Malzberg, he has been describing the challenges and joys of the professional science fiction writer in SFWA's *The Bulletin*.

Maybe, somehow, we could even factor all that in if he did everything on the run. Get it written, don't worry about quality, get it to the editor, and move on. But now we are confronted by another curious fact: Mike Resnick has won pretty much every award, major and minor, the field has to offer. The sheer number of nominations he's collected for these various awards is staggering. E.g., he's been on the final ballot for the Hugo, as of late summer 2009, thirty-three times.

He's also won numerous awards abroad for translations of his work. And it is the totality of these awards, more than anyone else in the field has been able to accumulate, and by a sizable margin, that forces us to an inescapable conclusion: Mike Resnick, the Mike Resnick we know, who hangs out at conventions and conferences, who loves parties, who seems to have been born to showbiz, who answers the phone whenever another writer or an editor calls for help, is only a front man. He's the P.R. guy. I have it on good authority that he takes long naps, enjoys spending his spare time with dogs, and is a regular attendee at the Kirinyaga weekly poker sessions, where he's established a reputation for bluffing opponents out of their socks.

The actual writing is done by a team of relatives, mostly cousins. The African stories, for example, were really written by Louie Resnick, who has ridden safari through the jungles, and got his start when his Chicago scout troop was adopted by a local politician, who raised money to send them on a camping trip to the slopes of Kilimanjaro. (He was later accused of having diverted some of the funds, but that's another story.)

Most of the anthologies were assembled by Kathie Resnick who, according to insiders, is the sharpest member of the family. Kathie does her editing during her spare time. (She's actually a nuclear physicist, and has been playing a major role in the effort to create a safe atomic drive. She is reported to be close to success, and a manned mission to Neptune is expected by the end of the next decade. And if you're wondering why you've heard nothing about this, it is being kept quiet for political reasons.)

Harv Resnick specializes in bigger-than-life characters. He's given us unforgettable rides with The Forever Kid and Three-Gun Max and Catastrophe Baker and Lucifer Jones and the Dragon Lady. Rumor has it that he also created the purely evil Conrad Bland and his nemesis Jericho, the ultimate assassin, both of whom you will meet in *Walpurgis III*.

January Resnick has always had a passion for the epic fable. She won her spurs with the *Santiago* novels, featuring characters who might easily have come out of the American west: Halfpenny Terwilliger; the journalist Virtue McKenzie (whose name and reputation don't quite match up to reality); Father William, a clergyman who employs homicide for good causes; and Santiago himself, of whom it is said is the product of a meeting between a comet and a cosmic wind.

In recent years, we've had the Starship novels, by James (Ohio) Resnick. None of the Resnicks trust government very far, but Ohio is possibly the most skeptical of all. The starship of the title is the *Theodore Roosevelt*, which has led some to suspect that the series was actually written by Ohio's older brother, Louie. But a recently published interview makes it clear that Ohio intended the name as a homage to Louie.

In any case, *Starship: Mutiny* introduces us to Wilson Cole, the Charles Lanrezac of his era. Cole is always right, and consequently succeeds in annoying his superiors. Eventually Cole and his crew take the ship and break away from the Republic, launching a series of high-wire adventures whose latest incarnation, *Starship: Flagship*, has recently been released.

And so, we arrive at a collection with a title guaranteed to drive off the Sunday School teachers, the faint of heart, and parents across the Bible Belt. I'll confess I'm not certain which of the Resnicks actually wrote the five stories and two novels that comprise this collection. In fact, internal evidence leads me to believe the novels had separate authors, and that at least two others were involved with the stories. (At this date, it appears that at least seventeen different Resnicks, none of them named Mike, have contributed to his *oeuvre*.)

I'm not convinced that any of the views implicit here actually constitute blasphemy. Resnick books have traditionally demonstrated the effects of tribalism, the willingness of people to believe anything, in spite of common sense and all evidence to the contrary, so long as it is presented by authority, and that we are sufficiently young upon first indoctrination. And we tend all too often to overlook the consequences and implications of that belief. Do we, e.g., really admire Abraham because he was willing to kill his child to save his own skin? Do we believe God actually considered that act virtuous? Do we really think those innocent Egyptian kids should have been massacred during the Passover? How could millions of Germans buy into the Nazi line and feed their neighbors to the fire?

Thus, the various citizens support the Republic in the Starship novels, and even believe they live in a Republic, though it is clearly no such thing. But most of them will fight to defend it, probably never asking any questions.

Resnick examines our tendency to believe in various authoritarian systems, to accept them at their word, and to behave accordingly. And he doesn't approve. That's only blasphemy or treason to the people pushing the official story. The Velvet Comet (from the *Eros* novels) is an interstellar house of ill repute. But the characters who spend their time in the place, whether professionally involved, or as customers, are both interesting and likable. However, in *A Miracle of Rare Design*, Xavier William Lennox shows up at an alien religious ceremony only to be tortured and nearly killed.

It may be that the most dangerous authoritarian systems are those that cannot be questioned. Those that claim penalties beyond the grave for lack of adherence. Those whose practices and dogma are determined, not by a panel of experts, or even by a group of politicians, but by a collection of written documents assembled thousands of years ago, and put forward as the infallible word of God.

The two novels and the five stories collected here have a common theme: It has nothing to do with what we really believe. Rather, the issue is whether we claim to believe given notions without ever really having considered the implications of that belief.

Have those of us who accept the existence of Lucifer ever really considered what his status might be in a future world, when mankind has spread out among the stars, many groups claiming worlds exclusively for the like-minded? Thus, it would be no surprise to find a Quaker world, and a Methodist world, Buddhist and Islamic and Jewish worlds. And, possibly, as the author suggests in *Walpurgis III*, a world given over to Devil worship.

Then there's the issue of the Messiah. The Jews were expecting a well-armed military genius who would lead them against their assorted enemies in the Biblical world. Who would grant victory to the armies of God. And Jesus showed up. To the believers of that era, he simply did not qualify as a Messiah. Means well, but he's not what we're looking for. So where did things go wrong?

In *The Branch*, the real Messiah arrives on the scene. He doesn't quite fit the image either. It's the twenty-first century, and his name is Jeremiah the B.

The five stories are memorable for a variety of reasons.

"How I Wrote the New Testament, Ushered in the Renaissance, and Birdied the 17th Hole at Pebble Beach" makes my short list for all-time great titles. It's also a brilliant comic take on the Wandering Jew.

"God and Mr. Slatterman" pits the Almighty against a guy who hangs out in casinos. And, like so many of us, either can't or won't listen.

"Genesis: The Rejected Canon" describes a creation effort that goes awry.

Mike has never been uncritical of human folly. But his reaction to our cruelty and barbarism is usually leavened with a sense of humor. We are what we are. Pity, but there it is. The light touch, however, is utterly missing in "The Pale Thin God," which draws the darkest conclusions about us that I've seen in his work.

And, finally, the PR guy from the Resnick Foundation, who is considerably more reasonable than Slatterman, sits down with God in Sid & Sylvia's 5-star deli to ask the questions we'd all like to ask (or maybe not) in "Interview with the Almighty."

This is a collection for people who don't mind asking questions. And aren't reluctant to hear the answers. If indeed, there are any answers. In any case, it's an opportunity to sit back and enjoy some vintage Mike Resnick. Unlike some of the characters we will encounter, we can't go wrong.

Jack McDevitt
September 2009

Blasphemy

Genesis: The Rejected Canon

ⲒN THE BEGINNING GOD CREATED THE HEAVENS and the earth.

The earth was without form, and void; and darkness was on the face of the deep. And the spirit of God was hovering over the face of the waters.

And God said "Let there be light," and there was light.

And, five days later, after some heavy-duty creating, God said, "Let Us make man in Our image, according to Our likeness; let him have dominion over the fish of the sea, over the birds of the air, and over the cattle, over all the earth and over every creeping thing that creeps on the earth.

God then created Eden, and said, "It is not good that man should be alone; I will make him a helper comparable to him."

Out of the ground the Lord God formed every beast of the field and bird of the air, and brought them to Adam to see what he would call them. And whatever Adam called each living creature, that was its name.

So Adam gave names to all cattle, to the birds of the air, and to every beast of the field. But for Adam there was not found a helper comparable to him.

And the Lord God caused a deep sleep to fall upon Adam, and

he slept; and He took one of his ribs, and closed up the flesh in its place.

And when Adam awoke, he saw his helper, and said, "You are now bone of my bones and flesh of my flesh," and together, they went hand in hand through the Garden of Eden.

And Adam turned to his helper and said, "My name is Adam." And his helper smiled coyly and replied, "My name is Raoul."

God's next attempt to populate the world was with tap-dancing giant sloths. It didn't work out a hell of a lot better.

✤ ✤ ✤

Walpurgis

Prologue

"There is some soul of goodness in things evil."
—Shakespeare

"Every evil to which we do not succumb is a benefactor."
—Emerson

"Our greatest evils flow from within ourselves."
—Rousseau

They were all wrong.

"There is no explanation for evil. It must be looked upon as a necessary part of the order of the universe. To ignore it is childish; to bewail it senseless."
—Maugham

He came close.

"Evil is its own Justification. It therefore renders meaningless even such questions as power, pleasure, and profit."
—Conrad Bland

He knew. But of course, he would.

*H*E KILLED ELEVEN MILLION MEN IN THE DEATH camps of Pilor IX during the brief reign of the mad Emperor Justacious.

He killed seventeen million men on Boriga II in a manner that made the gas ovens of ancient Earth and its Reich seem compassionate.

He killed five million women and children on New Rhodesia.

He killed three thousand seventeen men on Cambria III, each in a different way.

He invented torture devices that even Spica VI, which was in revolt against the Republic, would not use.

No photograph, holograph, or videodisc of him was known to exist. He had never been fingerprinted. There was no voice or retina identification pattern on him in any computer. He had no bank account on any world, no financial or property holdings that anyone had been able to trace. His planet of origin was unknown. Many men had served him; all but seven were dead, and none of those seven had ever seen him.

He was a fugitive.

His name was Conrad Bland and he was, for the moment, safe.

Chapter 1

"If you kill one man, you are an assassin.
If you kill millions, you are a conqueror.
If you kill everyone, you are a god."
—Conrad Bland

Orestes Mela walked past the snakes and scorpions, past the elephants and lemurs, past the eight-legged Rigelian herbivores and the bloblike Vegan carnivores and the armored Spican omnivores, marveling that they had all managed to adapt to the hothouse climate of Serengeti, the zoo world of the Terrazane Sector. He began to wipe the sweat from his pudgy face, then decided that he didn't want to call even more attention to the small briefcase that was chained to his wrist, and stopped in midmotion.

He checked his handout map, pinpointed the aviary some six miles away, and flagged down a robotic cart. Serengeti wasn't *that* fascinating, and there was no sense arriving at his destination too winded to talk.

The cart left him off a few minutes later, and he produced a token that gained him access to the screen-covered path that wound its way through the sanctuary. He walked along it for almost a mile, wondering why they kept the birds of different worlds separated, and trying to get used to the odor.

Finally he came to a circular area filled with benches and tables and an automated refreshment stand. Three men and a woman sat at various tables, and an ancient, uniformed attendant was painfully picking up rubbish from a number of deserted benches.

Mela surveyed the four. Two of the men were too young, and the woman seemed too frail, though she was a possibility. But the other man seemed to fill the bill: a huge, towering man with hard, gray eyes and a deep scar on his left cheek. A gust of hot wind caught the man's empty paper cup and sent it flying off the table, but he caught it before it could land, moving with a fluid animal grace.

Well, thought Mela, at least he looks the part.

Mela waited, uncertain of how to initiate his approach, and a moment later the huge man stood up, stretched like some savage jungle cat, and strode off. Puzzled, Mela thought of walking after him, but chose to remain seated. The two young men left about five minutes later, and a moment after that the woman followed them.

The grizzled attendant approached him.

"Do you mind if I sit down for a moment, sir?" he said in a voice weak with age. "It's hot, thirsty work, cleaning up after the tourists."

"I'd prefer you sat elsewhere," said Mela irritably. "I'm waiting for someone."

"Not any longer," said the attendant, pulling up a chair.

Mela peered at the ancient face.

"Jericho?" he asked at last.

The attendant nodded.

"Well, I'll be damned!" exclaimed Mela.

"Shall we proceed?" said Jericho, and his voice was no longer that of an old man.

"Right here?" asked Mela, frowning.

"We won't be interrupted," said Jericho. "I've seen to that."

Mela shrugged.

"Is there any reason why you picked this particular world for our meeting?" he asked, lifting his briefcase to the table and punching out a fourteen-digit combination on its computer lock.

"I've never been to Serengeti before."

"Odd," commented Mela. "It seems like an ideal place for you to keep your hand in, so to speak. I understand they sell hunting licenses in certain areas."

"I never kill for pleasure, Mr. Mela," said Jericho emotionlessly.

"Well, to business," said Mela, withdrawing a number of packets. "This," he said, holding up a thick package of discs, "is what he's done. And this," he added, holding up a single disc, "contains everything we know about him. We filled only about two minutes' worth of it. In point of fact, we don't even know, after eighteen years, if he *is* a him. After all, Conrad Bland is only a name; doubtless he has others."

"Doubtless," said Jericho noncommittally.

"You'll want to go through these, of course," said Mela, sliding the large package across the table. "I've arranged a temporary security clearance for you, so you can take them with you and study them carefully."

"Keep them," said Jericho.

"Keep them?" repeated Mela incredulously. "But they contain all the details of New Rhodesia, all the pertinent information about Boriga and Quantos and Pilor and—"

"What Conrad Bland did on Boriga and the other worlds is of no concern to me."

"Don't you want to know the nature of the man you'll be facing?" insisted Mela, finally mopping away some of the sweat that streamed down his face.

"I never draw moral judgments," replied Jericho. "It's enough that you want him dead and that you've agreed to pay my fee. I am merely an executioner."

"More to the point, you are a professional assassin who has been commissioned to terminate a man that the Republic can't extradite," said Mela, twitching his nostrils as the avian odors assailed them. "And I might mention in passing that we know even less about you than we do about him."

"You know that I'm on your side, Mr. Mela. That ought to be sufficient."

"I hate to think how many of *us* you may have killed over the years," said Mela bitterly. "I find the whole concept of hiring a killer to exterminate another killer distasteful in the extreme."

"And yet here you are, doing just that," noted Jericho.

"It's not a matter of choice. I have my orders. By the way, Jericho isn't your real name, is it?"

"Does it make a difference?"

"Not really," said Mela. "But I suspect that it's a code name or an alias or something, just as I suspect you're a much younger man than you presently appear to be."

Jericho stared calmly at him and made no reply.

Mela met his gaze for a long moment, then shook his head. "Damn it!" he said. "I was expecting someone who looked more like a killer!"

"What does a killer look like?" inquired Jericho mildly.

"You blend right in with the scenery!" continued Mela, wondering why he felt so outraged. "Normal height, normal weight, no speech patterns. You're probably the penultimate Average Man under all that makeup."

"I strongly suggest that you stop worrying about my appearance," said Jericho. "You will never see me again after this meeting is over."

"I'll at least have to know what you intend to look like and what identity you expect to be using so our people can be forewarned."

"That won't be necessary."

"The entire planet is under military quarantine," Mela pointed out. "How will you get there?"

"The same way I got here," said Jericho. "Which leads me to another point, Mr. Mela. There are seventeen Republic ships in orbit around Serengeti and some three hundred operatives on the planet itself. Obviously they are not here for your protection, and just as obviously they are not here to defend the planet from any real or imagined attack. I must therefore assume that they are here to scrutinize me and gather such information as may prove useful should you wish to arrest or eliminate me at the conclusion of our transaction. I must warn you that should any member of the Republic make any such effort to invade my privacy at any time in the future I will consider it to be a breach of good faith and will feel free to call the entire affair off without returning your down payment—which I trust you remembered to bring with you."

Mela nodded, withdrew a small titanium container from his briefcase, and handed it to Jericho, who opened it, spilled a number of precious gemstones onto his hand, nodded, and replaced them in the container.

"Don't you want to examine them more closely?" asked Mela irritably.

"No," said Jericho. "I've no intention of beginning my assignment until they have been appraised and converted into currency."

"How long will that take?" demanded Mela, raising his voice to be heard over the screeching of the birds.

"Less time than you suppose," replied Jericho. "And now to business. There are certain things I need to know about Bland."

"I thought you didn't want our information," said Mela petulantly.

"The wholesale slaughter of planetary populations is a matter of complete indifference to me," said Jericho, his gaze leaving Mela's round, sweating face to follow the flight of a hawk as it swooped down to snare a sparrow amid much squawking and fluttering of wings. "But it stands to reason that the Republic wouldn't seek my services unless and until they had lost a number of their own operatives. How many men have tried to assassinate Conrad Bland, and how did they fail?"

"We have sent twenty-three men after him, fifteen on their own and four two-man teams," admitted Mela. "None of them has been heard from again."

"Who were they?" asked Jericho.

"The best men the Republic had," said Mela. "Including Rinehart Guntermann."

"Your people should have known better than to send a used-up old warhorse after someone like Bland."

"I beg your pardon!" snapped Mela, struggling to control his temper. "It so happens that Guntermann was the hero of the Battle of Canphor VII!"

"Which he fought from the flagship of an impenetrable fleet," said Jericho dryly. "Apples and oranges, Mr. Mela; if Bland was where the Navy could get at him, you wouldn't have sought me out and I wouldn't have allowed you to find me."

"*Allowed* me?" repeated Mela as a hot breeze blew over him, again making him unpleasantly aware of the myriad of pungent odors that surrounded him.

"Of course," said Jericho. "I watched you make awkward and blundering attempts for almost a year, displaying considerably more obstinacy than skill. It was your very persistence, the frantic nature of your efforts, which convinced me you had to be after Conrad Bland."

"You expected us to come to you about Bland?"

"Sooner or later," said Jericho.

"And you look forward to the challenge?"

"Not at all," answered Jericho. "I look forward to the reward, which is commensurate to the challenge."

"Twenty-three decent and honorable men went after him with no thought of reward," said Mela bitterly.

"Little good it did them," responded Jericho emotionlessly. "By the way, were they all killed on Bland's current world?"

"No," said Mela. "He's been running from us for almost five years. We made our first attempt on Lodin, two more on Bareimus II, another on Belsanidor, three on Nimbus VIII, and the rest on other planets along the way."

"I'll want dossiers on all twenty-three operatives," said Jericho. "I want to know their skills, their specialties, and their previous accomplishments in similar situations, if any."

"It's all in there," said Mela, gesturing toward the thick packet, which Jericho now reached for and took.

"Don't look so angry, Mr. Mela," said Jericho. "Your down payment is nonrefundable. Regardless of your feelings toward me, it is in both of our best interests that I accomplish my mission."

"I am here because I was ordered to come," said Mela coldly. "I will cooperate with you in every way possible. But that doesn't mean I have to like it."

"Fair enough," said Jericho, tossing a few tidbits of food and garbage through the protective fence to a bird that was patiently watching them from the other side. "And now perhaps you'd better tell me something about the planet."

"It's called Walpurgis," said Mela. "Walpurgis III, actually."

"So you informed, me," commented Jericho. "I couldn't find it on my star charts. Is it newly settled?"

"Within the past century or so. You'll find it listed as Zeta Tau III."

"Walpurgis," repeated Jericho. "An interesting name."

"It's an interesting world," said Mela. "A psychologist could have a field day with it."

"In what way?" asked Jericho, and Mela sensed that though there was no change in his expression he had suddenly become more attentive.

"During the Great Opening," began the Republic man, "every damned special interest you can think of laid claim to a planet or two. General Combine got four, United Silicon picked up a pair, even the Jesus Pures got a little world of their own."

"Jesus Pures?" inquired Jericho.

"Church of the Purity of Jesus Christ," explained Mela. "There were so many worlds that even the fringe groups started staking claims."

"And what particular fringe group does Walpurgis represent?" asked Jericho.

"Witchcraft," said Mela.

"You're kidding!" said Jericho, smiling for the first time.

"I wish I were," replied Mela, raising his voice again as another flock of birds began screeching.

"But witchcraft doesn't work."

"Neither does believing in the purity of Jesus Christ," said Mela. "The fact remains that a number of covens and Satanic cults staked a claim to Walpurgis, the claim was allowed, and they settled the planet."

"All right, they believe in witchcraft," said Jericho. "How does this cause a problem?"

"Because Conrad Bland fled to Walpurgis and claimed sanctuary." Mela wiped his face again. "My God, it's humid here!"

"I still don't see the problem," said Jericho. "It's a Republic world, isn't it?"

"It's not that simple," said Mela. "These people worship evil, if not in practice then at least in principle. They have a civil government, but in point of fact they're ruled by a theocracy, and the theocracy won't give him up. And after the problem we had on Radillex IV, we're not about to go in after him in force."

Jericho nodded thoughtfully. Radillex IV had given sanctuary to two escaped convicts, the Republic had demanded their return, the planet had refused, the Navy had moved in, and when the dust cleared three million Radillexians were dead and the Republic had a brand-new government. Their successors remained more than a little sensitive about showing their muscle to any colony planet, especially when there were so many alien worlds in real or imagined need of subjugation.

"So we clamped an embargo on Walpurgis and placed it under quarantine," continued Mela, "which probably didn't do a hell of a lot of good, since they never had any commerce with the rest of the Republic anyway."

"And you're sure he's still there?" said Jericho.

"We've got that world sealed up so tight nothing can get in or out," said Mela. "He's there, all right. In fact, we've had some recent secret communications with the civil government concerning him."

"And?"

"They've begged us—literally *begged* us—to terminate him."

"Did they give any reason?" asked Jericho.

Mela shook his head.

"I'll need histories, guidebooks, and anything else you can give me concerning Walpurgis," said Jericho at last.

"We don't have a damned thing," said Mela.

"Not even a map?"

"Topographical, yes; roads and cities, no," said Mela. "You must understand: the founders viewed themselves as an oppressed minority, and they cut themselves off totally from the rest of the Republic. Both immigration and emigration have been severely restricted throughout their history. They have no commerce with any other world of the Republic—or with any alien world, for that matter. They willingly pay the higher taxes that result from refusing conscription. They allow no video transmissions in or out. Hell, they don't even honor the credit; instead they've got some archaic mixture of dollars, pounds, yen, and rubles."

"I see," said Jericho. "Have you any operatives there at the moment?"

"One, if he's still alive," replied Mela. "A man named Ibo Ubusuku."

"Where is he stationed and how can I contact him if the need arises?"

"We've heard from him only once," said Mela. "He's in a city called Amaymon in the southern hemisphere, and he can be contacted through a coded classified advertisement which is on one of your discs. He hasn't broken radio silence since his initial message, since the Republic isn't very popular on Walpurgis these days."

"Is there anything else I should know?" asked Jericho.

"Probably," said Mela. "Unfortunately, no one in the government is in a position to give it to you."

"Then," said Jericho, rising to his feet, "I think we can consider our meeting concluded. Please make no attempt to follow me."

"One last thing," said Mela. "I am empowered to authorize the purchase of any weapon you feel you may need."

"I'm sure I can find what I need on the planet," said Jericho.

"But our weaponry is much more sophisticated!" protested Mela.

"Mr. Mela," said Jericho slowly, as if weighing each word, "this may come as a surprise to you, possibly even a disappointment, but there are many men and women who are better shots than I am, just as there are many others who are more proficient in hand-to-hand combat. You are not hiring a marksman or a brawler. You are hiring an executioner. I'll get what I need on the planet."

A huge scarlet eagle floated effortlessly down toward the ground, then screeched and pounced on a small mammal. Mela turned momentarily to see the cause of the commotion. When he turned back, the man who called himself Jericho was gone.

Chapter 2

"Murder is merely a passion, but slaughter is an art."
—Conrad Bland

It was not, at first glance, all that odd a world.

Jericho had prepared for it as best he could. The physical portion was easy, consisting of simply adjusting the ship's systems to give him the feel of the lighter gravity and somewhat higher oxygen content of Walpurgis, so that he could maneuver on the planet without giving himself away through a sudden, unexpected show of strength or agility, or by the slow intoxication that occasionally overtook a body unused to the enriched atmosphere.

He spent three weeks reading everything he could find on the various cults and covens of Earth prior to their departure for Walpurgis III 123 years ago—but since societies were living, evolving things, he had the feeling that his information would be, for the most part, outdated and archaic.

When his preparations were complete, he proceeded to the next stage of his plan. Replacement ships were continually joining the cordon of Republic vessels blockading Walpurgis, and one of those ships, within three days of taking up its position, found its orbit decaying and had to set down on the planet for minor repairs. No member of the crew had been aware of Jericho's presence on board the ship; none knew that the malfunction was carefully calculated to allow them to land in the southern hemisphere; no one saw him leave the ship shortly after nightfall.

A major city lay adjacent to the spaceport, and using the cover of night he made a quick but expert tour of the nearest shopping center. Once he had determined from examining various window displays that the local clothing bore no symbols of rank, class, or occupation, he methodically looted four haberdasheries, taking a shirt from one, pants from another, an outer jacket from a third, and shoes, socks, and cash from a fourth. Though he was certain that no one had seen him leave the spaceport, he also changed his appearance from that of a pudgy blond man in his early thirties to a somewhat slimmer man of about fifty. Since he couldn't be sure of the local hairstyles—store mannequins were frequently out of date—he decided that it would be best to give himself a sparse, thinning head of hair, receding in the front, balding at the back, light brown on top and gray at the sides. He decided against a mustache or beard, but gave himself an impressive scar extending from his upper lip to his jaw, just in case he needed an excuse for his bare face.

Feeling himself to be relatively safe from immediate detection, he took a second, slower tour of the area, trying to get the feel of the place, and walking toward what he took to be the center of the city. There were a number of stores specializing in this world's equivalent of religious tokens and charms, and a few more herb shops and palmists and phrenologists than he would expect to see in a normal Republic city of comparable size. Many of the shops selling what he considered to be "normal" goods—clothing, groceries, hardware, and the like—had cabalistic designs painted or etched on their windows, and almost all of them had small charms and amulets in among their merchandise. None of them, however, were advertising cut-rate surefire curse removals or virgins for sacrifice, and this disturbed him. It would be far easier to infiltrate a society so new that it still belligerently exhibited and commercialized the signs of its beliefs than to pass unnoticed in a society where those beliefs were so commonly held that the tokens became unimportant.

Suddenly he heard voices off to his left, and he quickly ducked into a recessed doorway. A moment later a number of bare-breasted women, dressed uniformly in shoulder-length gloves and thigh-high boots made of rubber, walked past him, moaning and chanting what seemed to be a prayer, though the language was unfamiliar. Two of them carried a small litter between them, and on it sprawled the body of a dead cat that had evidently been crushed by some type of vehicle.

That it was a funeral procession for a familiar, in the form of a cat, seemed obvious. As for the clothing of the mourners, he could make no sense of it—or of its failure to attract any masculine attention.

He walked another block, then again ducked out of sight as two hooded figures, clad totally in black, approached him in the company of three men wearing what he took to be standard business suits. They seemed to be having a vigorous but good-natured discussion about some sporting event or other, but he couldn't catch the details. None of them seemed to be aware of the incongruity of their outfits.

He continued walking, observing and making mental notes about the city. It was starting to show its age in places, despite the obvious care taken by its sanitation department. The streets were devoid of dirt and litter, the smooth sidewalks glistened as if they had been polished, trash atomizers were on every corner—but here and there were the signs of deterioration: level upon level of patch-work placed over pothole-prone sections of the street, a building in need of sandblasting, a small shop between two large office build-ings obviously being allowed to run down so that it could be con-demned and replaced by still another steel-and-glass tower of enterprise.

As he walked along he passed a number of churches, most of them mock-Gothic in architectural style, each with goats grazing on its lawn. He thought he heard screams and moans coming from one of them, and he actually did see a few nude bodies doing a frantic dance through the window of another, but he had no intention of inspecting them more closely until he knew more about the cus-toms of the planet. One rather small church, perched at the top of a slight incline, actually had a circle of fire around its doorway, through which the congregants presumably had to leap in order to pay homage to their particular god or demon.

He realized that he was still a couple of miles from the heart of the city, and he reached it just before dawn. When the businesses began opening a few hours after sunrise, he decided to buy a local newspaper. He passed five vending machines, ascertained to his relief that he was indeed in Amaymon, and not wishing to draw attention to himself by inserting the wrong coin, sought out a human-operated newsstand, preferring an excessive amount of change to the possibility of underpaying from ignorance.

He stopped next at a seedy-looking restaurant, had some coffee and an odd-tasting roll, and decided that finding lodgings was his next order of business. He avoided the larger hotels, since he didn't know what kind of identification or credit information they would require. He would have much preferred a rented room in a private home, but he was too unfamiliar with the city and felt that the sight of a strange man wandering through a residential area was far more likely to draw unwanted attention than he would receive if he remained in the business section. He walked a few blocks until the surroundings grew a bit more squalid, then entered the lobby of a particularly dismal-looking hotel, the type which in most societies would have rented its rooms by the hour rather than the night.

"Name?" said the bored desk clerk.

Jericho looked around to make sure the lobby was empty.

"Conrad Bland," he said, watching for a reaction.

"Don't tell *me*, feller," said the clerk, shoving a book toward him without any hint of recognition. "Write it down here."

Jericho picked up a pen and scribbled the name so badly that a score of handwriting experts could spend days trying to decipher it without success.

"Any luggage?" asked the clerk.

"Just what I'm wearing."

"Right," said the clerk, unsurprised. He handed Jericho a small slip of paper with the room combination written on it. "Do you belong to the Cult of the Messenger or the Church of Baal?"

Jericho shook his head.

"Okay. If you belong to any other cult or sect requiring the sacrifice of living animals, you must inform the management and a stipend will be appended to your bill. You don't look like you've got any candles with you, but if you decide to go out and get some, we allow cold candles only. No hots. Got it?"

"Got it," replied Jericho. "Where's my room?"

"I'm not through yet," said the clerk irritably. "Any charms attached to the walls in a manner that the management considers permanent will become the property of the hotel. Any ritual weapons found in your room by the maids will become the property of the hotel. No visitors of either sex are allowed after midnight. And we demand a week's rent in advance."

"What if I don't stay a week?" said Jericho, certain that this reaction was expected of him.

"Then you apply for a refund," said the clerk.

"I don't like it," grumbled Jericho.

"No one pulled you in off the street," said the clerk. "You don't like it, all you got to do is turn around and walk out."

Jericho glared at the man for a long minute. "How much?" he asked at last.

The clerk smiled. It was the grin of a man who played this scene out several times every day and knew both ends of the dialogue by rote. "Seventy sterlings," he said, holding out a huge hand.

Jericho turned his back and pulled out a handful of bills, checking the denominations and handing the proper amount over to the clerk. He allowed the clerk a long look at his bankroll.

"That's a fair-sized wad you got there," commented the clerk, staring intently at him. "Nice new clothes, too."

"I got lucky," replied Jericho, again watching for a reaction.

"If it starts burning a hole in your pocket, I might know a couple of interesting places to spend it," said the clerk. "For a small consideration, of course."

"Perhaps later," said Jericho. "How about my room?"

"Three-ten," said the clerk. "Up three flights and down the corridor. The lift is broken; you'll have to take the stairs."

Jericho nodded. A quick glance at the elevator convinced him that it had been in a state of disrepair for months, probably years, and he walked over to a concrete staircase. A moment later he had reached his room, punched out the combination on the computer lock, and entered.

It was a dingy, barren room, pentagonal, as he suspected all of them were. It possessed a narrow bed with a stain on the spread, a much abused dresser, one chair, and a nightstand. He pulled out the top drawer of the dresser, hoping for a phone book, but found only a throwaway pack of tarot cards and a cheaply bound copy of the *Malleus Maleficarum*, an ancient grimoire dating back to the days when Man was still Earthbound. There was no phone, no video set, no radio, nothing that he could possibly use to gain a further working knowledge of the world. The bathroom contained a small chemical commode and dryshower of the type used on spaceships, but he couldn't tell if water was especially hard to come by or if the hotel was simply too cheap to pipe it in.

Having examined the premises thoroughly, he returned to the bed, sat down on the edge of it, and began reading the newspaper he had purchased. It was thin, too thin to service a major city, which implied that most of the news was disseminated through newstapes and discs or by means of video transmissions. It also meant that he would get only major news stories rather than the local color he was after.

The lead story concerned the economy, which was growing a little too erratically to suit those who controlled it. Also on the front page was an editorial that managed to castigate the Republic thoroughly for eleven paragraphs without ever once mentioning Conrad Bland. The third page made brief mention that the Brotherhood of Night and the Cult of the Messenger had both closed their branches in the city of Tifereth, and a quick check of the financial page showed that the Tifereth commodities market had ceased trading almost a month ago, ostensibly because of a major decline in volume.

Possibly the city had fallen on hard financial times. Possibly it was due to Bland. He couldn't tell based on such minimal information, but he put a visit to Tifereth on his list of priorities.

The clerk and the news story had both mentioned a number of cults, and, on a hunch, he turned to the advertisements listing the local churches. It was as he had feared. There was no one religion whose tenets he could quickly assimilate. Rather, there were such sects as the Cult of the Messenger, the Church of the Inferno, the Daughters of Delight, the Church of Baal, the Order of the Golem, the Sisterhood of Sin, the Church of Satan, and literally dozens more, almost as many splinter groups as Christianity had possessed in its heyday.

He sighed. There was more to this world than met the eye. Intermixed with ads for furniture and clothing and real estate were occasional ads selling protection against both good and evil forces, ads for amulets, for voodoo dolls and love potions and immortality elixirs.

When he had finished with the advertisements and notices, and had thus obtained a reasonable approximation of the value of his money, he went through the paper thoroughly to see if his thefts had been reported, though he suspected it had been printed too early to cover them. He was correct, but in the process of looking for the stories he made another discovery: not a single crime had been written up. He couldn't believe that a city of Amaymon's size, which he estimated to be well over a quarter of a million, could go through an entire day without its share of murders, robberies, and rapes, especially on a world that had a religious passion for such things. This implied one of two things: either the news was being carefully managed, or else the concept of crime had undergone an almost unbelievable metamorphosis on Walpurgis.

He suspected the former. No matter how much lip service Walpurgis paid to the concept of evil, no society could ignore felonies without falling into anarchy; and while he could only guess at the framework of this society, anarchy was the one thing he had seen no trace of.

Still, censored news could work to his advantage. If Bland was entrenched solidly enough to make the civil government ask for help in eliminating him, there was no way that Jericho was going to be able to march into his headquarters, wherever they might be, and simply gun the man down. Bland would have layer upon layer of protection, or else he wouldn't have survived long enough to get to Walpurgis. Which in turn meant that Jericho would have to approach Bland indirectly. He didn't know how long he could hide his presence, and it was at least comforting to know that in all likelihood the government would make no more mention of his actions than he himself would.

Having learned everything he could from the paper, he cast it aside, stretched out on the bed, and went to sleep.

It was just after sunset when he arose. He showered, shaved, put on his identity, and went out of the hotel for dinner. He chose a restaurant frequented by people who were dressed like himself and spent some time studying the menu. After he had eaten he again walked through the city, listening to snatches of conversation, and then went to a Tri-Fi cinema. If he had hoped to learn something about Walpurgis he was disappointed, for it was a conventional love story during which the audience laughed hysterically every time the heroine made some sacrifice to Beelzebub. He gathered that it fell into the realm of lighthearted historical romance, but be didn't dare ask anyone.

He spent the next hour checking into three more hotels, signing names he had memorized from the Tri-Fi's credits at each. He returned to his original hotel and emerged ten minutes later as a middle-aged and semi-obese man with close-cropped red hair. In this guise he visited two bars about a mile from the hotel, got himself thrown out of both for unruly conduct, and then lumbered into an all-night restaurant, ostensibly for black coffee. When he left half an hour later he had a steak knife tucked under his belt.

Then, because he had to learn more about the police and their efficacy, he went hunting. Two blocks from the restaurant he spotted his prey, a mild-looking man in his late fifties, who was walking along the sidewalk alone and unconcerned.

Jericho fell into step behind him like some awful jungle animal that had marked its dinner. He didn't hurry, never seemed to increase his pace, often appeared to be traveling in a different direction on the deserted streets; but slowly, inch by inch, he narrowed the gap between them with a dreadful patience. Within ten minutes they were eighty feet apart, then forty, then twenty—and then, with the swiftness and surety of a cobra, he struck.

The man never made a sound, never felt a stab of pain, never even knew his throat had been slit. He was dead almost before he hit the pavement.

And Jericho, like some besmocked technician who has added a dangerous element to a solution in a laboratory, settled back to observe what happened next.

Chapter 3

"No matter how heinous a deed you contemplate, the operative
question is not Is It Evil, but rather Is It Possible?"
—*Conrad Bland*

John Sable stood at the pentagonal obsidian table in the corner of
his office, genuflected before the statuette of Cali, lit an oddly
shaped red candle, and murmured a brief prayer to Azazel over it.
This was followed by two more candles, with prayers to Asmodeus
and Ahriman. He then held his amulet up to the baphomet that
hung on the wall above the table, made a Sign of Five in the air,
and walked over to his desk. He sat down, leaned back with a sigh,
and once again promised himself that he really would make more of
an effort to wake up early enough to go through his morning invocation at home.

After a moment he pressed an intercom button.

"Any word on that body yet?"

"Yes," came the reply. "Parnell Burnam, age fifty-seven. Lived at
834 on the Avenue of Despair. He was a welder by trade."

"Sect?" demanded Sable.

"Cult of the Messenger."

"Shit!" muttered Sable. He hit another button. "Get me Benito
Vertucci on the vidphone." He waited a moment for the connection
to be made, then turned and faced the camera that was positioned
to the side of his chair. "Vertucci, this is John Sable."

"I know who you are," said the tall, black-hooded figure in stentorian tones.

"I thought we had an agreement," said Sable harshly.

"What do you mean?" asked Vertucci.

"Two ritual murders a year," said Sable, trying to control his
anger. "That was the deal."

"We have committed only two this year," was the reply. "Both
were registered with your department."

"Then explain Parnell Burnam to me!"

"The name is unfamiliar," said Vertucci.

"He happens to be a member of your cult!" snapped Sable. "At
least, he was until he got his throat slashed last night. Murder happens to be a capital crime, even in Amaymon. We agreed to close
our eyes to two killings a year apiece from your group and the
Church of Baal, provided you kept it within your own sects. But

you've crossed the line on this one, and I'm going to nail you for it."

"The Cult of the Messenger does not mutilate necks, ritually or otherwise," said Vertucci. "I am as anxious to see the murderer brought to justice as you are, Detective Sable. You must believe me about this."

"Are you willing to face the truthtell machine?" demanded Sable.

"I am."

"I'll have the dose turned up to lethal."

"Satan is with me," said Vertucci serenely. "Send one of your operatives by for me at your convenience."

"One hour," promised Sable, breaking the connection.

He hit another intercom button. "Have someone bring Benito Vertucci in for questioning, and find out if there's ever any variation of the standard procedure for a Messenger ritual killing. Oh—and tell Langston Davies that I want to see him."

He pulled out a cigar, was about to light it, realized that he would have to offer one to Davies, and put it back in his pocket with a wry smile as he realized that even the Chief of Detectives was starting to feel the pinch of inflation.

Davies entered his office a moment later, a tall, cadaverous man in his mid-thirties who had been attempting to cultivate a beard with only moderate success.

"You sent for me?" he asked, pulling up a chair.

"You've been on the Burnam thing all morning, haven't you?" asked Sable.

Davies nodded. "Looks open-and-shut to me. The guy was a Messenger."

"What if I told you Benito Vertucci is coming in to face the truthtell machine?"

"He's bluffing," answered Davies firmly.

"I don't think so," said Sable. "I've got someone checking on it right now, but I think we're going to find that it wasn't a ritual killing."

"It's got to be. The man had three thousand yen in his pocket and one hell of a gold amulet around his neck. It sure as blazes wasn't a robbery."

"Lovers' quarrel?" suggested Sable.

"Not hardly," said Davies with a chuckle. "The guy lived alone, and according to his medical file he's been impotent for the better part of twenty years."

"Couldn't *that* produce a frustrated lover?" inquired Sable mildly.

"I'll check it out, but I think you're reaching," said Davies. "By the way, you wouldn't happen to have one of those wonderful cigars of yours lying around, would you?"

Sable smiled ironically and withdrew a pair, handing one to Davies and lighting the other himself. "Did Burnam have any problems at work?" he asked at last.

"I doubt it," said Davies. "The guy inherited a bundle a few years back. Gave most of it to the Cult of the Messenger, but he kept enough to live very comfortably. He'd refused a couple of promotions in his machine shop because he liked what he was doing, and I don't imagine letting people skip over you in seniority is apt to produce too many enemies."

"What was he doing last night?"

"Getting killed."

"Before that," Sable said irritably.

"I don't know," said Davies. "He lived alone, ate most of his meals out. Probably he was at some bar or watching a Tri-Fi. Or he could have been with the cult. They deny it, of course, but that's how I see it. They slit his throat for some reason or other and then dumped him downtown."

Sable shook his head slowly. "I've got a gut feeling that says the Messengers didn't do it. We get our share of murders in this town, but usually they're ritual killings or else very obvious crimes of passion or profit. This one smells different. It *feels* wrong."

"It's a pity you gave up voodoo when you married Siboyan," said Davies. "I understand they've got a ceremony that's really great for ferreting out criminals."

"You understand wrong," said Sable. "Voodoo's like any other religion; long on comfort and short on results."

"So you keep telling me," said Davies with a smile. "Yet it remains one of the most popular sects."

"Almost every black man starts out in voodoo," replied Sable. "Most of us leave it sooner or later. It's a little too barbaric for my tastes. And now perhaps we'd better get back to the subject at hand, equally barbaric though it may be."

"To tell the truth, it wasn't all that brutal a killing," said Davies. "It was quick, clean, efficient. I doubt that Burnam knew what happened to him."

"You'd better check the local bars and restaurants and see if anyone was getting out of hand last night," said Sable. "I'll handle the Messengers, but I don't think they're going to be able to help us on this one."

"Anything else?" asked Davies.

"Yes," said Sable. "See if the Church of Baal has any grievances against the Messengers. Maybe Burnam's murder was just a warning to them, though I doubt it."

Davies left the office, and Sable leaned back, folded his hands behind his head, and savored the aroma of his cigar.

It was puzzling. He knew he was sending Davies on a wild-goose chase, though of course he had to explore every possibility. But if Burnam was the Church of Baal's calling card they had forgotten to sign it, and he couldn't believe they were that careless. There was an order to the universe, a surplus of motives rather than a lack of them, and he knew if he proceeded methodically and vigorously he would come upon the motive for this murder sooner or later, and then everything would fall into place. In fact, he reflected wryly, that was his job in a nutshell: preventing the chaos of the human psyche from spilling over into the structured order of daily life. Still, it could have been worse; at least he lived on a world where the normal aggressions and hatreds of the race were channeled into spiritual outlets rather than suppressed to the point where they began popping up all over the landscape, and for that he was grateful.

His reverie was broken by a call from Siboyan, who informed him that their younger son had contracted a mild case of the flu and asked him to bring home some asafetida and vervain from the herbalist and to buy some more ceremonial candles when he had the time. He dutifully jotted down her requests, added a note to pick up a toy for the boy, and then explained that he had to get back to work.

He waited for Vertucci in the truthtell room, got the negative responses he had expected, and released him.

More information kept crossing his desk all morning and afternoon. The murder weapon had not been found. The Church of Baal didn't have any arguments with anyone. The Cult of the Messenger's ritual murders were always performed by a knife thrust through the heart while the victim lay on an altar. There were no fingerprints on the body. Burnam had eaten at the Roost, an inexpensive restaurant in the center of town, but his whereabouts for the next three hours were unknown. A fat, redheaded man that no one could identify had been thrown out of a couple of bars, seemingly in too intoxicated a condition to hold a knife, let alone wield it like an expert, thought that would bear some looking into. Burnam was the most popular man at his place of work, without an enemy in the world. Burnam had not been seen in the company of a woman for almost two decades, nor could any homosexual contacts be uncovered. Burnam's rent was paid for three months in advance, and the bulk of his money was drawing interest in a local bank.

Yet there *had* to be a motive. Sable knew that this wasn't the work of a madman or some fanatic in a state of drug-induced or religious frenzy; it was much too cold-blooded and efficient for that.

He half wished that he himself had been a little less efficient in the past. That way, at least, there might be other unsolved murders to link this one to, other killers still prowling the streets of Amaymon. But there weren't. He had been Chief of Detectives for seven years, and his record was perfect: forty-three murders, forty-three arrests, forty-three convictions. There was nothing in the past to which he could tie this killing.

Sable lit another cigar—his fourth of the day, he noted guiltily—and concentrated on the facts before him.

All right. It wasn't the Cult of the Messenger. It wasn't the Church of Baal. It wasn't a lover of either sex. It wasn't a thief. It wasn't this. It wasn't that.

Then who could it be?

Sable lowered his head in thought, then sat bolt-upright.

Bland?

Sable considered the notion for a moment, then rejected it. Bland was still in Tifereth, and besides, they were on his side. More, they were the only people in the whole Republic who were on his side. He'd know better than to turn on them.

All right. If not Bland, then who?

And if it wasn't tied to the past, could it perhaps be tied to something else?

He stared blankly at the baphomet on his wall, considering all the possibilities.

Then, suddenly, John Sable began to get very excited. He had a totally wild notion, a longshot among longshots, but deep down in his gut, where such judgments were weighed and made, it felt *right*.

Chapter 4

"Suffering serves no useful purpose, but it does delight the eye."
— Conrad Bland

Jericho returned to each of his four rented rooms after the killing, disturbing the covers and making enough of a mess in the bathrooms so it would appear that they were actually being used. Then he went out, looted two more stores, and moved into the Talisman, a middle-class hotel. He slept until sunrise, breakfasted, purchased a better grade of clothing, disposed of the clothes he had stolen, and spent most of the morning and early afternoon watching the video set in his room. He concentrated on soap operas, hoping to glean more about the customs and habits of Walpurgis.

What he saw confused him. There were differences between Walpurgan society and the rest of the Republic worlds, but the differences were very subtle. He was not surprised to discover that an expression of "Gezundheit!" when someone sneezed was looked upon as an insult or a curse, since these people had no desire to wish devils out of their bodies. But try as he might, he couldn't understand why a prayer to Belial was a source of amusement while the same prayer offered to Baal was supposed to draw tears from the audience, or why a woman would submit to sexual ravishment at the hands of one black-cloaked figure and would take offense when another merely tried to hold her hand.

There was, for example, a Cult of Cthulhu, a demon that he knew from his research to be a totally fictitious creation, but as far as he could tell no one worshiped or even mentioned Lucifuge Rofocale, who was supposed to be the commander of the armies of Hell. Some of the actresses dressed like an adolescent boy's kinkiest fantasy, replete with rubber, leather, whips, and spurs, while others covered themselves from head to toe, and he was simply unable to pinpoint any correlation between their behavior and their dress modes.

It was after watching a half-dozen video shows that he knew he would have to seek out Ibo Ubusuku, the Republic's undercover operative, and get a thorough backgrounding on the society that he was going to have to infiltrate. He hadn't wanted to make his presence known to anyone, not even a Republic agent, but he simply had too many areas of ignorance, too many wrong manners and habits to begin approaching Bland yet.

He checked the hour and decided that it was time to see how the police were progressing. He had given them all morning to come to the conclusion that they weren't dealing with any normal, run-of-the-mill murder. He had already given them a timetable: If they weren't looking for an obese redheaded drunkard by nightfall and searching through his four cheap hotel rooms by late the following afternoon, they wouldn't pose much of a problem to him in the future. And if they ran ahead of schedule, well, it was best to know now what trouble they could cause him later.

Keeping the guise of a blond man in his mid-thirties, which he had assumed after the murder and had decided upon as his primary persona during his stay in Amaymon, he went out and began walking the mile or so to the first of the two taverns he had visited the previous night

He had gone only three blocks when he was accosted by a scarlet-robed man who carried a pile of leaflets and wore a distinctive jeweled amulet.

"Excuse me, citizen," said the man, "but can I offer you one of these?"

He waved a leaflet under Jericho's nose.

"Why not?" said Jericho with a smile, taking it from his hand.

"What's your position on Conrad Bland?" continued the man.

"I haven't any," said Jericho.

"But you've heard of him?"

"Vaguely, in passing."

"Our position—and the position of all the churches—is that Bland is the savior of Walpurgis," said the man passionately. "It's all spelled out in the leaflet."

"Who does Walpurgis need saving from?" asked Jericho.

"From the Republic. You know that they've demanded his extradition and that we've refused?"

"I don't read the papers," said Jericho.

"You won't find it in the papers," said the man. "The government—the *civil* government—isn't happy about it at all. They wanted to turn him over to the Republic, but the Council of Sects put enough pressure on them so they had to back down."

"Then what's the problem?"

"They've clamped down on the news media. Hell, a third of the people don't even know Bland's on Walpurgis, and those who do are like you, meaning no offense. We may someday have to go to war over Bland, so we're trying to educate the lay public about him."

"Then I'd better take this home and read it," said Jericho.

"That's all we ask," said the man, spying another pedestrian and heading off to give him a leaflet.

Jericho took a quick look at the handout. It told him nothing new about Bland; indeed, it was nothing but an impassioned tract praising him as the personification of evil, and neglecting to mention those deeds that might have supported the argument.

But while it told him nothing about Bland, it told him quite a bit about the political situation on Walpurgis. The theocracy wasn't as all-powerful as Mela had led him to believe, or else it wouldn't be trying to win the public over to its side by force of argument. The civil government still held most of the reins of power, certainly they controlled the media, and they represented a real obstacle to the theocracy on this particular issue. But the most interesting finding of all was that the man in the street was not likely to be a devout advocate of saving or protecting Bland. Indeed, a lot of men in the street didn't even know who Bland was, which was borne out by the ignorance of the desk clerk at the first hotel he had visited.

He tossed the leaflet into the next garbage atomizer he came to, then continued on to the tavern. Nothing much was happening there, no police were visible, most of the evening crowd hasn't gotten off work yet, so he ordered a local brand of beer and nursed it slowly, his eyes riveted to the mirror above the bar, watching every movement on the street.

An hour passed, then another. Jericho was undisturbed; he had spent most of his professional life waiting in one manner or another, and he was used to it.

It was late afternoon now, and the streets began to get a little more congested with both people and vehicles. And then a tall, thin man with a sparse beard entered the tavern.

The man walked up to the bartender and began conversing in low tones. The bartender listened attentively, shrugged once, then nodded. The man said something further, and the bartender shook his head vigorously.

Finally the man broke off the conversation and walked to the middle of the room.

"Excuse me," he said in a loud voice, holding up a small golden emblem for any interested bystanders to see. "I am Langston Davies, assistant to Chief of Detectives Sable, and I'm looking for a heavy-set man with red or brown hair who was in here last night. Does anyone recall seeing him?"

There was general murmuring of negatives. Jericho considered speaking up and laying another false trail, but decided against it. Sooner or later they would realize they had been lied to, and since only one person would have any reason for lying, he would have revealed his ability to move into and out of identities at will.

"He would have been very drunk," continued Davies, looking hopefully around the room. "He either came here from the Devil's Den or else went there directly after leaving this place. We've posted a reward for any information that anyone may have."

"How big a reward?" asked a woman who was sitting alone at a table.

"That depends on how useful the information is," said Davies. "I'll leave my card here in case anyone decides to get in touch with me."

There was no response, and Davies paused for a moment and then left.

Jericho checked the clock on the wall.

Right on schedule. Davies would check the Devil's Den and the restaurant before dark. Possibly he'd find someone who had actually seen him; probably he wouldn't. Midafternoon habitués of bars and coffee shops usually weren't around at midnight.

Davies would report back, and they'd realize that hunting for witnesses was a dead end. By early evening they'd be staking out all the hotels in the area, and by midmorning at the latest they'd realize they were following a cold trail. Then would come the methodical checking of every recently rented hotel room and a search of those rooms. They'd find his four rooms by late afternoon tomorrow.

Par for the course. Efficient but uninspired. Jericho allowed himself the luxury of a tiny, unseen smile.

He paid his tab and walked out the door, almost bumping into Davies, who was gesticulating wildly and arguing with what was obviously a colleague.

"But what in blazes does he want us to do?" Davies was demanding.

"I don't know," came the reply, "but he says we're wasting our time, that there isn't any fat guy."

"And he doesn't want to start checking out the hotels?" insisted Davies.

Jericho wanted to listen further, but even dropping something on the ground and pausing to pick it up might be too obvious. So, frustrated, he continued walking.

He didn't know who the "he" was that the two detectives were referring to. Probably this Chief Sable. But whoever it was, he'd caught on a little too quickly for comfort.

He made his round of the four rooms again, making each look lived in, then returned to his headquarters hotel and took out the disc containing the information on Ubusuku.

What he learned wasn't all that encouraging. Ibo Ubusuku had been a minor functionary in the diplomatic corps who had accepted the assignment on Walpurgis merely to jump up a couple of notches in his job rating and pay scale. He was a tall, black man of Zulu heritage with an excellent academic background but no training in espionage, undercover work, or covert operations of any kind—nor, for that matter, was there anything in his record to imply that he knew the first thing about cults and covens. He had applied to the Walpurgis Immigration Bureau, had been one of only twenty secular applicants accepted during the past two years, and had reported back to his superiors only once.

The gist of that report, short and simple, was that he had seen no trace and heard no mention of Conrad Bland, and that any operative who wished to get in touch with him could take out an ad in the classified section of the Amaymon newspaper stating that he wished to purchase a Red Letter facsimile edition of the *Compendium Maleficarum* in the original Latin. Ubusuku would reply to the advertiser's box number and a meeting could be arranged.

Jericho put the disc away and considered his situation. Someone had already seen through his disguise, and without doing the necessary legwork. It was not unreasonable to suppose that that same man would be waiting for him to make contact with an operative who was already in place. He couldn't know that the operative was Ubusuku; or, if he did, Ubusuku would already be in custody and beyond Jericho's reach.

Jericho had to proceed on the supposition that Ubusuku was at large and free from suspicion. Now, if his adversary didn't know how to waylay the incoming messages at Ubusuku's end, it made sense to try to stop them at their source. The police couldn't very well tap every vidphone in the city, but Jericho had already checked and discovered that Ubusuku had either no vidphone at all or an unlisted one. This Sable didn't figure to be a fool; he'd know he was starting off a couple of steps behind, and wouldn't waste his time with vidphones and the mails. He'd proceed on the assumption that Jericho was in the dark about Ubusuku's whereabouts, just as Jericho had to assume that Ubusuku's whereabouts didn't include a jail or an interrogation camp.

Jericho lay back on his bed, staring at the somewhat inexpert rendering of a Black Mass on the ceiling, and tried to extrapolate Sable's next move. The detective would keep a watchful eye on all means of public contact, of course, and that would include personal ads. There was nothing in the message to arouse suspicion, but now that Sable had figured out that he could alter his appearance, *any* stranger placing an ad would be suspect.

Still, he couldn't proceed any further without some kind of backgrounding, so he hit upon a compromise: He would place an ad, but not the one that would trigger a response from Ubusuku. If it sparked no official interest, he would place another within the next day or two.

He stood before the mirror, giving himself a head of thick, bushy gray hair. When this was done he inserted lifts into his shoes. The end result was to add the illusion of between two and three inches to his height. He didn't know if it would help much, since they were looking for a faceless chameleon, but there was at least an outside chance they'd be looking for a somewhat shorter man, and he hadn't gotten this far by not being thorough and cautious.

His new disguise in place, he walked six blocks to the paper's local office, inserted a personal notice to the effect that he was searching for a blond woman he had met at a party two weeks ago, paid for the ad in cash, gave the address of a hotel across the street that he could observe from his window, and returned to his own room. He shaved, showered, took a brief nap, and reclaimed his standard identity.

Then he pulled a chair up near the window, sat down, and kept a watchful eye on the nearby hotel. And as he waited for any sign of discovery, he put himself in Sable's shoes and tried to figure out what he would do next.

Chapter 5

*"The screams of the dying can be sweeter music than
any symphony."*
— *Conrad Bland*

Try as he would, Sable could never get used to the outward manifestations of affluence. He sat uncomfortably now, leaning back on a leather vibrochair, wondering if he dared to light up a cigar and certain that if he did his host would immediately offer him a far more expensive one. His gaze swept the massive room, passing over a number of jeweled artifacts and beautifully wrought oils, coming to rest on a solid gold statue of a winged Lucifer who seemed to be laughing at some very private joke.

"Well, John, what'll it be?" asked Pietre Veshinsky, tall, distinguished, immaculately dressed, the very picture of a Walpurgan aristocrat. "A little liquor, a happy pill, or perhaps something a little more exotic?"

"Just coffee," said Sable.

"That's not like you at all," said Veshinsky with a smile. "What's happened to that voracious Sable thirst?"

"Oh, it's still around," said Sable, returning his smile. "But I'm here on business this time."

"Oh?" Veshinsky raised his eyebrows. "You know I'm always glad to see you at my home, John—but if this is business, shouldn't you have gone through my office?"

"I tried, but they gave me the runaround."

"I'll have to speak to them about that," said Veshinsky calmly.

"They've got a lot of company. No one in the government seems to want to return my calls, and since I've known you for the better part of fifteen years, I thought I'd better have a little talk with you."

"I'm happy to oblige. What seems to be the trouble, John?"

"I have reason to believe that the Republic has placed an operative on Walpurgis with the intention of assassinating Conrad Bland."

Sable expected Veshinsky to make the Sign of the Horns, or utter a curse, or do *something*. But the tall man merely sipped his drink as if they were doing nothing more than discussing the weather.

"Why did you seek *me* out?" asked Veshinsky at last.

"You're a member of the City Council," said Sable, wondering at the lack of a reaction.

"What has one to do with the other?" asked Veshinsky.

"My department is having a difficult time getting necessary documents on this case," said Sable. "Files, records, all manner of things. No one is exactly denying us priority, but they're dragging their feet, and I don't think I've got much more than forty-eight hours to nail this killer."

"Just out of curiosity, John," said Veshinsky, picking up a Satanic idol and fingering it absently, "what makes you so sure you've got an assassin on your hands?"

"We had a killing downtown the night before last."

"Oh? Who was killed?"

"The name isn't important. What *is* important is that the killing was a very efficient, very professional job, and we were unable to find any motive for it."

"And from this you deduce the presence of a Republic assassin?" Veshinsky laughed. He set the idol down, walked across the thick carpet to the bar, and poured himself a refill.

Sable shook his head. "No. From that we could only deduce that we had a very skilled killer in our midst. But when our standard procedures couldn't turn up any clues we expanded our investigation, and found out that a Republic ship had set down at the spaceport for repairs the night before the murder."

"If you'll permit me to say so, John," said Veshinsky, returning to his chair and carefully setting his glass on an onyx coaster atop an altar-shaped end table, "that is an awfully tenuous chain of logic. If I were you I'd forget the whole thing before I made a public fool of myself."

"There's more," said Sable, trying to control his temper.

"I should hope so," said Veshinsky mockingly. "John, take a little advice from an old friend and give it up. Even if you're right, Conrad Bland is thousands of miles away. He's not your concern."

"No, but Parnell Burnam is."

"Who's that?"

"The dead man. This assassin has committed a murder in Amaymon, and it happens to be my job to solve crimes that occur in Amaymon. Since he could have put his ship down in half a dozen other places on the pretext of needing repairs, I can only assume that he has a contact here. I figure he'll make that contact in the next two days, and if we haven't nailed him by then, he'll be gone."

"What are you doing about him right now?" asked Veshinsky, staring at Sable from beneath half-lowered eyelids.

"I've posted watches on all offworlders who have settled in Amaymon during the past two years. If I had a little more manpower, I'd extend it to all immigrants for the past five or ten years, but I don't."

"What if your supposed killer's contact is a native of Walpurgis?"

"Then we're out of luck."

"I think you're out of luck in any event. You've given me no reason why you should assume Burnam's killer is a Republic assassin."

"Oh, I have a reason, all right. Yesterday afternoon he tried to place a personal advertisement in the paper. Probably it was a code of some sort to apprise his contact of his arrival."

"Why should you think so?" asked Veshinsky, returning to the bar for yet another drink.

"Because he gave his address as the Hotel Hanover."

"So?"

"The Hanover is a hotel for women only!" said Sable, his dark eyes shining fiercely. "Our assassin didn't know that. He'd obviously observed the place, seen men entering the restaurant and bar, or going up to visit the residents in their rooms, but he hadn't actually been there himself. More to the point, the hotel is owned by the Sisterhood of Sin. He didn't recognize their talisman, didn't know what it stood for. Only an offworlder would commit a blunder like that. When the hotel got a pair of vidphone calls asking for the phony name he had used, the desk clerk contacted us. Our killer has made his first blunder."

"Oh, come now, John," scoffed Veshinsky. "How do you know that it wasn't just a prank?"

"I don't *know* anything," explained Sable patiently. "I am simply making an educated guess. If I waited for hard information on a man like this, he'd have completed his mission and left the planet before I had a single verifiable fact on him."

"All right, John," said Veshinsky, his face suddenly hard. "Let me ask you a few simple questions, all right?"

"Go ahead."

"Have you found any connection between Parnell Burnam and Conrad Bland?"

"No."

"Have you any tangible proof that anyone got off the Republic ship?"

Sable shook his head. "No."

"Have you any reason to believe that any immigrants are working for the Republic?"

"Only the presence of the assassin."

"*If* there's an assassin," corrected Veshinsky. "Have you any proof that other departments are dragging their feet on this?"

"Hard proof? No."

"Then allow me to suggest that perhaps what you need is not a manhunt but a vacation," said Veshinsky. "If I were you, I wouldn't jeopardize my health by remaining on the job one minute longer than I had to."

"It's out of the question," said Sable firmly. "We've got an assassin on our hands, and he's not going to wait around Amaymon until we're ready to trap him. He's going to make his contact, and then he'll be off to Tifereth."

"If not a vacation, then perhaps a medical leave of absence," said Veshinsky. "I'll see to it that you don't lose any pay."

"Why don't you spend a little less time worrying about me and a little more worrying about Bland?" said Sable. "Despite the fact that I seem unable to convince you, there *is* an assassin in Amaymon, and Bland has got to be his target."

"Ah, John," sighed Veshinsky, "subtlety was never your strong suit, was it? You have convinced me that what you said is true; I only wish I could do the same."

"What are you talking about?"

"What do you think of my house, John?" said Veshinsky.

"Why?"

"Just answer the question."

"It's a very nice house."

"It's more than a very nice house. It's a palace. It has seventeen rooms, video-cinema tie-ins in each room, fireplaces and bars almost beyond counting, thick white carpeting, objects of art that you couldn't afford if they multiplied your salary by a factor of ten. I have four butlers, two maids, a robot housekeeper, two manservants, a doctor on twenty-four-hour call. I have—"

"I know what you have," interrupted Sable. "What's the point?"

"The point, my friend John, is that I didn't acquire all of this by sticking my nose in where it didn't belong."

"Let me get this straight, Pietre," said Sable. "Are you *bribing* me not to get involved in this thing?"

"Nothing of the sort, John," answered Veshinsky. "A man has been murdered. You are Chief of Detectives. It is certainly your job to try to solve it."

"But my job ends three thousand miles south of Tifereth, is that it?" persisted Sable.

"I never said that, John," said Veshinsky. "Though, of course, it's quite true."

"Are you seriously telling me that the government knows that someone's out to kill Conrad Bland and they won't lift a finger to stop him?"

"I am telling you no such thing."

"But you would if you were free to," said Sable.

"Nonsense."

"Then I presume that I can depend upon you to facilitate my job?"

"I'll do what I can," said Veshinsky. He reached behind the bar and pulled out a large box. Opening it, he handed six carefully wrapped cigars to Sable.

"Take these with you. I think you'll enjoy them."

"I really shouldn't," said Sable, but he reached out and took them anyway.

"Aren't you going to have one now?" asked Veshinsky as Sable put the cigars into a lapel pocket.

"These are too good to smoke while I'm working. I'll have one a night. And thanks."

"My pleasure. I'll walk you to the door."

"I can find my way out," said Sable. "Goodbye, Pietre."

"Goodbye, John," replied Veshinsky. He touched a button behind the bar and surrounded himself with quadraphonic holograms of his favorite symphony orchestra.

Sable left Veshinsky's home, signaled to his driver to pick him up, and was back in his office twenty minutes later, wondering why the government didn't seem concerned about the threat to Bland, but indeed seemed to welcome it. He spent a little while thinking about that, finally shook his head as if to rid himself of the problem by a physical action, and summoned Davies and six other members of his staff, two men and four women.

"How did things go with Veshinsky?" asked one of the women when all were seated.

"Not very well," replied Sable. "How about our offworld travelers?"

He had wanted to interview the five Amaymon businessmen who had recently been to other planets for the simple reason that while the assassin was a stranger to Walpurgan customs, neither Sable nor anyone on his staff had ever been off the planet and thus couldn't begin to know precisely how their customs differed from those of the other Republic worlds. He was hoping someone would be able to tell him how to differentiate between eccentric behavior and *wrong* behavior.

"They're making lists," replied Davies sardonically. "What else are experts good for?"

"Any word when they'll be ready to talk to us?"

"Nope. I also get the distinct impression that certain powers in the government would prefer that we didn't rush them."

"It's an impression I share," said Sable. He surveyed his seven senior staff members for a long moment. "All right," he announced at last. "I'm no expert, but I have a feeling that if we wait for our bona fide authorities to help us out we're all going to die of old age. So let me lay out some broad general guidelines for you to pass on to the people working under your supervision.

"First," he continued, "forget about language. There are already a number of accents on Walpurgis, and everyone in the Republic uses the same base tongue. If our killer knows the name of a distant city, and he must by now, all he has to do is say he comes from there.

"Second, forget about physical descriptions. He's a chameleon, and you can bet that by the time you think you know what he looks like, he's already discarded that identity."

"So what *do* we look for?" asked another of the women.

"Little things," replied Sable. "Things he hasn't had a chance to learn yet. Don't watch for huge blunders, because he isn't going to make any."

"Give us a for-instance," she persisted.

"All right. If he's as thorough as I think, he'll make sure his hotel maid sees burnt-out candles and offerings to the demon of his choice. I think we should look for a room where the candles are placed in a strange configuration, or where he offered, say, fruit to Belial. I think we should look for a man who is ignorant of the letter of our customs, but not of the customs themselves. For example, *we* know that a man who makes the Sign of Five will never make the Sign of the Horns or the Sign of Satan, but *he* probably doesn't know it yet, and he won't know it until he makes a mistake and someone notices. He can also be expected to have a little trouble with our symbols at first: he may very well deduce that a man wearing the Talisman of Saturn over his left breast is a member of the Order of the Golem but he may never know that the same token worn over the right breast makes the wearer a warlock in the Church of the Inferno. If you see him on the street wearing the talisman *you* may not know that he's blundered, but sooner or later he's going to walk into the wrong church or make the wrong sign and *someone* will know."

"It makes finding a needle in a haystack look easy by comparison," said one of the men.

"The whole trick is to approach the problem at the proper angle," said Sable. "Look directly at a godsnake in a patch of silverweeds for an hour and you might never see him; blink once and cock your head and there he is, big as a mountain. We've got to get used to blinking—and we've got to get used to it soon. With every minute that passes his education continues—and the obvious corollary is that the more he learns about us, the less likely we are to learn anything about him."

"Not to sound defeatist," said the other man, "but this doesn't sound very hopeful. Maybe a massive dose of publicity, even public panic, might prod this guy out into the open."

Sable shook his head. "Not this man. One thing he's not going to do is lose his composure."

"What makes you so sure?"

"Because the Republic hasn't sent in an amateur. We're dealing with a man to whom this is strictly routine. He does it all the time, knows all the tricks of the trade, probably feels right at home hiding out in a crowd. He came in absolutely cold, and he's managed to maintain at least two identities and pull off a murder right under our noses. He's made only one mistake, and it was a very minor one." Sable looked around the room grimly. "Just how many more mistakes do you think a man like this is going to make?"

He received no answer, nor had he expected one, and a moment later his staff filed silently out of his office.

"Think it'll do any good?" asked Davies, who stayed behind.

"Who knows?" shrugged Sable. "But we've got to do *something*. I'm open to alternatives."

"I wish I had one," admitted Davies.

They sat in silence for perhaps five minutes. Then his secretary put through a vidphone call from Pietre Veshinsky.

"Hello, John."

"Hello," replied Sable. "I hadn't expected you to get back to me so soon."

"There wasn't much sense waiting," said Veshinsky. "I made a few calls, spoke to a few people, and didn't see any sense procrastinating."

"Can you help us?"

"No, John, I can't."

"Can anyone?"

"That's an awkward question, John."

"It's an awkward situation, Pietre. The man's a hired killer. He's already murdered a citizen of Amaymon. I can't just sit on my hands."

"I know that, John."

"Can I expect out-and-out physical or legal hindrance if I catch him?"

"I doubt it."

"You *doubt* it?" demanded Sable. "You mean to say that there's a chance of it?"

"No, John. Let me word that more definitely: No one will hinder you in any way."

"They just won't help me, is that it?"

"In essence."

"Well, fuck them, Pietre!" snapped Sable. "I don't know the first damned thing about Bland, but I know my job and you can tell your friends I'm going to do it!"

He broke the connection and started stalking around his office, feeling constricted by the walls, the ceiling, the government, his clothing, everything.

"Well said," said Davies.

"Don't be an ass, Langston," snapped Sable.

"Huh?"

" 'I know my job!' " he repeated mockingly. "Damn it, Lang, right now my job consists of sitting around waiting until he kills someone else!"

He walked over to the window and looked out onto the winding streets of Amaymon, cursing under his breath and wondering if the killer was even now within his field of vision—or, if not, where he was and what he was doing.

Chapter 6

"Evil has no friends, and therefore need not concern itself with loyalty."

—*Conrad Bland*

Ibo Ubusuku stepped off the lift, walked down the corridor to his apartment, and punched out the combination to his lock. As the door opened he tossed his red satin cape onto an ebon clothespole that had been carved to resemble an enormous phallus. Then he walked through the foyer to the kitchen, deposited two canisters of liquor he had purchased on the way home from work onto a counter, poured himself a tall drink from one, dialed a pair of ice cubes from his freezer unit, and went to his study with the intention of doing a little reading. When he got there he found a blond man of nondescript features sitting at his desk, staring emotionlessly at him.

"Who the hell are you and what do you think you're doing here?" demanded Ubusuku.

"I thought perhaps you'd like to purchase a Red Letter facsimile edition of the *Compendium Maleficarum* in the original Latin," said Jericho.

Ubusuku threw back his head and laughed. "You scared me half to death! Why didn't you contact me through the newspaper?"

"I ran a test ad yesterday afternoon to see if there would be any reaction."

"And they spotted it?" said Ubusuku. "Well, so much for my great idea about covert contact."

"Nobody spotted anything that I know of," said Jericho.

"Maybe I'm missing something, but if the ad went through, why didn't you follow it up with the real one?"

"Instinct," replied Jericho. "Nothing I could put my finger on. But something told me not to try it again, and I didn't make it this far by not listening to my instincts."

"How did you find me, then?" asked Ubusuku, offering Jericho his drink, which he refused.

"It wasn't that difficult. I knew there had to be a list of resident aliens somewhere in the city, and it stood to reason that the post office would possess it. So I broke in there last night, found your address, and came here."

"You broke into the post office?" repeated Ubusuku with a smile.

"Sneaked in is perhaps a better way of describing it," said Jericho. "Everything is as it was, nothing was taken, no trace of my presence was left. The video monitors will show anyone who checks them out that no one entered or left after hours."

"And you just strolled over to my apartment and made yourself at home?"

"It wasn't quite that simple," said Jericho. "I had to make sure that no one saw me enter, and that's quite a little lock you've got on your door. It took me almost ten minutes to break the code."

"Ten minutes!" exclaimed Ubusuku. "Do you know how much I paid for that damned lock?"

"I wouldn't worry about it," said Jericho impassively. "I doubt that anyone else on this planet could break in here except by force."

"Well, you're here and you're safe and sound and that's all that counts," said Ubusuku, trying to put the ease with which Jericho had gotten there out of his mind. "I've been waiting for the Republic to send someone down here for almost a year. I think you'll enjoy Amaymon. It's got a beautiful climate and the people are—"

"I didn't come here to enjoy myself," said Jericho.

"Sorry." Ubusuku grinned. "But I've got to warn you to get rid of all your preconceptions about witchcraft and devil worship. They simply don't apply."

"Oh?"

"I thought the same as everyone else when I arrived," said Ubusuku, his enthusiasm growing. "I thought there'd be people ripping babies open by the light of the full moon and all that kind of shit. But it's not like that at all. I took a good, hard look at what these people were doing and what they had, and by God—or by Lucifer, I suppose I should say—I converted!"

"I noticed the trappings," said Jericho, looking about the room, which was littered with Satanic artifacts. "This is the first private dwelling I've been in since I got here. Is it typical?"

"Not for everyone," said Ubusuku, adding with a touch of pride. "Just for *my* cult."

He put his glass down and started walking around the room, pointing out the various things that made it unique to him. "See this baphomet, now? All of them have goat's heads, but the beard makes it the property of the Order of the Golem. And this big round thing over here that looks like an oversized talisman? It's the Seal of Solomon, which is the seal of my cult."

"And all the pornographic paintings on the walls—are they religious symbols too?" asked Jericho with a smile.

"Absolutely!" said Ubusuku. "My cult is a little more hedonistic than most, which is really saying something for a Walpurgis cult. We're very conscious of the need for pleasure, so we surround ourselves with enchantments, so to speak. Old Nellie here," he said, giving a fond pat to the posterior of a shapely young woman who was copulating with three man-sized toads at once, "is my favorite. She was painted by a fellow who lives in the building, if you'd like to meet him—but no, of course you wouldn't. Excuse me for running off at the mouth. What's your mission here and how can I help you accomplish it?"

"I'm afraid its nature is confidential."

"It's got to have something to do with Conrad Bland, right?" said Ubusuku with a smile.

"Why should you think so?"

"Oh, come on!" Ubusuku laughed. "What else could the Republic be interested in on this planet? My guess is that you're here to kidnap him or kill him—not that I personally give a damn, mind you."

"Why not?" asked Jericho, fingering a sacrificial dagger graven with images of toads, snakes, and lizards.

"What's he to me?" said Ubusuku. "The man's a goddamned butcher, isn't he? That's got nothing to do with Satanism."

"Isn't Satan supposed to be a butcher?" asked Jericho mildly.

"No!" exclaimed Ubusuku. "You see, that's where your preconceptions lead you astray! We believe in pleasure, in indulgence, in gratification. Oh, we're opposed to turning the other cheek and a lot of that lily-white crap, but we're a religion that's based on satisfaction of the senses, not termination of them."

"From what I understand, Bland gets his satisfaction from terminating other people's senses," commented Jericho dryly.

"That's why I don't give a damn what happens to him!" said Ubusuku, seemingly unaware of the faulty logic behind his statement.

Jericho decided to let it pass. He was not, after all, here to engage in a theological debate.

"Getting back to your offer," he said at last, "you can help me by giving me some background on the society."

"History or religion?" asked Ubusuku.

"Neither, at least in an academic sense. But I'm going to have to pass for a native, and I've got to know enough about it so that I don't make any mistakes that will identify me."

"How long have you got?"

"I'm not sure," replied Jericho, wondering how close Sable was to guessing the truth. "Maybe a day, possibly two."

"It can't be done," said Ubusuku. "Oh, I could tell you what the major sects are, and how they differ in their beliefs, and what constitutes a major social blunder, and how we got to be this way . . . but I can't pass you off as a Walpurgan in two days."

"I adapt very quickly."

"No one adapts *that* quickly," said Ubusuku. "It took me months, and I had nothing else to do with my time except learn how to fit in. It's tricky, because it's so much *like* any other world of the Republic. We eat the same food, we use the same transportation, we live in the same buildings, we pay for products with currency. But on a deeper, subtler level, it's as different as a society can be."

"For example?"

"For example, I say a Regie Satanis instead of an Our Father. I don't use credits unless I'm dealing with another Republic world. I buy steaks and bread and wine, but I also buy bat wings and dead spiders. I'll walk under a ladder, but I make the Sign of the Horns whenever I hear a clap of thunder. But I speak the same language as you do, I put my clothes on the same way, I can't imagine that my sexual techniques are a hell of a lot different. Do you begin to see the problem?"

"Let me approach it another way," said Jericho. "Does everyone make the Sign of the Horns at the sound of thunder?"

"Of course not," said Ubusuku. "The Daughters of Delight do, but the Brotherhood of Night makes the Sign of Five, and I doubt that the other sects do anything much except get in out of the rain or open their umbrellas."

"Good!" said Jericho. "You've made everything a lot simpler."

"I have?"

Jericho nodded. "Now I don't have to learn every gesture and symbol around. What I need from you is a list of those symbols, reactions, beliefs, whatever, that *everyone* displays, no matter what their sect is."

"I can do that," said Ubusuku. "I *will* do that. But it won't be enough."

"Why not?"

"Because if you don't practice *some* form of religion you're going to stick out like a sore thumb. Look: spaceflight is cheap, worlds are cheap, and Walpurgis is on its fifth or sixth generation. Anyone who didn't believe in Satanism or witchcraft to some greater or lesser degree didn't emigrate to Walpurgis to begin with, and of course the children have been brought up with their religious principles intact for more than a century. We don't have any Christian or Buddhist underground here. Why would we, with tens of thousands of planets for the asking, and the motive power to get there affordable to just about everyone? You don't have to be a Golemite or a Messenger or an Infernal, but you've got to be *something*." He lit a cigar, offered one to Jericho, who refused, and began using various portions of an obscene little statue as an ashtray.

"I see."

"I could school you on the Order of the Golem," offered Ubusuku, trying unsuccessfully to hide his eagerness.

"I think not," said Jericho. "After all," he lied, "if I should be captured during the course of my mission, I wouldn't want anything about my manner or my trappings to lead them to you."

"You've got a point there," said Ubusuku. "Well, at the risk of sounding like a salesman, what sort of religion are you looking for?"

"A popular one," said Jericho. "One of the largest."

"Funny," came the reply. "I would have thought you'd have preferred one of the tiny ones."

"It's easier to get lost in a big crowd than a little one," said Jericho. "And I want a religion where the layman carries no symbols or tokens around with him, where he just goes to the rituals, mumbles a few words, and goes home."

"Well," said Ubusuku, nodding, "I suppose you'll want to become a member of the Church of Satan. Voodoo's almost as big, but most of them are black and you'd be too obvious."

"If voodoo appeals to blacks, how come you didn't join?" asked Jericho.

"And spout a bunch of mumbo-jumbo and say the Lord's Prayer backward and all that crap?" said Ubusuku with a grimace. "No, thanks! Even if I didn't agree with their principles, I would have joined the Order of the Golem just for the sex alone! Let me tell you, friend, you can lose twenty pounds the first month before you convince yourself it's not all a dream and everything will still be there tomorrow."

Jericho remained silent.

"Well, suppose I dial us up a little dinner and we'll get to work?" said Ubusuku. "I'll also see if I can get us into a Satanic service tonight. In the meantime, my home is your home, although I realize that I'm offering it to you somewhat after the fact."

"Does that include your library?"

"Absolutely," said Ubusuku, rising and walking toward the kitchen.

"Do you have any maps in your study?" asked Jericho.

"Top left-hand drawer of my desk!" called Ubusuku from the kitchen.

Jericho knew where the maps were, of course; he had had about two hours to go over every inch of Ubusuku's apartment before he returned home, and the maps were the first thing he had sought out. However, to make a suitable impression on his unsuspecting host, he pulled out the map of Amaymon and spread it on the desk.

He then pulled out a somewhat less detailed map of the entire planet—the map he needed. If the police hadn't figured out who he was yet, they soon would; and they'd probably warn Bland to be on the lookout for a Republic assassin coming from Amaymon, which was almost three thousand miles south and a bit east of Tifereth.

He had already decided against the two most obvious and direct routes before Ubusuku arrived home, and now he began searching for alternatives. Finally he found what he had been looking for: a little town some two hundred miles north and east of Tifereth. It was called Malkuth, and had a population of about fifty thousand. He decided that his best bet was to approach Malkuth from the north, assimilate himself into the population if possible, and go south to Tifereth from Malkuth. If Bland didn't have an army he would at least have an enormous security force, and if they conscripted from beyond Tifereth itself, Malkuth seemed one of the likelier principalities. Possibly he could even manage to get himself drafted into Bland's forces; it was worth a try.

He studied the map further. Walpurgis was relatively newly settled, and the population wasn't going to be able to cover its adopted world with a network of cities and villages and hamlets for quite a few centuries yet. In fact, the mere existence of almost one hundred cities spread across the planet was unusual in itself; most colony worlds started with one or two central villages that radiated outward and evolved into hugely diverse cities in a matter of a few decades but left most of the planetary surface untouched. Probably Walpurgis had developed as it had because the sects found each other's beliefs inimical, but he made a mental note to check on it.

He spent a few minutes committing the vital portions of the map to memory, then folded it neatly and replaced it in Ubusuku's desk. He felt no need to remove his fingerprints; he had had none for fifteen years.

Then, rising, he walked through the apartment, scanning the titles of the books and tapes that cluttered the shelves. Most of them were either treatises on chlorine-world entomology or else works of pornography, which he took to be his host's academic and nonacademic fields of interest and expertise.

He went next into Ubusuku's bedroom, which was filled almost to overflowing with paintings and statues and holograms of demons and women locked in various perverted forms of sexual congress. He paid them scant attention and walked quickly to the mounds of books and journals that were piled carelessly on the floor. He hadn't had time to get to them before, and he was hoping they might include some local publications. To his disappointment, most of them were scholarly journals relating to insects.

He returned to the study just before Ubusuku came in with a huge smile on his face.

"I know it sounds corny as all hell," he said, "but how would you like deviled eggs?"

"They'll be fine," said Jericho. "And after dinner, perhaps you can recommend a couple of books or magazines that might help me."

"We'll discuss the universal customs and superstitions while we eat," said Ubusuku, "but you won't have any time for reading after we're through with dinner."

"Oh?"

"I've got a friend who's a member of the Church of Satan. He's been trying to convert me for months, and he agreed to get us into a Black Mass tonight."

"Good," said Jericho, following Ubusuku from the kitchen to the dining room.

"We'll be having some steak with our eggs," said Ubusuku, placing a pair of plates on the table and seating himself. "Which brings up the first of many points we've got to cover: There aren't many food taboos on Walpurgis, but the ones we have are pretty broad-based."

"Such as?"

"Such as never eating goat or any goat product."

"Why not?"

"The goat is one of our sacred symbols. It crosses just about all religious lines."

"Then why would anyone offer it on a menu?" asked Jericho, cutting into his steak.

"Because we've got about two million of them on the planet," said Ubusuku. "And some of the restaurants will serve goat meat or goat milk for the whites."

"What are whites?"

"White witches," said Ubusuku. "There aren't a lot of them, but there are enough in every city so that a few restaurants will cater to them."

"How does a white witch differ from any other one?"

"They believe in using magic for good," said Ubusuku.

"Seems kind of unrewarding on a world like Walpurgis," commented Jericho.

"It is," agreed Ubusuku. "Which leads me to another taboo: Don't wear white."

"I've noticed that hardly anyone does."

"There's a reason for it," explained Ubusuku. "Black is the holy color of most of the sects. White will identify you as a white witch, and there are so few of them that one of them will probably spot you as an impostor. Also, you'll run into trouble if you try to get into any place that's forbidden to them."

"Such as?"

"It's too involved to go into. Just make sure you don't wear white."

Jericho nodded. "Can a man be a white witch?"

"Certainly. Of course, we'd call such a man a white warlock, but it comes to the same thing. The witches aren't too thrilled with them, though; they've got enough troubles without them. Women have a rather ambiguous position on Walpurgis."

"In what way?"

"Politically they're equal to men in every respect, just as they are in the rest of the Republic. But our religions require them to practice various forms of enchantment. Most of these enchantments are ritualistic, but some of them are sexual, and this creates some conflicts. A number of women have risen to positions of enormous power: there's the Magdalene Jezebel, who's the head of the Daughters of Delight, and even the Cult of the Messenger has a High Priestess. But all in all, most of the religions are holdovers from the days when women were objects of lust and desire, and some of them have trouble balancing their positions in the church with the economic and political power they possess outside of it. It's a bad situation, and it's going to boil over one of these days. I hope I'll be peacefully dead and buried before it happens."

"How are women treated by men?" asked Jericho.

"I just told you."

"I mean on the streets."

"Ah!" said Ubusuku, his face lighting up. "Well, as I've said, they are political equals, and of course we believe in the principle of selfishness, so don't go opening doors for them, or tipping your hat, or treating them any differently than you'd treat a man. Chivalry is a *Republic* custom. And, on the subject of the Republic, try not to say anything civil about it. There's been a worldwide hate campaign going ever since the Republic tried to get Walpurgis to extradite Bland. And if you know any Republic slang, I'd advise you to forget it until you leave the planet. We've had so little contact with the other worlds that any slang that's cropped up in the past few years would be pretty easy to spot."

"What else?" said Jericho, finishing his steak and starting on the deviled eggs.

"Offhand, I wouldn't shake hands with anyone if I were you," said Ubusuku. "Rudeness is not the social stigma here that it is elsewhere, and there are so damned many secret handshakes that you'll never know which one you're getting or how to respond to it. Oh yes, and you'd better have a secret name."

"A secret name?"

"Everyone has one. Again, it's an almost universal trait among cultists. And it's best to be prepared—if you try to join a church, they may ask for yours. My own," he said with a touch of pride, "is Ehlis."

"Then I think I'll take Judas," said Jericho with a secret smile.

"That's not a demon," Ubusuku pointed out.

"I feel a certain kinship to him nonetheless," said Jericho.

"Whatever you want," said his host with a shrug. "And you'd better have a home town."

"What's wrong with Amaymon?"

"It's the biggest city on the planet, and most people have been here at one time or another. I think you'd be better off choosing a smaller city that almost no one goes to so you'll be less likely to be tripped up if someone questions you about it."

"Can you suggest one?"

"Well," said Ubusuku, "there's a tiny little town called Tannis about five hundred miles west of us. I know they've got a Church of Satan there, and I've only met three people from it in a year. Also, if anyone questions you closely, you can lie about it, which you can't do about Amaymon."

"Why should that be?"

"Amaymon was the first city on the planet, but a lot of the cults didn't like the religious freedom and tolerance Amaymon was forced to display as the home of maybe seventy sects. So they started their own outposts, which over the years have grown into cities. Most of them are on the River Styx, since barge traffic is still the cheapest way to ship goods between cities, but a lot of them are closed to outsiders once you get past their docking facilities. Since Amaymon has the only spaceport capable of handling the really big ships, it has always had more of a mix of religions."

"Have you been to any of the other cities?" asked Jericho.

"Why should I?" asked Ubusuku. "I like it here just fine. And besides, some of those other places take their religion a little too seriously."

"I thought you were serious about yours," commented Jericho.

"I'm serious about fucking a lot of women and having a good time for myself," said Ubusuku. "Some of those cities pay more than lip service to evil, let me tell you. I don't think Bland wound up in Tifereth by accident; it was a pretty strange place long before he got there. But to get back to some of the things you'll have to watch for, I'd strongly suggest that you never mention God, or Allah, or Jehovah, or whatever name He goes by in your culture, in conversation or even when cursing." He smiled. "We tend not to mention the enemy here. Also, don't whistle."

"Why not?"

"Many of the sects have secret identifying whistles, just as they have secret handshakes and passwords. Whistle the wrong thing and you might find yourself in a hell of a lot of trouble."

"I notice that you use 'hell' and 'damn' frequently in your speech," said Jericho. "Is that usual?"

"Except among the whites," said Ubusuku. "And while I'm thinking of it, some people will make the Sign of the Horns or the Sign of Five the way Christians make the Sign of the Cross. Your church doesn't have any such sign, so don't go trying to emulate it when you see someone else make it."

"Anything else I should know about the Church of Satan?"

"Just that your talisman is a goat's head inside a five-pointed star, which in turn is inside a circle. You'll see it a lot around Amaymon."

"I've seen a lot of talismans," said Jericho.

"Well, avoid the others. Most of the sects own various bars and restaurants and businesses, and when they display their talisman it's like hanging up a sign that says 'For Members Only.' You can get in a lot of trouble if you disregard it."

"You wouldn't happen to have a book on the local customs, would you?" asked Jericho.

"I've got a little giveaway pamphlet that they handed to me when I arrived," said Ubusuku. "And it's probably only valid in Amaymon."

"I'd like to take a quick look at it before we leave for the church."

"No problem," said Ubusuku. "I'll show it to you after dinner."

"Good," said Jericho, shifting carefully in his chair so as not to dislodge the sacrificial dagger he had taped to his leg.

Chapter 7

"I would never make a pact with Satan. I need no underlings."
—Conrad Bland

The Church of Satan, brand-new and glistening in the moonlight, was a huge Romanesque building with Moorish undertones. It was set back almost two hundred feet from the street, and was encircled by a black wrought-iron fence topped by razor-sharp spikes. Discordant electronic music emanated from within, and the exterior was illuminated by smoky red lights.

Ubusuku and Jericho stopped a few yards short of the gates, and while Jericho stood where he was and observed the people who were entering the church, Ubusuku walked up to one of the hooded men guarding the entrance and whispered a few brief words. The guard nodded, went off for a moment, and returned with a small, caped man whose only distinguishing feature was a thick shock of unruly gray hair.

"I didn't really think you were going to make it!" he exclaimed, grabbing Ubusuku by the shoulders and giving him an affectionate hug. "And where is your friend?"

Ubusuku led him over to Jericho. "This is Gaston Leroux," he said, gesturing toward the little man, "and this is my friend—"

"Orestes Mela," interrupted Jericho, stepping forward but not extending his hand.

"Well, I'm pleased to meet you, very pleased indeed," said Leroux with a cordial smile. "We'll have time to get acquainted later, but the service is due to begin any minute now."

"Big crowd?" asked Ubusuku as Leroux led the way up the stone walk to the doors of the church.

"For a weeknight," said Leroux with a shrug. "We've been drawing so well on weekends that we've had to hold two masses an evening."

"I don't think I'd have the energy for two Golem services an evening," laughed Ubusuku.

"My friend the lecher," said Leroux to Jericho with a huge wink.

"I was always a lecher," said Ubusuku. "But on Walpurgis I've found a religion that condones it. However, I'm willing to be shown the error of my ways—but I warn you, it's not going to be easy."

"The way of Lord Lucifer rarely is," said Leroux. "But we'll give it our best shot, and at least you're willing to listen. We'll sit in the back so I'll be able to explain what's going on without disturbing the priests." He looked at them for a moment. "Matter of fact, we'll *have* to sit in the back, in the Laymen's Gallery. Neither of you is wearing a ritual cape."

They passed through an ornate foyer, and he turned left, leading them into and out of a short series of dark corridors, finally emerging at a row of cushioned seats about fifty yards away from an onyx altar. Frescos of debauchery and bloodless torture dominated the walls and ceiling, illuminated by literally thousands of oddly shaped ritual candles. On the wall behind the altar hung a gold-and-black Church of Satan talisman, which Jericho estimated to be a good forty feet in diameter.

Dozens of speakers throughout the church amplified the music, which Jericho found atonal but compelling, possessed of an insistent primal rhythm and punctuated by screams and moans, both passionate and pained, which might or might not have been human in origin.

The arm of every seat had a small orifice for inserting a candle, and Leroux produced one for each of them. As Jericho lit and positioned his candle, Leroux explained that these candles differed from those of the other sects in that they were made from human rather than animal fat, all graciously willed to the Church of Satan by its membership. Ubusuku looked somewhat distressed, but Jericho showed no reaction and continued observing the scene around him.

In the front three rows were a number of men and women whose bare arms suggested that they were wearing little, if anything, beneath their cloaks. After that came perhaps twenty-five rows of men and women—mostly men—dressed much as Leroux was. There was a gap of six more rows, and then came the Laymen's Gallery, which this evening possessed only about thirty men and women, most of them seated singly and in pairs, and none so close that Leroux would bother them with his whispering.

Then, as Jericho's gaze moved back to the altar, a tall man appeared beside it. He was dressed all in black, and wore a black cowl possessing a pair of horns that were meant to appear ominous but that Jericho thought looked rather foolish.

"That's Dennison, our Major Priest," whispered Leroux. "Rumor has it that he's going to be elevated to High Priest of Amaymon within the next year or two."

Dennison waited until the audience was perfectly still, then withdrew a wand from his cape and touched five points in the air before him.

From somewhere a gong rang out, and the priest spoke:

"I reign over thee, saith the Lord of the Flies, in power exalted above and below."

"Follow the audience," whispered Leroux, and Jericho moved his lips as the congregants murmured, "Regie Satanis!"

"Behold, crieth Satan," chanted Dennison, "I am a circle on whose hands stand the Twelve Kingdoms. Six are the seats of living breath, the rest are as sharp as sickles, or the horns of death."

"Regie Satanis," intoned the audience.

This continued for another five minutes, at which time the priest touched his five imaginary points with his wand again, and cried out *"Shemhamforash!"* and the audience responded with the same word.

"It's our most holy invocation of Satan," whispered Leroux. "What's occurred so far is standard for our services. Now we'll get a sermon of some sort, which I hope won't be too boring, and then we'll get on to the mass itself."

Jericho nodded and looked back to Dennison.

"My parishioners!" cried the priest, to the accompaniment of another gong. "I must speak to you now about the man who may be the Awaited One."

"Oh, shit!" whispered Leroux. "Not again!"

"I speak of he who has come to be called the Dark Messiah," said Dennison. "He who has single-handedly staved off the forces of the dread Republic. He who represents the pinnacle of all we cherish and worship. He who has called upon the sects of Walpurgis to help him. Can we, *dare* we, refuse aid to this man?"

"Great Lucifer, but I wish he'd find some other subject!" whispered Leroux.

"Conrad Bland is the embodiment of Satan, the spirit made flesh!" cried Dennison. "Yet even as I speak to you, Republic ships of war encircle our planet, threatening instant retribution if our people do not comply with their demands. Will we do so?"

"No!" screamed the audience.

"No indeed!" echoed Dennison. "For just as the church must not impose its will upon the state"—Ubusuku and Leroux both chuckled at that—"so the state must not dictate to the church. And the sects of Walpurgis will not relinquish this savior of the believers in Satan!"

"Savior my ass!" snorted Leroux under his breath.

"What do you mean?" asked Jericho pleasantly, as Dennison droned on.

"I haven't been to Tifereth myself, you understand," whispered Leroux, "but I've got a friend who has, and he says Bland has turned the whole damned city into a charnel house."

"You don't say!"

Leroux nodded. "I guess there's corpses lying everywhere, and the torturing has gotten so out of hand that even the Messengers have left the place. This Bland has gone on a killing spree that's already wiped out half the town."

"It makes it rather difficult to worship evil," said Jericho wryly.

"Bland's not evil!" said Leroux hotly. "He's crazy! He's got nothing to do with my religion. What the hell does he know about pleasure or contemplation or—"

"Lower your voice," whispered Jericho, noticing that they were attracting some attention.

"Sorry," said Leroux. "But I get sick and tired of hearing about that madman." He turned back to Dennison, a scowl on his face.

"Beware the Republic!" the priest was saying. "Even from their vast distance they can still distort, they can still influence, they can still subvert. I tell you that Conrad Bland is nothing less than Satan unchained, Satan made flesh!"

Dennison parroted the clergy's line for another fifteen minutes, and the gong sounded again.

"Well, at least that's over!" sighed Leroux. "Have you ever attended a Black Mass at a Church of Satan before, Orestes?"

Jericho shook his head.

"Well, no matter what my friend Ibo may have told you, it's a very symbolic ceremony with a reason for everything that occurs. Laymen don't participate, but if you'll note the people in the first three rows, they'll be joining in later."

A young woman got up from her chair in the first row, walked up to the altar, unfastened her cloak, let it fall to the ground, and turned once around to show the congregants that she was entirely nude. She then lay on her back on the onyx altar.

"The purpose of the Black Mass is to invert the traditional Roman Catholic mass," whispered Leroux. "I've heard that some churches to the north of Amaymon take it so seriously as to actually sacrifice babies or virgins, but this is mostly a ritual with us. The girl represents an altar, which is about as blasphemous to Christianity as an altar could be."

A black-hooded priest came up and placed a black candle in the girl's left hand.

"The candle is ostensibly made of the fat of unbaptized babies," commented Leroux, "though of course it isn't. Still, it's the symbol that's important."

A bare-breasted woman wearing a parody of a traditional nun's habit walked up to the altar, deposited a small bowl on the girl's belly, and stood behind her, holding a cross upside down.

"More blasphemy," explained Leroux. "The nun is holding the cross in an inverted position, and the bowl is supposed to contain the blood of a prostitute. Since there are no prostitutes on Walpurgis, we use the blood of a sacrificial goat."

Jericho wanted to know how they managed to sacrifice an animal they held sacred, but decided against asking.

A caped priest, not Dennison, approached the altar, holding a small object on a tray.

"That's a black-stained turnip he's got on the tray," whispered Leroux. "He'll rub it against the girl's labia and then use it to draw a pentagram around both of them."

"Any particular reason why?" asked Ubusuku.

"I suppose it's the most blasphemous thing he could use for the purpose," said Leroux with a shrug. "Now he'll start speaking in Latin. It's a dead tongue, but what he's doing is chanting Christian prayers and psalms backward, with various obscenities thrown in to confuse any angels who happen to recognize certain key words."

"This symbolically conjures Satan?" asked Jericho.

Leroux nodded. "He's almost done with the Latin. Now he'll speak in a language we can understand."

The priest accepted a cat-o'-nine-tails from the mock nun and gently began passing it over the nude girl's body.

"I suppose I needn't point it out," said Leroux, "but he is symbolically flaying the shit out of her."

"Before the mighty and ineffable Prince of Darkness, and in the presence of all the dread demons of the Pit," intoned the priest, "I renounce all past allegiances, I proclaim that Satan rules the universe, and I ratify and renew my promise to recognize and honor Him in all things, without reservation, desiring in return His manifold assistance in the successful completion of my endeavors and the fulfillment of my desires."

The priest then took a bite of the turnip and sipped the goat's blood, after which a second bare-breasted nun picked both up and began passing through the first three rows of the audience with them.

"Ave, Satanis!" cried the priest, and the church echoed with the repetition of the words.

Then a man, totally nude except for a goat's-head mask, raced out and leaped into the pentagram.

"Satan?" asked Jericho dryly.

Leroux nodded without taking his eyes off the proceedings.

The Satan-priest took the whip from the priest and cracked it two or three times. Then he brought it down hard once on the nude girl, who shrieked but didn't move. Throwing it aside, he went through a number of gestures and antics that made no sense at all to Jericho and that Leroux didn't bother to explain. Finally he drew the girl toward him and began rhythmically thrusting his erect penis into her as the congregation began chanting "Ave, Satanis!" with each movement of his pelvis. At last the girl shrieked again and wrapped her legs around him. He lifted her off the onyx altar and they completed their orgasms as he whirled her around the border of the pentagram. When they were through he put her back on the altar, turned her onto her belly, did a few obscene things with an unlit candle, and disappeared into the darkened recesses of the church.

"That's it?" asked Jericho.

"It's just beginning!" said Leroux, sweat streaming down his excited face. "Now all the participants will enact much the same thing for the rest of the congregation."

Jericho watched, remembering details and certain phrases in case he ever needed them, while Ubusuku and Leroux joined the rest of the congregants in chanting "Ave, Satanis!" at the appropriate times.

When the last exhausted participants had returned to their seats, Dennison reappeared, gave a final curse/blessing in Enochian, the official Satanic language, and the congregation got up to leave.

"Well, what did you think?" asked Leroux excitedly, as he walked out the door with Jericho and Ubusuku.

"I saw a bunch of men fucking a bunch of women," said Ubusuku.

"No, Ibo!" said Leroux. "What you saw was a symbolic invocation of Satan, and a total inversion of the Roman Catholic mass for demoniac purposes. It's a shunning of Good for Evil, a casting off of the beliefs that held men in thrall for ages. Do you understand?"

"Of course I understand." Ubusuku grinned. "A bunch of men fucked a bunch of women."

"You're hopeless!" said Leroux with mock anger. "How about you, Orestes? Did you like what you saw?"

"Hey, I liked it just fine!" protested Ubusuku with a laugh.

"It was interesting," said Jericho. "I'd like to come again for a different ceremony."

"I'd be glad to have you as my guest," said Leroux. "Possibly you'd like to take instruction in the Church of Satan?"

"Possibly," said Jericho.

"Well, then the evening wasn't a total loss," said Leroux. "See, Ibo, who needs you? I've got me a convert, and I'll bet the police aren't even interested in *him*."

"What are you talking about?" said Ubusuku.

"Oh, Sable's office," said Leroux offhandedly. "They called this afternoon to ask some questions about you. I told them you were a solid citizen and a credit to the community. They certainly hassle immigrants with red tape, don't they?"

"They certainly do," said Ubusuku, his eyes clouded with worry.

"Exactly what kind of questions did they ask?" said Jericho softly.

"Oh, nothing in particular," said Leroux. "Just the typical sort of inane bureaucratic stuff you'd expect."

"I see," said Jericho.

"Well, who's for a drink?" said Leroux. "I'm buying."

"Fine," said Jericho. "I know a little bar not too far from here."

"Lead the way," said Leroux, and Jericho started off, turning left at the corner and moving farther and farther from any major thoroughfares.

"I'm really glad you came," said Leroux as they walked down the empty avenues. "The Black Mass isn't one of our major ceremonies, but it's flashy, if you know what I mean."

"It looks just like a Golem orgy," said Ubusuku.

"It's not the same thing at all," said Leroux. "You do it for plea-sure, we do it to defile everything that Christian religions stand for. It represents a travesty and a perversion of God and goodness and all that self-denying crap. We have our orgies, too, but they're not like this. If this wasn't so steeped in religious significance very few of the women would be willing to participate as the altar; it's too degrading. But they do, because they understand what it means, even if a Golemite like you snickers."

He went on praising his church and explaining some of the

more obscure blasphemies that they had witnessed for another ten minutes, then suddenly came to a stop. "Are you sure that bar's near here?" he asked Jericho. "This looks awfully residential to me."

"Just another block or so," said Jericho. "By the way, did anyone drop a token or a talisman on the street?"

"Of course not," said Leroux. "Why?"

"Because I see something shining by the curb there."

Leroux leaned over to get a closer look, and Jericho brought the edge of his hand down hard on the back of the little man's neck. There was a loud cracking sound, and Leroux collapsed lifeless to the pavement.

"You didn't have to do that!" raged Ubusuku.

"Keep your voice down," said Jericho softly.

"He was my friend!"

"He was a connection. He could have led them to me through you. Better to be done with him here and now."

"What about me?" demanded Ubusuku.

"What about you?" said Jericho.

"I'm a link to you too—and the police have probably got my apartment staked out."

"I know," said Jericho.

"You've got me into a mess of trouble! What do you intend to do about it?"

"I've given the matter serious thought," said Jericho.

He reached down to his leg and unwrapped the tape.

Chapter 8

"The aftermath of carnage is a pleasant time for reflection."
—Conrad Bland

Jericho reached his hotel two hours later, taking a complex route to make sure he wasn't being followed. He had already decided that his blond identity was finished, as was his need to remain in Amaymon. It was time to start drawing closer to Bland.

He took the lift to his floor, punched out the combination on his lock, and entered the room. A young woman, no more than twenty years old and dressed all in white, sat on his bed.

"Hello, Jericho," she said. "You've been a naughty boy."

Chapter 9

"The prime advantage Evil has in its battle with Good is that
its opponents always assume it must ultimately be irrational."
                                        — *Conrad Bland*

John Sable turned on his bedlamp, reached out to activate his vidphone, and mumbled a groggy "What's up?"

"Officer Belasco, sir," said the earnest, young man whose picture appeared on the screen. "You said you wanted us to call you if anything unusual happened."

"Yes," said Sable, trying to focus his eyes. "What time is it?"

"Three o'clock. There have been two murders, sir," said Belasco. "One of them was Ibo Ubusuku."

"Who's that?"

"An offworlder."

"And the other?" asked Sable, shaking the cobwebs from his brain.

"Gaston Leroux, sir. A friend of Ubusuku's. We spoke to him yesterday afternoon."

"How were they killed?"

"Ubusuku was stabbed to death. One thrust, from his abdomen to his breastbone. Leroux seems to have had his neck broken. We found them lying about fifty feet apart."

"How long have they been dead?"

"Less than an hour, according to the medic."

"I'm on my way to the office," said Sable. "Have Davies there, and take the bodies to the forensic lab. I want to see them before you ship them to the morgue."

He broke the connection, decided that he didn't have time to shower or shave, and dressed himself in less than a minute. He stooped over the bed, kissed his sleeping wife, left a message on the home computer that he didn't know whether he'd be home for dinner, and arrived at headquarters ten minutes later.

Davies was waiting for him, and they went down to the forensic laboratory, where the two bodies were stretched out on metal tables.

"Good professional job," Sable muttered as he examined Ubusuku's wound. He walked over and looked at Leroux, then turned the body onto its stomach and examined the back of its neck. "One blow. Very neat."

"Looks like our man," said Davies.

"Was there ever any doubt?" said Sable, leaving the lab and walking down the long corridor to his office. He stopped in the outer receiving room just long enough to ask a secretary to bring him some coffee, then went inside, where he found Belasco waiting for him, absently studying the numerous citations and commendations hanging on the wall.

"I don't suppose anyone's turned up any clues yet?" he asked, plopping down onto his vinyl chair.

"No, sir," said Belasco. "We've still got a team out there searching the area, but nothing's turned up so far."

"Where did you find them?" asked Sable.

"The 4700 block of the Street of Avarice."

"What the hell were they doing there?"

"Two eyewitnesses said that Leroux had two guests for a service at a nearby Church of Satan," said Belasco. "One of them fits Ubusuku's description."

"And the other?" asked Sable, clasping his hands behind his head and staring at his little statue of Cali.

"Hard to say, sir," said Belasco. "One of them thinks he was a blond man in his late twenties, perhaps six feet tall. The other remembers him as a man with light brown hair, maybe forty years old, about five feet nine."

"It doesn't matter anyway," said Sable with a sigh. "He's not going to use that identity again." He turned to Davies. "Well, that's it, Langston. There's no reason for him to stay in Amaymon now. He's killed the only contact he's got, and the only man who could place him with that contact."

"We've got other offworlders here," said Davies. "Can we be sure this was his only contact?"

"I think so," replied Sable. "If he had more, he wouldn't frighten them off by killing Ubusuku so quickly."

"So what do we do now?" asked Davies.

"Lock up the city," said Sable. "Nothing comes in, nothing goes out. We watch for Satanists, but he's bright enough not to appear as one yet. We close the airports and the train terminals and the river, and we blockade all the roads, and then we'll also call ahead to warn Conrad Bland, because personally I think we're just going through the motions. Closing down the city probably isn't going to keep this man in it one minute longer than he wants to be kept. Still, I don't know what else we can do. Let's set everything in motion, because if we wait until morning there's an excellent chance he'll be gone."

"Right," said Davies, walking to the door.

"And Langston," Sable called after him.

"Yes?"

"Just because I don't think it's going to work is no reason to do a half-assed job. Everyone works overtime until we've caught him or we know he's flown the coop. Give me an hour to make some calls and you can start borrowing men from other departments as well."

Davies nodded and left the room.

"Well, Officer Belasco," said Sable, lighting a cigar as soon as Davies was out of sight, "how do *you* reconstruct the killings?"

"I wouldn't exactly say the man is taunting us, sir," began Belasco, "but he sure as hell isn't worried about us. He could have set it up to look like they'd killed each other, but he didn't; after all, a man with a broken neck isn't going to stab his attacker, and a man with the kind of knife wound I saw wasn't going to break another man's neck and then walk fifty feet away to die. And if he wanted to hide the fact that they were killed by the same man, all he had to do was move one of the corpses a couple of blocks away. After all, he killed them by different methods; it might have taken us a couple of days to link the murders."

"Very perceptive reasoning, Officer Belasco," said Sable. "Go on."

"Well, as I see it, he probably killed the man with the broken neck first."

"Why?"

"Because why kill a man with your bare hands when you've already shown him that you've got a knife?"

"Makes sense," agreed Sable. "I don't suppose we've found the knife yet?"

Belasco shook his head. "From the size of the wounds, it looks like he used a ceremonial dagger of some sort. Not like the little steak knife he used on the last one, if indeed it's the same killer."

"It's the same killer, all right," said Sable. "You've done a commendable job, officer. I've got a few calls to make now. Why don't you see if you can help Davies, and keep me informed if the squad turns up anything at all at the scene of the crime."

Belasco left the room just as the coffee arrived. Sable took a long swallow, sighed, and started calling other department heads, soliciting aid. Within an hour he was able to present Davies with a gift of six hundred more men to help cordon off the city.

He waited until six o'clock, then punched an intercom button.

"Yes?" said a secretary.

"Get me Tifereth on the vidphone. I want to speak to Conrad Bland. If he's sleeping, have someone wake him up."

A moment later the secretary reported that Bland accepted no personal calls, and that the Tifereth exchange wouldn't give out his number.

"Well, get me *somebody* up there!" snapped Sable.

"Who?"

"I don't know! Try Bland's chief of security."

"I'll do what I can."

About ten minutes later he was connected to a middle-aged man wearing a plain, gray military uniform. The man stared into the camera at his end of the line without speaking.

"This is John Sable, Chief of Detectives in Amaymon. Who am I speaking to?"

"Jacob Bromberg."

"You have access to Conrad Bland?" inquired Sable.

"When necessary," said Bromberg.

"Good! I have reason to believe that a Republic assassin has been hired to liquidate Bland. He's in Amaymon now, but I suspect we're not going to be able to contain him much longer."

"So?"

"What do you mean, *so?* I'm telling you that someone is out to assassinate your leader!"

"He'll have to get in line," said Bromberg with a smile.

"I assure you this isn't a joke!" said Sable hotly. "This man is a highly skilled professional, and he's been here long enough to start assimilating some of our customs. We'll help you in any way we can, but I cannot overstate the seriousness of the situation."

"We appreciate your warning," said Bromberg, "but I assure you that it is unnecessary. No one is going to murder My Lord Bland."

"Will you at least tell him?" demanded Sable, glaring at the screen.

"If I get around to it," said Bromberg, breaking the connection.

Sable cursed under his breath, then rummaged through his desk, pulled out his personal vidphone directory, and placed a call to Casper Wallenbach, his counterpart in Tifereth.

"Yes?" said Wallenbach, who was obviously an early riser, for he was seated at what appeared to be a breakfast table.

"Detective Wallenbach? This is John Sable, from Amaymon."

"Mr. Sable," said Wallenbach with a smile. "How good to see you again. What can I do for you?"

"I've got a little problem that I hope you can help me with," said Sable.

"Just name it," said Wallenbach. "My department owes you a couple of favors."

"There's a Republic assassin currently at large in the city of Amaymon. We've cordoned off the city, but I don't know how long we can keep him here."

"I'd be happy to loan you reinforcements," said Wallenbach, "but my staff is almost depleted at present."

"That's not it," said Sable. "If we can contain him we won't need any help, but if not, he's going to be headed up your way. I think he's after Conrad Bland. I called Bland's chief of security, a fellow named Bromberg, but I don't think he took me seriously, so I thought I'd better let you know what's up."

"An assassin, you say?"

Sable nodded.

"Good at his trade?"

"He's had us running in circles for three days. He kills very efficiently, and he can change identities quicker than I can change clothes."

"Very interesting," said Wallenbach, gazing thoughtfully into space.

"I'll let you know as soon as I think he's gotten out," said Sable. "I really don't give us much chance of detaining him for long."

"Yes, Mr. Sable," said Wallenbach distractedly. "You do that."

"Will you need any help?"

"Oh, I doubt it," said Wallenbach, the trace of a smile playing about his thick lips. "I think we'll know exactly how to handle the situation."

What the hell is going on here? thought Sable. Bland's security chief thinks it's a joke, and the Chief of Detectives acts like he couldn't care less.

"Fine," he said aloud. "I'll keep in touch."

"I'll be here," said Wallenbach. He reached out and broke the connection, leaving Sable to wonder why the possible assassination of the Dark Messiah of Walpurgis didn't seem to upset anyone in Tifereth.

Chapter 10

"If I were told that I had but one hour to live, the first thing
I would do would be to kill the man who told me."
                                            —Conrad Bland

"Who are you?" demanded Jericho softly, locking the door behind him.

The girl in white smiled up at him from the bed. "Believe it or not, I'm a friend."

"Not," said Jericho. He crossed the room, closed his window, and turned up the volume on the video.

"Before you kill me," said the girl, obviously unworried, "I should tell you that if you go to Malkuth, as you now plan to do, you'll be killed there."

Jericho stared at her for a long moment. "You've just bought yourself three minutes," he said at last, sitting down on a hard-backed metal chair. "Let's hear what you have to say."

"As I mentioned, going to Malkuth would be a mistake."

"*Am* I going to Malkuth?"

"Oh yes, Jericho."

"What makes you think my name is Jericho?"

"Actually it isn't," said the girl, smiling again. "It's merely the name you've chosen to use."

"To use for what?"

"For the assassination of Conrad Bland."

"I've never heard of anyone named Conrad Bland," said Jericho. "Why should I wish to kill him?"

"Don't be coy, Jericho. You've already killed Parnell Burnam, Gaston Leroux, and Ibo Ubusuku."

"Who are they?" asked Jericho, his expression never changing.

The girl sighed. "If we can't be honest and straightforward with one another I don't see how I'm going to be able to help you. You killed Leroux and Ubusuku only two hours ago."

Jericho stared at her again for another long minute, then walked across the room and positioned himself in front of the door.

"All right," he said at last. "You haven't told me anything that Sable's department doesn't know or can't find out. I can only assume that you are a member of that department. Perhaps you'd like to tell me why I should let you live?"

"You're a very difficult man to talk to," said the girl, looking mildly amused. "What if I were to tell you that, under a different name, you assassinated Gustav Gagenbach on Sirius V some twelve years ago?"

"I'd say you were guessing," said Jericho. "Or does Sable plan to pin every unsolved murder in the galaxy on me?"

The girl shook her head. "I guess I'll have to be as forthright as I wish you to be." She paused for a moment, then delivered her bombshell. "I know that you killed Benson Rallings on Belore VII."

Jericho almost allowed his surprise to break through his emotionless mask. That had been one of his earliest commissions: Belore VII was an uninhabited mining world, Rallings's body had been completely disposed of, and his employer had died of natural causes before he could report the success of his mission. No one except Jericho knew that a murder had been committed.

"Ah," said the girl, smiling again. "You almost look impressed."

"I am," he said. "How did you find out about that?"

"There are no secrets from the White Lucy."

"You're the White Lucy?"

"Oh, no," said the girl. "I merely serve her. My name is Colas."

"Who or what is she?"

"You'll find out very soon," promised Colas. "She wants to meet you."

"Why should I want to meet her?"

"Because you cannot enter Tifereth without her help," said Colas. "And if you do not enter Tifereth, you cannot kill Conrad Bland."

"Everyone else on this world seems to worship him as some kind of god," said Jericho. "Why do you and this White Lucy want him dead?"

"Because he is the living embodiment of evil," said Colas passionately, "and as such his continued existence is intolerable."

"Do all the white witches on Walpurgis feel that way?" asked Jericho.

"I have no idea," said Colas, shrugging her narrow shoulders. "The White Lucy and her acolytes are a cloistered sect. We have no contact with the white witches. They claim, of course, to work for good rather than for evil, but those are just words. Concepts of good and evil can get very confused on Walpurgis, in case you hadn't noticed."

"Do all the members of your sect have the power to read my mind?" asked Jericho.

"No," said Colas. "However, I don't have to be a mind reader to know what you're thinking, and I must warn you that if you kill me the White Lucy will reveal you to the authorities no matter where you may hide."

"Why hasn't she already done so?" asked Jericho. "It seems to me that if I was this Sable character, the White Lucy would be the first person I'd seek out for information."

"First of all," said Colas, "he doesn't know where to look for her."

"Bad answer," said Jericho. "I'm sure he could find her if he wanted."

"And in the second place, he doesn't know that the White Lucy possesses this power."

"It's a hard thing to keep hidden if she spends her time helping destroy anyone she considers evil," commented Jericho.

"She has never helped anyone before," said Colas. "Good and evil are merely abstract concepts—or at least they were until Conrad Bland came along. We don't care who kills who as long as we are left alone."

"Then why all the fuss about Bland?"

"Because if he remains alive, he will kill every other living thing on Walpurgis," replied Colas. "His philosophy is repugnant to us, to be sure, but no more so than many others that abound on this planet. The difference is that he has the will and the power to put his beliefs into practice."

"I appreciate your concern," said Jericho at last. "But I work alone."

"If you continue to do so, you will also die alone," said Colas with certainty.

"I'll take my chances," said Jericho.

"You will meet with the White Lucy, or you will surely die in Malkuth," said Colas with conviction. "She knew where you were, she knew the combination to your room, she knew what you had done in the past, she knew who you had killed this evening, she knew your plans for approaching Bland, and throughout she has maintained her silence as a show of good faith. She empowered me to reveal some of her power to you, which is also a show of good faith, since only a handful of people know of it."

"I appreciate that," said Jericho.

"Then appreciate this: At any time since your arrival she could have revealed your whereabouts to John Sable, and she did not. She is on your side, Jericho, and she says that you cannot enter

Tifereth without her. Is it not in your best interest to meet with her?"

"I'll consider it," he said after some thought.

"Good," said Colas. "About one hundred miles north and west of Amaymon there is a newly constructed bridge across the Styx. Be there tomorrow at sunset and you will be taken to her."

"By you?"

"Probably not," replied Colas. "John Sable has already found the bodies of the two men you killed tonight, and all means of egress from the city have been closed. I may not be able to leave."

"But you expect *me* to be one hundred miles away by tomorrow afternoon?" asked Jericho with the hint of a smile.

"The White Lucy says that you will not need our help to escape from Amaymon. I would accompany you, but she says that you have things to do that I can't be any part of."

"When did she say that?"

"Just now, as we were speaking," Colas answered calmly.

He stepped aside as she walked to the door and punched out the combination on the lock with swift, sure fingers. The door swung inward, and a moment later she was gone. Jericho considered following her, but decided not to chance discovery while he was still in the guise of the blond man who had been seen at the Church of Satan.

He stood before a mirror, working quickly but carefully, and a few minutes later he had become a balding, slightly paunchy man whose age could have been anywhere from forty to sixty. A change of clothes made him look a little more prosperous, and very flat shoes took about an inch off his height.

He inspected himself carefully, could find no trace of the blond man who would never again be seen, and went out into the cool, dry Amaymon night for the last time, his makeup kit tucked inside his shirt.

The sun would not rise for another two hours, and the streets were almost deserted. This made his task more difficult, but not impossible. He walked, with seeming aimlessness, along the empty avenues of the city until at last he found what he had been looking for.

A pedestrian.

He didn't have time to stalk this one the way he had his first victim. Rather, he turned into an alleyway, raced the length of the block, and positioned himself just out of sight around the corner. When the pedestrian came into view Jericho leaped out, dealt him one swift blow to the neck, and stepped nimbly aside as the body hit the pavement.

He walked almost a mile before he found a second victim, tottering home alone from some tavern. The same procedure brought the same result, and he began walking back toward the center of town.

The next pedestrian he saw was a woman, but he decided to avoid her. He didn't want the police to think this was the work of a sex killer.

He found his third victim almost within the shadow of the Devil's Den, one of the bars he had visited before killing Parnell Burnam. This one he stabbed, leaving Ubusuku's dagger beneath the corpse.

Then he waited for sunrise. When it came, he positioned himself in the lobby of a small office building in the heart of the city. Six uniformed policemen passed in front of the building before he spotted the one he wanted, a slender, dark-haired man of approximately his height and weight. He walked out the front door of the building and fell into step behind the policeman, never nearer than fifty feet, never farther than half a block. Within a few minutes the policeman had stopped at a small coffee shop, and Jericho did the same. He sat down next to him, managed to spill a little coffee on his sleeve, and apologized profusely. When the policeman went to the lavatory to clean his hands and dab the sleeve with water, Jericho followed him.

Three minutes later Jericho, dressed as an officer of the Amaymon metropolitan police force, emerged from the washroom, looked around, found a small storage room half filled with canned goods, and a moment later had transferred the naked corpse of the policeman there. His own clothes were dumped into a small disposal unit in the washroom.

He picked up both tabs from the counter, paid for them on his way out, and took a local bus to the end of the line. From there it was only a half-mile walk to the edge of the city, when he found a number of policemen manning an efficient-looking roadblock.

He joined them, turned back a trio of pedestrians in the next half hour, and observed the police as they explained the situation to inbound vehicles before turning them away.

Thereafter he lingered on the far side of the roadblock, and took his turn sending irate drivers on their way. When an intercity bus pulled up just after ten o'clock, it was Jericho who walked out to tell the driver that he could not enter Amaymon. The driver protested, other policemen walked over to press home their point, and finally, amid much muttering and dire warnings about what his company would do to the officials of Amaymon, the driver turned his large, lumbering bus around and went back the way he had come, leaving behind one less uniformed policeman than had been there to meet him.

Chapter 11

"Confusion and Chaos are the handmaidens of Evil."
—*Conrad Bland*

"We just found a third one," said Langston Davies, stepping into Sable's office.

"Same killer?" asked Sable.

"Neck's broken," said Davies. "Looks like a single blow with the edge of the hand."

"Any prints on that knife yet?"

Davies shook his head. "It doesn't seem to have been wiped clean, but there are no prints. The lab says there are some impressions, but he must have been wearing gloves, or maybe he's had his prints surgically removed."

"Figures," said Sable. He glared at his baphomet, which seemed to be laughing at him. "Dammit, Lang! Something's very wrong here, and I can't put my finger on it!"

"What's wrong is five corpses in one night," said Davies, pulling up a chair.

"No, that's not it," said Sable. "Sooner or later he figured to kill Ubusuku, and it stands to reason that he'd kill Leroux too, since he could obviously identify him. That made sense. But why these next three?"

"We don't know anything about the latest victim," Davies pointed out. "It might be another offworlder."

Sable shook his head. "I'm not a betting man, but I'll wager a week's pay that he was just as innocuous as the last two. I just wish I knew what the three of them had in common. I figured once our assassin killed Ubusuku he'd be on his way to Tifereth. Could I have been wrong? Is there something right here in Amaymon that he's after?"

Davies offered a silent shrug, and Sable, still muttering to himself, stood up and began pacing around his office.

"Why did he leave the dagger?" he said at last. "And why did he kill them so neatly? He's not a stupid man, Langston; you think he'd change his method now that we know what to look for."

"Bragging?" asked Davies. "Taunting us?"

"He's a professional," said Sable. "And professionals don't take risks. They don't brag about what they've done; they *hide* it." He flung himself back into his chair. "I just don't understand it! I mean, so what if he didn't leave any fingerprints? He had to know we'd trace that dagger to Ubusuku—why leave it at all?"

A small computer on Sable's desk suddenly came to life.

"Data on the latest one," said Davies, walking over to read it. "Name, Hector Block. Age, thirty-seven. Profession, grocery store manager. Address, Ninth Circle—it's a local hotel owned by the Brotherhood of Night. Never been off the planet, no contact with any known offworlder. Cause of death: broken neck."

"A nobody," muttered Sable. "Another damned nobody! What the hell is the connection?"

"Maybe he recognized him," offered Davies without much enthusiasm.

"And ran a mile away from the nearest murder?" scoffed Sable. "No chance. He never knew what hit him, never felt he had any reason to fear for his life. We'll check it out, but I'll bet none of the three even knew the other two."

He started pacing again, absently withdrawing a cigar and lighting it up. "Well, at least we know he's still in Amaymon."

"But we don't know if he's completed his mission or not," said Davies.

"True," admitted Sable. "Still, we can't just sit on our hands and do nothing. We've got to turn up some kind of clue or lead before this guy goes back to work." He shook his head in wonderment. "Six killings in what—fifty-four hours? We've *got* to stop him!"

Sable spent the next two hours personally visiting the scenes of the previous evening's murders and examining the victims. Then, just before noon, he returned to his office to await further developments and try to reason things out.

It just didn't add up. If the assassin was after Bland, he had nothing to gain by remaining in Amaymon after his contact had been eliminated; more, he had every reason to leave, since he was less apt to give himself away through some blunder while on the move than ensconced in a city where the police were hunting for him, however futilely. On the other hand, if his objective was in Amaymon, why had he alerted Sable to his presence by killing Parnell Burnam? There was something very wrong, but try as he would Sable couldn't put his finger on it.

And then, just after noon, Davies burst into his office.

"We found another one!" he exclaimed breathlessly.

"Same as the others?" asked Sable.

"Uh-uh. This one was Vladimir Kosminov."

"*Our* Vladimir Kosminov? From the burglary detail?"

Davies nodded. "We found him in a storeroom in the back of a restaurant. Or, more properly, we were called in when the owner found him."

"How was he killed?" demanded Sable.

"A broken neck," said Davies. "One blow, just like the others. One thing is different, though: He may have been sexually assaulted."

"What makes you think so?"

"Because he was stark naked."

"Oh, shit!" snapped Sable. "We've lost him!"

"Lost who? What are you talking about?"

"The killer, the killer!" snarled Sable. "He's gone! Call off the roadblocks."

"What do you mean?" asked Davies, genuinely puzzled.

"Kosminov," said Sable, slumping back in his chair, totally exhausted. "He was the missing piece. Now it all makes sense."

"Not to me it doesn't," said Davies.

"Think, Langston," said Sable. "Why did he kill three men who couldn't have had anything to do with him? Why didn't he try to disguise his method? Shit, we even asked the right questions and still couldn't come up with the answer!"

"I still can't," said Davies.

"Use your brain, Langston," said Sable. "He knew we'd try to shut down the city once he killed Ubusuku. He knew we'd keep an eye on every escape route, because he had no reason to stay. So what did he do? Killed the first three people he could find, to make us think he still had business here. Those three men were sucker bait, and we fell for it! It bought him almost half a day's head start. The important killing, the one that counted, was Kosminov. He probably walked right out of Amaymon three hours ago dressed as a cop!"

"Then let's send out an APB."

"Great Lucifer!" Sable laughed bitterly. "You don't think he's *still* wearing Kosminov's uniform, do you? All he needed was a means of getting past our roadblock and a couple of hours' head start. He knew we'd find Kosminov before the day was out, but it didn't matter to him. He just needed enough time to sneak out. Who the hell can know what he looks like by now? How can you put out an all-points bulletin on the whole damned planet?" He threw an ashtray against the wall, spraying glass in all directions. "Damn! I can't believe it! We knew everything we had to know and he still slipped through our fingers!"

Davies waited until his superior's rage had diminished somewhat, then broached a question: "What's our next step?"

"There's nothing we *can* do," said Sable bitterly. "He's gone. He's out of our jurisdiction. All I can do is get back to Wallenbach and Bland's security chief and try to convince them that this guy plays for keeps."

"Is there anything you want me to do?" asked Davies.

"No," said Sable with a sigh. "You've been up all night too. Go on home and get some rest."

Left alone in his office, Sable sat back and glared out his window for a long time. Then, remembering somewhat belatedly that a new day had dawned some hours back, he genuflected to Cali, lit his ceremonial candles, and murmured his prayers to Azazel, Asmodeus, and Ahriman. He held his amulet up to the light, made a half-hearted Sign of Five in the air, and returned to his desk.

A moment later he had Casper Wallenbach on the vidphone.

"Mr. Sable," said Wallenbach. "I hadn't expected to hear from you again so soon."

"He's on his way," said Sable bluntly.

"The assassin?"

Sable nodded. "I wish I had better news."

"That's all right," said Wallenbach. "We'll know how to deal with him if he gets this far."

"He's killed five more men," said Sable. "I don't mean to disparage your department, but I just don't think you know what kind of man you're going to be up against."

"Suppose you tell me."

Sable spent the next twenty minutes covering what had happened during the past three days. When he had finished, Wallenbach looked down and straightened some papers on his desk.

"Well, I thank you for your thorough briefing, Mr. Sable," he said. "And I'm sure that with this added knowledge we'll soon bring this criminal to justice."

"Don't underestimate him," persisted Sable, feeling terribly frustrated.

"I wouldn't dream of it," said Wallenbach. "And now, if you've nothing further to add, I really must start passing the word to my staff."

Sable shrugged, broke the connection, and stared, perplexed, at the blank screen. He didn't look forward to making the next call, but given Wallenbach's attitude, he saw no way around it.

"Yes?" said Jacob Bromberg.

"This is John Sable from Amaymon. We spoke yesterday."

"I know who you are," said Bromberg.

"I'm calling to say that the assassin has made his way out of Amaymon and is undoubtedly on his way to Tifereth."

"What do you expect *me* to do about it?" said Bromberg with a dry laugh.

"Dammit!" yelled Sable. "What's the matter with everybody up there? I'm telling you that the most skilled killer I have ever come across in my career is on his way to Tifereth to assassinate Conrad Bland! Doesn't that mean anything to you?"

"It means that he's going to be one very sorry killer when he gets here," said Bromberg, smiling.

"Look—let me speak to Bland, just for five minutes," said Sable, trying to control his temper. "*Someone* in Tifereth had better start taking this seriously!"

"Oh, I take it seriously," said Bromberg, suppressing another smile. "What do you want me to do—shit in my pants because another nut wants to kill My Lord Bland?"

"You just don't understand!" said Sable, wishing there were some nearby object that he could hit or kick. "This man is no nut! He's an efficient, highly skilled professional!"

"Mr. Sable!" said a strange, high-pitched voice that seemed to crackle with electricity.

"Who's that?" demanded Sable.

"This is Conrad Bland," said the voice. "I have been monitoring your conversation. I thank you for your concern. Now please leave us alone."

"Just give me a few minutes to convince you of the seriousness of the situation, sir," said Sable.

"I fully understand the situation," said Bland. "A very formidable killer is coming to Tifereth to assassinate me. If he gets this far, which I doubt, he will learn that I am not wholly without resources myself."

"This man is different," said Sable.

"They are all different," said Bland. "And yet I am still alive, and they are dead."

"At least let me prepare your security forces for what they will be facing," said Sable. "I could fly up to Tifereth and spend a couple of days with them."

"That's out of the question, Mr. Sable. You are not welcome in Tifereth."

"But—"

"Mr. Sable, customs differ from city to city on Walpurgis, but there is one that remains constant: churches are sacrosanct, and what occurs within their confines is of no concern to the outside world."

"What does that have to do with what we're discussing?" asked Sable.

"Mr. Sable," said Bland, his voice rising in pitch and intensity, "*Tifereth is my church. Keep out!*"

An unseen hand broke the connection.

Chapter 12

"There is a certain poetic beauty in destroying that which you love."
—*Conrad Bland*

Jericho got off the bus twenty miles south of Amaymon. A few minutes later he managed to flag down a southbound truck. He dispatched the driver with bloodless efficiency, appropriated his clothes, and placed the corpse in the back of the truck. He then cut over the median strip and proceeded north, giving Amaymon a reasonably wide berth and picking up a highway that roughly paralleled the River Styx. When he was within seven miles of the appointed meeting place he waited until there were no other vehicles in sight, then drove the truck into the water, jumping clear at the last instant. Even though it vanished beneath the surface he had no doubt that it would be found in the next day or two; the river wasn't all that deep, and it would probably impede barge traffic. But a day or two was all the head start that he needed, especially now that he was beyond Sable's jurisdiction and free to choose a new identity.

It took him a little more than an hour to walk through the gathering darkness to the new bridge, and he arrived just as the planet's two small moons were producing a beautiful counterpoint to the last stages of the sunset. A few minutes later a woman dressed all in white approached him.

"Jericho?"

He nodded.

"Follow me, please." She turned on her heel without waiting for an acknowledgment or acquiescence.

He fell into step behind her and they walked, unspeaking, along the riverbank for a little more than a mile. Then she led him up a relatively steep incline to the top of a rocky bluff overlooking the Styx, and he found himself facing a large concrete building. Night had fallen, and the interior of the building was aglow with artificial light.

The woman entered, gestured him to follow her, and led him down a long corridor. He looked for some symbols or tokens to indicate which sect the White Lucy belonged to, but the whitewashed walls and ceilings were devoid of any religious artifacts or ornamentation. They passed a number of rooms, each sparsely and austerely furnished, then stopped before a heavy, wooden door. The woman paused for a moment, then nodded her head and opened it, and Jericho quickly stepped through the doorway. Seated on a wooden chair, her arms resting on its arms as if they were too feeble to move, was a very old woman. A teenaged girl sat at her feet. Both were dressed in white.

"Come in. Sit down," said the old woman in a stronger voice than he had expected. He looked around, found a chair in the shadows by the window, and walked over to it. The woman who had acted as his guide left the room, closing the door behind her.

Jericho sat down and looked at the old woman. Her hair was long and gray, done up in a bun atop her head, and her face was so wrinkled that he couldn't begin to guess her age.

She turned her face to him and he saw that her eyes were covered by thin, white membranes.

"You're the White Lucy?" he asked.

"I am," she said. "You may leave us now, Dorcas." The girl at her feet stood up and left the room. "A nice girl, Dorcas, but I don't need her now that you're here."

"I don't understand," said Jericho.

"Your eyes," she said. "I need someone's eyes to see through."

"You're seeing what I'm seeing?"

"Oh, yes," said the White Lucy. "I almost wish I wasn't, though. I used to be a very pretty woman."

"I'm sure you were."

"About a century ago," she continued. "I am one hundred and twenty-eight years old. Can you believe that?"

"I have no reason to doubt you," he said.

"Of course you don't," she said. "And you couldn't hide it if you did. You have a curiously flat mind, Jericho; I don't think I've ever found one quite like it."

"Oh?"

"Indeed. Most people would be very apprehensive about meeting with a woman who can read their innermost thoughts. You seem not to care at all. A very curious mind: no hills or valleys at all. No passions, no hates, no fears, no lusts. Just flat and businesslike. I think the reason you accept my age without question is not that I am telling you the truth, but that it makes no difference to you whether I am or not. Such a clean, uncluttered mind! It might be interesting to shock it out of its straight lines and carefully measured angles, just to see how it reacts. I could, you know."

"I don't doubt it," said Jericho. "Since you're inside my head already, why are we speaking?"

The White Lucy chuckled. "Because *you're* not a telepath. I can read your thoughts, but you can't read mine. That's why I sent for you: so that we could speak face to face. Though if you'd like to look out the window, I would enjoy that: I like to see the stars."

"All right," said Jericho, turning his gaze to the night sky. "You sent for me. I'm here. Now what can you do for me?"

"To begin with, I can warn you not to go to Malkuth," said the White Lucy.

"Why?"

"Because Conrad Bland has scheduled every last man, woman, and child in Malkuth for extermination. Within a week nothing will be left alive there, and even you, with all your skills, would not be able to escape the city or its destruction."

"Interesting," remarked Jericho. "What has Bland got against Malkuth?"

"Nothing."

"But—"

"Ah!" exclaimed the old woman. "So *that's* what your mind looks like when it's puzzled! Such curious patterns! I wish you could see it."

"Why does Bland want to destroy Malkuth?" repeated Jericho.

"Because he is an evil man."

"That's no answer," said Jericho. He slowly, deliberately, closed his eyes.

"What happened?" said the White Lucy, suddenly confused. "Ah! Now I see. Isn't that a little juvenile, Jericho, cutting off a poor, weak old lady's vision?"

"There's nothing poor or weak about you," said Jericho coldly. "I just thought I'd bring you back to the subject at hand: Why should Bland want to destroy Malkuth?"

"Because it is his nature to destroy things," said the White Lucy.

"You're saying he's some kind of madman?"

"No!" snapped the old woman. "Conrad Bland is totally rational, as rational and as much in control of himself as you are. I don't know if the concept of good is embodied anywhere in this universe. I only know that there is evil and there is everything else, and that the evil resides within Conrad Bland."

"You make it sound rather mystical," said Jericho.

"And now your mind is saying that you've wasted a trip, and that I'm nothing but a demented old religious fanatic after all," said the White Lucy. "But your mind hasn't been where mine has been. I tell you truthfully that left to his own devices Conrad Bland will destroy every living thing on this planet."

"That doesn't make any sense. Walpurgis is the only planet in the Republic that was willing to grant him sanctuary."

"He will not do this because it makes sense," said the White Lucy, "but because it is his nature. No alternative to destroying Walpurgis has ever occurred to him. No alternative ever will." She paused. "Why do I see confusion in your mind?"

"You've convinced me of your sincerity," he said with a sardonic smile. "But since you can read my mind, you knew exactly what to say to convince me. However, it makes no difference. I personally couldn't care less why you want Bland dead. I want to know how you think you can help me, and why you think I can't kill him alone."

"You need our help because you have made a serious blunder," said the White Lucy, shifting slightly on her chair.

"The newspaper ad?" he asked.

"A minor thing," she said. "No, your blunder was killing Parnell Burnam."

"Who was he?"

"The first of your victims."

"I had to find out what—"

"I know your reasons," she interrupted. "But it got John Sable involved, and he turned out to be a lot smarter than you thought. Even then I didn't interfere, but now he's told Bland everything he knows, and I couldn't put off our meeting any longer."

"Why?" said Jericho. "Bland doesn't know who he's looking for any more than Sable did. I won't be using any of my Amaymon identities again."

"Bland knows exactly who he's looking for," said the White Lucy, scuffing the floor with her right foot. "Oh, he may not be able to pinpoint you the way I could, but he knows a Republic assassin is on his way to Tifereth. Today alone he has killed more than seven hundred people who were traveling within a two-hundred-mile radius of Tifereth. Tomorrow he will kill more. He will surround himself with death and desolation, and will kill any living thing that approaches him."

"Then I fail to see how you can help get me into Tifereth," said Jericho.

"Amazing!" said the White Lucy.

"What is?"

"The fact that he's killing all these innocent people doesn't mean a thing to you, does it?"

"A professional in my line of work can't afford to be emotional."

"Even after all I've told you, you have no more concern for Bland than if he were an insect. You don't especially care whether he lives or dies, except as it effects the remainder of your fee."

"What difference do my motives make to you as long as I kill him?" said Jericho. "Every minute I waste here is another minute he has to prepare his defenses. I appreciate the fact that you want him dead. I appreciate the fact that you can read his mind. I appreciate the fact that you can also read the minds of his security forces. But I fail to see how that can help me if he's mowing down everything that approaches the city. Besides, you can't send your thoughts to me once I leave here, even if you learn something useful."

"Oh yes I can," she said. "I have receiving stations posted all over Walpurgis."

"Your white witches?"

"My people—and we're not white witches. We practice no magic or devil worship. We are merely women with a gift."

"Why do you wear white?" he asked.

"Protective coloration. You, of all people, should understand that."

"And you've got people like yourself all over the world?" he continued.

"Not exactly like myself. Most of them can only receive. A few can send. Only I can do both."

"It strikes me that you're a pretty dangerous person in your own right," said Jericho, getting up from his chair and stretching.

"Don't be foolish," she said. "Why would I keep your identity and whereabouts a secret from the police and expose my own powers to you if I weren't on your side?"

"I don't know," admitted Jericho, walking around the room and staring idly at various smudges on the wall. "I wish I did."

"You're a very untrusting man," said the White Lucy. "Your mind has been conditioned that way. I am telling you the truth, but, to borrow your own words, what difference does it make? We both want Bland killed, and I have offered you my help."

He stared at her long and hard, trying to scrutinize her withered face, and simultaneously he became very aware of the fact that she was probably digging around inside his head, seeking weak spots, points of least resistance that would allow her to convince him to accept her aid. Suddenly, as he tried to make his mind a blank, a series of grotesquely erotic images shot across it. Embarrassed, he tried to expunge them, and found that the harder he tried the more they persisted.

"Very good, Jericho," said the White Lucy with a smile. "That's usually the initial reaction I get when someone finds out I am reading his mind. I would call this a delayed reaction . . . Oh! That's a new one!"

He fidgeted uncomfortably. Finally he dredged up a picture of the body of Benson Rallings in its death throes. It was neither pleasant nor unpleasant. He concentrated on it.

"Ah, you learn quickly. If it will ease your discomfort, I will withdraw from your mind."

He felt no different, and wasn't sure he could trust her. He drew a mental picture of how he might disembowel her, then watched her for a reaction. There was none.

"All right," he said at last, still not sure she had kept her word but seeing no alternative to believing her, at least for the moment. "How can your people help?"

"I have arranged to put you aboard a freighter that will be coming up the Styx tomorrow morning before daylight," said the White Lucy. "Dorcas will accompany you."

"No," he said firmly. "I work alone."

"I know you do," she said. "Now please let me finish. Dorcas will accompany you until such time as I feel that remaining on the river is no longer safe. She will then be instructed to return home, and you will go ashore and make your way north to Tifereth. In most of the cities of Walpurgis my people function as fortune-tellers and palmists. Since they can have me read a customer's mind and tell them what they need to know, we are naturally a little more successful than our competitors, and hence we make enough money to support ourselves. I have women stationed in most of the cities between here and Tifereth. They will be able to tell you of any new developments, of the disposition of Bland's forces, of any further attempts being made to determine who and where you are. They will know which cities are still safe, which of your disguises have been penetrated."

"There are a lot of fortune-tellers around," said Jericho. "How will I know which ones are yours?"

"They'll be wearing white."

"So do white witches."

"But white witches don't tell fortunes," said the White Lucy.

"Have you any people in Tifereth itself?" he asked.

"I did. They're dead now."

"Why? Did Bland figure out who they were?"

"No."

"Then why did he kill them?" persisted Jericho.

"Because it is his nature to kill everything," said the White Lucy.

"He enjoys it?"

"No more or less than you enjoy breathing," she said.

"I don't understand."

"It is the nature of evil to do evil things. You kill by choice and by calculation. He kills from compulsion. You find a certain beauty, a sense of symmetry, in a well-planned hunt and an efficiently performed execution. He finds no beauty or symmetry or satisfaction in taking life, because he has never considered, and will never consider, *not* taking it. You are polar opposites, you and he. You kill because you can, and he kills because he must. I find a certain irony in considering that you will be the instrument of his destruction, or he of yours."

"He of mine?" repeated Jericho. "What are you talking about?"

"I can direct you to him," said the White Lucy. "I can help you past his defenses. But I cannot strike the death blow. Only you can do that."

"Are you implying that I won't be able to?"

"Oh, you have the capacity to kill," she said. "There can hardly be any doubt about that, can there? And of course we pray that you succeed, because if you fail, Walpurgis is going to become one enormous funeral pyre. But Conrad Bland is unlike any man you have ever faced before. He is a man to whom destruction is just another natural function. You were trained to murder, but he was born to it."

She paused, turning her sightless, covered eyes to him. "He is the very essence of evil, while in your mind I can find no trace of evil at all. I can only hope that this does not give him an insurmountable advantage."

"This is getting a little too metaphysical for me," said Jericho. "He's flesh and blood like any other man, and he can be killed like any other man. I'll start for Tifereth in the morning."

"True," said the White Lucy. "Metaphysics has no part in this business. I shall leave my final question unasked."

He displayed no interest whatsoever, but a thousand silent voices from across the planet nudged her, urged her to state the question, and so, relenting, she did:

If he has the power to kill the ultimate Evil, then is he not an even greater threat himself?

Chapter 13

"There is a difference between refusing a helping hand and dismembering it. I would never refuse one."
—Conrad Bland

Jericho and Dorcas stood at the railing of the ship, watching the water rush past them as the sun began rising in the east. Suddenly he turned to her.

"Well?" he asked.

"Well what?" said the girl.

"I was wondering how many miles it is to Tifereth if I manage to stay on the river," he said. "I thought you could read minds."

"No," replied Dorcas.

"Then I'm confused," he said. "What use are you going to be if you can't get messages from the White Lucy?"

"That's an entirely different matter," she said.

"Oh? How?"

"Let's get some breakfast and I'll explain it to you while we eat," said Dorcas, leading the way to the ship's galley.

They found themselves alone, the small crew having eaten earlier. Dorcas had eggs, cereal, and toast, while Jericho stuck to soybean products.

"It's not that I wouldn't like the taste of what you're eating," he said when she queried him about it. "It's just that not every world had the foresight or the money to import colonies of farm animals from Earth, but just about all of them managed to bring along some soybeans. You've lived your entire life on Walpurgis; I've been on perhaps two hundred worlds, each with different home-grown food. My system had trouble adapting to the constant changes after a while, so I stick to soybean creations whenever I can. They taste pretty much the same—a little blander, perhaps—and I don't get sick from them."

"I find it hard to imagine such a successful killer having a belly-ache!" laughed Dorcas.

"I *don't* have them," he pointed out. "It's one of the things that makes me successful: attention to detail. And I believe you were going to explain another detail to me now?"

"Yes," she said, swallowing a mouthful of cereal and washing it down with a glass of milk. "What you must understand is that we're not superhuman beings. We're just people with a gift. A very limited gift. I'm a receiver, not a reader. I can receive thoughts sent by the White Lucy or one of the other senders, of which there are about two thousand. But I cannot read your thoughts, or the thoughts of anyone who doesn't have the capacity to send them. Only the White Lucy can do that."

"How many of you are there?" asked Jericho.

"In the galaxy? I have no idea."

"No. On Walpurgis."

"About six thousand, so far," said Dorcas, starting on her eggs. "The White Lucy has gathered us together from her excursions all through the Republic. Of course, she hasn't made any lately; the last one was more than five years ago."

"I'm surprised she can make it from one room to the next," remarked Jericho, "let alone travel between planets."

"She's a strong woman, the White Lucy. Stronger than you suspect. She's forced herself to live this long while she's tried to find a successor."

"To herself?"

Dorcas nodded, waiting a moment to speak until she had swallowed her food. "We're all just partial telepaths, all except her.

She'll stay alive until we find another one with her powers."

"She's well over a century old," said Jericho. "What makes her think that there will ever be another one like her?"

"She's already found one," said Dorcas. "A woman on Gamma Epsilon IV. But she was insane."

"And that's the only one?"

"Yes. But the existence of one implies the existence of others. That's where most of our senders are—on other worlds trying to find a true telepath. And in the process they recruit more partials for Walpurgis."

"Recruit?" asked Jericho. "You make it sound like a military operation."

She giggled.

"Have I said something funny?" he asked.

"Comparing us to an army," she said. "I find *that* funny. Haven't you figured out why we've banded together?"

"Suppose you tell me."

"We're *lonely!*"

"Why?" said Jericho with a smile. "In the kingdom of the blind, the one-eyed man is king."

"Not if they all live in the dark," replied Dorcas. "Growing up in a normal society is like, oh, I don't know—like turning on your radio and finding that no one in the world can broadcast a signal."

"Why Walpurgis?"

"Why have we all come here? Because the White Lucy is here."

"And why is *she* here? She doesn't believe in all this supernatural hocus-pocus."

"But *they* believe in *us*," said Dorcas. "This is an isolationist society, which means that except for you we don't have any busybodies from the Republic nosing around. And it's composed of some pretty strange beliefs and customs, which makes it very tolerant of the odd talent. They leave us alone and let us earn a living while we try to find out how to reproduce our gift."

"Reproduce it? How?"

"I don't know. Here, I'll let the White Lucy tell you." She closed her eyes for a moment, then looked back up at him. "To begin with, it's sex-linked, since only women have even a partial power. And it's probably recessive, but we can't be sure if it's a simple or complex recessive, because we have no way of testing male carriers. I'm just repeating what she told me; does it make sense to you?"

"Some," said Jericho. "It seems to me that your best bet would have been to breed the hell out of your White Lucy."

Dorcas closed her eyes again for a few seconds. "She's sterile. So is the one on Gamma Epsilon IV. The White Lucy thinks that anyone with her abilities will be sterile, but she doesn't know why."

"I'm not the person to ask," said Jericho. "Maybe you'd better ask the White Lucy if Bland has tightened his defenses since last night."

"She says that he hasn't, that they're not defenses in the normal sense of the word so that he has no need of tightening them."

"What does she mean?"

"That he's killing anyone within his radius, regardless of whether he has reason to suspect them or not."

"Including his own men?"

"When he feels like it," said Dorcas.

"Interesting," said Jericho, pursing his lips. He fell silent for the remainder of the meal, then spent the rest of the day on deck, watching the barren landscape as the ship continued at a steady rate.

It was a strange world—nothing he hadn't been led to expect from the map he'd seen in Ubusuku's apartment, but strange nonetheless. Every few hours they'd come to a city or town, but in between was nothing: no suburbs, no exurbs, no country estates. There were a few farms, and these he questioned Dorcas about.

"Most of them are cooperatives, owned by city dwellers," she told him. "Most Walpurgans don't like country life."

"Who works them?" he asked, wondering if farmers were relatively free from Bland's scrutiny.

"Robots."

"Nonsense," he said. "No one uses robots these days."

"Walpurgis does."

Another anomaly. Men had given up on robots when it turned out that enforced leisure was not all that it was cracked up to be. They weren't outlawed, merely shunned. And yet since Walpurgis, thanks to its isolation from the Republic's community of worlds, was an essentially agrarian society, here robots formed the basis of a planetary economy.

"Have they any human supervisors?" he asked aloud.

"Very few," said Dorcas. "They're pretty sophisticated machines."

"They wouldn't be humanoid in structure, would they?"

She shook her head. "Why would anyone want a human structure to work a farm? They're harvesters and threshers and combines, all with functional brains. The White Lucy says that it was a nice idea, though."

"Thank her for me," Jericho replied ironically.

Three more days passed without incident, and Jericho, for lack of anything better to do, furthered his education concerning the ways of Walpurgan society. It was easier than he had anticipated, since the White Lucy was one of the original settlers—one of only three still alive, in fact—and was able to shed some historical light on many of the customs that mystified him.

The trick, he learned, was not to assume that anything he had discovered in Amaymon necessarily applied to any other city. Amaymon was a thriving river city, a melting pot of Walpurgan culture, and a debarkation point for visitors. Its rituals were more symbolic than substantive, and while the people paid lip service to all religions, they believed deeply in none of them.

Most of the other cities were different. They did more than mouth platitudes about evil and devil worship and black magic: they practiced them, sometimes to the point of anarchy. The White Lucy assured him that as he drew closer to Tifereth he would see sights that would shock even his flat, passionless mind. There would be torture rituals, not like the ones Bland seemed compelled to conduct, but rather born of a fervent religious belief; there would be ceremonies that had evolved from grotesque rites back on ancient Earth; there would be perversions—not just sexual—that existed nowhere else in the galaxy. The White Lucy would help him sort out one city's customs from another's, but since he would frequently be unattended by her receivers, she was already teaching him the basics of protective coloration on this world.

She related scores of small details to him, details of the type Ubusuku could only hint at, that would help him protect his identity and his life. And always, overriding everything else, was the constant reminder not to underestimate the sincerity and the conviction of these people. The concept of live and let live might apply to the White Lucy and the rest of the outside world—but in their own cities one obeyed their rules, both legal and religious, or one suffered the consequences, none of which were likely to be very pleasant.

On the morning of the fifth day, when they were a little more than halfway to Tifereth, Dorcas looked up at Jericho suddenly during breakfast.

"It's time," she said softly.

"The White Lucy?" he asked.

Dorcas nodded. "She says we'll reach a blockade within the next three hours."

"Should we chance it?" he asked, though he had already made up his mind to go ashore.

"No. The crew will be tortured, and sooner or later one of them will admit to having taken us on board just north of Amaymon. Once that happens you will never escape alive."

"What about the ship?"

"The captain is one of the few outsiders who knows of the White Lucy's abilities. When I tell him to turn around and head back to Amaymon, he will do so without question."

"I see," said Jericho. "Well, there's no sense calling attention to myself by taking a rowboat. I think I'd better swim. Wait for ten minutes after I've made it to shore, then speak to the captain."

"All right," said Dorcas.

"What's the nearest town?"

"Kether. It's about eighteen miles north, along the river."

"Don't let the ship get that far before you turn it around. I don't want any connection between me, the ship, and Kether."

"I understand."

He went to his cabin, gathered together those few things he felt he would need, put them into a waterproof bag, and went back on deck.

"I hope this Kether is one of the cities where the White Lucy has a contact," he said.

"It is," Dorcas assured him. "A fortune-teller named Cybele. You can find her shop at the Plaza of Forras, a shopping center in the heart of the city."

"All right," he said, throwing a leg over the railing. "Remember: ten minutes."

Without another word he dove into the cold, murky water of the Styx and vanished beneath the surface.

Chapter 14

"Once you have set yourself a goal, why should a little thing like slaughter deter you?"

—*Conrad Bland*

Once he was ashore and out of sight of the ship, Jericho shed his wet clothing and donned a workingman's outfit he had placed in the watertight bag. Then he went to work, giving himself a large scar on his right cheekbone and another, somewhat smaller one, above his left eye. Within a few minutes his eyebrows were bushier, his complexion more sallow, his hairline in a distinctive widow's peak, his age somewhere between thirty-five and fifty.

He began walking toward Kether, keeping away from the few

roads he saw, and pausing when he was perhaps ten miles from the city to brush the dust from his shoes and clothes. He then sought out a major thoroughfare, waited unseen beside it until a truck from one of the nearby farms went by, and flung himself at the back of it. His fingers closed on the wooden panels that kept the produce from spilling out the sides, and shortly thereafter he entered Kether, crouched in the back of the truck. He took the opportunity to put a pair of apples in his pockets; he disliked them intensely, but at least he wouldn't have to waste any time in a restaurant until well past nightfall.

Jericho waited for the truck to turn onto an almost-empty street, then jumped off. He landed lightly, made sure he hadn't drawn any undue notice, and quickly began walking in the opposite direction.

After he had proceeded for three short blocks, he came to a large intersection. He crossed the street, paused leisurely for a moment as if trying to remember something, turned left, and repeated the process until he wound up where he had started. As best he could tell no one was following him.

Still unconvinced, he went two more blocks, then walked between two buildings, found himself in an alley, and stood motionless, hidden by shadows, for almost ten minutes. No one came after him, and he then returned to the street, confident that if anyone *had* been tracking him they would now be waiting for him to emerge one block over.

Jericho had never seen a map of Kether, but it didn't take much imagination to piece together an idea of the city's layout from what little he had seen of it. It seemed to be laid out in a pattern of concentric circles—he supposed there would be nine of them, if only for religious reasons—with a number of major boulevards that would intersect at its center. Since he didn't know exactly how far from the center of the city he was, he couldn't be sure how many boulevards formed the spokes of the wheel, but he guessed at either eight or twelve, since Dorcas had told him that Kether was not a large city, housing something less than 100,000 people.

The architecture was quite different from Amaymon's. It owned no debt whatsoever to Gothic churches or Victorian haunted houses. Kether was all steel and glass and angles, and as he began walking toward the heart of the city he saw why: All of the buildings were solar-powered, which made a great deal of sense, since Kether, like most of the other cities on Walpurgis, was quite isolated from its neighbors and probably couldn't have afforded the money for a fusion plant when it had been settled. As the city grew and spread over the landscape, the city fathers had probably seen no reason to erect a plant when all the houses and businesses were already being powered by sunlight.

He wanted to buy a newspaper, the quickest way he knew of learning about a city, but he decided against it since he didn't know what currency was in popular use in Kether. As he passed through a small, commercial area he paused for a moment to look at a video display in a store window, but they were showing the endless soap operas that seemed so popular on Walpurgis and from which he could learn nothing further; indeed, some exterior scenes convinced him that they weren't even set in Kether.

He passed a crippled beggar, reclining legless in a handmade cart, hat in hands, and took a quick look at the hat, hoping to get a handle on the local currency. It didn't help much: the beggar was having a poor morning, and he couldn't identify the few coins in the hat without drawing undue attention to himself.

As he continued walking, he saw a large crowd gathered on the street about two blocks ahead of him. His first inclination was to turn up a side street and avoid them, but then he decided that he might learn a little more about the city by listening to snatches of conversation and picking a few pockets. As he drew nearer, he heard the screams and shrieks of a child emanating from the center of the crowd.

Suddenly he heard a gong, and, looking up, he saw enough Satanic designs on the building next to the crowd to convince him that it was a church. He reached the outskirts of the mass of humanity, lifted two wallets in a matter of seconds, then realized that he was standing in a rather ragged line.

He didn't know where the line led or what was expected of him, but he decided that he was less likely to expose himself by doing what everyone ahead of him did rather than attempting to leave. In a few minutes he was able to see clearly what was going on.

A black-robed priest and priestess, both hooded, stood before the door of the church on a large pentagonal platform that was raised about six inches off the ground. Before them was an obsidian altar, and strapped onto the altar was a nude boy whose age Jericho estimated to be between ten and twelve. Each citizen in line, as he or she reached the altar, took a knife from the priestess and pressed it into the boy's belly, while the priest intoned a chant that Jericho couldn't understand, in a tongue which he guessed was either Latin or Enochian.

At first he thought he had stumbled onto a ritual killing, but as he moved up in line he realized that if that were the case the boy should long since have been dead. He was ignorant of Satanism, but killing was his business, and he knew that not one man in fifty was capable of inflicting an abdominal wound designed to maim but not kill.

As he moved closer still, the nature of what he was seeing was finally made clear to him. The boy had various cabalistic signs drawn on his chest and stomach with black paint and the congregation—as he now took it to be—was painfully tattooing the design onto him by means of the dagger. It was probably some painful but normal rite of passage into manhood, since no one seemed very surprised or upset by the boy's cries.

When only two people remained in line ahead of him, he concentrated on their actions. Each pressed the blade to his lips, murmured some words that he couldn't quite make out, and traced the pattern for perhaps an inch. Now he saw that as the dagger was returned to the priestess, the priest quickly rubbed some sort of salve over the freshly lacerated flesh.

Finally it was his turn. Jericho stepped out onto the five-sided platform, took the dagger from the priestess, murmured something so softly no one could hear it, and added another inch of mutilation to the boy's belly. Then he returned the blade, stepped off the platform, and continued on his way to the center of Kether.

He had gone two blocks when a firm hand gripped his shoulder. He turned and found himself looking into the cold blue eyes of a tall, well-dressed, balding man.

"Nice show you put on there," said the man.

"What do you mean?" replied Jericho.

"The Ceremony of Belphegor," said the man. "You even fooled the priest."

"I don't know what you're talking about."

"I think you'd better come with me," said the man.

He grabbed Jericho's left arm. Jericho resisted for a moment, checking the street to make sure no one was within thirty or forty yards. Then he reached forward with his right hand, stabbing the man's eyes with his thumb and forefinger. Startled, the man released his grip and threw back his head, exposing his throat. Jericho caught his Adams's apple with the edge of his hand once as he stood that way, again as he was falling. He was dead before he hit the ground.

Jericho looked around, saw a number of people beginning to

whisper and point, and raced into a building. He found a back exit, hit it at full speed, ran down an alley for almost two hundred yards, then entered the back entrance of another building. He found a service lift, took it to the fifth floor, and picked the lock of the first door he came to. It was a small apartment, and he quickly found a closet filled with a man's clothes. He removed his outfit, appropriated a cheap suit and shirt, and was on the verge of leaving when he heard a toilet flush. He waited outside the bathroom, killed the man quickly and painlessly when he emerged, and took a few extra minutes to give himself a new face and a head of short, curly, black hair.

Then he walked down the hallway to the tenant's lift, descended to the main floor, and walked out into the street. He heard the sirens of the police vehicles a quarter mile away, but no one hindered or even noticed him as he continued toward the heart of the city.

At last he reached it, a huge circular plaza perhaps a half mile in diameter, housing the tallest office buildings in the city, though none of them approached the larger buildings of Amaymon in size. He walked the perimeter of the circle until he came to a huge shopping complex. There was a statue of a man with a long beard sitting astride a horse and holding a spear in his right hand. A plaque told him that this was a representation of Forras, also known as Forcas or Furcas, a Knight of Satan and the Grand President of Hell, who commanded twenty-nine legions of demons in the defense of the Infernal Empire.

He paused for a moment, as if admiring the artistry of the sculptor, then began walking in and out of various shops and stores, finally stopping at a sign advertising Madame Cybele's.

He looked around, found a flight of stairs leading to a dingy little basement room, and followed them down. As he entered a cat hissed and scuttled into the shadows, and a tall, dark-haired woman dressed all in white approached him.

"Please be seated," she said, pointing to a chair beside a small ivory table.

He did as she told him, and she joined him a moment later, placing a crystal ball between them.

"What do you wish to know from Madame Cybele?" she asked.

"You're the fortune-teller," he said. "You tell me. Start with my name."

She stared into the crystal ball.

"I don't know your name, but the White Lucy says that you are to be called Jericho. She also says that you are in more trouble than you realize."

"I've taken care of it."

"You have not. The first man you killed was one of Bland's agents."

"How did he spot me?"

"You handed back the dagger hilt first."

"Damn!" he muttered. "As little a thing as that!"

She nodded. "The priestess was too intent upon the boy's agony to notice at the time, but the White Lucy says that when she concentrates upon it she will remember, and then Conrad Bland will know not just that there is a killer loose in Kether, but that the killer is unfamiliar with our customs. From this he will deduce that it is the same killer John Sable has warned him about."

"Then I guess I'd better be going. How much time does the White Lucy think I've got?"

"A few hours. No more."

"That fast?"

"You were seen killing him. They may not connect it with your second murder, but they don't have to. Someone will remember that both of you were at the Ceremony at Belphegor. They will question the priest and priestess, and they will then know why he accosted you and why you had to kill him. It will not take long."

"How far away is the next town on the road to Tifereth?"

"Almost two hundred miles," replied Cybele.

"And who is my contact there?"

"You have none."

"I thought the White Lucy had agents in all the cities," said Jericho.

"She did. This one is dead."

Jericho nodded. "I see."

"I doubt that," said Cybele. "But if you make it to Yesod, you *will* see."

"Yesod? That's the name of the city?"

"Yes."

"Ask the White Lucy what my chances are of getting to Yesod in a stolen vehicle."

She closed her eyes for a moment. "She says that even trucks are not allowed on the roads north of here, that nothing may travel between cities except authorized vehicles."

He shrugged. "Then I guess I'll have to borrow a police car, won't I?"

He stood up and left the shop.

Chapter 15

"Satan lost his war. Only a fool would pay homage to him."
—Conrad Bland

"Mr. Bromberg, this is John Sable again."

"Dammit, Sable!" snapped Bromberg, glaring into the camera at his end of the vidphone. "This is the fourth time in five days!"

"Just routine," said Sable, striving to control his temper. "Has he turned up yet?"

"I keep telling you: If he does show up we are quite competent to handle matters without your assistance."

"And I keep telling you," said Sable, "that he's wanted for six murders in Amaymon. If you capture him, we want him back."

"I know," said Bromberg. "Now why don't you just leave me the hell alone and I'll let you know when we've got him."

"Goodbye, Mr. Bromberg." Sable sighed. "I'll be checking in with you again tomorrow."

"Don't bother!" snapped Bromberg.

"It's my job," said Sable, and broke the connection.

He checked the clock on his wall, above and to the left of the baphomet, and was amazed to find out that it was only midafternoon. He lit a cigar, his second of the day, or maybe his third—he'd given up counting them since the second and third murders—and leaned back in his chair.

Theoretically it wasn't his problem any longer. The killer was gone from Amaymon, was completely beyond his legal jurisdiction, and no one seemed to want his help. Also, his superiors were still dragging their feet. He had gone to them, urging them to make contact with Bland's headquarters at a higher level than he could reach and offer any assistance that Bland's security men might need—but so far, to the best of his knowledge, neither side had moved off dead center. Bland didn't want help, and the civil authorities seemed quite content not to offer it.

It was puzzling. He had no intense personal interest in Bland; in fact, based on their one brief conversation, he didn't like him at all. But almost half the population of Amaymon revered the man. Even his wife, Siboyan, had been lighting candles and offering symbolic sacrifices for his safety. Why did no one in authority, either here or in Tifereth, show any concern?

Even discounting the presence of a Republic assassin, there was a lot more to this business than met the eye. This didn't trouble him, or even seem especially unusual: after all, his job was unraveling mysteries. But he had pulled every string he possessed and he was still in the dark—and *that* bothered him.

Finally he sat up in his chair and pushed an intercom button.

"Yes?" said his secretary.

"I'm going home," he announced.

"Will you want any vidcalls transferred to you?"

"No."

"Under any circumstances?"

"Not unless they come from Conrad Bland himself," he said with a chuckle.

He locked his desk, put on his lightweight jacket, and left the office. He decided not to take his usual bus home; instead he walked the three miles, poring over those few facts he knew and trying to guess at the many he didn't know.

As he walked, the neighborhood began changing, first from commercial to residential, then from apartment buildings to homes. He walked past the black houses of the Messengers, the reds of the Brotherhood of Night, the violets of the Daughters of Delight, even an occasional white house owned by one of the white witches. At last he turned onto his own street, which was a little poorer and a little smaller, but well kept up. His own house was brick, and he had resisted Siboyan's urgings to paint it the black and gold of the Cult of Cali. Possibly it was because he had changed religions when he married her, possibly there was some other reason he couldn't yet fathom, but he had no desire to make public his beliefs; and besides, with three young children he had better ways to spend his money.

"Hi!" said Siboyan as he walked in the door. "You're home early, aren't you?"

"That's a hell of a greeting," he said. "If it bothers you I can go back to the office."

She brushed a wisp of blond hair back off her forehead. "Don't be silly," she said, walking up to him and kissing him on the cheek. "I'm just surprised to see you, that's all."

"I'm sorry."

"Are you getting pressure over the killings?"

"No," he said, frowning. "Not even a little."

"Curious," she commented.

"Isn't it?"

"Will you be wanting dinner soon?"

"Not for a couple of hours," he replied. "I think I'll go out back."

He changed into a pair of coveralls and a heavy shirt, then went to the backyard to work in his garden. He had begun it some six years ago, a little vegetable patch to help stretch his paycheck; but over the years he had become obsessed with it, to the point where it now covered almost the entire yard. He enjoyed the regularity of it, the predictable patterns of growth. There were no unknown motives lurking in this garden, no forces working at cross purposes, no threats to life or limb or logic. It was a pleasant way to spend a few hours at the end of each day, anticipating something new and beautiful rather than reconstructing something old and terrible, forming the patterns rather than hunting for them. He had added flowers to the vegetables, then some of the hardier exotic plants. Working here relaxed him, cleared his mind, renewed his spirit—except that today it did none of these.

He spent two hours there among his growing things, tending to them and trying unsuccessfully to make his mind relax. Then Siboyan sent the two boys out to tell him that dinner would be ready in half an hour and that he'd better wash up. He wrestled with them for a few minutes, listened to them complain about school and church, promised to help fix a broken toy after dinner, then went into the bathroom and showered, emerging a few minutes later in pajamas and a robe.

He shaved with a straight razor—the Cult of Cali insisted, for reasons he still did not comprehend—and joined Siboyan and his sons and daughter in the dining room, noticing yet another stain on the red flocked wallpaper which he himself had hung the previous spring to save the cost of a craftsman, and which the children seemed determined to deface a little more with each passing day. He made his obeisance to the small statue of Cali atop the buffet, an onyx queen of demons wearing a necklace of tiny golden skulls, took his seat at the head of the table, and led the family in a brief prayer to Azazel.

Dinner was composed of soybean products, as usual. Inflation and three growing children limited them to very infrequent meals of real meat, though the kids hardly noticed the difference, and even Sable had difficulty telling one from the other on occasion. Afterward the boys went off to do homework, and his daughter, who never procrastinated on school assignments and always had them done before dinner, posted herself in front of the video.

Sable and Siboyan remained at the table, sipping a little wine and talking about the events of the day. She shared his frustration at not being able to impress Bland with the seriousness of the situation and the skills of the assassin, though Sable wondered if her feelings weren't caused more by her reverence for Bland than her sympathy for his own position. Not that it mattered—he wasn't out for sympathy, just for answers that no one seemed able to supply.

She recognized his restlessness and suggested going out to a cinema, but he begged off, claiming he was too tired. It didn't ring true—he just didn't want to waste the money when he knew he wouldn't be concentrating on the entertainment—but she didn't press the issue, and finally he went down to his cellar workshop to try to fix the broken toy. He had just about gotten it repaired when Siboyan walked to the top of the stairs and called down to him:

"John—vidphone!"

"I told her not to forward any calls!" he called back, reluctant to set aside the toy when he was so near to having it done.

"I think you'd better come," said Siboyan. Something in her voice made him put the toy down and run up the stairs.

He picked up the extension in the kitchen, activating both the camera and the screen.

"Sable here."

"Mr. Sable," said a high-pitched voice, "this is Conrad Bland."

"Hold on a minute, Mr. Bland," he said. "There's something wrong with my screen. I'm not getting any picture."

"I'm not transmitting one," said Bland. "I am unfortunately not in the vicinity of a vidphone. My voice is being carried to one on an intercom system."

"What can I do for you?" said Sable.

"You are a very difficult man to reach," continued Bland, ignoring his question. "My chief of security informs me that you will speak to no one except myself."

"Not so," said Sable. "But when I'm at home, my time is my own. That's neither here nor there; you obviously have something important enough to merit contacting me yourself. What is it?"

"Direct and to the point," said Bland with a chuckle. "I like that, Mr. Sable. Yes, I have something important to tell you: We have captured your Republic assassin."

"You're sure?"

"I do not make mistakes, Mr. Sable," said Bland coldly.

"Well, I'm very glad I was able to warn you in time," said Sable. "Is he still alive?"

"Alive and well," replied Bland. "He is currently incarcerated in Tifereth, though we apprehended him a good deal south of here."

"I appreciate your letting me know. I suppose the next step is for us to extradite him."

"My own sentiments precisely," said Bland.

"I'll file the papers first thing in the morning."

"That won't be necessary," said Bland. "I am the only government here in Tifereth. I give him to you freely."

"That's somewhat irregular," said Sable. "But to quote an old proverb, I don't believe in looking a gift horse in the mouth. How would you like to arrange the transfer?"

"I think it would be best if you came to Tifereth," said Bland. "My work here makes it impossible for me to get away."

"You needn't deliver him personally," said Sable.

"I realize that. Nevertheless, I think it would be best for all parties concerned if you came to Tifereth."

"If you wish," said Sable with a shrug. "I'll fly up there tomorrow morning."

"I'll send my personal plane for you," said Bland. "Can you be ready to leave in, shall we say, six hours?"

"You needn't go to all that trouble," said Sable. "I'm a qualified pilot and I have access to a departmental plane."

"Mr. Sable, you force me to be blunter than I would wish," said Bland. "I cannot guarantee your safety unless you come in my own plane."

"Oh?" said Sable, frowning.

"The local airport in six hours," said Bland. "Be there."

The connection was broken.

Sable turned to Siboyan, who had been listening to the entire conversation with a rapturous expression on her face.

"Well?" he said. "What do you think?"

"About what?" she asked him.

"Weren't you listening?" he said.

"Of course. They've caught the killer."

"I'm talking about the rest of it," he said patiently. "What's going on up there that they're shooting down airplanes?"

"What difference does it make to us?" she replied. "All you have to do is go up as his guest and bring your prisoner back."

"Something's wrong," he said, shaking his head. "Something's still very wrong."

"I don't see what," said Siboyan. "He's sending his own private airplane, he's offering to cooperate with you, he's turning over the man the Republic sent here to kill him. If it was me I wouldn't do that: I'd see that he died very slowly and very painfully for even attempting to assassinate a man like Conrad Bland."

"The law applies even to your new hero," he said with a sardonic smile. "Murder takes precedence over attempted murder. Our assassin will have to stand trial in Amaymon."

"How soon do you have to leave?" she asked.

"Almost immediately," Sable answered. "Bland may not care about his extradition forms, but I care about doing it right at this end. I'll have to stop by the office and see what's needed, and since Enoch Toomey down in Legal won't be around I'll probably have to call him in to help me. I've never extradited a killer before."

"So much for our quiet evening at home," she said with a rueful smile.

"Cheer up. There'll be others."

He went into the bedroom to change. He decided not to pack a suitcase, since he planned to be in Tifereth only long enough to take charge of the prisoner, but he did put one change of clothes into an overnight bag in case they were grounded because of bad flying weather.

He stopped by the front door on his way out and took Siboyan in his arms.

"See you soon," he said.

"I've never been to Tifereth," she said. "Bring back something unusual."

"I will," he promised.

Chapter 16

"I have never denied that Truth has a value. The fool pays homage to it; the wise man twists it to his own advantage."
—Conrad Bland

Sable slept through most of the uneventful flight, waking as the plane banked steeply just prior to landing. He looked out the window as they touched ground, and discovered that rather than landing at the Tifereth airport the pilot had brought the plane down on a private strip.

Jacob Bromberg was standing at the end of the runway, and came up to greet him as he walked down a ramp that a pair of mechanics had wheeled up to the hatch door.

"Welcome to Tifereth, Mr. Sable," said Bromberg, though he seemed indisposed to extend his hand. "Did you have a pleasant flight?"

"I really couldn't say," responded Sable with a smile. "I was asleep most of the way." He looked around him at the barren plain surrounding the strip. "By the way, where are we?"

"This is My Lord Bland's private airfield, about eight miles north of the city. If you'll follow me, I'll drive you into town."

"Fine," said Sable, hefting his overnight case and falling into step behind Bromberg. The air was damp and heavy, with a stale smell to it that he couldn't immediately identify.

Bromberg led him to an open military vehicle, relatively new and highly polished, which sported some insignia Sable hadn't seen before.

"Please put your bag in the back, Mr. Sable."

Sable did as he was told, then climbed into the passenger's seat and lit a cigar, the last of the handful Veshinsky had given him a few days earlier.

"How did you catch him?" he asked after Bromberg had turned on the ignition.

"I really couldn't say, Mr. Sable," said Bromberg, taking a hard left and turning onto the main road to Tifereth. "I had nothing to do with it."

"Who is he?"

Bromberg shrugged. "I have no idea."

"Has he said anything yet?"

"Not to my knowledge."

"Then, at the risk of sounding impertinent, how do you know you have the right man?"

"Oh, we've got the right man, all right," said Bromberg with a smile. "My Lord Bland doesn't make mistakes."

"What does he look like under all the disguises?"

"I personally haven't seen him, Mr. Sable," replied Bromberg. "Anything I told you would be hearsay."

Sable fell silent. He puffed on his cigar, allowed the flavor of the tobacco to permeate his mouth, then blew out a thin stream of white smoke.

Bromberg obviously knew nothing at all about the assassin, and he was Bland's chief of security. That was curious in itself. And the fact that they had caught the killer so quickly and easily was even more curious. It was possible that they had the right man, of course, but the more he thought about it the more he doubted it. Well, when he got him back to Amaymon he'd hook him up to the truthtell machine and then he'd know for sure. Or possibly Wallenbach had a truthtell machine right here in Tifereth, which might save a lot of trouble and a possible suit for false arrest. He made a mental note to check with Wallenbach on that before he left with the prisoner.

Tifereth began to loom large before them, and although it was midday he got the impression that the city was somehow dark and filled with lengthening shadows. Probably it was just the way he was looking at it, or the angle of the sun against some of the steepled buildings, but it was a curious sight nonetheless.

And then, as they entered the city, the stench reached his nostrils. It smelled of decaying, rotting matter, and at first he thought it was uncollected garbage, but then he saw the source: bodies, some of them newly dead, some rank and fetid, littered the streets and sidewalks, singly and in groups, naked and clothed, some lying in pools of congealing blood, some with a single bullet hole or laser burn in them.

"What the hell is going on here?" demanded Sable, stunned by the extent of the carnage.

"We had a little insurrection a few days ago," said Bromberg calmly. "My Lord Bland decided to leave the bodies on display as a warning to others who may object to the rule of law."

"A few days ago?" repeated Sable. "Some of those bodies look as if they're still warm."

"You must be mistaken, Mr. Sable," replied Bromberg.

After they had gone six blocks into the city the bodies became more numerous, and Sable could swear he saw two of them, an old man and a very young girl, still twitching.

"Stop the car!" he demanded.

"Why?" asked Bromberg.

"A couple of those people are still alive!"

"They couldn't be," said Bromberg. "The insurrection was put down almost a week ago."

"Let me out!"

"I really can't," said Bromberg, hitting the accelerator. "We're already late."

The scores of corpses became thousands as they neared the center of the city, and Sable saw that those buildings that weren't burned out or blown apart were locked and shuttered. Not a living soul walked the streets of Tifereth. Not a dog or a cat lurked in the shadows. Even the vermin seemed to have taken up residence elsewhere. The only living things in the area were the thick clouds of flies that swarmed over and around the bodies, lighting here and there, then rushing off to land on an even more decayed piece of flesh.

"Some insurrection!" snorted Sable, feeling the need to break the deathly silence.

"Indeed it was, Mr. Sable," replied Bromberg.

"How many of your own forces were killed?"

"None."

"Somehow that doesn't surprise me."

"We're a very efficient unit, Mr. Sable," said Bromberg.

"So I see," replied Sable. "What I don't see is a single weapon on any of the corpses."

"We've confiscated them," said Bromberg with a smile. "No sense leaving them around for more revolutionaries."

"Very incisive reasoning."

"Thank you, sir."

"Now if you're all through bullshitting, why don't you tell me what's really happening here?"

"I just told you, Mr. Sable."

"Forget it," said Sable. "I'll talk to Bland."

"That would be best, sir," said Bromberg.

They drove for another two miles, the carnage around them unchanging, then pulled into a parking lot in the basement of a hotel.

"Bland lives here?" asked Sable as the vehicle screeched to a halt.

"No," said Bromberg. "But he's in conference at the moment. He's arranged for you to have a suite of rooms. You'll be sent for shortly."

"Why don't I just wait outside his conference room?" said Sable uneasily.

"I do not question My Lord Bland's orders," said Bromberg, getting out of the vehicle and taking the overnight bag in his hand. Sable followed him, a glass door slid back, and they walked to a lift. It let them off on the top floor—the thirteenth—and Bromberg led him to a door at the end of the hall. He punched out the combination, the door opened inward, and Bromberg and Sable entered a truly luxurious penthouse suite. There was an enormous and expensively furnished sitting room, complete with fireplace and well-stocked bar, which had a view of the central city. To the right was another, smaller sitting room, to the left a bedroom with a pneumatic mattress that could have accommodated ten people, and beyond that a marble bathroom with a sauna.

"The accommodations are satisfactory?" asked Bromberg.

"They're fine. How long will I be here?"

"Not very. My Lord Bland will send for you shortly. In the meantime, enjoy your stay in Tifereth. I can guarantee that you won't be disturbed. You're the hotel's only tenant."

"What happened to the others?"

"Oh, that's a long story, Mr. Sable," said Bromberg. "Perhaps we'll discuss it over dinner."

"I was rather hoping to leave town before then," said Sable.

"Then some other time, perhaps."

"By the way, I don't happen to see a vidphone anywhere around here. Is there one?"

"Whom do you wish to communicate with?"

"I want to call my wife and tell her I've arrived safely."

"It's been taken care of."

"And I want to speak to Caspar Wallenbach."

"I'm afraid that's quite impossible," said Bromberg. "He died last night."

"How?"

"Heart attack, I believe," said Bromberg. "And now, if you've no further questions . . ."

"I've got plenty of them," said Sable.

"Then I suggest you ask My Lord Bland," said Bromberg with a smile. He walked to the door, punched the combination, and left.

Sable walked over to the door, tried it, and wasn't surprised to discover that it wouldn't open without a combination. He then checked the huge picture windows in the sitting room. There was no way to open them, and he didn't see any sense shattering them and trying to climb down over the sheer side of a thirteen-story building.

He began inspecting the suite more closely, feeling very much like a caged animal. There were no religious artifacts of any kind, no reading material, no video or radio sets. All the closets were empty, the cabinets and dresser drawers were barren, even the chest above the vanity in the bathroom was vacant.

He checked the bar, found a corkscrew, and spent the next twenty minutes futilely trying to pry open the door to the outer corridor. He toyed with breaking a bottle and keeping a sliver of glass for a weapon should he need it, but rejected the notion: he was more likely to inadvertently slash himself with a concealed piece of jagged glass than do injury to anyone else.

So, instead of breaking a bottle of liquor, he opened one and poured himself a drink. He downed it in a single swallow, tried the door again without much hope, then stripped off his clothes and took a shower. While he was drying himself off Bromberg entered the suite, found him in the midst of getting dressed, and announced that Bland had sent for him.

"So I'm really going to get to see him?"

"Of course."

"I was beginning to feel like a prisoner."

"These are security precautions, nothing more. There are certain elements still at large that unfortunately make Tifereth less safe than we desire."

"Did the same elements give Wallenbach his heart attack?" asked Sable caustically.

"I really couldn't say."

"I know," said Sable. "You were elsewhere at the time and you don't know anything about it."

"Right." Bromberg grinned. "Are you ready?"

"Should I leave my bag here or take it along?" asked Sable.

"Oh, I think you might as well take it with you. After all, if you're fogged in, you can always bring it back here, can't you?"

Sable grunted, picked up the bag, and followed Bromberg to the lift. When they reached the basement parking lot he was once again very conscious of the stench of death, but he made no comment and quickly took his seat.

They drove for just under a mile, passing row upon row of armed guards during the final few blocks, and stopped before the gates of a large building, which Sable took to be a Church of Baal from which all sectarian symbols had been removed. Bromberg uttered a password, a guard opened the gate, and they proceeded up a long driveway, stopping at a covered portico.

"Here we are," said Bromberg, getting out of the vehicle. "Let me carry your bag."

"Fine," replied Sable, following the Security Chief to the entrance. They walked through two huge wooden doors, both of which had scenes of depravity and degradation carved into them by the hand of a strange but masterful artist who obviously had a morbid fascination with his subject matter. A moment later they found themselves in an enormous lobby with polished red floors and walls, and armed guards posted every five feet. Bromberg nodded to one of them, who immediately left his post, walked down a long corridor, and returned a few minutes later. He made a slight gesture, and Bromberg took Sable by the arm.

"He'll see you now," he whispered, leading Sable down the corridor. When they reached the end of it they came to a heavy, iron door, and Sable knew Bland must be behind it. He and Bromberg waited for a team of men to laboriously pull it open. Then they entered the room together.

Sable had to fight back the urge to vomit on the spot. The smell of decaying flesh was superseded by the pungent odor of blood, the salty, sickly scent of gallon upon gallon of blood.

Men and women, all nude, hung from the rafters that crisscrossed the huge domed ceiling, some held in place by meathooks, some tied by the thumbs, the toes, the genitals. Others were crucified to the walls. Still more cluttered the floor. Some were dead; most were alive but in no condition to move or even to scream in agony.

Sable stared dumbly at the scene before him. Slowly he became aware of an insistent tugging on his arm, and he finally let Bromberg lead him past the dying and the dead, toward the center of the auditorium. He felt as if he were sleepwalking, as if this *had* to be a nightmare. Then a woman, her face and body no longer covered by skin, reached out and grabbed at his leg, and he realized that this was really happening, that the hideous scenes on the doors of the church now had a counterpart in life.

At the far end of the auditorium, sitting on a plain wooden chair, was a small, slender, golden-haired man, clad immaculately in white. As Sable forced himself to approach him, he saw that the man's face was cherubic and unblemished, his fingers lean and delicate, his hair carefully groomed, his features almost feminine.

"Mr. Sable," he said in a high-pitched voice when Sable was within fifteen feet of him. "How nice of you to come."

"You're Conrad Bland?" said Sable, fighting the urge to run from the auditorium and never look back.

"In the flesh!" said Bland with a smile.

"What's going on here?" Sable asked weakly.

"Nothing that need concern you," said Bland. "But I *am* delighted to see you. I was very much wondering what you'd look like."

Sable looked dully around him. "What sort of butchery is this?"

"The sort I like," said Bland easily. "In time you may come to enjoy it yourself. You have figured out, of course, that we have not captured your assassin?"

"Of course," repeated Sable without inflection. "Why did you send for me?"

"Curiosity," said Bland with a laugh. "I wanted to see what kind of man would try to extradite a butcher from a slaughterhouse."

"I didn't know . . ." said Sable, his voice trailing off again, trying to keep his attention focused on Bland but unable to stop himself from looking at the quivering meat around him. "*Nobody* knew . . ."

"They *will* know, never fear," said Bland. "Without exception, they will all know."

"What happens to me now?"

"Why, you will remain in Tifereth as my honored guest," said Bland. "You fascinate me, Mr. Sable. You really do."

"Why?"

"Because you are the first man, other than my mercenaries, who ever felt compelled to protect or prolong my existence."

"It was my duty," said Sable dully.

"So much the better. You are a man of honor, a man of duty and decency. In short, you are the Enemy. You are the embodiment of what I must destroy. I must study you well, Mr. Sable. Indeed I must."

"Suppose I don't want to stay here?" asked Sable, once again forcing his eyes away from the horror that surrounded him and focusing on Bland's face.

"Suppose away." Bland laughed. "You will remain here as my guest nonetheless."

"For how long?"

"Until you cease to amuse me."

"And then what?"

"I should think, Mr. Sable, that the answer to that would be obvious," said Bland.

Chapter 17

"If blood were green, then green would be my favorite color."
— *Conrad Bland*

Jericho kept off the streets of Kether until nightfall. Then, just before midnight, he took up a vigil near a small, all-night restaurant on the outskirts of town. Before long a police vehicle pulled up and two officers emerged. When they came out of the restaurant half an hour later he was waiting for them. There was a brief, bloodless, silent scuffle that attracted no attention from the other patrons, and a few moments later, after loading their bodies into the trunk and appropriating their hand weapons, he was driving along the almost-deserted highway from Kether to Yesod.

He gave some thought to bypassing Yesod entirely and driving on to Netsah, the next major city on the road to Tifereth, but he decided that the failure of the dead officers to report in to their headquarters would have aroused suspicion by then. The three hours it would take him to reach Yesod was about all the time he felt he could buy in this particular vehicle.

He was within fifteen miles of Yesod and could see the lights of the city twinkling in the distance when an unmarked car going toward Kether crossed over the median strip and began following him. A moment later a siren sounded, a light on the car's dashboard began flashing, and Jericho decided that he'd better pull over to the shoulder. Both cars came to a stop simultaneously, and three men immediately emerged from the unmarked vehicle and began approaching Jericho's car.

"Out," said one of the men.

Jericho emerged from his vehicle into the humid night.

"What's the problem?" he asked.

"We'll ask the questions, if you don't mind," said the man. "What's your business in Yesod?"

"I'm a detective from Kether," said Jericho. "Officer Parnell Burnam. I'm on police business."

"*What* police business?"

"If you'll show me your credentials, I'll be happy to tell you," said Jericho.

The man pulled out a wallet and displayed a plastic card.

"No good," said Jericho. "Being from a private security force from Tifereth doesn't give you the right to stop and question me."

"Jason," said the man to one of his companions, "put in a call to Kether and see if they've got a Parnell Burnam on their force. Call in the license plate, too."

"No sense going to all that trouble," said Jericho hastily. "Actually, I was supposed to be here a few hours ago. I stopped for a couple of drinks just outside Kether and kind of lost track of the time."

"That's *your* problem."

"Look," he persisted desperately. "You're going to get me in all kinds of trouble if they find out that I'm just now getting to Yesod. Let me just show you my ID and get out of here."

"Let's see it," said the man noncommittally.

Jericho fumbled nervously inside his jacket as if searching for his ID card, then calmly pulled out one of the hand weapons he had taken from the dead policemen and fired it at point-blank range. The man died without a sound, and an instant later his two companions also lay lifeless upon the highway.

Jericho turned to the police car, fired a burst into the radio, then searched the three corpses until he found the keys to the unmarked car. He pulled the bodies off the road just as a light drizzle began to fall, got in the car, and a few minutes later drove into Yesod.

Yesod was a compact little town of perhaps 100,000 people, an architectural hodgepodge of Victorian and Gothic buildings, of spires and steeples and cobblestone streets, all brand spanking new and all aspiring to look centuries old. He was a mile into the city when the radio on his dash panel began buzzing. Since he didn't know the car's call letters or passwords, he ignored it, and in less than another mile two police cars, sirens screaming, were hot on his heels.

He increased his speed on the wet street and began weaving through the sparse traffic, tires screeching as he turned every few blocks. But it didn't help, for now five cars were chasing him, waking the whole area with the ear-splitting sound of their sirens and the blinding flash of their lights. He knew they were in radio contact with each other, and that he'd be blocked off in another two minutes at most.

He peeled into an alley, slowed down slightly, opened the door, grabbed his makeup bag, and jumped out, rolling into the shadows as he hit the ground. He was on his feet instantly, standing stock-still until a trio of police cars raced by him. He heard his car crash a few hundred feet up the alley, then raced between two Victorian houses and made his way to the sidewalk before anyone had emerged from the houses to see what had occurred.

He quickly untucked and unbuttoned his shirt and walked rapidly up to the end of the street, turning right for half a block and then turning again into the alley. A number of other men and women who had heard the crash were also approaching the site of the wreck, most of them in their nightclothes, some with umbrellas.

He waited until he got within view of the police, then began buttoning his shirt back up.

Two of the cars had left the scene before he joined the little semicircle of onlookers, and he knew they were searching for the missing driver. One of the officers who had remained with the car asked the bystanders if they had seen anyone fleeing from the scene of the wreck, and dispersed them a few minutes later when no one was able to provide any information. Most of them hurried home to get out of the rain.

Jericho turned back the way he had come and walked away at a leisurely pace. Police cars were still patrolling the area, and he knew he would have to get off the streets shortly, before he attracted their attention. He spotted what seemed to be a church a few blocks up ahead and he headed toward it, planning to wait out the remainder of the morning there until the manhunt moved elsewhere.

When he arrived he saw that the symbols on the door and the portico were identical to the Church of Satan he had attended with Ubusuku back in Amaymon, and as he entered he looked about for some sign directing him to the Laymen's Gallery. There wasn't any.

He then opened a door that led to the main auditorium of the church. A man at the head of the aisle handed him a cheaply fashioned cloak and hood, both bearing Satanic and cabalistic designs, and he realized that there were no laymen in Yesod's Church of Satan.

The church was almost empty, and he sat alone in the back, his head lowered as if in prayer. He estimated that it would be dawn in another hour, and he decided to remain inside the church until early afternoon.

From time to time a man or woman would enter the church, approach the onyx altar, make some form of obeisance, and then take a seat in one of the pews. No priests were present, and the only staff member he could see was the one whose sole duty seemed to be the dispersal and retrieval of cloaks and hoods.

He remained where he was for more than an hour. Then, as the church got a little more crowded, he rose and walked to the back of the aisle, returning the cloak and hood and seeking out a restroom. He quickly altered his identity, then sat, fully clothed, in a toilet stall for another hour. When he reemerged he found a new man on duty, took a new cloak and hood, discovered that the church was more crowded and that most of the people were seated at the front, and joined them.

The number of congregants continued to increase, and by noon the church was almost entirely filled. Finally, at what he assumed to be high noon, a gong was struck and a black-hooded priest strode out to the altar.

"We will recite the Eighteenth Enochian Key," he announced, and began chanting in a language that was totally unfamiliar to Jericho but which the other congregants repeated unhesitatingly.

When they were done the gong was struck again, and the priest raised his hand for silence.

"O thou mighty light and burning flame of comfort, that unveilest the glory of Satan to the center of the Earth," he intoned, "be thou a window of comfort unto me. Move, therefore, and appear! Open the mysteries of your creation! Be friendly unto me, for I am the same, the true worshiper of the highest and ineffable King of Hell!"

The congregation responded with a number of heartfelt cries of "Hail Satan!" and "Regie Satanis!" and then fell silent again.

"My brethren," continued the priest, removing his hood, "I had a sermon prepared for today. I shall not give that sermon. We have more important things to do." He paused for effect, then thundered out his next sentence. "An assassin hired by the Republic to kill the Dark Messiah is in Yesod at this very minute!"

There was a stunned silence.

"He must be stopped!" cried the priest "He must not be allowed to reach Conrad Bland. It is said that he is a master of disguise. Therefore, you must disbelieve your neighbor, doubt your spouse, scrutinize your children. Shoot first and question later. It is far better that a thousand innocent men and women die than that this man be allowed to leave Yesod! If you hesitate, if you pause, you are no Satanist and you do not belong in this church!"

The people began shifting uneasily, scrutinizing those seated next to them.

"We must ask for help, for strength, for guidance!" cried the priest. "We must offer a Sacrifice of Supplication!" He looked out at his suddenly intense audience. "Who will stand among the chosen?"

Five young men, an old man, and a middle-aged woman stood up immediately. Three other women and another man rose a few seconds later.

"Excellent!" said the priest. "Let it never be said that the membership of our church lacked zeal!" He pointed to one of the young men, who approached the altar while the others sat back down.

"You shall sit at Lord Lucifer's left hand this day," said the priest, and the young man, wild-eyed and with a fanatical glow on his face, nodded vigorously.

"And who will strike the blow?" cried the priest. This time everyone but Jericho rose to his feet, and Jericho stood up a moment later.

The priest pointed to an elderly woman in the third row, who quickly approached him.

"With this hallowed blade shall you present Lord Lucifer with our supplication," he said, handing her an ornate dagger.

The young man took off his clothes and stood, hands clasped behind him, facing the audience.

"The congregation will join me in the Chant of Supplication," said the priest.

He began intoning another chant, and as the congregation joined in, the woman pulled her cloak tightly about her, completely covering her dress. Then she touched five imaginary points in the air with the dagger, placed it next to the young man's abdomen, and pushed it inward and upward. He screamed, gurgled, spit up a mouthful of blood, but remained standing.

"Satan smiles upon us!" cried the priest "For the more suffering Lord Lucifer enjoys, the more power shall he return to us for our efforts. Regie Satanis!"

The young man suddenly fell to his knees and stared glassily at the priest, who ignored him.

"Hear me, Lord Lucifer!" cried the priest "Heed our supplication, embrace our sacrifice! Make keen our eyes, make powerful our arms, bless our quest, and destroy our enemies!"

The young man fell on his face, twitched a few times, and then lay still.

The ceremony went on for another hour, turning into a grimmer, more sordid version of the Black Mass Jericho had witnessed in Amaymon.

This time the living altar was a fifteen-year-old girl who was carried to the front of the congregation, where she was stripped naked, strapped to the onyx altar, and sodomized by the priest and three of the congregants. When this was over she lay motionless except for the rapid rising and falling of her breasts, while black candles were affixed to her hands by means of dripping wax.

A bare-breasted nun appeared, urinated in a bowl, and placed the bowl on the girl's belly. After a few more chants, the three men and the priest drank from it.

The priest then took a whip from the nun and began whipping the girl and the three men, intoning still more chants with each stroke. A moment later a nude man in a goat's-head mask leaped into a pentagram which had been drawn with a black turnip dipped in the urine, took the whip from the priest, flayed the girl in earnest, and began a series of grotesque contortions which seemed to consist primarily of pelvic thrusts. The girl was sodomized again as the congregation chanted "Ave Satanis!" with each thrust. He then took an unlit candle, inserted it first into her vagina and then into her anus, and, finally withdrawing it, raced off into the darkness surrounding the pentagram.

The Satan-figure's departure seemed to signal the onset of an orgy among the entire congregation, and Jericho found himself forced to follow suit. He stripped himself naked, was handed a whip, followed the other members up to the altar, and tried to ignore the pain as his neighbors lashed out indiscriminately with their own whips. He found a reasonably attractive girl who was momentarily unencumbered by a partner and pulled her to the floor. He was about to have normal sex with her—as normal as was possible under these circumstances, anyway—when he looked about him and saw that normal sexual relations were definitely not the order of the day. He quickly turned the girl onto her belly and sodomized her, while she screamed Enochian chants at the top of her lungs.

More whips lashed him as he was withdrawing from her, and he found that his participation was far from finished. During the next half hour, with a variety of partners of both sexes, he found himself being expected to perform acts of degradation he hadn't believed existed outside of the twisted imaginations of some of the Republic's grosser pornographers. But since the alternative was the exposure of his identity, he undertook the task as coldly and efficiently as he undertook the more usual task of murder.

When he was beginning to wonder just how much more of this he could take (or, to be more accurate, how much more of it he could administer), the gong rang again and the congregants, with scarcely a glance at their momentary partners, walked back to their seats, physically and emotionally spent. They took a few minutes getting dressed, catching their breath, tending to minor abrasions, and otherwise composing themselves, then joined the priest in another twenty minutes of prayers and chants. Finally the priest exhorted them one last time to catch the assassin, after which he left the auditorium. A black-hooded woman carrying a medical kit approached the girl who had been the living altar and began ministering to her, two minor priests picked up the corpse of the young sacrifice and carried it off, and the people started filing out. Jericho quickly worked his way into the midst of the crowd, handing back his cloak and hood on the way out.

Most of the congregants walked to a nearby parking lot, and Jericho lagged behind. When the last of them had driven off he inspected the few remaining empty cars, selected one that worked by computer-lock ignition rather than keys, quickly broke the code, and drove out of the lot. He went north through the center of town, never moving out of the slowest lane of traffic, then veered to the west when he had passed out of the commercial and industrial areas.

After a few minutes he spotted a brightly labeled Air Parcel truck making a pickup. He slowed down and began discretely following it. The truck made several more stops, but he knew that it would eventually wind up at Yesod's airport, as indeed it did just after nightfall.

Jericho parked a goodly distance away from the air-freight terminal, walked unseen to the truck, waited until the driver climbed into the back to begin unloading his merchandise, and then dispatched him quickly and bloodlessly. He appropriated his uniform and identification card, then made his face up to resemble the driver's ID photo. He picked up a pair of small packages, locked the driver's body in the back of the truck, and walked into the freight dispatcher's office, his credentials pinned to a breast pocket. While waiting in line behind a number of other couriers he got a look at the flight schedule that was posted on the wall, and saw that a plane was leaving for Hod in the next half hour.

This was better than he had hoped for. Netsah was only two hundred miles north of Yesod, but Hod was within three hundred miles of Tifereth itself. If he could get on the plane, he could bypass Netsah and four other cities. He stepped out the door, changed the addresses on the tow parcels to read "Hod," then waited fifteen minutes and reentered the building. The line was gone and he walked straight up to the dispatcher.

"What have you got for me today?" asked the dispatcher pleasantly.

"Some priority stuff for Hod," he replied matter-of-factly.

"I don't know," said the dispatcher. "The plane is loaded up and is due to take off in just a few minutes."

"Look, I don't know what the hell is in these packages, but if they don't get to Hod tonight I could lose my job. Isn't there anything you can do?"

"They're *that* important?" said the dispatcher, rubbing his chin thoughtfully.

Jericho nodded.

"All right," said the dispatcher. "I'll radio the pilot and tell him to open up a hatch and wait for you. Drive it out to Runway Seven."

Jericho thanked him profusely, went out to the truck, and drove to within forty yards of the plane that was gunning its engines on the runway marked "7." He got out of the cab, waved to the pilot, and tossed the packages and his makeup bag into the cargo hold.

"Are you clear?" called the pilot.

"All clear!" shouted Jericho above the drone of the engines.

He waited until the pilot hit the button that slowly closed the hatch door, then leaped upward and pulled himself into the hold just before the door slammed shut.

He would have preferred to kill the pilot rather than chance discovery at the other end, but while he could pilot a spaceship he was totally ignorant of the workings of planetary airplanes.

A moment later he was airborne, heading for the distant city of Hod and wondering if the White Lucy's contact there was still alive.

Chapter 18

"Torture, like the violin, is merely an instrument. Only in the hands of a master does it become an art form."
—*Conrad Bland*

Sable had spent an almost sleepless night in a small room in a turret of the church. Though not as luxurious as the hotel where he had been temporarily incarcerated, it provided for all of his needs—except freedom. The door was made of steel, the combination lock could be punched only from the outside, and two burly men stood guard, one on each side of the door. Such minimal sleep as he had been able to achieve had been broken by the screams and moans of the dying and the overpowering stench of the dead.

About an hour after sunlight began flooding into his room through a barred window, his door was unlocked and he was escorted down a winding staircase past scores of tortured bodies, some living, some recently dead, and out a side door.

He was then led down a flagstone path, and found his eyes tearing from the bright sunlight. A number of birds flew overhead, attracted by the smell of the rotting bodies, and he found himself idly wondering if any of them ever made it inside the church.

After walking for perhaps two hundred feet, they reached a small, heavily guarded rectory, and Sable was roughly ushered inside. Bland was waiting for him, seated in a large library that he had filled with books and tapes from all parts of the Republic. An octaphonic sound system played the bittersweet strains of some symphony that sounded vaguely familiar but which Sable couldn't identify.

"Good morning, Mr. Sable," said Bland pleasantly. "I trust you slept well?"

"As well as could be expected," replied Sable, looking around the room. Along with the books and tapes there were numerous paintings and statuettes, though none of them was even mildly Satanic in nature. There seemed to be no mementos of any kind representing Bland's bloody career.

"Have a seat," said Bland, gesturing toward a wing-backed chair opposite him. "I apologize for the inelegance of my domicile, but one must accept certain inconveniences from time to time."

"But one needn't like them," said Sable coldly.

"Come, come, Mr. Sable. You're not being very friendly or amusing, and we mustn't forget that your sole purpose for being here is to amuse me."

"Or humor you."

"You think I'm crazy?" Bland laughed. "Well, why not? It helps to have the enemy underestimate me. But let me tell you this, Mr. Sable: When I was twelve years old I was taken to a psychiatrist after my mother found me vivisecting our family pets. I am perhaps the only man of your acquaintance who has a certificate stating categorically that I am *not* insane." He laughed uproariously at that.

"Your psychiatrist had an interesting notion of innocent childish pranks," said Sable, watching Bland for a reaction and surprised when he got nothing more violent than a smile.

"Well, I'm sure if he were alive he would appreciate that. I killed him when I was thirteen." Sable decided it would be safer not to comment again, but Bland, vastly enjoying the sight of the detective struggling with his urge to detect, prodded him on. "Aren't you curious to know *why* I killed him?"

"Only if you wish to tell me."

"I knew that a great destiny, a magnificent destiny, lay before me. I didn't know what it was, but even at that early age I knew that I didn't want anyone around who would be able to identify me or supply any information about me to my enemies. To that same end, I killed both of my parents, but except for that and a few other isolated instances, I had a rather normal adolescence. But enough about me, Mr. Sable. Tell me about yourself."

"For instance?" asked Sable, his eyes scanning the various windows and doorways.

"For instance, why in the world would *anyone*—and especially a moral man like yourself—wish to protect my life? And I strongly suggest that you stop looking for a means of escape. You would find your life much less pleasant, and of far shorter duration, if you actually made it out of this house before I released you."

Sable sighed and waited for the tension to flow out of his muscles. Bland might be a madman, but he wasn't a stupid madman, and he hadn't lived this long by being careless. He took him at his word that escape was out of the question.

"I'm a police officer, sworn to uphold the law. When I discovered that the Republic was out to assassinate a man to whom my government had given asylum, I felt it was my duty to prevent it."

"And would you do the same thing now that you've been to Tifereth?" asked Bland pleasantly.

Sable stared at him, took a deep breath, and answered the question. "I would no longer lift a finger to protect you."

"Oh?" said Bland, amused. "Do you know how many innocent men and women your assassin has murdered since he's been on Walpurgis?"

"Six."

"You've been out of touch, Mr. Sable. The count is up to at least fourteen, and possibly as many as twenty."

"You haven't caught him yet?"

"We will soon."

"Where is he?"

"Somewhere between Kether and Tifereth. Probably in Yesod."

"He's gotten that far?" said Sable, surprised.

"He's a highly skilled killer. But of course he hasn't gotten close enough to be a real irritant yet. When that time comes—and it's coming soon—he will be stopped. But tell me, Mr. Sable, why you no longer wish to hinder a paid professional assassin, a killer who has been strewing the countryside with innocent victims."

"Are you expressing moral outrage at someone killing off innocent people?"

"*He is poaching on my territory!*" cried Bland, his eyes blazing fiercely. Suddenly his face contorted into the semblance of a smile again. "Forgive me. I happen to feel deeply about my prerogatives, and occasionally I express myself too strongly."

An intercom buzzed on the wall, and Bland walked over to it. "Yes?"

"Sir," said a voice that sounded like Bromberg's, "there's no question about it: he's escaped from Yesod."

"I rather thought he might," said Bland calmly. "How long will it take him to reach Netsah?"

"Three hours, maybe four."

"Wait five hours and then destroy it."

"The whole city?"

Bland didn't even deign to answer, but merely switched off the intercom.

"So much for your assassin," he said. "May I offer you a drink, Mr. Sable?"

Sable shook his head.

"As you wish," said Bland with a shrug. He returned to his chair. "You look distressed, Mr. Sable. Is it the destruction of Netsah?"

"You're killing thousands of innocent people," said Sable, trying to control his fury.

"They're only people," said Bland. "Sooner or later they would die anyway. Some people, such as yourself, amuse and entertain me. Some, such as your much-heralded assassin, challenge me. But I must truthfully admit that I care for none of you." He gestured to his books and tapes. "The best of Man, all that is worthwhile, is *there*. The rest is just meat."

"Like your parents?" said Sable coldly.

"Mr. Sable, you strike me to the quick. In point of fact, I am quite ashamed of killing my parents."

"Then why did you do it?"

"Let me rephrase that," amended Bland. "I do not regret their deaths, but rather the *nature* of their deaths. I behaved like some slinking night-stalking carnivore—or," he added with a smile, "like some Republic assassin. They were the two people whose suffering I would have most enjoyed, and I dispatched them quickly, secretly, leaving no traces. They never knew what happened to them, and consequently I never fully savored the thrill of their death agonies. I have become much more skilled in recent years, but alas, one can murder one's parents only once."

Sable tried to disguise his disgust and horror, and felt it would be unsafe to make any comment.

"You look distressed, Mr. Sable. There is no need to be. It is my nature to do certain things; it is my strength that I do them well. I destroy things because the only alternative is *not* to destroy them, and I find that unpalatable. Tell me truthfully: Have you never had the desire to kill your parents, or your wife, or your children?"

"Of course I have," replied Sable. "But it's just an animal impulse. It can be overcome."

"Ah, but what if a man chooses not to overcome it? What if, instead, he learns to direct it? What might that man not do, given intellect and drive and opportunity?"

"One of the things he might not do is convince me that he's right."

"Wonderful!" cried Bland, clapping his hands together in delight. "I *knew* you would prove amusing. How shall I reward you? Ah, I have it! You may ask me anything you wish, with no fear of repercussion, for the next five minutes. Surely you have stockpiled a number of questions?"

"Let's start with a simple one," said Sable, not at all sure the wrong questions would be free of repercussions. "What is your goal—to conquer Walpurgis?"

Bland laughed and shook his head.

"What, then—the whole Republic?"

"My dear Mr. Sable, how you misjudge me in your ignorance! I have no wish to conquer anything. I have neither the desire nor the capacity to rule over an empire."

"Then why all this slaughter?"

"You must not confuse wars of conquest with wars of destruction."

He walked to a window and opened it, and Sable could hear the muffled shrieks and screams of Bland's victims coming from the church.

"Do you hear that?" said Bland, his eyes aglow. "*That* is the symphony I love the best, Mr. Sable."

And, along with the sound, came a hot breeze bringing the stench, the smell of rotting, decaying flesh, of blood, of vermin, of death. Sable was sickened by it, and simultaneously amazed that he had grown moderately accustomed to it during the night. He began to understand how some of Bland's guards could lose their objectivity and come to love their work; it was only when you stepped out of the charnel house and then reentered it that you began to realize the full extent of what was happening.

"Why did you come to Walpurgis in the first place?" asked Sable, covering his nose and mouth with a handkerchief until Bland reluctantly closed the window and returned to his chair with a regretful sigh.

"This is a world that worships Satan," said Bland at last. "I was born to come here, and this planet was born to have me. We were made for each other. It has been a perfect marriage, and it will remain so—until I kill the bride, that is." Sable, still fighting the urge to vomit, said nothing, and after a moment Bland continued. "To be painfully honest, Satanism and devil worship is, if anything, even sillier than theism, but if the planet's belief in it can be used to my advantage, I have no strenuous objections to it. Never forget: It was your clergy, your moral leaders, who first offered me sanctuary. And now they think to ingratiate themselves with me by proclaiming me their Dark Messiah." He laughed. "What need has Satan for servants?"

"*You* have them," Sable pointed out. "Bromberg and the rest."

"And before I am done, I shall kill them. I would expect no less of Satan, nor should your clergy." He glanced at his timepiece. "Ah, but I see I shall have to terminate our little discussion, Mr. Sable. There are certain functions about to begin next door that I simply cannot avoid. Perhaps you would like to watch?"

"I'd prefer not to."

"So be it," said Bland, rising. "After I leave, you will be escorted back to your quarters. You may order anything you wish from our rather limited menu, and of course my library is at your disposal. In the meantime, I'd suggest that you prepare a list of those members of your civil government who are opposed to me and might be persuaded to pay a little visit to you during your stay here in Tifereth."

Sable was about to object, but Bland silenced him with a raised finger. "Have you ever heard of Cambria III, Mr. Sable?"

"No."

"I had the opportunity to spend almost a year there, after I was forced to flee from New Rhodesia. It was not a totally wasted period of time, since I had certain theories I wanted to put to the test. I killed three thousand men on Cambria—three thousand seventeen, to be accurate. Each of them firmly stated that there were certain things he would never do, secrets he would never reveal, vows he would never break. Each of them, without exception, did those things, revealed those secrets, broke those vows. They were strong men, Mr. Sable; far stronger than you—nor were they weakened by religion or a sense of duty. You might consider that, Mr. Sable, before we have our next little chat."

Chapter 19

"Evil admits of no alternatives."
—Conrad Bland

The south end of Hod wasn't just a meat shop; it was a barbecue shop.

Jericho had no trouble sneaking off the plane and leaving the airport. His problem was making sense out of what remained of Hod.

Once a teeming city of 200,000, filled with tall angular buildings and bustling thoroughfares, its population had been cut in half, its structures burned and bombed, its streets destroyed. He was certain that Bland couldn't have been expecting him here this soon; it had to be the result of some morbid, bloody whim on Bland's part, nothing more.

The streets—such portions of them as remained intact—were littered with garbage and glass and burned-out wrecks of vehicles of all shapes and sizes. And in among all the other useless rubble on the streets were the bodies: some shot, some slashed, some charred beyond recognition, all of them dead.

Jericho had gone less than half a mile from the airport when he realized that a whole and healthy man would attract more attention than just about anything else in Hod. He walked into the blackened skeleton of a small home and went to work, emerging a few minutes later with burn marks all over his body, his left arm in a bloody sling, his clothes tattered and bloodstained, and a severe limp. Then, with a properly glassy-eyed expression on his face, he began trudging through the ruins.

To his surprise, he passed some other people who were in even worse condition that he himself appeared to be. The sick, the wounded, and the maimed paid him no notice, and there was no one else around to question his identity. From time to time he could hear the explosive sounds of projectile weapons in the distance, but since the city had been slaughtered rather than occupied he couldn't imagine who the shots were being directed at.

He limped on, unhindered, for the better part of four miles, taking in the carnage. There had been massive firebombing, but the pilots who had dropped the bombs had hardly shown pinpoint accuracy. Certain sections of the city had been hit three and four times, others—though not many of them—had been totally missed. But even in those relatively destruction-free areas his battered appearance seemed to be the rule rather than the exception and he drew no unwarranted attention.

He didn't know where to begin looking for his contact, but it stood to reason that if she was still alive she would have to be in a section of the city that the firebombs had missed. He toured the largest such area with no success, spent the night with a number of lost, butchered souls in the lobby of a burned-out hotel, and proceeded to a different unscathed area the next morning.

The sound of gunfire became more frequent, and twice it was so near that he instinctively hurled himself to the ground. No one was around to see the agility he had displayed on either occasion.

And, at noontime, he found it: a locked palmistry shop with a photograph of a white-clad woman in the window and an "Out of Business" sign pasted on the door. He waited until a few walking wounded had moved out of sight, then quickly jimmied the door and entered a small anteroom. Tense and alert, he walked to the back of the room, pushed aside some beaded curtains, and stepped into the main room.

A middle-aged woman sat by a window, staring dully into the alley.

"We're closed," she said tonelessly, without looking at him.

"Not anymore," he replied, taking a seat.

She turned and scrutinized him. "You want a hospital, if there are any left; not a seer."

"Suppose you let me be the judge of that," replied Jericho, idly fingering a pack of tarot cards that lay on a pentagonal end table next to him. "The White Lucy thinks I need a seer."

"Jericho?" she said hesitantly, staring at him in morbid fascination.

He nodded.

"What happened to you?" she said at last.

"Nothing."

"But you're all—" She stopped herself short. "But of course: what could be less conspicuous in a slaughterhouse than one of the cattle?"

"Why didn't the White Lucy tell you what disguise I'd be wearing?" he asked, only now taking his arm out of the sling and stretching it. "I would have thought she'd be following my progress every step of the way."

"She's very ill," said the woman.

"What happened to her?"

"Stroke, old age, who can say? She's kept in sporadic contact, but most of her thoughts have been irrational and rambling. I suspect she's dying."

"Has she managed to tell you anything useful in her moments of lucidity?"

"Yes. The only city between here and Tifereth where you'll have even a minimal chance of survival is Binah."

"Binah," he repeated. "That's only about eighty miles from Tifereth, isn't it?"

She nodded.

"By the way, what's the reason for all the gunfire I've been hearing?"

"You are," said the woman.

"Me?"

"Bland figured out sometime yesterday afternoon that you had bypassed Netsah and were on your way to Hod. He had his men announce that if you weren't killed in Hod, he'd be back to destroy what's left of it. So far they've killed about fifty people in the hope that one of them was you."

"He'll be back anyway," said Jericho.

"Of course he will. Hod was bombed almost two weeks ago, before he even knew of your existence. He bombed Hod because it pleased him, and he'll be back for the same reason."

"How many men has he got stationed here?"

"No more than two thousand."

"And how do they travel between here and Binah?"

"Let me ask the White Lucy," she said, closing her eyes and frowning. She looked up at him a moment later. "It's no use. She's practically deranged. Nothing she's sending makes any sense."

"All right," said Jericho. "Perhaps you can tell me a couple of things without having to call upon the White Lucy."

"I can try."

"First of all, why do these people put up with this? Why don't they either mount an attack on Tifereth or get the hell out of here?"

"You must understand: They worship Conrad Bland. He is their Dark Messiah, and in their eyes he can do no wrong. If he thinks that Hod must be obliterated and its population wiped out, then he must be correct. These are not the half-hearted devil worshipers you encountered in Amaymon or even Kether. They are true Satanists, with all that implies. They believe in the power and the might of evil, they revere deception and humiliation and degradation, they dwell in sin and corruption and wouldn't have it any other way. They freely administer death to each other, they have no fear of dying, and they are fully prepared to start serving Lucifer in the pits of Hell."

"That's ridiculous. Nobody wants to die. Even the martyrs of old Earth, given the choice, would have preferred to change their societies without dying."

"True," she answered. "But their religious beliefs didn't glorify death and suffering."

"They glorified Jesus, who was tortured on a cross," Jericho pointed out.

"That's because he suffered *for* them. No one suffers for Satanists."

"It's crazy."

"Could Conrad Bland have accomplished so much on a sane world?" was her answer.

He shrugged. "That takes care of my next question. I assume that even here, even after what's taken place, there is no underground that I can work through."

"None."

"And if this is what Hod is like now," he said, glancing out the window at the broken buildings in the distance, "I don't imagine I'll have a contact in Binah."

"Yes you will, if she's still alive," said the woman. "Her name is Celia."

He considered it for a moment, then shook his head. "It's not worth the risk, not if the White Lucy is demented."

"As I said, she does have moments of rationality. It may not be worth the risk *not* to make contact with Celia."

"I'll take it under advisement," said Jericho noncommittally.

"One last question: Is any kind of nonmilitary traffic at all moving between Hod and Binah?"

"Not to my knowledge. It's possible, of course, but I doubt it."

"Well, I guess that's everything," he said, rising and inserting his arm back into the sling. "Will you be safe here?"

"I'll be much safer here than you will be where you're going," responded the woman.

He forced a friendly smile to his lips, then limped out through the anteroom and into the street.

He continued walking through the city, eyes and ears and nose alert, his brain editing out the misery and the suffering, hunting for a means of egress from Hod. Finally, in midafternoon, he passed by a pair of troop transport trucks, both under heavy guard. He hobbled along the street, seeming to pay no attention to them, and kept walking until he was out of sight. Then he doubled back.

He entered the charred remains of a nearby office building, waited inside it until nightfall, and then went back out. The gunfire had increased somewhat in frequency, for it was much easier to mistake a friend or neighbor for a Republic agent in the darkness than in daylight, but none of it was coming from his immediate vicinity.

Finally he approached the trucks again, hiding as close as he dared in the shadows of some still-intact buildings, and waiting. Eventually one of the guards—there were six that he could see, and probably a couple of others hidden from view by the trucks—walked off in his direction, obviously on his way to a bathroom or a restaurant. Jericho backed away, waited for the man to pass him, then struck him a powerful blow on the back of the neck and another to the Adam's apple. He carried the lifeless body into the nearest building, immediately appropriated the man's clothes, and a few minutes later had assumed his face and identity as well.

A quick search of the man's few papers told him that he was Jacinto Vargas and that he made his home in Netsah, but Jericho could find nothing to tell him where the transports were going.

He considered returning to the trucks, for Vargas's continued absence would soon draw attention, but he decided against it: the last thing he needed was to find himself driving south. So he waited, out of sight, until members of Bland's forces began wending their way to the trucks in groups of two and three and four.

Finally a lone uniformed man approached, and Jericho dragged him into the shadows, throwing him onto his back and pressing a knife against the side of his neck.

"Where are those trucks going?" he whispered.

"Binah!" stammered the man, his entire body trembling.

"Where else?"

"Just Binah! I swear it!"

Jericho killed him without using the knife. The Vargas identity, though he'd had it for only an hour, was too dangerous to use now, and he didn't want any signs of blood on his next uniform. He quickly traded clothes with his victim, approximated his facial features as best he could under the circumstances, found that his name was Daniel Manning, and transferred Manning's identity papers to his own person. He toyed with leaving Vargas's papers on Manning's corpse in an effort to confuse whoever finally found the body but decided that they might come in handy in Binah, and stuffed them into a back pocket.

Throughout his journey he had always been able to keep his makeup kit with him, either in a small bag, a wrapped package, or else stuffed inside his shirt, but he knew that any packages or bulges would draw too much attention on the troop truck. Therefore, he withdrew a single tube of facial putty, another of black hair dye, and a small packet of facial rouge that could suggest a different complexion, and regretfully left the rest of the contents behind.

A moment later he approached the trucks, and shortly thereafter he was huddled in the back of one of them, next to the tailgate, his head slumped on his chest, feigning sleep and rubbing shoulders with Bland's troops while the trucks raced through the humid night air to distant Binah.

Chapter 20

"Of course all men have souls. Otherwise I might just as well waste my time killing animals."
—Conrad Bland

It was still dark when the troop trucks reached Binah some five minutes apart.

Jericho, sitting by the tailgate, knew that his disguise could never stand the scrutiny of Manning's friends in the daylight, and as the truck slowed down and made a sharp left turn he leaped out. He doubted that any of the sleeping soldiers were even aware that he was no longer among them, but he took no chances and was running at right angles to the truck the second his feet hit the ground.

When he had gone a quarter of a mile, weaving in and out of buildings, he ducked into a doorway and paused for breath. There were no sounds of pursuit.

He remained where he was for another hour, emerging only after the sun began rising. Then he got his first good look at the city.

Whatever he had expected, Binah wasn't it.

First of all, it was relatively free from destruction. There were a certain number of bodies littering the streets, or hanging by hooks from lampposts, but the uniformly low buildings were intact, the streets weren't pockmarked by bomb craters, and the electricity seemed to be working.

Second, despite the corpses, he saw none of the walking wounded that had seemed endemic to Hod. Evidently in Binah you were either personally marked for destruction or you were not, and those people he saw on the streets seemed quite happy and healthy.

Almost all of the men wore black or red cloaks decorated with the insignia of their sects, and most of them were armed with both knives and hand weapons.

The women, for the most part, were dressed in the same kink-and-leather he had seen during his first night in Amaymon, when he had stumbled onto the cat's funeral procession. Bare breasts and backs and buttocks were on display almost everywhere, regardless of the shape and age of the women, and Jericho found himself wishing that ninety percent of them would don some more clothing, if only for aesthetic reasons. He also idly wondered what they wore during the frigid Walpurgan winters.

A few soldiers appeared on the street, and he noticed that none of the citizens seemed to draw back from them. They were not cheered as conquering heroes, to be sure, but they were accepted with no discernible resentment.

He didn't know if any of the soldiers were from Manning's unit, and he had no wish to call attention to himself by searching for Celia's establishment in his current outfit. Therefore, he turned into an alley, standing motionless with a terrible patience, waiting for a lone male to wander by. Within twenty minutes he had his victim, and a minute later he was wearing a red cloak over his military uniform. Then, feeling more secure, he stepped back onto the sidewalk.

Binah was a small city, extending no more than a mile in each direction from its core, and Jericho had hopes of finding his contact before noon. As it turned out, he didn't come to her place of business until late afternoon, and even then he almost missed it until he realized that protective coloration also had to be adaptive, and that the medium standing by the window wearing nothing but a white corset and boots was the woman he was searching for.

The building was a moderately new structure made of brick and some hardwood he couldn't identify, and her suite was half a flight up from the ground level. He climbed the stairs and knocked twice on a door that proclaimed in small gold lettering that she was Madame Celia, Medium and Phrenologist.

"Good afternoon," she said, opening the door and leading him past a pair of tufted leather love seats to a large chrome-and-leather chair. "Won't you please be seated?"

"Thank you."

"And how may I serve you?" she said, sitting across from him on a matching chair, totally oblivious to any effect her naked breasts and exposed thighs might be having upon him.

"I wish to make contact with someone," said Jericho.

"What is the name of the departed?"

"The White Lucy."

"You're Jericho?"

He nodded. "Is she still alive?"

"Just barely," said Celia sadly. "Even when she's awake she's almost never cogent anymore. I just hope we can keep together after she's gone; she was the glue that bonded us."

"Then she had no message for me?" said Jericho.

"Just one. I received it a few hours ago."

"What was it?"

"She still doesn't know if you will succeed in your mission," said Celia. "But if you do, you must not kill John Sable."

"Sable's in Tifereth?" asked Jericho, surprised.

"Yes. You will not be able to escape without his help."

"How will he help me?"

"The White Lucy says he'll know what to do."

"That's all?"

She nodded.

"Did she have any suggestions concerning how I'm to get to Tifereth?" asked Jericho.

"No," answered Celia. "She's very weak, and rarely rational. I think it took almost all of her remaining strength to transmit that message to me."

"I see," said Jericho. He stood up and walked to an antique, full-length mirror that hung on the wall between various charts of human heads and hands. He studied himself for a moment, then turned back to her.

"Can you tell me what kind of garb I'm wearing?"

"Your robe and insignia proclaim you to be a warlock in the Church of the Inferno."

"And you?" he asked, staring at her barely concealed body.

"I am dressed as a Daughter of Delight," she replied. "It is by far the major sect among the women of Binah."

"I've been going out of my way not to stare. Is that correct?"

She laughed. "Do you have any idea how uncomfortable whalebone and stays and garter belts can be? Of course you're supposed to admire us. Our mode of dress is for enchantment, not practicality."

"I've passed about two dozen Daughters of Delight. Would my lack of reaction have drawn any attention?"

"I doubt it," said Celia. "After all, a native of Binah sees us every day, and could be expected to be preoccupied from time to time. No, I think you're safe."

"Good. Can a member of the Church of the Inferno go to Tifereth without being stopped?"

"Not a chance. Only Bland's security men can get into or out of Tifereth."

"Have I a contact in Tifereth?"

"No. I'm the last. Once you leave Binah you're on your own."

"Have you got anything further to tell me? I don't like staying in one place too long."

"No. That's everything."

"Then thank you for your help," he said. "And allow me to say that I greatly admire your dress code."

"Thank you," she said unselfconsciously. "And good luck."

He was walking toward the door when a sudden movement in the street caught his attention. He looked out the window for a moment, then turned back to Celia.

"There are two soldiers headed straight for this building. Do they have any business here?"

"None that I know of," she replied.

"How many other stores and offices are there in the building?"

"Five."

"Then there's probably nothing to worry about," he said. "Just the same, I think I'd better hide until they're gone. Have you got another room?"

"Just a bathroom," she said, pointing toward a door.

"That'll do fine," he replied, walking into it and leaving the door cracked open.

He had been there for no more than a minute when the front door opened and the two soldiers—one tall, one medium height, both lean and well muscled—strode into Celia's suite.

"You are Madame Celia?" demanded the tall soldier.

"Yes."

"You were born on the planet Beta Tau VIII, otherwise known as Greenveldt?"

"Why?" she asked, frightened.

"If you do not respond to the question, I must assume your answer is affirmative."

"Yes, I was born on Greenveldt."

"You will come with us, please."

"What is this all about?"

"My Lord Bland has issued orders that all offworlders be transferred to Tifereth for questioning."

Suddenly the blood drained from her face and her entire body tensed. "But I know nothing of use to Conrad Bland."

"That is no concern of ours," said the soldier. "Let's go."

"No," she said. "Please!"

The taller soldier shrugged and nodded to his companion. Then the two of them walked over and grabbed Celia roughly by her arms.

"Jericho! Help!" she cried.

Jericho stepped out of the bathroom and calmly shot each soldier in turn. As they slumped to the floor he knelt down and began rummaging through his nearer victim's uniform.

"Go through the other one's pockets," he said. "If they were taking you to Bland they've got to have some kind of pass or permit to get out of Binah and into Tifereth."

Celia did as she was told, and a moment later each of them were holding small cards signed by Bromberg.

"This will get *me* in," said Jericho. "But these passes are only valid for soldiers. They don't seem to have any extradition papers with them."

"Then you'll have to leave me behind," said Celia, visibly relieved.

"I can't," he replied. "Someone must have sent them here. Sooner or later more soldiers will show up looking for them."

"Then I'll leave."

"It won't do any good," he said, shaking his head. "You can't get out of Binah without a pass. It won't take them long to find you, and when they do I'm sure they have ways of making you talk."

"I'd never tell them anything about you!"

"Yes you would. You called out my name a moment ago when you merely thought that they *might* hurt you. I can't allow you to fall into their hands." He stared at her for a long moment. "I'm sorry," he said regretfully.

He pointed his weapon at her and fired.

He spent a few minutes rearranging the bodies, trying to make it look as if she had been killed defending herself from the soldiers. Then he removed his robe, folded it neatly, went out into the street, and threw it into a trash atomizer.

He found a car that worked by computer code, appropriated it, showed his pass at the edge of the city, and was soon driving across the flat arid plains toward Tifereth.

Chapter 21

"Why should anyone wish to wind up in Hell, except to take charge of it?"
—*Conrad Bland*

Sable paced off the boundaries of his room for perhaps the thousandth time: twelve feet by ten, with a sink and a toilet in one corner. The room was no longer under guard; the door was no longer locked. After their conversation two days ago, Bland had given him run of the church.

The problem was that he didn't *want* the run of it. The only place free from the sight of torture and unendurable agony was this room, so he remained here, refusing to set foot outside of it until Bland commanded his presence once again.

The room had been stripped of all religious artifacts, as had the rest of the church. A photograph of Bland, taken at night on some distant planet, hung above the bed, and Sable hadn't quite mustered the courage to remove it. There was a small bookcase, filled with magazines containing short articles Bland had written over the years for various fringe groups and extremist political factions. Sable had read them for lack of anything better to do with his time, and decided that Bland had had his tongue tucked firmly in his cheek as he discussed his philosophic principles, which usually were in full agreement with the sponsoring group.

Finally, tired of pacing and in no mood to read any more of Bland's tracts, he sat down on a small wooden chair, put his feet up on the side of the bed, clasped his hands behind his head, leaned back, and thought of home. He hoped Siboyan was keeping the boys out of his garden and remembering to water it, and he made a mental note to naturalize some more daffodils in the front yard if he ever managed to get out of Tifereth alive. He thought his daughter had a birthday coming up, but when he tried to remember the date he found to his chagrin that he couldn't. He could picture her now, studying in her room before dinner, writing pedantic essays with the dignity only a nine-year-old schoolgirl who is out to impress her teacher can muster, and planning what video shows to watch after dinner. Later Siboyan would give the two boys their nightly lecture about getting their homework done on time and send them shuffling and grousing to their room (where they would lock the door, make properly studious noises, and probably engage in a hot game of cards).

He had taken them all—even Siboyan—for granted for years now. If he came out of this alive, he would never do so again. The more he thought of his family the more he physically ached to be with them, to wrestle with the boys and let his daughter explain some obscure scientific or legalistic principle to him, to fall asleep with his arms around Siboyan and his head on her small breasts which looked so firm but felt so soft.

If he got out of this alive.

If . . .

Suddenly his door opened and a tall, redheaded woman, wearing the costume of the Daughters of Delight, entered the room.

Sable studied her with a practiced eye. She had been quite lovely once, and she was attractive still, but he could see the tiny scars where silicon forms had been inserted into her breasts, and the too-smooth skin around her eyes was a dead giveaway of a recent facelift. Her hair was a little too red to be natural, her lips were too bright, and even her nipples showed touches of body rouge. He put her age at fifty, though from a distance of thirty-five feet she could have passed for half that.

She stood before him, aware of his gaze, and stared right back at him, unblinking.

"So you're John Sable," she said at last. Her voice was low, and with a discernible effort she made it sound almost husky.

"Who are you?" he asked.

"I am the Magdalene Jezebel."

"The High Priestess?"

"The High Priestess *emeritus*," she corrected him with a smile that somehow made her face look harsher. "The Magdalene Hecate is the High Priestess of the Daughters of Delight these days."

She walked over to the bed and sat down on it, absently testing the springs. "It's very uncomfortable," she announced at last.

He shrugged.

"Believe me, Mr. Sable—beds are my specialty, and this is much too lumpy."

"Possibly you can get me a better one," he said.

"I'll speak to My Lord Bland about it."

"I assume you are not a prisoner here," he said dryly.

"That's correct."

"Why did you come to my room?"

"Just curiosity," said the Magdalene Jezebel. "My Lord Bland seems quite taken with you, so I wanted to meet you for myself."

"And is your curiosity satisfied now?"

"Not even a little bit. For instance, I notice that you wear the amulet of the Cult of Cali. I had rather expected you to be a practitioner of voodoo."

"Why does everyone assume that all black men must necessarily believe in voodoo?" he said irritably. "*You* go around chopping chickens' heads off and singing Gregorian chants backward and see how you like it."

"I'm sorry if I offended you," she said easily. "Besides, personal beliefs don't really make much difference now that Conrad Bland has arrived."

"Speaking of Bland, do you know what he plans to do with me?"

"He's grown very fond of you for some reason. He truly doesn't want to kill you."

"So he's kidnapped me as a companion?" said Sable with a bitter smile.

"Not a companion," said the Magdalene Jezebel, unconsciously shifting her body to present it to best advantage. "More like a mascot. You amuse him. You make him laugh. As long as you continue to captivate him, he'll treat you in much the same way that you would treat a pet." She held up a hand as he opened his mouth to speak. "It's not as demeaning as it sounds, Mr. Sable. After all, there *are* alternatives."

"I've seen them."

"He *does* have certain eccentricities," she said uneasily. "But one must look beyond that."

"At all the other corpses?" he replied with a harsh laugh.

"You don't understand!"

"I understand perfectly. He's out to kill every last man, woman, and child on Walpurgis, and when he's done with that he'll probably start in on the animals."

"It's not the way you make it sound at all! He is the Dark Messiah!"

"He's the Butcher of Boriga II!" said Sable hotly. "All he knows how to do is kill!"

"You're wrong!" she shouted at him, her eyes blazing. "He has to eradicate the old order before replacing it with his own!"

"There won't be anything left alive to join his new order!"

"There will! He has gathered about him a few of us, those who were farsighted enough to understand what he is doing, to form the nucleus of the new age that he will bring about. I was the High Priestess of the Daughters of Delight, Mr. Sable. I had power and respect and wealth. Why do you think I gave it all up to come to Tifereth?"

"I couldn't even hazard a guess," he said with dry irony.

"Because I saw the power he wielded, the might he displayed. I realized that all of the rest of us were just dabblers on the surface of things. Why worship Satan when Conrad Bland walked among us, the devil made flesh?"

"In other words, you wanted to get in on the ground floor," he said with a cold, hard smile.

"Why deny it? He is the most potent force in the universe. Why *not* flock to his banner? Why do you suppose the Messengers disbanded in Tifereth? Because they saw that the Master had arrived, and they had no further justification for their existence. He will create a new world, a new Republic, and we who had the foresight to serve him from the first will help to preside over it."

"Can't you see that he's going to kill every last one of you, followers as well as foes?" said Sable with just a touch of pity in his voice. "Don't you know yet what he is?"

"He is the living embodiment of the power and the might of Lord Lucifer."

"And that is what you worship and serve—his might and power?"

"Yes."

"What if this Republic assassin gets through and kills Bland? Will you then worship *him* as an even greater killer?"

"He won't," she said decisively.

"But *if* he does," persisted Sable.

"He won't!" she repeated. "He'll be stopped before he leaves Binah."

"He's reached Binah?" said Sable, startled. "He's actually gotten that close?"

She looked uncomfortable. "My Lord Bland made a statement to that effect this morning."

"Then you'd better give some serious consideration to my question," said Sable. "It may not be academic too much longer."

"He will be stopped in Binah!"

"I thought I could stop him in Amaymon, when he knew nothing of our customs," Sable pointed out. "And Bland has wiped out a couple of cities trying to stop him."

"He would have destroyed those cities anyway," she said uneasily.

"I know. That's why I hope the assassin succeeds."

"I find this entire subject distasteful."

"So do I," agreed Sable with an ironic smile. "What else do you wish to discuss?"

"Nothing. But perhaps I will bring you My Lord Bland's writings."

"I've read them," he said, gesturing toward the stack of magazines.

"Those were written for political expediency," she said, nodding toward the magazines contemptuously. "He is currently at work on a massive tome that codifies his entire personal philosophy."

"Who will be left alive to read it?"

"You're a very difficult man to talk to, Mr. Sable," she said irritably. "I can't understand why My Lord Bland has let you live!"

"I amuse him," said Sable wryly.

"Well, you don't amuse me!"

"On the other hand, you've satisfied your curiosity," he noted with a smile.

"Not entirely," she said, studying him carefully. "Perhaps I should go to bed with you. Possibly you have certain qualities that aren't immediately apparent."

"Doesn't it seem a little contradictory—speaking of pleasure in a place like this?"

"Where better than a place like this?" she countered, starting to remove her clothing.

"I don't know exactly how to tell you this, Magdalene Jezebel," he said, "but I am a married man. I have made a pledge of fidelity to my wife."

"Of course—the Cult of Cali," she said contemptuously. "Now my curiosity is assuaged, Mr. Sable." She got to her feet "You haven't a single thought or trait that I consider admirable or amusing."

"I'm sorry you should feel that way."

"After I speak to My Lord Bland, you may be even sorrier," she promised.

She gave him one last scornful look and left his room.

Chapter 22

"The triumph of Evil is as inevitable as the changing of the seasons."
—Conrad Bland

Jericho pulled off the road halfway between Binah and Tifereth. Then, because he suspected that he would have to do some shooting at greater than point-blank range on the way to Bland's headquarters, he picked up half a dozen small rocks, lined them up at six-inch intervals on a low-hanging tree limb, stepped back about fifty feet, took aim, and tested the accuracy of his projectile pistol.

The first bullet lodged itself in the branch a good four inches below and to the left of where he was aiming, and he made a minute adjustment to the pistol's sights. He then fired three shots in quick succession, shattering the three rocks he was aiming at into dust.

The stolen car contained a laser pistol, and he now returned to the vehicle, pulled it out, and went through the same procedure until he was satisfied that it was as accurate as he could make it.

He didn't bother with his knife. It was not only his favorite weapon, but also his weapon of last resort, and he would never think of throwing it at a potential victim and thereby losing possession of it.

Then, because he had no intention of reaching Tifereth before dark, be hoisted the car up on a jack and pretended to be working on a tire just in case any passing vehicles spotted him and wondered what he was doing on the roadside.

As it happened, no traffic came by from either direction, and in the fading moments of sunset he put the jack away, got back into the car, and headed north to Tifereth. He passed the remains of three tiny hamlets, which were now nothing more than blackened ruins, and within half an hour he had reached Bland's first line of defense around the city. He presented his pass, waited calmly while it was checked through a portable computer, and received permission to proceed.

He was stopped twice more, questioned perfunctorily both times, and again allowed to continue.

A final check was made at the city line, and it was far more thorough than the others. His face—on which he had used the last of his makeup—was compared to his credentials, his pass was sent through a computer again, his car was searched for hidden passengers, and his projectile pistol was checked out against its registration number. The laser weapon was confiscated when he was unable to prove ownership of it.

He was detained for almost an hour at this final outer checkpoint, but eventually he was allowed to pass, and Jericho, with just the smallest trickle of sweat starting to roll down his face in the humid night air, drove slowly and inexorably into Tifereth.

Chapter 23

"Neither mercy nor regret exist in the lexicon of Evil."
—*Conrad Bland*

"Satan has kept the Republic's churches in business for eons," said Bland. "It is time to redress the balance."

Sable had been summoned from his room just before midnight. Bland had slept until noon, as he frequently did, and was just now getting around to having dinner. He had wanted companionship, and insisted that Sable join him.

The detective was escorted down to the main floor of the church, and into a large room that had once served as an initiation room where novices learned the sacred Rites of Baal, but which Bland had turned into a dining room.

A broad, polished table some thirty feet long dominated the room. The walls were covered with photographs and holographs of Bland, and with small plaques displaying what he believed to be his more incisive observations. Bland, surrounded by four armed guards, sat at the head of the table, and Sable was directed to a chair at the other end. He had been offered food, but the stench was stronger down here and his appetite, never strong since his arrival in

Tifereth, vanished completely. Bland seemed to enjoy the odor, or at least not to mind it; at any rate, noted Sable, it certainly hadn't affected the obvious relish with which he wolfed down his dinner.

"What's the matter, Mr. Sable?" asked Bland between mouthfuls. "Have you no opinion on the matter?"

"You know my opinion," said Sable coldly.

"Well said, Mr. Sable!" laughed Bland. "Such diplomacy! You delight me, you truly do! Like all men of good intentions, you even now believe in manners, and gentleness, and turning the other cheek." He paused and laughed again. "Of course, you realize that these are also the very qualities that farmers breed for in their sheep."

"You can't murder a sheep."

"Don't judge me so harshly, Mr. Sable," said Bland. "If there is a God, then He has passed a death sentence on every human being from the moment of conception. I am but a talented amateur."

A soldier walked into the room, approached Bland, and whispered something in his ear. Bland frowned, then issued some orders in a voice too low for Sable to hear. The soldier saluted and left.

"I must compliment the Republic," said Bland. "Their killer has made it to within a mile of us."

"Did you capture him?" asked Sable.

"We will momentarily. We have him surrounded. But he got a lot closer than I expected him to. I think I shall have to inspect my defenses tomorrow morning." He shot Sable a cherubic smile. "But enough of such sordid matters. The reason I have invited you to join me, Mr. Sable, is that we are to be entertained by the Magdalene Jezebel after dinner is over."

They heard the sound of gunshots in the distance.

"Well, that's that," said Bland. "It saves me the trouble of deciding whether to kill him or hire him. You look disappointed, Mr. Sable; don't be. Nothing can kill me, and this saves you from the possibility of being hit by a stray bullet or laser beam. Would you care for some pie?"

"No, thank you."

"Be a little generous, Mr. Sable," said Bland. "I don't offer to share my possessions—even my meals—with many people."

Sable shook his head, and Bland shrugged.

"Well, if that's your final decision, I suppose I shouldn't be too upset. It means there will be more for me."

He began gobbling his pie, then suddenly stopped.

"Damn!" he said irritably, picking up a napkin and dabbing at a small stain on his white jacket. "I do many things efficiently, but I simply cannot get through a meal without spilling something." He dipped the napkin in a glass of water, then began rubbing the stain more vigorously.

Sable heard two more bursts of gunfire, this time noticeably closer. A moment later another soldier rushed into the room.

"Well?" demanded Bland, looking up from his jacket.

"He got away, sir," said the soldier, shifting his weight uneasily from one foot to the other.

"How?"

"We haven't been able to get a report, sir. I think he destroyed their radio."

"Get out!" screamed Bland. "Get out and don't come back until he's dead!"

The soldier needed no second invitation to remove himself from the presence of his enraged leader. Bland glared at the door for a long moment after he had left, then returned to his pie. He toyed with it for a few seconds, then flung it off the table with a sweep of his hand. The plate shattered into a hundred tiny pieces.

"Damn damn *damn!*" he shouted. "Who does this fool think he is, marching into Tifereth as if I were just some *ordinary* man he could kill at will? This is Conrad Bland he's after!" His voice became a high whining shriek. "What's the matter with your government, Mr. Sable? First they offer me sanctuary and now they won't lift a finger to stop this murderer!"

Sable sighed. "If you haven't figured it out by this late date, I don't see how I'm going to be able to explain it to you."

Bland's face contorted in fury for a moment—and then, suddenly, as if nothing had happened, he stood up with a pleasant smile on his lips.

"Please excuse my little show of temper, Mr. Sable. It's really not like me at all. Anyway, as long as dinner seems to be over, I think it's time for a little entertainment."

He motioned to Sable and two of his guards to join him, and walked to a door at the back of the room. It led to a dimly lit corridor, which they followed for perhaps two hundred feet, emerging at last into a small room that had once been a private chapel. A number of cushioned seats were still bolted to the tile floor, but the altar had been removed, replaced by a large rectangular structure that had a curtain draped over it.

Bland seated himself in the first pew and gestured to Sable to do likewise. Sable saw a number of electric cables leading from the covered structure to a small panel that one of the guards now brought to Bland.

"Let's have a little music," said Bland, and a moment later a bizarre symphony was piped into the chapel through the intercom system.

Bland nodded to the guards, who pulled the curtains away, revealing a large tank of water. Inside the tank, dressed in the jewels and leather of her order, was the Magdalene Jezebel, her hands and feet loosely tied to support poles along the sides of the tank. It took Sable almost a full minute to realize that she was entirely submerged and no longer breathing. Her hair floated behind and above her, moving gently as it was carried to and fro by tiny currents in the water.

"Why did you kill her?"

"She came to me this afternoon and told me to destroy you," said Bland. "Ultimately I will do so; I may even do so tonight. But no one gives orders to Conrad Bland. *No one!*"

He pressed a button on his panel and Sable heard the hum of electricity. An instant later the Magdalene Jezebel's body jerked ferociously as the charge reached the water.

"You see, Mr. Sable," said Bland with a chuckle, "one need not be alive to be an entertainer."

For the next twenty minutes, as the music built to a discordant crescendo and Bland matched it note for note on his control panel, Sable watched the Magdalene Jezebel's dance of death with horrified fascination.

Finally it was over, and Bland, suddenly uninterested, ordered his guards to replace the curtains.

"I think I'll try it with a living woman next time," he said confidentially. "Of course, only the first few steps will be different, but even that could prove interesting, don't you think?"

Sable, still stunned by what he had seen, made no answer.

"Come, come, Mr. Sable," said Bland. "Surely you have seen less pleasant sights in your official capacity. And waste no sympathy on our Daughter of Delight. She had a purpose, and she served it admirably."

"Her purpose was to entertain you like *this?*" demanded Sable.

"No," said Bland. "Her purpose was to die."

"For no reason at all."

"Precisely," said Bland with a smile. "Consider my position, Mr. Sable. If I treat the innocent like this, think how the guilty will fear me."

"You're mad!"

"It pleases my enemies to think so." Bland laughed. "It also weakens them." More gunshots rang out, still closer to the church. "All but one, anyway," he added, concern momentarily clouding his face.

"They haven't caught him yet," said Sable, amazed. "He's still out there!"

"We shall catch him, never fear," said Bland harshly. "That I promise you, Mr. Sable."

"You promised me that three days ago," said Sable.

"You seem to be confused in your loyalties," said Bland, smiling. "In case you've forgotten, you came to Tifereth to protect me."

Sable snorted contemptuously.

"Are you telling me, Mr. Sable, that if your assassin walks through the door this minute that you won't sacrifice your life to save me?"

"If he enters the room right now, I'll strew his path with flowers!" snapped Sable.

"Poor deluded man," said Bland with a sigh. "You still haven't learned that I'm invincible. What he does with those fools in the street is one thing; what he does here is another. I assure you that this building is impregnable."

"We'll see," said Sable with more conviction than he felt.

"This whole conversation is probably academic," said Bland. "I haven't heard any more gunfire." He turned to one of the guards. "Find out if we killed him yet."

The guard left the chapel, and Bland played idly with his control panel, though he could no longer see the Magdalene Jezebel's spasmodic contortions.

"You are ceasing to amuse me, Mr. Sable," he said at last. "I hope you haven't outlived your entertainment value."

Sable made no reply.

"Come, come, Mr. Sable," continued Bland. "I am surrounded by fools and cowards and sycophants. I should hate to see our relationship come to an end."

"What do you want me to do to amuse you—an underwater juggling act?" said Sable, glaring at him.

"That's more like it, Mr. Sable!" said Bland with a chuckle.

"That's the kind of spirit I like to see, that wonderful sense of humor while staring into the very maw of death!"

A moment later the guard returned to the room and Bland got to his feet and walked over to speak to him. They conversed in low whispers for a few seconds, then Bland pulled a small pistol out of his belt and shot him between the eyes.

"There's a lesson in this," he said, turning to the other guard, who hadn't moved. "Never bring me bad news twice in one day."

"What happened?" asked Sable.

"All of our communications lines are down," said Bland, frowning.

Sable laughed.

"What's so funny?" snapped Bland.

"You still don't understand what's happening, do you?"

"I told you: our communication lines are dead. It's a technical failure, nothing more."

"Your communication lines aren't dead," said Sable. "But your communicators are."

"Nonsense! I've got five thousand men out there!"

"And one lone man has got you surrounded!" Sable laughed.

"*Don't laugh at me!*" screamed Bland. He lowered his head in thought for a moment, then looked up. "Come along, Mr. Sable. I see that it's time to take an active hand in this."

"You'll never stop him," said Sable, more confidently this time.

"Yes I will!" snapped Bland, walking to the door. "But don't think I will forget that you laughed at me. For the next few hours I shall direct my every effort toward destroying this upstart who thinks he can attack Conrad Bland with impunity. But the instant I have finished with him, Mr. Sable, I shall turn my attentions to you—and I promise you that it won't be a pleasant experience."

Chapter 24

"One need not hate what one kills."
—*Conrad Bland*

"One need not hate what one kills."
—*Jericho*

Bland led Sable and his bodyguard to the main auditorium, picking up another five guards along the way. There were somewhat fewer bodies than the first time Sable had been there, which implied that despite his many protestations to the contrary, Bland had been too preoccupied with the assassin's progress during the past few days to pay much attention to this most terrible of rooms.

"How many of the troops within the church grounds have communications units?" Bland asked.

"About a dozen, sir," responded one of the guards.

"Good. Get a radio in here and set up a command post. I want to keep in constant touch with them—and woe betide any officer who doesn't respond immediately when I try to establish contact with him."

The soldier saluted, sent out for a radio, and got to work cordoning off a section of the room.

Sable looked around him, and reflected ironically that proximity to Bland had changed his viewpoint more than he had expected. The carnage within the room, the skinless bodies, the corpses and near-corpses suspended from the rafters on meathooks, all filled him with moral outrage—but the numbing sense of shock was gone, the urge to vomit was minimal, the need to escape from the room was prompted solely by self-preservation. The wholesale nature of Bland's brand of torture and slaughter had deadened something deep within him, and he resented that almost as much as he resented the mindless brutality and suffering that surrounded him. Possibly it was his capacity to empathize that was gone, possibly it was something else—but whatever it was, he hoped that he hadn't lost it forever. Always supposing, he added with a wry mental footnote, that he came out of this mess alive, a prospect which seemed less and less likely as time wore on.

Bland had appropriated two more handguns from his guards and was checking them over carefully, making sure they were loaded and in proper working order. Finally satisfied, he tucked them into his pockets and began pacing around the room, kicking any writhing bodies that happened to be in his path.

Finally he turned to Sable.

"Who is he, Mr. Sable?"

"I don't know," replied Sable with a shrug.

"He must have a name, a face, an identity," persisted Bland.

"I don't know his name, and he's used up more faces and identities than you've got corpses in this room."

"How can he still be alive?" said Bland, his voice shrill and whining again. "Why haven't we captured or killed him yet?"

He walked over to the command post, which had just been activated, and began checking with his officers by radio. No one had seen any trace of the assassin; the church was still secure.

"Do you want us to send some men outside to see if he's been taken yet, sir?" asked one of the officers.

"Yes," said Bland, then quickly changed his mind. "No! No one leaves the church until he's dead!" He began pacing furiously, ranting into the microphone. "If I find that anyone has left his post, I'll make what goes on in this room seem like a picnic! I cannot and will not tolerate disloyalty! Satan help anyone who goes over to the other side, for *I* certainly will not!"

"The other side?" replied the officer, his voice crackling with static as it came over the radio. "I understood that it was just one man."

"Shut up!" screamed Bland. "Count your men! Count them right now! I want to know they're all where they're supposed to be!"

"But—"

"*Count them!*" shrieked Bland.

There was a brief silence on the radio, then the voice spoke again: "They're all here and in position, sir."

"Good!" snapped Bland. Then his eyes narrowed. "What's the password?"

"Password?" repeated the voice. "This network was just established within the last five minutes. No one has given us a password."

"Who are you?" demanded Bland.

"Marcus Cooper, sir."

Bland grunted and turned off the radio.

"You see, Mr. Sable?" he said, suddenly smiling again. "Still secure. Your assassin has gotten as close as he's going to get. I am not a man who is noted for my compassion, but I must confess to feeling sorry for him. It was a noble effort, and one he can well be proud of during the few short minutes of life that remain to him."

Suddenly oblivious to the situation that had so captured his attention for the past half hour, he began wandering through the room, admiring his handiwork. Even in their dismal condition his victims recognized him, and tried to draw back as he walked among them. He continued his tour, smiling at the living and the dead, giving them affectionate pats on backs and shoulders much as a proud general might do to the members of a crack unit.

Sable merely stared at him, finding his behavior more fascinating and terrifying than anything that had yet been done to the poor souls in the room.

Then, suddenly, came the sound of gunfire again.

Bland raced to the radio and picked up the microphone.

"What's going on out there?" he yelled.

"He's somewhere on the church grounds, sir!" said Marcus Cooper's voice. "He's disguised as one of our soldiers, and we've got so many men out here that it's impossible to spot him!"

"Kill them all!" ordered Bland.

"But sir—"

"You heard me," repeated Bland, calmer now. "Kill every last soldier."

"But sir, I can't just—"

There was another sound of gunfire, and the radio went dead.

Bland tried his eleven other communications officers; only seven responded, and there was obvious confusion and chaos everywhere. He ordered each of them to open fire on anything that was alive and moving.

"Sir," said one of Bland's bodyguards, "I'm sure it's only a matter of minutes until they kill him. However, just to be on the safe side, perhaps we should move to the chapel or one of the smaller rooms. They would be much easier to defend."

"No," said Bland firmly.

"But—"

"I like it here," said Bland, giving a fond pat to the buttocks of a dead man who was suspended from the ceiling a few feet away. "I feel at home here. Here is where I shall remain."

"I can appreciate that, sir, but—"

Bland pulled a pistol out of his pocket and killed the guard with a single shot.

"Does anyone else care to dispute my orders?" he inquired mildly.

Nobody did, and he turned to Sable.

"Well, it may cost me my army to get him, Mr. Sable," he said, "but I've lost armies before. I shall soon raise another."

"If you live long enough," said Sable meaningfully.

"First *him*, then *you!*" snapped Bland.

"You're not going to stop him!" said Sable with a triumphant smile. "He's within a hundred yards of you right now!"

"And he'll get no closer!" yelled Bland.

"He's probably gotten closer just since we've been speaking," said Sable. "How does it feel, to know that your death is inexorably approaching and there is nothing you can do to stop it?"

"An excellent question, Mr. Sable," said Bland, fingering his pistol lovingly. "Consider it carefully, and then give me your answer."

"Isn't it ironic," continued Sable, still smiling viciously, "that Conrad Bland, supposedly the greatest killer of them all, will be brought down neither by age or disease nor revolution, but by an even greater killer?"

"Be quiet," said Bland ominously.

"I think it's proper and fitting that you should die in this room, where you have killed so many others."

"My patience is not endless, Mr. Sable," said Bland, raising the pistol and pointing it at his chest. "I think I would stop speaking right now if I were you."

Sable closed his mouth and glared at Bland defiantly.

Bland smiled back at him for a moment, then went back to his radio. This time only three officers replied.

Suddenly Bland turned almost white.

"The doors!" he screamed. "Why are the doors not locked?"

The five guards raced to the dozen doors that led to the auditorium and began bolting them, as a number of soldiers raced past in the corridor, guns drawn. As the last door was locked, another burst of gunfire rang out no more than sixty feet away.

"I told you he would not reach this room, Mr. Sable," said Bland.

"You told me he wouldn't reach Kether and Hod and Binah," Sable pointed out with a contemptuous laugh.

"Blights upon the map," scoffed Bland. "I would have destroyed them anyway."

"I know," said Sable.

Bland returned to the radio. "Did you get him?" he demanded.

"We're not sure, sir," said a hoarse voice. "There are so many dead bodies out here it's going to take hours to sort them out, but if he was in any of the corridors in the last couple of minutes he'd be among them."

"Well, that's that!" said Bland, smiling and rubbing his delicate hands together.

Sable said nothing.

"What's the matter, Mr. Sable?" gloated Bland. "Have you no congratulations for my heroic forces, no plaudits for their leader? Surely you are more generous than that!"

"If you're so sure he's dead, open the doors and dismiss your guards," replied Sable.

"All in good time," said Bland. "But before I do, I have some other business to conclude, as you may recall." He paused, waiting for a reaction from Sable, but there was no change in the detective's expression. "I offer you one last chance to amuse me, Mr. Sable. Surely your life is precious enough for you to make the effort. Say something that strikes my fancy, and possibly I may let you live until tomorrow."

"I'm not at my wittiest during bloodbaths."

"A little cynicism, a modicum of defiance, a soupcon of wit," said Bland with a small chuckle. "I'm going to give you an eighty on that one, Mr. Sable. Passing, but just barely."

"Thank you," said Sable caustically.

"Think nothing of it," replied Bland. "Think, rather, of your next witticism."

Sable sighed and glanced around the room, struck by the utter insanity of trying to amuse a madman in the middle of a mad-house—and suddenly he had the feeling that something was differ-ent. He couldn't immediately put his finger on it, but there was something. . . .

And then he knew.

Where there should have been five uniformed soldiers guarding the bolted doors to the corridors, there were six. He lowered his eyes and turned his head away, not wanting Bland to see him staring. But Bland was wandering among his beloved bodies again, stroking dead and dying limbs, offering cheerful chatter to men and women who were beyond hearing anything ever again, and Sable dared another quick look.

Three . . . four . . . five . . . six!

Yes, he was right: the man was here, now, in this room!

But why didn't the others know he was among them? Couldn't they count?

Finally he understood. The six men were stationed all around the room, guarding the various doors, and none of them could see all five of the others. Only he and Bland, standing in the middle of the auditorium, were in position to count all six guards, and Bland was too obsessed with his victims to notice.

Then what was the assassin waiting for? Why didn't he pull out his weapon and shoot Bland down like the mad dog that he was?

And then he remembered: This was no impassioned revolution-ary, no mythic avenger out to eradicate a monster from the face of the planet. This was a hired killer—an even more efficient killer than Bland—who had absolutely no intention of sacrificing his life for anyone or anything. There were five other armed men in the room besides Bland; he wouldn't make a move until he had dispatched them or somehow negated their effectiveness.

Bland continued walking and talking, and the tension within Sable grew so great that he felt he would have to scream to give it an outlet before it tore him apart. But somehow he managed to maintain an outward appearance of calm, and after a few minutes Bland approached him again.

"I have heard no more shots, Mr. Sable," noted Bland. "The man is dead. There's no question of it any longer."

"If you say so," replied Sable, trying to keep the excitement out of his voice.

"I do. And now we come to a problem of somewhat lesser import, but one which we must address anyway: What are we to do with you, Mr. Sable?"

And, for the first time all evening, Sable was scared. When the assassin was just a shadowy figure working his way through the city, when there was absolutely no hope of rescue, he had been resigned to his own death. But to come this close to remaining alive, only to die mere minutes ahead of Bland—he felt more than terrified; he felt *cheated*. Yet he knew that the assassin wouldn't lift a finger to help him. His job, after all, was killing people, not saving them.

"Well, Mr. Sable," said Bland, his face aglow with anticipation, "I am waiting. Surely you have some opinion on the matter, some input you wish to offer?"

Sable glared at him, his knees weak, his hands starting to tremble, but said nothing.

"Guard!" shouted Bland, and all six men turned to him. "I have the feeling that Mr. Sable is just a trifle warm. Two of you come over and strip off his clothing while I give some serious thought as to how we may take his mind off his present discomfort."

Two of the guards began approaching Sable, who looked desperately beyond them at the other four. *Now!* he wanted to scream. *Now, while you're all within each other's field of vision! Now, before they start counting!* The four guards remained motionless for the longest twenty seconds of Sable's life. Then one of them, who had been holding his handgun casually as he leaned against a door with his arms crossed, turned ever so slightly, and an instant later the grim silence of the auditorium was broken by three quick explosions. The three other guards who had remained at their posts crumpled to the floor.

The two remaining guards, who had almost reached Sable, were dead before they could turn around to determine the source of the gunshots.

"Don't touch it, Mr. Bland!" said Jericho coldly as Bland's hand inched down toward his pocket.

"Who are you?" demanded Bland.

"Stand aside, Mr. Sable," said Jericho.

Sable backed away, almost tripping over a dead guard in the process.

Bland's eyes narrowed. "All right," he said, his voice suddenly cool and unperturbed. "Someone has hired you to kill me. Whatever they gave you, I'll give you more not to."

"What have you got that I could possibly want?" replied Jericho.

"Half my kingdom," said Bland, making a grand gesture with his arm.

"What use have I for twenty-eight lifeless planets?"

"Money, then," said Bland. "More money than you ever dreamed existed! Dollars, rubles, yen, credits, pounds—name your currency. A million, a billion, even a trillion; it makes no difference to me. Think of what a billion credits can buy! Think of the power that accrues to the possessor of a trillion yen! Name your price!"

Kill him! Sable wanted to scream. *Don't listen to him! Do what you came here to do!* But he didn't dare make a sound or a gesture that might take the assassin's attention from Bland, and so he stood motionless and silent, waiting with a dull certainty for Bland to find the chink in the killer's armor.

"I *did* name a price," said Jericho softly. "And it has been paid. That's why I'm here."

"We're alike, you and I," said Bland, visibly struggling to retain his composure. "We kill things. We revel in death, we grow drunk through destruction. Join me, become my general—no, my partner, my *equal* partner—and I'll give you such opportunities to kill and slaughter as you never imagined existed!"

"I take no pleasure in killing," said Jericho.

"Women, then!" cried Bland. "Women of every color, every persuasion, every talent, yours for the asking!"

Jericho allowed a smile to cross his lips. "On *this* world, Mr. Bland? I'm afraid that's not much of an offer."

"Then," said Bland, a look of triumph on his face, "if I can't make you rich, or powerful, or passionate, I will make you *me.*"

Jericho cocked an eyebrow, but made no reply.

"There are no photographs or holograms of me on record anywhere, no fingerprints or retinagrams. Except for my followers in Tifereth, no one in the entire galaxy who has ever seen me is now alive. Let me live and we will trade our identities, our very essences. Think of it! Let me escape, let me leave and never return, and you can remain here and *become* Conrad Bland!"

Sable stared, tense and unblinking, at the assassin. For the first time he thought he detected some interest, a willingness to weigh the possibilities, a slight wavering of purpose.

"An interesting offer," said Jericho at last. "In fact, your *only* interesting offer. But every profession has its code of honor; mine requires me to fulfill a contract once I've accepted a commission."

"You can't do this to me!" shrieked Bland, his voice a screechy falsetto. "*I'm Conrad Bland!*"

Jericho pointed his pistol at Bland and casually took aim.

"*No!*" roared Bland. "You can't do this! My work is just beginning! I must destroy Walpurgis, and then Earth and Deluros and —" Bland's hand darted toward his pocket as he ranted.

Jericho fired his weapon, and Conrad Bland's head was splattered all over the room.

"Thank God!" said Sable softly.

"I thought you didn't believe in God, Mr. Sable," said Jericho, putting his weapon back into its holster and walking over to inspect Bland's corpse.

"Thank God and thank Satan," said Sable, "but mostly, thank *you*."

"It's not necessary," said Jericho. "I'm being well paid for this."

"I thought I was a dead man," said Sable, realizing that he sounded silly but unable to stop talking.

"Not a chance," said Jericho with a smile. "I was never going to let you die."

"I don't understand," said Sable.

"You're going to get me out of this cesspool."

"How?" asked Sable, confused.

"I haven't the slightest idea," admitted Jericho. "But I've been told on excellent authority that you would be my ticket out of here."

"Who told you?"

"I'm afraid I'm not at liberty to reveal that just now." Jericho turned Bland's corpse over with a foot. "Damn!"

"What's the matter?" asked Sable, again feeling foolish at being unable to keep from asking questions, but so busy luxuriating in the simple fact of still being alive that he didn't care how he appeared to Jericho.

"His clothes are all bloodstained."

"So?"

"So I can't masquerade as Bland to help get us out." Jericho sighed. "It wouldn't work anyway. I haven't got my kit any longer, and his hair's the wrong color. I'm afraid it's up to you, Mr. Sable."

"I don't know what to do," said Sable, silently berating himself for sounding so stupid.

"Then you'd better start thinking of something quick," said Jericho. "We're not going to be alone too much longer."

"How many men are out there?"

"A few thousand less than there were before," said Jericho grimly. "But enough."

"You killed *that* many?"

"I killed very few," said Jericho with an amused smile. "Mostly, they killed each other. And now, while you're busy considering our position, there's one more thing I must do."

He walked over to one of the dead guards, the one who had accompanied Bland and Sable from the chapel, and removed a laser weapon from his belt. Then he began walking through the room, methodically firing a beam into each of the broken and twisted bodies. When he returned a few minutes later, he and Sable were the only living entities in the auditorium.

"I can understand why you wanted to put them out of their misery," Sable said harshly. "But not all of them were beyond saving."

"I know that."

"What do you mean?" demanded Sable, a sudden chill creeping up his spine.

"We will be much safer without witnesses, Mr. Sable," said Jericho. "*Especially* those who are not beyond saving."

Suddenly Sable began to wonder if he hadn't been better off with Conrad Bland.

Chapter 25

"Emotions clutter up the mental landscape."
—*Jericho*

"Why can't we just try to sneak out the same way you got in?" asked Sable.

"Because we're surrounded," said Jericho patiently, without any hint of tension in his voice. They were standing at the center of the auditorium, and as they spoke Jericho kept a watchful eye on the various doors. "It was easy to pass as one of Bland's soldiers while I was in their midst, but this is a different situation. The second they spot Bland's body they'll know who I am, regardless of my uniform."

His obvious calm bothered Sable. Jericho had just killed a man half the planet worshiped, he was surrounded in a hostile city on a hostile world, he found himself in a tightly constricting time frame, he lacked any weaponry more effective than projectile and laser pistols—and yet he seemed totally unperturbed.

More than that, he seemed *formidable.*

"Well, there's no sense making it too easy for them," announced Jericho. "Give me a hand, Mr. Sable."

Jericho walked to the nearest of the dead guards and began undressing him. Sable got the idea immediately, and within two minutes five more laser-scorched naked bodies were added to the pile of Bland's hapless victims, completely indistinguishable from the rest.

They then removed Bland's clothing and, at Jericho's insistence, hung his corpse on an empty meathook.

"But why?" asked Sable.

"People tend to look down rather than up," said Jericho, wiping his forehead with the back of his hand as he returned to Sable's side. He then aimed his laser weapon at Bland's corpse and obliterated everything above the neck. "That ought to make him a little harder to identify."

Sable stared at him and shook his head, amazed. This was just *business* to Jericho, nothing more. He was simply attending to necessary details now, much as a grocery clerk would carefully lay out his produce for its best effect.

"All right, Mr. Sable," said Jericho. "Let's start figuring out how to get out of here. Obviously I can't disguise myself as Bland. And, just as obviously, I can't pretend to be one of the guards."

"I still don't see why not."

"Because then I wouldn't have had to let you live," said Jericho dispassionately. "No, the answer lies in your presence here. You're the cipher." He paused. "What are you doing here in the first place? Why aren't you in Amaymon?"

And suddenly Sable knew how they were getting out.

He searched his pockets and pulled out a folded sheet of paper. They had never returned his overnight bag, so he hadn't had an opportunity to change clothes or to pack the paper away.

"What's that?" asked Jericho.

"An order empowering me to extradite you to Amaymon," said Sable.

"For what crime?" asked Jericho, suddenly interested.

"The murder of Parnell Burnam."

"Good! Then we don't have to represent me as Bland's potential assassin."

"What do you mean—*potential?*"

"You don't think we can get out of here if they know Bland is dead, do you?" asked Jericho with an ironic smile.

"I don't—" began Sable. Then his eyes fell on the radio. "You're crazy. It'll never work!"

"I heard enough of his voice to mimic the tone," said Jericho. "You're going to have to give me a little help with the way he structured his sentences."

"They won't buy it!"

"You would be amazed at what men under pressure will buy, Mr. Sable," said Jericho calmly. "They are dying like flies beyond this room and they don't even know who the enemy is. They will be easier to direct than you might think." He paused. "Did anyone besides Bland know that I killed Parnell Burnam?"

"His security chief—a man named Bromberg."

"Do you know his first name? Has he a military rank?"

Sable shrugged.

"Very well," said Jericho. "We'll just have to make do with Bromberg. In the pile of clothing were a number of pens and at least two notebooks, Mr. Sable. I want you to write down—precisely as Bland would express it—a message to the effect that he has captured the assassin and is tending to him personally, whatever that may imply. If *he* would be explicit, *you* must be. Then I want him to summon Bromberg to this room, and arrange for an armed squad to show up in about five minutes to escort you and your prisoner to his personal plane, which will fly us to Amaymon. I'm bound to get questions, so I want you to fill up a separate page with some rather terse remarks I can make to establish my authority and their inability to challenge or even question my commands."

"All right," said Sable, going off to a pile of clothes and emerging a moment later with pen and notebook. "But even if it does work, we're going to look awfully lonely when Bromberg shows up and doesn't see anyone else."

"There are hundreds of people in this room," said Jericho. "It'll take him a few seconds to figure out that only two of them are alive."

Sable wrote up the speech, and then Jericho switched on the radio, picked up the microphone, and began reading in Bland's high-pitched voice, matching the whining inflections so perfectly that he almost fooled Sable, who was watching him with both awe and a growing sense of alarm. It wasn't so much that Jericho seemed on the verge of accomplishing the impossible, but rather that he was accomplishing it so *easily*.

Bromberg knocked on one of the doors a moment later, and Sable let him in, immediately closing the door behind him. He was less than ten feet into the room when Jericho shot him down with the laser pistol.

"We've got to work fast!" Jericho told Sable, tossing his laser pistol and his knife across the room and starting to strip the Security Chief. Sable joined in and a moment later they had added the nude body to Bland's grisly collection. Then they buried all the clothing under a pile of bodies.

Jericho tossed Sable a set of handcuffs he had removed from Bromberg's pocket. "Put these on me," he instructed the detective. "It's got to look legitimate. Then unlock the doors, take the projectile gun out of my belt, and point it at me."

Sable did so, and held the pose no more than ten seconds before a squad of six men entered the room.

"Where is My Lord Bland?" demanded the leader, as Conrad Bland's legs swung gently to and fro not three feet from his head.

"Gone," said Sable with a shrug. "The crisis is over."

The man looked suspiciously about the room, then turned back to Sable.

"My Lord Bland mentioned extradition papers. May I see them?"

Sable turned them over to him. The man read them carefully, then returned them.

"All right," he said. "Follow me."

Jericho went along meekly, and Sable, still expecting the world to cave in around his head, fell into step behind him. They carefully threaded their way through the mounds of dead flesh in the corridor, then went outside and walked to an open vehicle parked between a number of burned-out cars and tanks.

They were driven through the still, dead streets of Tifereth, sirens screaming, for almost half an hour before reaching Bland's private airfield just north of the city. Then Sable, his gun still trained on Jericho, walked up a portable stairway into the luxuriously appointed cabin, fighting the urge to look back and see if the highway was filled with vehicles racing to stop the plane after the discovery of Bland's body.

But nothing happened, and a moment later the plane taxied to the end of the runway, gathered speed, took off toward the north-west, banked hard to the left, and headed south for Amaymon.

Sable looked out his window as they passed over Tifereth. From overhead it looked just like any other city, except for a marked absence of traffic. An observer would never know, he reflected, that the ultimate butcher had just been brought down by the ultimate executioner.

Chapter 26

"To show compassion for a killer is an insult to his victims."
—Jericho

"To show compassion for a killer is an insult to his victims."
—John Sable

The cabin was lined with a white fur carpet made of the pelts of some rare type of arctic animal. The furniture, all heavy and hand-crafted and covered with coal-black brocaded satin, consisted of two chairs and an enormous couch. A table next to the couch opened up into a small bar at the touch of a button.

"You can take the handcuffs off me now," said Jericho, sitting comfortably on one of the chairs and holding his hands out toward Sable.

"No I can't," said Sable, seated on the couch. He kept his pistol trained on Jericho and briefly clutched at the arm of the conch with his free hand as the plane hit a momentary patch of turbulence.

"Why not?" asked Jericho, his face impassive.

"Because the first thing you would do is kill me," explained Sable. "Now that we're out of Tifereth you don't need me anymore, and I already know your views on leaving witnesses behind."

"If it makes you more comfortable, leave them on me," said Jericho with a shrug. "I trust you'll remove them when we land in Amaymon."

"I haven't decided yet," said Sable.

"May I point out that I saved your life in Tifereth, Mr. Sable?"

"I know."

"Well, then?"

Sable sighed deeply. "I'm not like you. You think on your feet, you act decisively; you never seem to have any doubts. I don't function like that. I have to build a case slowly and carefully, examine each piece of evidence, put it all into some kind of order before I can come to a conclusion."

"And what particular case are you working on now?" asked Jericho wryly.

"You," replied Sable, his expression troubled.

"What right do you have to judge me, Mr. Sable?"

"I saw you next to Conrad Bland," said Sable. "No one *but* me has the necessary background to judge you."

"You seem distressed."

"I am," admitted Sable. "You killed Bland, which had to be done; and you saved my life, for which I'm grateful—but I don't know if you can be allowed to live."

"Surely you are not comparing me to Bland," said Jericho with a smile.

"No, I'm not. You're *much* more dangerous than he was."

"Don't be silly, Mr. Sable."

"I'm being as honest as I can be," said Sable. "If the positions were reversed, could Bland have killed you?"

"I have no idea."

"Don't be coy with me!" snapped Sable. "Do you think we're playing some kind of goddamned game here?"

"All right, Mr. Sable," said Jericho slowly. "Under no circumstance could Conrad Bland ever have killed me."

"I know that."

"There is not, however, any valid basis for comparing us," said Jericho.

"Of course there is," replied Sable. "Both of you have killed profligately."

"But for different reasons."

"He killed from compulsion, you kill from calculation. I have to decide before we land in Amaymon which motivation is the more evil."

"Had I not chosen to kill Bland, he would have destroyed the entire planet."

"He had no choice," said Sable. "To him there was no discernible alternative. How many people did you kill on the way to Tifereth?"

"Twenty-one."

"Why?"

"It was necessary."

"Why did you kill Ibo Ubusuku?"

"He knew my mission—or, if he didn't know, he would shortly have guessed." There was no sign of regret or remorse on Jericho's face.

"So what?" said Sable. "He worked for the Republic. He was on *your* side."

"*No one* is on my side," said Jericho coldly.

"You considered letting him live?"

"Of course," replied Jericho. "As you yourself pointed out, I am not a compulsive killer."

"But you killed him anyway."

"It was necessary."

"And Gaston Leroux?"

"Another link."

"But he only saw you in disguise. He didn't know your name, he didn't even know how to find you."

"His life was unimportant compared to my objective."

"What would have happened if you had let him live?" persisted Sable.

"Probably nothing," admitted Jericho.

"Then why did you kill him?"

"I don't deal in probabilities, Mr. Sable, but in certainties."

"He was a human being!"

"Bland was slaughtering tens of thousands of human beings," Jericho pointed out.

"I know. Did you care about them?"

"About who?" asked Jericho, genuinely puzzled.

"Bland's victims."

"What difference does that make? I stopped him before he could kill any more."

"But it *does* make a difference. Why did you kill Bland?"

"I don't understand your question."

"You heard me: Why did you kill Conrad Bland?"

"It was my job. I accepted the commission."

Sable sighed again and spent the next few minutes staring out the window, considering what he had heard and what he had seen, comparing and contrasting, building his little pyramid of facts and judgments, and finally weighing his inevitable conclusion against the absolute necessity of Bland's extermination.

At last he tore his gaze from the terrain that was racing by far below him, straightened his posture, and looked directly into Jericho's expressionless eyes.

"You're reached your decision," said Jericho impassively.

"I have."

"And?"

"As of this moment." said Sable, "you are under arrest for the murder of Parnell Burnam."

And, almost two thousand miles away, the White Lucy smiled, closed her eyes, and died.

Chapter 27

"God and Satan are in their cages; all's right with the world."
—*John Sable*

Sable stood between Pietre Veshinsky and Orestes Mela in a small cemetery on the outskirts of Amaymon and watched a plain casket being lowered into the ground.

Events had moved rapidly during the past four days. Justice, always swift on Walpurgis, had raced forward as if Satan himself were breathing down its neck. Within two hours after his return to the city, Jericho had been tried in a small courtroom with no jury, no reporters, and no court stenographer in attendance; even Sable had been barred from the proceedings.

He had been found guilty, condemned to death, and taken to a maximum-security cell, where he killed two guards and got as far as a service stairwell before he was apprehended and returned to confinement. While Jericho's escape attempt was occurring, numerous dignitaries from both the government and the clergy were conferring behind locked doors. Their meeting broke up in the early evening and the sentence was carried out before midnight.

Jericho's burial was delayed until Mela, representing the Republic, arrived three days later. He had requested, and was given, measurements and photographs of the body.

And now Sable stood, ignoring the light drizzle that was starting to fall, and watched the grave being filled in with dirt and rubble.

"No headstone?" asked Veshinsky.

"We never knew his name," replied Sable.

"His code name was Jericho," said Mela, drawing his jacket more tightly about him, "but no one knows who he really was."

"Well," said Veshinsky, "the important thing is that he completed his mission."

"I quite agree," said Mela. "That was the Republic's main concern—and of course we regard the apprehension and execution of Jericho as an extra bonus."

"I wonder how he got so far without being stopped?" mused Veshinsky.

"Who?" asked Sable.

"Bland, of course."

"Who knows?" said Mela. "Anyway, the main thing is that he's dead."

"True," agreed Veshinsky. "We've even established a national day of mourning for him." He chuckled ironically.

"For that monster?" said Mela. "What will happen when the public finds out what really took place in Tifereth?"

"They won't," said Veshinsky.

"Sooner or later they've got to!" persisted Mela.

"Who will tell them, Mr. Mela?" asked Veshinsky dryly. "Will *you*, who commissioned his death? Will the government, who begged you to send Jericho after him? Will the clergy, who demanded that we give him sanctuary and then lost control of him? No, the only man who might have told them was Jericho, and he's dead now."

"What about the press?"

"We control the press," answered Veshinsky with a smile. "It is in everyone's best interest to believe that Bland was a martyr, just as it is in all of our best interests that the assassin has been brought before the bar of justice and made to pay the penalty for his heinous deed. Isn't that right, John?"

"Yes, Pietre," said Sable. "That's right." Even if, he added mentally, it's right for the wrong reason.

The rain began coming down in earnest, and the three men left the unmarked grave and returned to the parking lot. Veshinsky suggested that Sable's driver take Mela to the spaceport while he and Sable rode in his limousine.

"I just want you to know, John," said Veshinsky as his chauffeur steered the huge car along the slick streets, "that we're all very proud of you. You've got quite a bright future ahead of you."

"Thank you," said Sable.

"There will be a raise and a promotion, of course, and just between you and me, I understand that the City Council is also cooking up a little ceremony to honor you."

"I'm very appreciative."

"You certainly don't sound it, John," said Veshinsky, concern showing on his face. "You haven't been yourself since you got back."

"It takes a little time to adjust to things after Tifereth."

Veshinsky rubbed the mist from his window and watched the rain as it hit the street.

"What was it like?" he asked at last.

"You've seen the carvings on the Church of the Messenger?" replied Sable, and Veshinsky nodded. "This was worse."

"I see," said Veshinsky soberly. "Mela had been to New Rhodesia just after Bland escaped. He told me about it in some detail."

"Whatever he saw, it couldn't have been as bad as Tifereth."

Sable shuddered and turned up his collar as if for warmth.

Veshinsky paused for a moment.

"How's Siboyan?"

"Fine."

"How did she react to the news of Bland's death?"

"Like most of the others," Sable said quietly. "She's sorry I wasn't able to save him."

"You haven't told her about him yet?"

"I don't discuss my cases outside the office."

Veshinsky smiled. "That's a very wise policy, John." He lit a cigar and offered one to Sable, who refused it. "I've got a couple of tickets for the fight next week. Care to come along?"

"Thanks for the invitation, Pietre, but I think I've seen enough bloodshed to last me for quite some time."

The limousine turned onto Sable's street.

"There's one thing that's been puzzling me," said Veshinsky. "If Bland was everything you and Mela say, why didn't you let Jericho go?"

Sable stared long and hard at his old friend, and wondered if he could explain it to him; indeed, if he could ever explain it to *anyone*. Finally he shrugged.

"He broke the law."

Veshinsky looked at the end of his cigar for a long moment. "If that's the way you want it, John. The subject is closed." The limousine came to a stop in front of Sable's house. "I'll be seeing you. And don't look so glum—you're a hero!"

Sable waved to him as the huge car pulled away, then entered the house. The children were still at school and Siboyan was off shopping. Even the cat seemed to have disappeared.

He walked slowly from room to room, wondering if he would ever get the stench of Tifereth out of his system. As he passed the statue of Cali he toyed with taking it down and putting it away in a closet, as he had done with the statue and baphomet in his office, then decided against it.

Siboyan still believed, and the kids believed as deeply as kids were able to. If they ever came face to face with their own Tifereths—and he hoped they never did—they'd put the statue away quickly enough. In the meantime, it was just plaster and paint; it represented nothing more to him than he cared to have it represent.

He walked to the bedroom and slowly got into his gardening clothes. The rain had stopped, the sun was starting to break through the clouds, and he had work to do. The garden, like his life, was in a state of temporary disrepair; he would have to tend to both, each in its turn.

At least, he thought with a sigh, the weeds had been eradicated from his life. He had survived the dark and the cold of the night. It would take some time, but he would flourish and grow again.

He turned his attention to the garden.

❖   ❖   ❖

God and Mr. Slatterman

SO GOD, HE DECIDES TO GIVE IT HIS BEST SHOT, and He says, "Thou hast made mockery of My name for the last time!"

And Mr. Slatterman, he pretends he doesn't even notice that the craps table is missing and all the people have vanished, and he looks God full in the eye, and he says, "I didn't take your name in vain, especially if you're who I think you are, and besides, if you will just take the trouble to check the record you will find that my precise words were 'Baby needs a new pair of shoes!' "

And God glares at him, and says, very stentoriously, "How darest thou speak to Me in such a tone of voice!"

And Mr. Slatterman, whose eyes are all squinched up because of how bright the Almighty is, he comes right back bold as you please, and says, "Well, just you be careful about who you go around of accusing of things they didn't rightly do, and what's more, I don't think I believe in you."

"What you believe is of no import," said God, Who has a feeling that He is not getting His point across. "You have repeatedly broken My Sabbath and disobeyed My laws that I gave unto Moses. Thou are an abomination unto My sight!"

"Now just hold it right there!" snaps Mr. Slatterman. "Bartenders got a right to live too, you know, and if you weren't so all-fired anxious to make everyone suffer the tortures of the damned, or at least as close an approximation as the Internal Revenue Service can whip up on short notice, then maybe I wouldn't be so damned busy on your day off, and could even get in a little golf."

Now, this really rankles God, and suddenly He's not just *pretending* to be mad anymore, and He bellows, "Thou art—"

"I don't want to put you off or anything," interrupts Mr. Slatterman, who is feeling just a little bit disoriented, "but could you kind of go a little easy on the 'Thee' and 'Thou' bit?"

God, He stares at Mr. Slatterman and utters a tired, little sigh, and after He gets His composure back He starts again. "Bernard Slatterman," He says in His best Sunday go-to-meeting voice, "you have squandered your life in pursuit of earthly pleasures, and your immortal soul stands in serious danger of being damned to everlasting perdition."

"That's better," said Mr. Slatterman, the dizziness starting to subside. "And considering who you are and all, you can call me Bernie."

"Do you not understand what I am saying to you?" demands God in stentorian tones.

"Seems to me that this is all beside the point, inasmuch as I'm already dead," says Mr. Slatterman. "And while we're on the subject, you picked a mighty cruel and unfeeling moment to take me off that mortal coil."

"You are *not* dead."

Mr. Slatterman resists the urge to curse, and settles for a disapproving scowl instead. "Do you mean to stand there and tell me, bold as brass, that you just plucked me out of that game on a whim, with three Big Ones riding on the roll and me just about to dish up a natural six?"

"It will be a seven," rumbles God harshly.

"Four and three or five and two?" demands Mr. Slatterman promptly.

"Six and one," replied God, Who feels Himself definitely losing control of the conversation.

"I don't believe it," says Mr. Slatterman.

"I never lie," says God, drawing Himself up to His full height, which is considerable.

"Well, that's a hell of a note!" exclaims Mr. Slatterman. "How can you do something like that to a nice guy like me, who never did anybody any harm, and is fashioned in your own image to boot?"

And God, Who wishes He had made Man a little more like a horned toad or maybe a koala bear so He would stop hearing that excuse over and over again, He says, "You are not as much in My image as some, and now that I come to reflect upon it, I cannot recall having created *you* at all."

And Mr. Slatterman, he gets that old, predatory look around his eyes, and he says, "Well, make up your mind. *Did* you create me or didn't you?"

"Well, yes, of course I did," says God, backing off a bit. "I just said I couldn't remember doing it."

"I thought so!" says Mr. Slatterman triumphantly. "You got to get up pretty early in the morning to put one over on Bernie Slatterman!" He scratches his head while God just stares at him. "Where were we now?" he mutters. "Oh, yeah, I remember. Why do you have it in for me? Why aren't you giving this warning to killers and bigamists and corporate lawyers and other degenerates?"

"Because they are all predestined to serve in the fiery pits of hell, while *you* have the germ of Redemption within your soul."

Mr. Slatterman gives God a kind of skeptical look. "You sure this ain't all because you need some expert advice on the right kind of wine to buy?" he asks.

"It is because you are flesh of My flesh and spirit of My spirit, and I have unbounded love and compassion for all of My children." God pauses. "It can get to be quite a strain at times," He admits.

Then Mr. Slatterman, he gets a look on his face like God has just said something a little bit off-color, and he takes a couple of steps backward. "Let's you and me try to keep this here love and compassion under wraps while we talk a little business," he says. "Especially the love," he adds meaningfully.

"You have an exceptionally vile mind," says God disgustedly.

"Yeah?" shoots back Mr. Slatterman. "Well, *I* didn't molest no virgin or have no out-of-wedlock baby." Then he lowers his voice and says, kind of confidentially, "Someday you got to tell me how you did it. You see, there's this girl that comes by the tavern every Saturday night who insists that she's saving it for her wedding night, and—"

"Enough!" screams God, Who is getting a little puffy around the face and wondering how He'd got all the way from talking about Mr. Slatterman's soul to discussing a very personal incident that had happened a long time ago, when He was a lot younger and more impetuous.

Anyway, Mr. Slatterman, he shrugs and looks like he expected this kind of reaction all along, and he says, "Well, okay, if you're going to be like that about it—but don't you go asking me for no free advice on how to mix drinks. After all, fair is fair."

God concludes that He's really getting a little old for this kind of thing, but decides to take one last crack at it, so He says, "Listen to me, Bernard Slatterman. Your soul is at risk, and I am giving you a chance to redeem it."

"You make Heaven sound kind of like a pawn shop," says Mr. Slatterman.

"Heaven is absolute perfection," says God sternly. "I made it."

Mr. Slatterman looks kind of dubious. "Well, the one don't necessarily lead to the other," he says. "You made Phoenix, Arizona, too, and you probably had more than a little to do with the Chicago White Sox."

"Oh, ye of little faith," mumbles God, Who realizes that this is a pretty feeble thing to say, but He is having more and more difficulty trying to get a handle on the conversation.

"You mind if I smoke?" asks Mr. Slatterman, reaching into his pocket and pulling out a pack of Camels.

God nods His head absently, and Mr. Slatterman lights up. Then, remembering his manners, he offers a cigarette to God.

"Certainly not!" said the Almighty, and Mr. Slatterman shrugs and puts the pack back in his pocket.

"So," he says, deciding that maybe God isn't such a bad guy after all, and has probably just been working too hard, "you've got a nice spread, have you?"

"I beg your pardon?" says God, puzzled.

"Heaven," explains Mr. Slatterman. "That *is* what we're talking about, isn't it?"

Now God, He figures it's easier to answer Mr. Slatterman than to keep trying to steer the talk back on track, and besides, He's not sure that Mr. Slatterman's soul is worth all that much more effort anyway, so He says, "Paradise is magnificent."

"Big place?" continues Mr. Slatterman.

"Vaster than the mind of Man can possible imagine," says God, with a touch of justifiable pride.

"Yeah? How many acres do you keep in cash crops?" asks Mr. Slatterman.

God looks bewildered. "None," He says, with the uneasy feeling that He has lost touch with the mainstream of Modern Thought.

"It's all pasture, then?" says Mr. Slatterman, whose face clearly implies that this is a pretty inefficient set-up.

"The landscape of Heaven is a pastoral wonderland," explains God defensively.

Mr. Slatterman frowns. "Well, I'm sure it's pretty as all get-out," he says. "But soybeans are up thirty percent this year."

"If I *want* soybeans, I can *create* soybeans," says God with just a trace of petulance.

Mr. Slatterman looks unimpressed. "Yeah," he says, "but you still got to harvest and process them. How much do you pay your help?"

"The cherubim toil for free," says God wearily, wondering how much longer this will go on.

"For free?" repeated Mr. Slatterman, and even God can see, one businessman to another, that Mr. Slatterman is very impressed. "Do the authorities know about this?"

God sighs heavily. "I *am* the authority," He says.

Mr. Slatterman nods his head. "Right," he says. "I forgot about that." His cigarette goes out and he lights up another. "What about the Devil?" he asks.

God just stares at him, kind of confused. "I give up," He says at last. "What *about* the Devil?"

"Well," says Mr. Slatterman, "old Satan's toiling in the pits of Hell, isn't he? And *you* created Hell, didn't you? Seems to me like it's a mighty valuable little piece of real estate." He pauses long enough for God to catch up with his train of thought. "So how much rent are you charging him?"

Suddenly God grins. "Well, by Myself!" He exclaims. "I never thought of that!" Then His face falls. "But what use have I for money?"

"None," agrees Mr. Slatterman. "So what we got to do is set up a kind of barter system. He's using something *we've* got, so it's only fair that *we* use something *he's* got."

"*We?*" repeats God, arching a bushy eyebrow.

"Right," says Mr. Slatterman, nodding his head. "As in you and me. Now, what has Lucifer got that we need?"

"Nothing," says God, feeling just a bit overwhelmed by the speed as which decisions seem to be getting themselves made.

"Wrong," says Mr. Slatterman triumphantly. "What he's got is manpower—or soulpower, if you prefer."

God takes a deep breath and exhales slowly. "I have no need for *any* type of power. I am the Creator."

Mr. Slatterman smiles. "Just my point. You've spread yourself too thin. You ought to stick to upper-level management and leave the mundane chores to someone else. Why, the second I got here, wherever *here* is, I said to myself, I said, 'Bernie, maybe you hadn't ought to mention it, since you're just a guest of limited duration and uncertain standing in the community, but the fact of the matter is that God's looking just a little bit peaked around the edges. Poor guy's probably been working too hard.' That's what I said."

God confesses that He's feeling a little overburdened these days.

Mr. Slatterman nods his head sympathetically, and says, "Sure you are, and perfectly understandable it is, too. I mean, hell, being God is probably even harder than being a good bartender, and I'll bet you don't have an awful lot of fringes, either." He looks around for a chair and one magically appears, so he sits down, and then another chair pops out of nowhere in particular, and God joins him. "Now," he continues, leaning forward, "I'll be happy to help in an advisory capacity, but what you really need is a good contract lawyer who's had some experience in labor negotiations."

"You have someone in mind, no doubt," suggests God dryly.

"Well, truth to tell, there's no one better qualified for this little job than my brother-in-law Jake."

"Jacob Wiseman's soul is already earmarked for perdition," says God sternly.

"He hasn't cheated me out of any money, has he?" demands Mr. Slatterman suddenly.

"That is perhaps the only sin of which he is not guilty."

Mr. Slatterman looks relieved, and he says, "Then we got no problem that I can see."

The Almighty shakes His head. "I told you: his soul is damned for all eternity."

"Look," says Mr. Slatterman reasonably, "people who are bound for Heaven can sell their souls to Satan, can't they? So why can't Jake, who's bound for Hell, sell his soul to *you* in exchange for his services?"

God looks like He is considering the idea, which is certainly a novel concept and worthy of a little serious thought, and Mr. Slatterman leans back comfortably in his chair. "Of course," he adds, "I'll expect a little something for putting the two of you together."

"Your immortal soul, for example?" suggests God knowingly.

Mr. Slatterman smiles. "Well, *that* too, I suppose—but what I *really* had in mind concerns that friendly little game of chance that you're going to be sticking me back down in when we're all through here."

God looks at him with extreme distaste. "Gambling is a sin," He points out.

Mr. Slatterman shrugs. "Yeah," he says, "but considering all the overdue bills I got sitting on my desk, and all the people who'll go hungry if I don't pay them, I'd say that gambling and losing is a lot worse sin than gambling and winning." He shoots a quick look at God out of the corner of his eye. "Of course," he adds with forced nonchalance, "we can call the whole thing off if your conscience is going to bother you all that much."

God stares at him long and hard. "I find it difficult to believe that you are really one of My creations," He remarks at last.

Mr. Slatterman, he frowns and says, "You're not going to go all metaphysical on me again, are you?"

God sighs. "No, I suppose not," He says in resignation.

"Good," says Mr. Slatterman with a smile. "Then do I get to roll my six?"

God considers His long, perfect fingers for a moment and decides that it really is time to start thinking about a vacation, and that maybe He has even found Himself a short-term replacement. After all, the man seems forceful and decisive, and he certainly knows his own mind, and of course he will be able to work closely with Jacob Wiseman on the delicate negotiations that God has already decided are long overdue.

"Will a pair of threes be sufficient," asks the Almighty, "or would you prefer a two and a four?"

❖ ❖ ❖

The Pale Thin God

HE STOOD QUIETLY BEFORE US, THE PALE THIN god who had invaded our land, and waited to hear the charges.

The first of us to speak was Mulungu, the god of the Yao people.

"There was a time, many eons ago, when I lived happily upon the earth with my animals. But then men appeared. They made fire and set the land ablaze. They found my animals and began killing them. They devised weapons and went to war with each other. I could not tolerate such behavior, so I had a spider spin a thread up to heaven, and I ascended it, never to return. And yet *you* have sacrificed yourself for these very same creatures."

Mulungu pointed a long forefinger at the pale thin god. "I accuse you of the crime of Love."

He sat down, and immediately Nyambe, the god of the Koko people, arose.

"I once lived among men," he said, "and there was no such thing as death in the world, because I had given them a magic tree. When men grew old and wrinkled, they went and lived under the tree for nine days, and it made them young again. But as the years went by men began taking me for granted, and stopped worshiping me and making sacrifices to me, so I uprooted my tree and carried it up to heaven with me, and without its magic, men finally began to die."

He stared balefully at the pale thin god. "And now you have taught men that they may triumph over death. I charge you with the crime of Life."

Next Ogun, the god of the Yoruba people, stepped forward.

"When the gods lived on Earth, they found their way barred by impenetrable thorn bushes. I created a *panga* and cleared the way for them, and this *panga* I turned over to men, who use it not only for breaking trails but for the glory of war. And yet you, who claim to be a god, tell your worshipers to disdain weapons and never to raise a hand in anger. I accuse you of the crime of Peace."

As Ogun sat down, Muluku, god of the Zambesi, rose to his feet.

"I made the earth," he said. "I dug two holes, and from one came a man, and from the other a woman. I gave them land and tools and seeds and clay pots, and told them to plant the seeds, to build a house, and to cook their food in the pots. But the man and the woman ate the raw seeds, broke the pots, and left the tools by the side of a trail. Therefore, I summoned two monkeys, and made the same gifts to them. The two monkeys dug the earth, built a house, harvested their grain, and cooked it in their pots." He paused. "So I cut off the monkeys' tails and stuck them on the two men, decreeing that from that day forth they would be monkeys and the monkeys would be men."

He pointed at the pale thin god. "And yet, far from punishing men, you forgive them their mistakes. I charge you with the crime of Compassion."

En-kai, the god of the Maasai, spoke next.

"I created the first warrior, Le-eyo, and gave him a magic chant to recite over dead children that would bring them back to life and make them immortal. But Le-eyo did not utter the chant until his own son had died. I told him that it was too late, that the chant would no longer work, and that because of his selfishness, Death will always have power over men. He begged me to relent, but because I am a god and a god cannot be wrong, I did not do so."

He paused for a moment, then stared coldly at the pale thin god. "You would allow men to live again, even if only in heaven. I accuse you of the crime of Mercy."

Finally Huveane, god of the Basuto people, arose.

"I, too, lived among men in eons past. But their pettiness offended me, and so I hammered some pegs into the sky and climbed up to heaven, where men would never see me again." He faced the pale thin god. "And now, belatedly, you have come to our land, and you teach that men may ascend to heaven, that they may even sit at your right hand. I charge you with the crime of Hope."

The six fearsome gods turned to me.

"We have spoken," they said. "It is your turn now, Anubis. Of what crime do you charge him?"

"I do not make accusations, only judgments," I replied.

"And how do you judge him?" they demanded.

"I will hear him speak, and then I will tell you," I said. I turned to the pale thin god. "You have been accused of the crimes of Peace, Life, Mercy, Compassion, Love, and Hope. What have you to say in your defense?"

The pale thin god looked at us, his accusers.

"I have been accused of Peace," he said, never raising his voice, "and yet more Holy Wars have been fought in my name than in the names of all other gods combined. The earth has turned red with the blood of those who died for my Peace.

"I have been accused of Life," he continued, "yet in my name, the Spaniards baptized Aztec infants and dashed out their brains against rocks so they might ascend to heaven without living to become warriors.

"I have been accused of Mercy, but the Inquisition was held in my name, and the number of men who were tortured to death is beyond calculation.

"I have been accused of Compassion, yet not a single man who worships me has ever lived a life without pain, without fear, and without misery.

"I have been accused of Love, yet I have not ended suffering, or disease, or death, and he who leads the most blameless and saintly life will be visited by all of my grim horsemen just as surely as he who rejects me.

"Finally, I have been accused of Hope," he said, and now the stigmata on his hands and feet and neck began to glow a brilliant red, "and yet since I have come to your land, I have brought famine to the north, genocide to the west, drought to the south, and disease to the east. And everywhere, where there was Hope, there is only poverty and ignorance and war and death.

"So it has been wherever I have gone, so shall it always be.

"Thus do I answer your charges."

They turned to me, the six great and terrible deities, to ask for my judgment. But I had already dropped to my knees before the greatest god of us all.

How I Wrote the New Testament, Ushered in the Renaissance, and Birded the 17th Hole at Pebble Beach

*S*O HOW WAS I TO KNOW THAT AFTER ALL THE FALSE Messiahs the Romans nailed up, *he* would turn out to be the real one?

I mean, it's not every day that the Messiah lets himself be nailed to a cross, you know? We all thought he was supposed to come with the sword and throw the Romans out and raze Jerusalem to the ground—and if he couldn't quite pull that off, I figured the least he could do was take on a couple of the bigger Romans, *mano a mano*, and whip them in straight falls.

It's not as if I'm an unbeliever. (How could I be, at this late date?) But you talk about the Annointed One, you figure you're talking about a guy with a little flash, a little style, a guy whose muscles have muscles, a Sylvester Stallone or Arnold Schwarzenegger-type of guy, you know what I mean?

So sure, when I see them walking this skinny little wimp up to Golgotha, I join in the fun. So I drink a little too much wine, and I tell too many jokes (but all of them funny, if I say so myself), and maybe I even hold the vinegar for one of the guards (though I truly don't remember doing that)—but is that any reason for him to single me out?

Anyway, there we are, the whole crowd from the pub, and he looks directly at me from his cross, and he says, "One of you shall tarry here until I return."

"You can't be talking to me!" I answer, giving a big wink to my friends. "I do all my tarrying at the House of Young Maidens over on the next street!"

Everybody else laughs at this, even the Romans, but he just stares reproachfully at me, and a few minutes later he's telling God to forgive us, as if *we're* the ones who broke the rules of the Temple, and then he dies, and that's that.

Except that from that day forth, I don't age so much as a minute, and when Hannah, my wife, sticks a knife between my ribs just because I forgot her birthday and didn't come home for a week and then asked for a little spending money when I walked in the door, I find to my surprise that the second she removes the knife I am instantly healed with not even a scar.

Well, this puts a whole new light on things, because suddenly I realize that this little wimp on the cross really *was* the Messiah, and that I have been cursed to wander the Earth (though in perfect health) until he returns, which does not figure to be any time soon as the Romans are already talking about throwing us out of Jerusalem and property values are skyrocketing.

Well, at first this seems more like a blessing than a curse, because at least it means I will outlive the *yenta* I married and maybe get a more understanding wife. But then all my friends start growing old and dying, which they would do anyway but which always seems to happen a little faster in Judea, and Hannah adds a quick eighty pounds to a figure that could never be called *svelte* in the first place, and suddenly it looks like she's going to live as long as me, and I decide that maybe this is the very worst kind of curse after all.

Now, at about the time that Hannah celebrates her 90th birthday—thank God we didn't have cakes and candles back in those days or we might have burnt down the whole city—I start to hear that Jerusalem is being overrun by a veritable plague of Christians. This in itself is enough to make my good Jewish blood boil, but when I find out exactly what a Christian is, I am fit to be tied. Here is this guy who curses me for all eternity or until he returns, whichever comes first (and it's starting to look like it's going to be a very near thing), and suddenly—even though nothing he promised has come to pass *except* for cursing a poor itinerant businessman who never did anyone any harm—everybody I know is worshipping him.

There is no question in my mind that the time has come to leave Judea, and I wait just long enough for Hannah to choke on an unripe fig which someone has thoughtlessly served her while she laid in bed complaining about her nerves, and then I catch the next caravan north and book passage across the Mediterranean Sea to Athens, but as Fate would have it, I arrive about five centuries too late for the Golden Age.

This is naturally an enormous disappointment, but I spend a couple of decades soaking up the sun and dallying with assorted Greek maidens, and when this begins to pall I finally journey to Rome to see what all the excitement is about.

And what is going on there is Christianity, which makes absolutely no sense whatsoever, since to the best of my knowledge no one else he ever cursed or blessed is around to give testimony to it, and I have long since decided that being known as the guy who taunted him on the cross would not be in the best interests of my social life and so I have kept my lips sealed on the subject.

But be that as it may, they are continually having these gala festivals—kind of like the Super Bowl, but without the two-week press buildup—in which Christians are thrown to the lions, and they have become overwhelmingly popular with the masses, though they are really more of a pageant than a sporting event, since the Christians almost never win and the local bookmakers won't even list a morning line on the various events.

I stay in Rome for almost two centuries, mostly because I have become spoiled by indoor plumbing and paved roads, but then I can see the handwriting on the wall and I realize that I am going to outlive the Roman Empire, and it seems like a good idea to get established elsewhere before the Huns overrun the place and I have to learn to speak German.

So I become a wanderer, and I find that I really *like* to travel, even though we do not have any amenities such as Pullman cars or even Holiday Inns. I see all the various wonders of the ancient world—although it is not so ancient then as it has become—and I journey to China (where I help them invent gunpowder, but leave before anyone considers inventing the fuse), and I do a little tiger-hunting in India, and I even consider climbing Mount Everest (but I finally decide against it since it didn't have a name back then, and bragging to people that I climbed this big nameless mountain in Nepal will somehow lack a little something in the retelling).

After I have completed my tour, and founded and outlived a handful of families, and hobnobbed with the rich and powerful, I return to Europe, only to find out that the whole continent is in the midst of the Dark Ages. Not that the daylight isn't as bright as ever, but when I start speaking to people it is like the entire populace has lost an aggregate of 40 points off its collective I.Q.

Talk about dull! Nobody can read except the monks, and I find to my dismay that they still haven't invented air-conditioning or even frozen food, and once you finish talking about the king and the weather and what kind of fertilizer you should use on your fields, the conversation just kind of lays there like a dead fish, if you know what I mean.

Still, I realize that I now have my chance for revenge, so I take the vows and join an order of monks and live a totally cloistered life for the next twenty years (except for an occasional Saturday night in town, since I am physically as vigorous and virile as ever), and finally I get my opportunity to translate the Bible, and I start inserting little things, little hints that should show the people what he was really like, like the bit with the Gadarene swine, where he puts devils into the pigs and makes them rush down the hill to the sea. So okay, that's nothing to write home about today, but you've got to remember that back then I was translating this for a bunch of pig farmers, who have a totally different view of this kind of behavior.

Or what about the fig tree? Only a crazy man would curse a fig tree for being barren when it's out of season, right? But for some reason, everyone who reads it decides it is an example of his power rather than his stupidity, and after a while I just pack it in and leave the holy order forever.

Besides, it is time to move on, and the realization finally dawns on me that no matter how long I stay in one spot, eventually my feet get itchy and I have to give in to my wanderlust. It is the curse, of course, but while wandering from Greece to Rome during the heyday of the Empire was pleasant enough, I find that wandering from one place to another in the Dark Ages is something else again, since nobody can understand two-syllable words and soap is not exactly a staple commodity.

So after touring all the capitals of Europe and feeling like I am back in ancient Judea, I decide that it is time to put an end to the Dark Ages. I reach this decision when I am in Italy, and I mention it to Michelangelo and Leonardo while we are sitting around drinking wine and playing cards, and they decide that I am right and it is probably time for the Renaissance to start.

Creating the Renaissance is pretty heady stuff, though, and they both go a little haywire. Michelangelo spends the next few years lying on his back getting paint in his face, and Leonardo starts designing organic airplanes. However, once they get their feet wet they do a pretty good job of bringing civilization back to Italy, though my dancing partner Lucretia Borgia is busily poisoning it as quick as Mike and Leo are enlightening it, and just about the time things get really interesting I find my feet getting itchy again, and I spend the next century or so wandering through Africa, where I discover the Wandering Jew Falls and put up a signpost to the effect, but evidently somebody uses it for firewood, because the next I hear of the place it has been renamed the Victoria Falls.

Anyway, I keep wandering around the world, which becomes an increasingly interesting place to wander around once the Industrial Revolution hits, but I can't help feeling guilty, not because of that moment of frivolity eons ago, but because except for having Leonardo do a portrait of my girlfriend Lisa, I really don't seem to have any great accomplishments, and eighteen centuries of aimlessness can begin to pall on you.

And then I stop by a little place in England called Saint Andrews, where they have just invented a new game, and I play the very first eighteen holes of golf in the history of the world, and suddenly I find that I have a purpose after all, and that purpose is to get my handicap down to scratch and play every course in the world, which so far comes to a grand total of one but soon will run into the thousands.

So I invest my money, and I buy a summer home in California and a winter home in Florida, and while the world is waiting for the sport to come to them, I build my own putting greens and sand traps, and for those of you who are into historical facts, it is me and no one else who invents the sand wedge, which I do on April 17, 1893. (I invent the slice into the rough three days later, which forces me to invent the two-iron. Over the next decade I also invent the three through nine irons, and I have plans to invent irons all the way up to number twenty-six, but I stop at nine until such time as someone invents the golf cart, since twenty-six irons are very difficult to carry over a five-mile golf course, with or without a complete set of woods and a putter.)

By the 1980s I have played on all six continents, and I am currently awaiting the creation of a domed links on Antarctica. Probably it won't come to pass for another two hundred years, but if there is one thing I've got plenty of, it's time. And in the meantime, I'll just keep adding to my list of accomplishments. So far, I'd say my greatest efforts have been putting in that bit about the pigs, and maybe getting Leonardo to stop daydreaming about flying men and get back to work on his easel. And birdying the 17th hole at Pebble Beach has got to rank right up there, too; I mean, how many people can sink a 45-foot uphill putt in a cold drizzle?

So all in all, it's been a pretty good life. I'm still doomed to wander for all eternity, but there's nothing in the rulebook that says I can't wander in my personal jet plane, and Fifi and Fatima keep me company when I'm not on the links, and I'm up for a lifetime membership at Augusta, which is a lot more meaningful in my case than in most others.

In fact, I'm starting to feel that urge again. I'll probably stop off at the new course they've built near Lake Naivasha in Kenya, and then hit the links at Bombay, and then the Jaipur Country Club, and then . . .

I just hope the Second Coming holds off long enough for me to play a couple of rounds at the Chou En-Lai Memorial Course in Beijing. I hear it's got a water hole that you've got to see to believe.

You know, as curses go, this is one of the better ones.

The Branch

Prologue

IT WAS NOT THE BEST OF TIMES; IT WAS NOT THE worst of times. It was the *dullest* of times.

By rights, it shouldn't have been. The first half of the twenty-first century was an age of fantastic, glittering cities that spread like creeping cancers across the face of the planet. It was an age of bold new art forms, darksome pleasures, and bizarre indulgences. Every day saw the discovery of a new perversion, every month revealed the creation of a new spectator sport, every year boasted splendid new forms of entertainment. The fact that the perversions and sports and entertainments ultimately proved not to be so new after all, but merely the recycling of old, mundane diversions, could hardly be blamed on society, which continued its quest for the new and the unique with unrestrained vigor, while its members, individually and collectively, came to the unhappy realization that an excess of leisure was not quite the Valhalla that they had anticipated.

Religion had recently made a big comeback. So had philosophy. So had anything else that took up time. Every city possessed baseball, football, hockey, basketball, rugby, soccer, and lacrosse teams, as well as scores of professional and amateur golfers, bowlers, boxers, wrestlers, tennis players, and martial arts experts. Handicrafts were unbelievably popular—and the more complicated and time-consuming, the better. Watercolors and acrylics had given way to a resurgence of interest in oils among amateur painters; origami was sweeping the nation; indoor gardens, especially those requiring constant attention and uncommon conditions, were the order of the day.

Only the rich could afford clothing made of wool, cotton, or other natural fibers; but even the rich designed and sewed all their own garments, usually choosing the most colorful fashions from past eras.

Scarcely a household was without a pet. Cats were the most popular, since they adapted easily to the mile-high, million-windowed hovels that formed the supercities, but a few breeds of dogs—Keeshonds, Shih Tzus, Lhasa Apsos, and a handful of others—still existed in some quantity. These, like the cats, the rats, the mice, the fish, the birds, the crickets, and every other form of animal life, were inbred, linebred, outcrossed, shown, trained, and pampered.

Of course, to the people living through it, there was nothing very special about their day and age. They accepted what came, as people always have, hopeful of better and fearful of worse. None of them were hungry, few of them were oppressed, most of them were at least minimally employed, and all of them were bored.

They were not to remain bored for long.

December 11, 2047, seemed neither better nor worse, neither more nor less interesting, than any other day of recent vintage. Certainly the two men who were to change the face of their world seemed quite ordinary at first glance: one of them was a criminal, and the other a beggar. Nevertheless, although no one was aware of it—and least of all the two principal players—this day marked the onset of a tapestry of events that would soon jolt Earth's unhappy and apathetic billions loose from their lethargy, never to return.

It began, appropriately enough, at a circus. . . .

PART 1

1

Like most of the others in the crowd, the young man was attracted by the huge neon signs and electric calliopes. They had come for pleasure, he for business, but all were drawn like suicidal moths to the artificial flame.

A huge, luminescent banner, fluttering slightly in the cold breeze, proclaimed to all and sundry that this was the

> NIGHTSPORE AND THRUSH
> INTERNATIONAL TRAVELING CIRCUS
> AND THRILL SHOW

Direct from Vienna, as circuses of old used to proclaim, though this one was less circus than thrill show, and more recently from Cleveland than Vienna. It was huge, as it had to be, for the people came out of Chicago and its environs by the tens of thousands, wild-eyed and hopeful as they maintained the frantic pace of their life-long quest for amusement and diversion.

The barkers, the grifters, the hookers, the musclemen, all the night people had assembled there to meet the challenge.

"This way, ladies and gentlemen!" called the barkers. "This way to Madam Adam! Is she a man? Is he a woman? Step right up, come right in, let's keep it moving. The world's only authenticated her-maphrodite, a compendium of all that's most voluptuous and sex-citing in man and woman, is onstage right now, waiting to . . ."

"Three throws for twenty dollars, three for only twenty dollars! Hurt? Sure it hurts 'em, mister! Ask your girlfriend how she'd like to have you hurl a dart into her naked, pulsating flesh! Listen to them scream, watch 'em writhe! Six throws for . . ."

The young man paused for a moment before the Living Dart-boards, then continued walking down the seemingly endless rows of sheds, games, and exhibits.

"Mister Blister, that's what we call him—Mister Blister! No, he doesn't do any childish stunts like eating fire or walking on hot coals. No, sir, not Mister Blister. Now folks, do you see this blow-torch I have in my hand? Well, step a little closer and . . ."

"First time ever onstage: a full-scale production of Leda and the Swan. Now, I know there are doubters out there, I know there are skeptics. So I'll tell you what I'm gonna do. If any of you feel cheated after the performance, if anyone can honestly state that we don't deliver the goods, I'm gonna refund not just *your* money, but each and every . . ."

The young man turned up another aisle, past the Chamber of 1,000 Pains, with its shrieks and groans coming through loud and clear over a pair of outside amplifiers, past the even more exotic pleasurepain palaces.

Tonight would be a good night; he felt it in his bones. The crowd was immense, as well it should be. There were just so many Madam Adams and Sin Shrines and Pervo Palaces in the world, and when the thrill shows made their rare appearances the money flowed like water—and there was no reason why he shouldn't be able to siphon some off for himself.

The young man continued walking past the gaudy, exotic exhibits, fighting his way through the crowd. Finally he came to a small, unoccupied space about a quarter of a mile from a windowless office building, unloaded his backpack, withdrew a pair of very dark glasses and a white cane, and went to work.

There was a bit of work going on inside the office building too—as Mr. Nightspore and Mr. Thrush were finding out. A tall, slender man, immaculately but archaically clad in the fashion of more than a century ago, sat with his feet on Mr. Thrush's desk. His long, lean fingers were covered by white dress gloves, he wore a double-breasted, navy-blue pinstriped suit, and his black leather shoes were covered by shiny white spats. He pulled a large cigar from his lapel pocket and placed it in his mouth; it was immediately lit by one of the four burly men standing behind him.

"So you see, gentlemen," he said calmly, puffing thoughtfully on the cigar, "it's not that I have any aversion to your company, or wish you to vacate the premises and set up shop elsewhere. Chicago is a big city, big enough for all of us."

"Then why did you force your way in here?" demanded Mr. Nightspore.

"Please don't interrupt," he said with a smile that began and ended at the corners of his mouth. "As I was saying, there's money enough for everyone here: money for you, money for your employees, and money for me. Frankly, I'm at a loss to see what your problem is. If anyone will suffer because of your presence here, it will be me. After all, there's no more money to be spent today than there was yesterday, but now there are two more hands reaching out for it—*your* hands. I've looked your operation over, and it's my conservative opinion that you'll take in about nine million dollars a week." He paused, staring coldly at them. "That, gentlemen, is nine million dollars I *won't* be taking in. Do you begin to appreciate my concern?"

Mr. Nightspore started to say something, then thought better of it, and nodded.

"Well," continued the man, with another nonsmile, "I'm delighted to see that we understand each other. After all, we're not enemies: we're on the same side of the fence. It's the people out there"—he waved a hand in the general direction of the midway—"who are our opposition. They've got something we both want and there's no sense working at cross-purposes to get it. The three of us are operating on the same basic premise: if God didn't want them fleeced, He wouldn't have made them sheep." He swung his feet to the floor and leaned forward on the desk. "Now, shall we get down to business?"

"How much do you want?" asked Mr. Thrush suspiciously.

"You make it sound like a gift," replied the man. "Let me hasten to assure you that Solomon Moody Moore takes charity from no one. No, gentlemen, you still misunderstand me. My organization will perform certain necessary services, according to a contract that we'll draw up, and we will receive only a fair and reasonable payment."

"What services?" asked Mr. Thrush.

"A very good question," said Moore. "To begin with, my representatives will police your grounds day and night, serving as what might be called combination caretakers and security officers. You've got a lot of valuable equipment, gentlemen," he added pointedly. "Any vandal could do untold damage to it in a matter of minutes." He paused and took another puff of his cigar. "Furthermore, I noticed a number of gambling games as I toured your circus; upward of eighty, I would estimate. Most of them are designed to break between ten and fifteen percent in favor of the house. You've got them rigged for thirty, of course, but you've been taken in by a bunch of clumsy amateurs. They're robbing you blind and giving the suckers too close to an even break. My people, at no extra charge, will set your games for a fifty percent break, and will operate them for you."

"If all this is free, what's the final bill going to run us?" asked Mr. Nightspore suspiciously.

"One-third," said Moore.

"One-third of what?"

"Everything." Moore's cigar went out, and he waited patiently for one of his men to light it again. "View it as a business investment that will pay off in large dividends. I'll double your gross by the end of the week, so it will cost you virtually nothing, and when you leave town, all of my improvements will leave with you."

"And then our partnership is ended?"

Moore smiled. "Oh, no. That, like diamonds, is forever." He held up a hand to stifle their protests. "Believe me, gentlemen, if we find that you're not making more money than before, we can always renegotiate our contract." He took another puff of his cigar, then placed it in an ashtray. "Now let's get down to business. How many drug emporiums are you operating here?"

"None!" said Mr. Nightspore emphatically.

"I would prefer a little more honesty now that we're going to be partners," said Moore calmly. "I counted six, but I might have missed a couple. I repeat: how many are there?"

"Seven," said Mr. Nightspore with a sigh.

"That's better," said Moore. "There is absolutely nothing like openness among friends. I'll take you at your word that there are seven. If we find any more, we'll assume they're not operating under your auspices and will appropriate their stock. Now, how much do you cut your hallucinogens and your harder drugs?"

"Not at all!" snapped Mr. Thrush.

Moore stared curiously at him for a moment. "You know, I think you're just stupid enough to be telling the truth. We can be of service to you there, as well. Next point: how many people die here every week?"

"We're covered for that," said Mr. Nightspore defensively. "No one enters the scare shows or the sado tents without signing an iron-clad release. We've been to court four times in the past two years, and won all four cases."

"You didn't answer my question: how many people die at your circus every week?"

"About ten."

"Not enough."

"What?" shrilled both partners in unison.

"Not enough," repeated Moore. "People love blood even more than they love the grotesque. They're not coming here to see your Four-Headed Baby or your Vaseline Corpse. They want death. The more you give them, the more they'll talk about it and come back for seconds. Take your Russian Roulette exhibit: you've got a nine-cylinder gun with one bullet in it and you're offering a lousy thousand dollars to the man who'll play the game. Starting tomorrow, you'll put three bullets into a six-cylinder gun, offer a ten-grand prize, and triple your admission price. Ditto with your Pervo Palaces and all the other crap like that. Agreed?"

The two partners nodded reluctantly.

"As for your girls, get more of them. Prettier, too. And the place reeks of Caucasians. I want to see blacks, browns, reds, yellows, albinos, and polka-dots. If you can't get them, let my people know and we'll hunt them up. If they don't know the meaning of the word 'normal,' so much the better. Also, I want you to start two exhibits for women only; I'll supply what you need for them. Can do?"

"Well, I don't know . . . that is, I'm not—" began Mr. Nightspore.

"Can do?" repeated Moore coldly.

Mr. Nightspore nodded.

"Excellent," said Moore. "All the members of my organization will wear red armbands with your logo printed on them." He paused. "They are not to be interfered with. Is that absolutely clear?"

The partners assured him that it was.

"My people will be armed for your protection," continued Moore. "I think it would be best if no one else carried any type of weapon, and that includes any security men you may now have on your payroll. It will avoid unpleasant misunderstandings. If any member of my organization abuses your hospitality, or if every last penny is not accounted for, I will expect you to report it to me." He stood up and stretched. "And now, if you gentlemen will excuse me, I'd like to take another walk around our circus. My associates will provide you with the proper contracts. I had a feeling that we could come to an equitable agreement, so I took the liberty of having them drawn up before I left my office. My men," he added meaningfully, "will keep you company until the contracts have been signed. Since you won't be needing me for the next few minutes, I think I'll take my leave of you. I find these interviews personally distasteful."

He put on his bowler—another anachronism—and walked out of the building.

It was not, he reflected as he mingled with the crowd, a bad night's work. Nightspore and Thrush ran the same kind of show as everyone else: it was geared for fear, lust, and greed, with a fair share of side trips into the bizarre. It was also rigged to the teeth, which made it fair game for him.

He looked up at a Eurasian girl proudly displaying her four nipples as a come-on for the Freak Show. Yes, he reflected, people would shell out all kinds of money just to see something different, to get out of their ruts and worship somewhere other than at the altar of Humdrum. And as long as people like Nightspore and Thrush were willing to bilk them, he'd stay solvent by bilking the bilkers.

Of course, there were legitimate business interests to be considered too, and he'd been buying into quite a lot of them lately: a leatherworks factory in New Hampshire, a computer plant in Pittsburgh, thoroughbred yearlings in Kentucky and California, a professional basketball team in Albuquerque. With more and more time to fill, there were more and more ways to capitalize on the needs of one's fellow man. Although, Moore acknowledged grimly, even the capitalizers had to battle against boredom. He himself had more money than he could hope to spend in one lifetime, and a reputation that would take him several lifetimes to expunge, and yet he kept at it.

And why not? After all, what else was there to do? The moment he stopped feeding off humanity he would become indistinguishable from them, ripe for somebody else to come feed off him. He had started as a small-time burglar, learned the ropes, began gathering a meticulously selected organization about him, had been careful never to move prematurely, and because he was a little smarter and a little hungrier and a little more ruthless than the next guy, had taken over the next guy's territory, and the next guy after that, and after that. He had a good, solid structure behind him, peopled with the best men and women that money and the opportunity to escape from boredom could buy. Every one of them wanted his job—he had no use for anyone who willingly settled for second-best—and it kept both him and them on their toes, a reasonably healthy state of affairs in this day and age.

He'd been uncommonly successful in his chosen field of endeavor, although that didn't really surprise him. When all was said and done, everyone else was running away from dullness and drudgery, while he was running *toward* his problems, molding men and situations to fit his various needs.

A shrill yell broke his train of thought, and he looked up to find himself in front of the Chamber of 1,000 Pains. He grimaced. Why people would pay perfectly good money to have the hell flailed out of them was beyond his capacity to understand, and he had no greater empathy for the hundreds of spectators who shelled out still more money to watch. He shook his head, shrugged, and continued walking.

He circled the entire Thrill Show, feeling increasingly unclean from his proximity to the marks, and finally decided to return to the office building to pick up the contracts. As he approached it, he noticed a small crowd gathered around a young man with dark glasses. The man had a moth-eaten top hat in one hand and a white cane in the other, and was singing psalms in a less-than-outstanding tenor.

Moore stopped and looked into the hat. "Not much of a haul," he remarked. "You'd do better with bawdy ballads."

"You want one, you got one," said the young man, breaking into one of the three million or so verses of "The Ring-Dang-Doo."

"Enough!" laughed Moore a moment later, flipping a coin into the upturned hat.

"You don't like the songs of the masses?" asked the young man with a smile.

"I don't like anything about the masses," replied Moore. "Want to make some real money?"

The young man nodded.

"Five hundred dollars says you're not blind."

The young man felt around in his hat, fingering the coins. "Sixteen dollars and seventy-three cents says you can't prove it."

Moore lit a match and casually tossed it toward the young man's face.

There was no reaction.

"Not bad," said Moore, suddenly releasing a blow to the young man's midsection. The air gushed out of him and he fell to his knees. Some of the change rolled out of the hat, and his fingers traveled frantically over the ground, trying to retrieve the lost coins. Moore walked over to him and faked a kick at his face, which went unheeded.

Finally Moore helped him to his feet, then dug a wad of five-dollar bills out of his pocket, counted ten of them off in front of the young man's face, and placed them in the hat.

"Thank you, sir," wheezed the young man.

Moore paused a moment, then took the money back, withdrew his wallet, peeled off ten fifty-dollar bills, and dropped them into the ragged top hat.

"I was wrong," he said, giving the young man a pat on the shoulder and walking off toward the office building.

Then, as he reached the door, the young man called out after him: "Hey, Plug-Ugly, where the hell did you ever buy those godawful white spats? They make you look like a goddamned faggot!"

Moore wheeled around, but the young man had already vanished into the crowd.

And *that* was the first meeting between Solomon Moody Moore and Jeremiah the B.

Most historians would have swapped their fortunes, their spouses, and their eyeteeth to have been there.

2

Tuesday was smut day.

Or, more properly, Tuesday was the day of the week when Moore went over the reports of his publishing corporation and its affiliates and issued his directives for the coming week.

He sat now in what was quite possibly the most Spartan office in the entire Chicago complex. Unlike most executive suites it contained no televisions, no radios, no sound systems, no paintings, no couches, no exercise areas, no handicrafts alcoves, no wet bars. It was spare and barren, like the man who worked in it. There was one large desk, made of artificial mahogany, which supported a computer terminal, three telephones, and a quartet of intercoms. Facing it were six chairs, none of them very comfortable. There were doors on three of the walls, two of which were rarely used, and one of the walls contained a small, built-in safe. There was only one window in the room, albeit a huge one, and the view was invariably obscured by a row of blinds that had been layered between the inner and outer panes of glass. What pleasures Moore sought were found elsewhere; his office was a place for work, and nothing else.

"The reports, Ben, if you please."

The man sitting across the desk from Moore handed him a sheaf of computer readouts, along with a large breakdown sheet. Ben Pryor, his clothing as loud as Moore's was muted, his wavy blond hair a stark contrast to Moore's straight steel-gray, was Moore's second-in-command, in charge of the day-to-day management of all Moore's enterprises. He was shrewd, highly intelligent, and totally competent, possessed of a master's degree in business administration and another in economics. He was also openly ambitious, which was natural but regrettable; he knew far too much about the operation for Moore ever to let him go, and the day wasn't too far off when Moore would have to eliminate him in a more permanent manner.

Moore began reading the reports, making an occasional comment, issuing a rare order. The pornography industry was doing very well these days, as usual, and the problems of management had more to do with the vast size of the operation than with any legal or sales problems. Indeed, sometimes the scope of it amazed even Moore: he owned three publishing companies that specialized in erotic books, magazines, and newspapers, and two others that churned out pornographic videotapes and computer disks. Between them, they produced some three hundred different titles each month, with sales in excess of eighty million units.

But that was just the beginning. Pornography, though going through one of its cyclic periods of legality, was still far from being socially acceptable and was subject to occasional harassment, which meant that the huge, monolithic distributors who monopolized service in the densely populated metropolitan areas didn't care to handle the stuff, or at least didn't push it with the same verve and zest that they applied to the more suitable publications. So Moore had quietly bought up a number of existing secondary agencies and created still more, each of them specializing in the type of material the large, independent distributors didn't want.

From there it was just a small step to buying and building some four thousand pornographic emporiums that specialized in carrying his merchandise. Since many of them catered to prostitution and the more bizarre sexual desires of the public, Moore had also branched out very thoroughly into such services. Finally, he had purchased a huge printing plant that not only sufficed for all his needs but also printed a goodly portion of his rivals' output as well, and had built a small factory that manufactured most of the sexual gadgets he carried in his stores.

The money didn't just roll in; it *poured*. The average publisher needed to sell about forty percent of his print run to break even; Moore, who owned the publishing company, the printing press, the distribution agencies, the bookstores, and all the associated items, broke even with a sale of five percent. He sold more than five percent, though; more than eighty percent, in point of fact. It wasn't that his products were superior; they weren't. But when you control the distribution lifelines, you control the industry, and when you have the power to fire any distributor who puts a single copy of a rival's publication on display before all of your own are sold, you are a lead-pipe cinch to wind up with the lion's share of the market. Moore not only had the lion's share of the market, but held on to it with the tenacity of a lion defending his kill from all the scavengers of the jungle.

The orders came slowly as Moore studied the reports: fire this man, promote that woman, sell this store, print more copies of that magazine, kill this line of plastic sex aids, place ten more girls in that city. Pryor took it all down on a pocket computer and left to set the wheels in motion. He returned a few minutes later, a beer in his hand, and sat back down opposite Moore.

"That's your fourth today," noted Moore disapprovingly, gesturing toward the beer.

"Haven't your spies got anything better to do than measure my alcoholic consumption?" asked Pryor with no trace of surprise or concern.

"They're doing it."

"Maybe you ought to send them over to the Thrill Show. Your new partners have already been pulling strings to get out of their contract."

"Let 'em," said Moore coldly. "This is *my* town." He paused. "If they want to mess around with me, they'd better choose a city where I don't own half the politicians and all of the coroners."

"What's the show like?" asked Pryor. "I haven't had a chance to get out there yet."

"Maybe if you'd stop trying to seduce my secretary and my stockbroker and every other woman who's ever had anything to do with me, you could find the time," said Moore with a mirthless smile.

"Can't blame a guy for trying," replied Pryor easily. "Besides, not everyone can lead your ascetic life."

"That's what keeps us in business," said Moore. "The way *I* live, and the way *they* live."

Pryor stared across the desk for a long moment, mystified as always by the concept of a criminal kingpin who grew rich off his victims' lusts and seemed violently opposed to displaying any of those drives himself. Finally he shrugged.

"You still haven't told me what the show is like," he said, taking a swallow of his beer.

"Pretty typical," said Moore. "They're selling dreams, just like all the others."

"That's a good commodity these days."

"It always was," said Moore. He clasped his hands together and stared thoughtfully at his fingertips. "I wonder if there isn't a cheaper way to go about it, though."

"What are you talking about?" asked Pryor.

"Dreams."

"We're already in it, except that we call them drugs."

Moore shook his head irritably. "Drugs *create* dreams. I want to *fulfill* them."

"You mean like putting a harlot in every room?" chuckled Pryor.

"I'm being serious, Ben," said Moore coldly.

"You always are," sighed Pryor. "But I haven't got the foggiest notion of what you're talking about."

"Just what I said: Dream Come True, Inc. I wonder if it's feasible?"

"How the hell should I know? What's the angle?"

"The angle is simply this: we'll fulfill any dream for a price. After all, the Thrill Show isn't going to be here forever, and besides, they're long on promises and short on results."

"Give me a for-instance."

"Okay," said Moore slowly. "Let's say some guy finds his life unbearably dull . . ."

"Which he probably does."

"And he wants to have one all-out fling and some excitement."

"Such as?"

Moore shrugged. "I don't know. Let's say he wants to rob the First National Bank."

"You're not seriously suggesting that we do it for him?" said Pryor incredulously.

"No. But what if we help him do it for himself? We make up the plans, help him case the joint, supply all the muscle and expertise he needs, and guarantee that he gets away scot-free."

"There's got to be a gimmick," said Pryor skeptically. "Why do we take all the risks so he can grab all the dough?"

"Of course there's a gimmick," said Moore patiently. "We're not altruists, Ben. What if we charge him a flat fee of half a million, hold his take down to a hundred thousand, and split our fee sixty-forty with the bank? Everybody's happy, nobody goes to jail, and we all get a little richer." He paused. "Anyway, it's got possibilities. What do you think?"

"I think you picked a loaded example," said Pryor. "There are something like nine elephants left in the world, all worth tens of millions. What if he wants to shoot them all in one afternoon? Or take an example closer to home: I would love to kill my ex-wife and sire fifty bastard children within a year. What can this outfit do for me?"

"We could certainly supply you with fifty women over a three-month span; the rest would be up to you. As for killing your ex-wife

. . . well, that could probably be arranged for a substantially higher fee." Moore smiled. "Of course, you'd have to tell us exactly which of your many ex-wives you had in mind."

"And the elephants?"

"He'd have to be a very rich daydreamer," said Moore with a shrug. "Anyway, have our people work out a *schema* of what is actually possible with this notion, and have them get it back to me in a day or two. Why should I split all the dreamers' money with Mr. Nightspore and Mr. Thrush?"

"Are those really their names?" asked Pryor with a disbelieving grin.

"What's in a name? It's their business that interests me."

Pryor left a few minutes later, and Moore took a brief lunch break, after which he began working on some of those enterprises that the government did *not* know about. Most of it was accomplished by telephone, through so many middlemen that nothing could be traced back to him. No records, written or computerized, were kept anywhere, and even Pryor didn't know the full extent of the operation, though Moore knew that he spent a lot of his own time and money trying to find out.

Moore left the office in late afternoon, as was his custom, boarded an underground monorail, and, accompanied by a solitary bodyguard, went to the center of town. The area had once been called the Loop, because of the elevated train tracks that encircled it, and the sobriquet still held, though the tracks had long since been torn down and the vast business buildings, all interconnected on every level and covered by an enormous dome, took up three square miles of incredibly valuable real estate. The suburbs might know rain and snow, but the inner city was always clear and pleasant.

He rode the slidewalks and escalators until, half a mile above the ground, he came to his regular Tuesday-evening eateasy, a swank and illegal little restaurant with a grubby exterior that proclaimed to all nonmembers that it was a branch of a silicone surgery beautification chain. The government had been rationing meat and most other non-soya products for more than a decade, but men and women of means soon found entrepreneurs to cater to their tastes and hungers, and the eateasies had become some of the more affluent pillars of the huge underground economy.

Moore left his bodyguard outside and his umbrella at the door — it never rained within the enclosed downtown section of the city, but he carried it religiously—and was ushered to a small table in the back, where he dined on a felonious meal of genuine veal cutlets and whipped potatoes. He ordered blueberry pie for dessert (six months for selling it, one thousand dollars for eating it, courtesy of the United States Fair Food Administration), capped it off with a cup of real coffee, and paid the standard flat fee of six hundred dollars. Then, sated, he picked up his umbrella and, joined by his bodyguard, he reentered the world of soybean by-products and flavored water.

He toyed with the idea of returning to the Thrill Show, hunting up the phony blind man who had duped him yesterday, and offering him a job in the organization, but concluded that the man was sharp enough to have a different gimmick for every night of the week and would be impossible to spot.

He decided to go home for the night instead. As he approached the monorail station he reached into his pocket for a token, and felt his fingers come into contact with a piece of paper. He pulled it out and saw that it was a business card:

THE BIZARRE BAZAAR
Specializing in the Unusual
461 N. LaSalle—5th Level

Scrawled across the back of it, in nearly illegible handwriting, were the words: "Come alone."

It could be a trap, of course; after all, if his life weren't in continual danger, he wouldn't require a bodyguard in the first place. However, most of his bigger deals were consummated in just such a manner—a politician who couldn't be seen going into Moore's office, a rival's underling with some information to sell, a deserted lover ready to turn against a man or woman Moore was out to ruin. After a moment's debate with himself, he dismissed his bodyguard and rode the escalator to the fifth level of Wabash Street. Then he took a slidewalk to Randolph Street, transferred to a northbound slidewalk, got off at LaSalle, and began walking north on a stationary ramp.

When he crossed over the long-dry bed of the Chicago River, which now housed a park and a huge sporting complex, he became aware of a subtle change in the stores and shops. Gone were the huge, brightly lit department stores, the plush, velvet-walled jewelers, the fashion shops and gift emporiums and other high-quality specialty shops. In their place were grubby little antique stores, secondhand bookstores drowning in stacks and stacks of dusty, moldy volumes, bars and brothels and warehouses.

Finally he came to the address he sought. It looked like a little hole in the wall, a storefront out of some Western ghost town. The windows were covered by dark, opaque shades, there were no signs, stating either the name of the establishment or what it dealt in, and a distinct smell of incense emanated from its half-open doorway.

He took one last took around to make sure he hadn't been followed, then walked into the store. He found himself in a dimly lit maze, with the walls blackened up to the ceiling, and followed it carefully as it continued to turn back upon itself. Finally he emerged into a long, narrow room that was illuminated only by an occasional red light bulb.

There were two glass showcases, one running down each side of the room. On display in them were various grotesque torture devices: spiked necklaces, tongue ties, exotic branding irons, razor-sharp chastity belts, instruments for piercing or removing all limbs and organs not essential to the minimal maintenance of life. Hung on the walls (or nailed to them; he wasn't sure which) were shriveled human heads, hands, legs, fingers, genitalia, noses, eyes, and ears. Stacked neatly in a corner were dozens of spears, spikes, and prods.

"May I help you?" said a hoarse voice from behind him.

He turned and found himself confronted by a little man with a satin patch over one eye. The man extended a hand, which was missing two fingers and part of a thumb, and Moore mechanically took and shook it.

"Welcome to the Bizarre Bazaar," said the man. "My name is Krebbs. If there is anything you don't see, just ask. We have many more rooms, each designed around a single theme."

"I'm not a customer," replied Moore, showing the card to Krebbs.

"Ah, well," sighed the man, "there was no harm in asking. One must try to make a living." He smiled. "Surely you, of all people, can appreciate that."

"You sound as if you know me."

"I know *of* you, Mr. Moore," said Krebbs. "You're one of my idols, if truth be known. Ah, to wield such power, to maim and kill and destroy! It must seem like paradise itself!"

"You must have me confused with someone else," said Moore in cold, level tones. "I'm just a businessman."

"Whatever you say, Mr. Moore," said Krebbs with a grin.

"*That's* what I say. Now, why did you ask me to come here?"

"Oh, but I didn't," said Krebbs. "I assure you, Mr. Moore, that I am content to worship you from afar."

"Then who did?"

"I can take you to her if you like," offered Krebbs.

"To who?"

"Why, to the young lady you've come to see."

"What's her name?" asked Moore.

"You needn't be coy with me, Mr. Moore," said Krebbs. "I told you—I'm on *your* side. If you wish to conduct your liaisons in my place of business, I'm only too happy to oblige."

"Where is she?" asked Moore, deciding that further questions would be fruitless.

"She wasn't quite sure when you'd arrive," replied Krebbs, "so I had her wait for you in our Unique Boutique. I'm sure she'll find something suitable to wear there, and there's a huge bed just across the hall." He gave Moore a sly wink with his only eye and took him by the arm, leading him to a curtain of hanging beads. "Fifth room on the right."

Moore shook his arm loose and walked down the corridor until he came to the fifth, and last, right-hand door, then opened it softly and walked in. The room was as poorly lit as the rest of the shop, and seemed to be composed of nothing but clothes racks and mirrors. It was actually quite small, but the mirrors, which covered the walls, ceiling, and floor, gave it the appearance of extending to infinity in all directions.

A blond girl stood at the far end of the room, about twenty feet from him. She wore leather hip boots with long, sharp heels, shoulder-length leather gloves, a black waist cincher, and nothing else. In her left hand she held a small cat-o'-nine-tails, which had bright, little metal prongs at the end of each tail. Her face was covered by a catlike mask, replete with silver whiskers.

"I had a little time on my hands," she said in a low, husky voice, "so I decided to try out some of the merchandise." She turned around gracefully. "Do you like it?"

"I don't buy this shit; I sell it," said Moore distastefully. "Am I supposed to know you?"

"Would you like to?"

"Not especially," he replied. "Did you place the card in my pocket?"

"No."

"But you had it placed there?"

"Yes." She moved a bit closer to him, making the tails undulate rhythmically with a flick of her wrist.

"Why?"

"I have something to give you."

"What?"

"*This!*" she whispered, suddenly bringing the whip down toward his face.

Moore reached out his arm instinctively and absorbed most of the blow's force on the fleshy part of his biceps. He backed away, startled, and the girl came after him.

"Who sent you?" he demanded, dodging another blow. "What the hell is going on here?"

There was no response from the girl, except for a renewed effort to rip his face apart with the whip. He knew better than to keep using his arm as a shield, and he turned and ran down the narrow corridor to the room where he had met Krebbs. Once there, he looked around for the one-eyed proprietor, but the place was deserted. He raced to the stacked weapons and pulled a hooked spear off the top of the heap.

"All right," he said, leveling the weapon between her breasts as she entered the room. "Are you ready to tell me what this is all about?"

The girl screamed an obscenity and swung the whip again. He ducked and prodded her shoulder with the spear. A little trickle of blood appeared, but the girl didn't seem to notice it. Unmindful of the spear, she continued chasing him around the room. Finally he decided that he had no choice but to start defending himself in earnest, and he cut her twice on the arm, once deeply. She fought on like a cornered beast, totally ignoring the wounds. He practically severed her ear with the next swipe of his weapon, again with no effect.

"Of course!" he said suddenly. "You're one of the Living Dartboards!" He ducked as she picked up a glass jar from the counter and hurled it at him. "Who put you up to this—Nightspore or Thrush? Or was it the pair of them?"

Her only response was to kick out with her boot, trying to stab him with its long, murderously sharp heel. He stepped aside, grabbed her leg, and twisted it. She fell heavily to the floor, and he leaped on top of her, turning her onto her stomach and holding her motionless. It took six sharp blows to the base of her skull before he finally managed to render her unconscious.

He dragged her over to one of the red light bulbs and examined her back and neck very carefully. Yes, there were the tiny, almost invisible scars from the nerve-severing operation that had rendered her insensitive to pain.

He decided against waiting to question her when she awoke. After all, if she didn't want to talk, nothing he could do was going to change her mind—and for all he knew, Krebbs was still lurking around somewhere, waiting to put a bullet in his back. He toyed with the notion of covering the girl with a blanket, slinging her over his shoulder, and taking her with him, but he knew he wouldn't be able to control her if she regained consciousness, so he decided to leave her to the tender mercies of one of his security squads. Still worried about Krebbs, he pulled out a cellular phone and called Pryor.

"Ben? Moore here. It appears that one of our new partners has gotten delusions of grandeur. Maybe both of them. . . . Yeah. Right. . . . You won't believe me. . . . A naked blonde with a whip, if you must know." He grimaced at Pryor's reply. "I *told* you you wouldn't believe me. Anyway, I want you to collect the muscle and find out which one tried to whack me. And while you're at it, send a squad to a little joint on LaSalle Street called the Bizarre Bazaar, at 461 North on the fifth level, and do a job on it. You'll find the girl there. I think she's got an accomplice—a guy with a maimed hand. Bring him in if you find him hanging around the place. . . . No, I'll be fine. Catch you in the morning."

He hung up, walked to the nearest monorail platform, and within ten minutes was approaching the entrance to his apartment, part of an exclusive complex at the south end of the inner-city dome. He nodded to his security men and went in, locking the door behind him. Then, being a thorough man, he began a methodical search to make doubly certain nothing had been stolen or tampered with. When he was finally satisfied that everything was as it should be, he sat down in an antique leather chair, put his feet up on a stuffed armadillo that he used for a hassock, and mentally reviewed the events of the evening.

His conclusion was that they just didn't make any sense. Any fool would know that sooner or later he'd be able to spot the girl as being from the Thrill Show—and Nightspore and Thrush, while certainly malleable, hadn't struck him as fools.

Suddenly restless, he arose and began stalking around the apartment. Like his office, his personal dwelling was modestly furnished and did not interface with the outside world except for two telephones, both unlisted. Remaining aloof from the masses that he victimized had become almost a fetish with him, and he allowed himself none of their vices for fear that their accompanying weaknesses might rub off on him. Once, as a surprise, some of his bodyguards had imported a pair of women and ensconced them in his bedroom before he got home; he had rushed to the phone and fired them on the spot, then ordered Pryor to come over and take the women away. Sex, especially the kind the women had promised him in low, sultry voices, was hardly apt to be boring, but he was in the business of selling sex—among other things—and bartenders don't drink when on duty. For one week every three months he packed up and left everything in Pryor's charge. He never said where he went or what he did on these quarterly trips, nor did anyone ask him, but the betting around the office was that the bartender went on a binge four times a year.

The apartment contained no drugs, no alcohol, nothing that could possibly be construed as a means of escaping from reality. When he worked at selling fantasies he practiced only austerity: he partook of no sex, no stimulants, no hobbies or crafts. He had two indulgences: one was gourmet food, and the other was his library. From floor to ceiling all the walls were lined with books, some new, some incredibly old. They were neither neat nor ordered, but he knew where every title was, what knowledge or emotion each author had to impart to him. There were poets and playwrights, philosophers and biographers, modern fiction intermixed with ancient and future fact, and even an old, timeworn copy of the Bible.

It was to his library that he now turned for relief and relaxation. He picked up a couple of works by Wilde and Austen, chronicles of more civilized eras that had no need for a business such as his, returned to his oversized leather chair, sat down with a grunt, and prepared to read himself to sleep.

He was drifting in the halfworld between clarity and slumber when the buzzing of the phone brought him to instant wakefulness.

"Moore here."

"This is Ben. How's the ravisher of Living Dartboards?"

"Knock it off and get to the point."

"The point is that we've got a couple of problems," said Pryor.
"You've been to the Thrill Show?"

"Yes."

"And the Bizarre Bazaar?"

"No such place."

"The hell there isn't!" snapped Moore. "It's at"—he pulled the card out of his pocket "461 North LaSalle, on the fifth level."

"The hell there *is*," replied Pryor, not without a trace of enjoyment at Moore's distress. "We went through the whole four-hundred block, both sides, and it's just not there."

"I was there two hours ago!"

"You're sure it wasn't *South* LaSalle, or 461 North on some other street—Clark or Wells, maybe?"

"Damn it, Ben—I know where I was and I know what happened to me!"

"I'm sure you do," said Pryor. "But the fact remains that the store isn't there. Besides, the whole thing sounds like some adolescent fantasy. If I didn't know you better, I'd say you'd been drinking."

"I'll take you there myself, first thing in the morning," said Moore disgustedly. "What about Nightspore and Thrush?"

"I know this is going to sound like we're operating in two different worlds, but they didn't know anything about it."

"Horseshit!"

"That's the strongest word I ever heard you use," said Pryor, amused.

"They had to know something," persisted Moore, ignoring him. "We were pretty thorough."

"*How* thorough?"

"You are now the sole surviving partner of the Nightspore and Thrush International Traveling Circus and Thrill Show."

"Great," spat Moore. "Just what I always wanted." He sighed. "Damn it, Ben, I told you to *question* them, not kill them!"

"You also told me that one of them was behind all this, so we used enough force to get the answers we needed. It was just their hard luck that they happened to be innocent. I've got our legal eagles down at City Hall smoothing things over. I think we can handle it."

"Operating on the assumption—probably erroneous—that our muscle didn't kill them before they could tell the truth, who the hell sent this girl after me?"

"The only thing to do is find the girl and beat it out of her," replied Pryor. "I'd love to try."

"Lots of luck," said Moore, repressing an urge to laugh. "You've got a remarkably single-minded approach to problem-solving, Ben." He paused. "As for identifying her, hell, I probably wouldn't recognize her with her pants on. Check the Thrill Show and find out which of the Living Dartboards was missing for a couple of hours starting at about six o'clock this evening. Track her down and bring her back to the office. Then check out the Bizarre Bazaar again, and if it's really not there, assemble some muscle in my office tomorrow morning at nine sharp and we'll go hunting for it. And Ben?"

"Yeah?"

"Unless you want to find out what happens when I become seriously displeased with someone, don't mess up again."

He placed the receiver back on the hook, picked up Jane Austen, and tried to read himself to sleep again.

It wasn't so easy this time.

3

"You look even more frazzled than usual for this time of day," remarked Moore as Pryor entered his office the next morning. "Shall I assume that we haven't accomplished a hell of a lot?"

"A fair assumption," admitted Pryor. "I did manage to assuage the high moral principles of the city fathers, though. They now agree that both Nightspore and Thrush died of heart failure."

"Well, that's something, anyway," said Moore. "What about the girl?"

"We checked out the Living Dartboard show, and it seems that one of them—a Lisa Walpole—has been missing since four o'clock yesterday."

"Blonde?"

Pryor nodded. "And from what I can tell, she's just the type who'd rather whip you to death than stand back and shoot you. I've got a couple of men trying to pick up her trail, and we've stationed agents at all the airports and bus stations. If she's anywhere in the Chicago complex, we ought to turn her up in a day or two." He paused. "We learned one other thing about her, too: she was sleeping with Thrush."

"Are you sure?" asked Moore, frowning. "I thought when they severed the pain receptors, it deadened the capacity for pleasure as well." He paused, then shrugged. "Oh, well, I suppose there's no law that says a girl who sleeps with her boss has to enjoy it. But I still can't figure out the connection. If Thrush didn't put her up to it, then what the hell was she doing there?"

Pryor shrugged. "I imagine we'll have to catch her to find out."

"While you're at it, I've got someone else who needs a bit of catching: an old man named Krebbs, sixtyish, about five foot seven or eight. He's wearing a patch over one eye—I can't remember which—and his right hand is missing a couple of fingers and part of the thumb. Real slimy type."

"I'll skip the slimy part, and get the rest of the description to our men right away," said Pryor, entering the information on his ever-present pocket computer.

"How about the Bizarre Bazaar?"

"I checked it out again myself, and it's simply not there. The phone book doesn't have it listed either. Are you absolutely sure of that address?"

Moore produced the card and slid it across the desk to Pryor. "We'll make that our next order of business. Leave someone here to keep an eye on things, gather up half a dozen security men, and let's get this show on the road."

Half an hour later Moore, Pryor, and six security men turned onto the North 400 block on the fifth level of LaSalle Street. They walked past two back-number magazine shops and an exceptionally dirty soya restaurant, and then Moore pointed to a building some fifty yards away.

"There it is!" he exclaimed. "What the hell were you talking about, Ben?"

"All I see is an old religious-goods shop," said Pryor, quickening his pace to keep up with Moore. "I checked it out this morning, and it's legit."

The windows of the store were no longer covered, and as Moore looked in he saw nothing but a tiny shop, no more than fifteen feet deep, its walls and counters covered by Bibles, crucifixes, and other denominational keepsakes. An elderly woman stood behind one of the counters, looking through a pile of papers, which Moore took to be invoices or index cards.

"May I be of some help to you gentlemen?" inquired the woman as Moore and Pryor entered the store, followed by their security men.

"Where is Krebbs?" demanded Moore.

"Krebbs?" repeated the woman thoughtfully. "He must be one of our newer authors. I don't believe we have any of his works, though you are of course welcome to browse through our stock of books yourself."

Moore unrolled a large wad of bills and laid them on the counter. "Last night there was a man named Krebbs working here. I want to know where he is."

"Here? Last night? You must be mistaken. No one works here except me and my daughter-in-law. We have no one named Krebbs here."

"Let's try another one." He stared coldly at her. "Does the name Solomon Moody Moore mean anything to you?"

"No."

"Lie to me once more and it will," he promised. "How do I get to the back?"

"The back of what?"

"The back of the store," he replied. "It goes on for hundreds of feet."

The woman stared at him as if he could be expected to fall to the ground and begin foaming at the mouth at any moment.

"The store ends at the wall right behind me," she said at last, speaking as if to a child. "That's all there is, except for a bathroom over there."

She indicated a door on a side wall.

"I told you that's all there was," grinned Pryor.

"How long have you been in business at this location?" continued Moore.

"Thirty-seven years."

"Where were you last night?"

"Right here, of course."

"How late?"

"Until nine o'clock, as always," she replied. "Are you sure you're feeling well?"

"No, I am not feeling well!" snapped Moore. "I am feeling angry as all hell, and getting angrier by the second!" He gestured to the bills lying on the counter. "I'm going to ask you one last time: where is Krebbs?"

"I keep telling you—I don't know anyone called Krebbs."

Moore picked up his money and put it back into his pocket, then turned to the head of his security team.

"See that wall?"

"Yes, Mr. Moore."

"Break it down," he said, stepping back out of the way.

"Have you gone crazy?" said Pryor. "It's a goddamned Bible shop, nothing more!"

"If you talk like a fool, I'm going to have to start treating you like one, Ben," said Moore, deciding that it really was getting near time to dispose of Pryor. "I was here. I know what I saw."

"If you don't get out of here and stop harassing me right this minute, I'm going to call the police!" shouted the woman.

"On the contrary," said Moore. "You're going to stay right where you are until I say otherwise." He turned to his security team. "One of you men come over and keep an eye on her."

"Will a laser be okay, sir?" asked the man who was examining the wall.

"I don't care how you do it," replied Moore. "Just get it done."

The man pulled out a laser device and began tracing a line from left to right, about twenty inches below the ceiling. He came to a weak spot a couple of feet before reaching the southernmost corner.

"That's it!" he said, throwing a shoulder against the wall. It crumbled like the thin plasterboard it was, leaving a doorsized hole through which Moore, Pryor, and five of the security men passed.

They found themselves in the main room of the Bizarre Bazaar, with its weapons and torture devices and grisly souvenirs. Moore walked through the room and went down a dimly lit corridor to the Unique Boutique.

"What do you think of my adolescent fantasy, Ben?" he asked with grim satisfaction.

Pryor shook his head. "I was wrong. But if it had happened to me and I'd found this Bible shop here the next morning, I would have thought I dreamed it all."

"That's why I'm the boss of this outfit."

"I don't follow you."

"I never fantasize," replied Moore.

One of the security men approached them. "There's no one in any of the rooms, sir," he announced. "We did find a number of long, black boards, though, which must be the maze you described."

"Look around and see what else you can dig up," said Moore, dismissing him. "Ben, if you're all through sounding like a complete idiot, suppose you tell me what you think is going on here."

"Someone tried to kill you and missed," replied Pryor, "and then decided that it wouldn't be real healthy to stick around and wait for us to show up." He shrugged. "Makes sense. I don't imagine Al Capone ever gave anyone a second chance at *him*, either."

Moore shook his head. "Too simple. There's a lot more to this than meets the eye. Let's have a little chat with our religious fanatic up front and see if we can get some answers."

When they got back to the false front of the Bizarre Bazaar they found their security man lying dead in a pool of his own blood, a bullet lodged in his temple. The woman was nowhere to be seen.

Moore yelled for other security men, who arrived seconds later.

"Who knows anything about gunshot wounds?" he demanded. "Did the old lady do this?"

One of the men examined the corpse. "Not a chance," he announced after a brief inspection. "This came from an awfully powerful handgun. If she'd fired at close range, it would have taken most of his head off. I'd guess that somebody opened the door and fired from there. There must have been a silencer, too, or we'd have heard one hell of a bang."

"So we can assume Krebbs or the Dartboard was keeping the place under surveillance, just in case I came back," said Moore. He turned to Pryor. "Ben, you got a good look at the old woman; see what you can do about tracking her down. Two of you men take this place apart and see if you can turn up anything that might explain what's been going on. When you're through, rig the whole place up with an electronic watchdog system. You other three, come with me and see to it that I get back to the office in one piece."

He walked warily to the monorail system, half expecting to be shot down at any moment and cursing the day that individual transportation had been outlawed within the city limits, but nothing unusual happened and he was back in his office fifteen minutes later.

The moment he arrived he ordered round-the-clock security forces to be posted throughout the building and had sleeping quarters set up just down the hall from his office. Then, because he was nothing if not thorough, he ordered still more security men to patrol all the possible approaches to the building.

Pryor and his other agents reported in regularly, but nobody seemed able to turn up any information. Finally, when he found himself unable to concentrate on the mundane aspects of his business, he kept himself occupied by working out the basic details of Dream Come True with a few members of his staff, and ordered them to put it into operation.

Anyone would be able to walk in and order up a dream—but if the dream was illegal, as he expected most of them to be, a rigid check would be run on the potential customer to make sure he wasn't working for any of the government or law enforcement agencies. If he was cleared, preliminary plans would be worked out, after which a price would be agreed upon. Moore decided to set up the first office at the Thrill Show on the assumption that a lot of people would go there with money to spend, and he wanted a broad cross-section of dream requests to see which particulars of the operation still had to be smoothed out.

He spent the next two days involving himself in the administration of his little empire, and the next two nights tossing uncomfortably on rollaway bed in the adjoining office. Then, when he had just about made up his mind to go home, one of his security men entered the office.

"Yes?" said Moore.

"We've got her, sir."

"The old woman?"

"Lisa Walpole."

"Better and better," commented Moore. "Where was she?"

"At the airport. She had a one-way ticket for Buenos Aires."

"You did a good job," said Moore. "There'll be a bonus for everyone involved. Bring her in here, and then send for Abe Bernstein."

"Your doctor?"

Moore nodded.

"Any instructions for him, sir?"

"He'll know what to bring."

Lisa Walpole, dressed conservatively this time, was ushered into the office, her hands securely tied behind her back. Her left ear was swathed in bandages. Moore gestured toward a chair, and she walked over to it and sat down, glaring venomously at him.

"Please leave us now," said Moore to the security man. "Miss Walpole and I would like to be alone for a while."

As the door slammed shut, Moore leaned forward and studied the Living Dartboard. "I was right," he said with a smile. "I would never have recognized you with your clothes on."

She stared defiantly at him, her lips pressed together.

"I have a few questions I'd like answered, Lisa," he continued. "For starters, suppose you tell me who hired you to kill me three nights ago."

"Go fuck yourself!"

"Was it the late unlamented Mr. Thrush?"

"You'd like to know that, wouldn't you?" she said contemptuously.

"Indeed I would," agreed Moore. "And what's more, I *will* know very shortly."

"Are you going to torture it out of me?" she asked with a sarcastic laugh.

He shook his head. "No. I don't think a little thing like torture would bother you, even if you hadn't had your pain receptors severed. Of course," he added conversationally, "I could always slash an artery or two and threaten to let you bleed to death if you didn't tell me what I want to know, but it would stain the carpet—and besides, I suspect that you're just a little too infatuated with death for a stunt like that to serve any useful purpose. And your unfortunate condition precludes the use of our Neverlie Machine; after all, there's not much sense in shooting an electrical charge through your body every time you lie if you can't even feel it."

"Then how do you expect to drag it out of me?"

"I'm not going to drag it out of you at all," said Moore. "You're going to tell me of your own volition."

"Hah!"

Moore pressed a button on his intercom. "Is Bernstein here yet?"

"Yes," replied a feminine voice. "He's waiting in your outer office."

"Send him in."

The door opened a moment later and a small, portly, silver-haired man entered the room, carrying a dark leather bag in his right hand.

"Thanks for coming so fast, Abe," said Moore.

"I was downstairs in the sauna, sweating off another one of my wife's parties," replied Bernstein with a smile. "I hear you had a pretty exciting weekend, Solomon."

"I'll tell you about it later," said Moore. "In the meantime, we seem to have a little problem that requires your talents," he added, indicating Lisa Walpole.

"I saw Ben on my way in, and he told me about it—though I assumed as much when you couldn't use the Neverlie Machine." As he spoke, Bernstein opened his bag and withdrew a syringe and a small bottle. He filled the syringe, walked over to the girl, and injected its contents into a vein in her forearm.

"Give her about two minutes," he told Moore. "Her eyes will glaze over a bit, but she'll be able to speak cogently. Ask direct questions, and try to finish up within ten minutes."

"Thanks, Abe," said Moore. "You'd better leave now."

Bernstein nodded and walked out of the office, as Moore counted off two hundred seconds on his watch, just to be on the safe side.

"All right, Lisa," he said, rising and walking over to the girl. "We're going to have a little talk now. Did Thrush put you up to killing me?"

"No," she said emotionlessly.

"Nightspore?"

"No."

"Then it was Krebbs!" he exclaimed. "But why?"

"It wasn't Krebbs."

"Who was it, then?"

"Jeremiah."

"Jeremiah?" repeated Moore. "Who the hell is Jeremiah?"

"He's a young guy who hangs out around the Thrill Show," said Lisa, her voice a droning monotone.

"What's his last name?"

"I don't know. He calls himself Jeremiah the B."

"I never heard of him in my life," said Moore, frowning. "What has he got against me?"

"Nothing."

"Then why did he have you try to kill me?"

"Thrush told me that you had forced your way into the business, and that you had plenty of money."

"And you relayed that to Jeremiah?" asked Moore.

"Yes."

"When and where?"

"In bed, the same night Thrush told me."

"He's a fast operator, I'll give him that," said Moore. "Now suppose you tell me exactly what I was being set up for."

"Jeremiah figured you'd carry a big roll of cash with you."

"Then you were just going to rob me?" said Moore dubiously.

"No. A plain robbery wouldn't have been safe. We felt we had to kill you first."

"We? Does that mean you and Krebbs?"

"No. Jeremiah and me. He was in one of the other rooms, hiding."

"Brave fellow," Moore commented dryly. "How about Krebbs? Where does he fit in?"

"Jeremiah knew him, and promised him a piece of the action if we could use the Bazaar."

"And the little old lady in the religious shop?"

There was no answer.

"Did you know that Krebbs camouflaged his store as a religious-goods shop the next morning?"

"No."

"Do you know of an elderly woman who was involved with either Krebbs or Jeremiah?"

"No."

"One last question: where can I find this Jeremiah?"

"I don't know. Probably at the Thrill Show."

"Thank you, Lisa," said Moore, pressing a button on his intercom system that signaled for two security men. "You did very well. The fact that I'm going to let you live, at least for the time being, should not imply that I am a forgiving man. You'll remain here, in this building, until I decide what to do with you."

He cut her bonds and ordered the security team to incarcerate her on another floor, then summoned Pryor to his office.

"Abe mentioned that you were in. Any news?"

"None," replied Pryor. "I think we must have checked out every Krebbs in the city, and I had one of our porn artists, of all people, render a sketch of the old lady that I passed out to all of our agents. There's nothing left to do now but sit and wait." He lit a cigarette. "By the way, did you learn anything from the Dartboard?"

"Plenty," said Moore. "For one thing, Nightspore and Thrush had nothing to do with it."

"I told you they weren't lying," said Pryor smugly.

"And *I* told *you* that you killed them for nothing," replied Moore irritably.

"What's done is done," said Pryor, shrugging off their deaths with a single sentence. "Did you find out who's behind it?"

"It's hard to believe, but some Thrill Show grifter found out I carry a big bankroll, and the whole thing was just a setup to roll me."

"It must be catching," remarked Pryor cheerfully.

"What are you talking about?" said Moore.

"Just that this grifter isn't the only guy who's decided to spread the wealth around. Dream Come True had its first customer this morning." He withdrew a sheet of paper from his notebook and handed it to Moore. "Take a look."

Moore read it, then read it again to make sure his eyes weren't playing tricks.

Dream Come True, Inc.
Preliminary Application Form

HEIGHT: *6 feet, 2 inches*
WEIGHT: *187 pounds*
HAIR: *Brown*
EYES: *Blue*
DISTINGUISHING MARKS: *None*
AGE: *22*
NATIONALITY: *American*
RELIGION: *None*
CURRENT ADDRESS: *Refused to divulge*
MARITAL STATUS: *Single*
FINANCIAL STATUS: *Unclear at present*
FIRST CONTACT: *December 15, 2047*
DREAM DESIRED: *To murder Solomon Moody Moore and take over sole ownership of Dream Come True, Inc.*
SIGNATURE: *Jeremiah the B*

"Persistent son of a bitch, isn't he?" said Moore, replacing the form on his desk.

"I don't think I follow you," said Pryor.

"Jeremiah the B just happens to be the guy who tried to set me up at the Bizarre Bazaar."

"And now he's trying to use Dream Come True to do the same thing?" said Pryor, greatly amused by this revelation.

Moore nodded. "He's got guts, I'll give him that."

"Are we going to do anything about him?"

"I think we'd better—before he gets around to doing something about me. As soon as the Thrill Show shuts down for the night, send some muscle over to pay our friend Jeremiah a friendly little visit."

"And?"

"And kill him," said Moore.

4

The young man sat up in bed, fondly patted the bare, rounded buttocks of his still-sleeping partner, and began putting on his clothes. He knew they'd be coming after him before long, and the Thrill Show was the first place they'd look, which meant that it was time to make himself scarce.

He stuck his head out the door of the trailer, made sure that no one was lurking in the shadows, and slipped out into the night, avoiding the bright lights and gaudy neon signs.

Jeremiah had confidence in his ability to escape detection for as long as need be. Moore might own or control most of the vice dens in the Chicago complex, but he didn't *know* them. Jeremiah did, and that was all the advantage he needed.

Moore would turn the city upside down trying to find him, but it wouldn't do him any good. Jeremiah could stay buried until Moore gave up the search, and then make his pitch: a one-third partnership. He'd learned enough about Moore to know that he never destroyed what he could assimilate, and if Jeremiah could hold off the entire force of Moore's organization, he would have shown all the boldness and resourcefulness that Moore could demand of a would-be associate.

The setup at the Bizarre Bazaar had been just that—a setup. He hadn't expected Lisa Walpole to be able to kill Moore. If she had pulled it off, so much the better; but the likelihood was that she'd fail, and that Moore would find some way to extract his name from her. He knew nothing of her current whereabouts, but felt reasonably certain that Moore had her by now. However, he viewed the Dream Come True application as his masterpiece. If there was a better way of announcing his presence, he couldn't think of it.

The trick now was to stay alive, to keep Moore constantly aware of the fact that he was still in Chicago, and to wait him out. He'd been playing for pennies long enough; this was his chance to make the big time in one giant step, and he had no intention of blowing it.

He had already decided where to hole up: Darktown, that sleazy underground section of the city, just west of the old Loop, with its tawdry subterranean dens of drugs and sin. Whether you wanted to buy a woman, a man, a child, a murderer, a narcotic, a fingerprint graft, or whatever, if it was illegal or contraband you could get it wholesale in Darktown.

It wasn't an easy place to reach, though anyone who had business there knew the way. It existed, ghostlike and serene, a good quarter-mile below the huge, forty-foot-diameter sewers that ran beneath the city. The service elevators and escalators stopped at the mammoth pipelines, and after that one had to know exactly where to go to find his way into Darktown.

The construction of Darktown had consisted of one disastrous blunder after another. It had originally been commissioned by the city as a storm-water reservoir, then changed to a garbage dump. During the initial drilling and digging the contractors had, not once but three different times, come upon the Lake Michigan water table, practically drowning themselves and their huge work crews. Then, when they finally managed to avoid the water, they created an artificial cavern about half a mile square, only to have it collapse within the first month of its existence. These setbacks were followed by ventilation and temperature-control problems, and finally, as costs continued to skyrocket, the project was abandoned, leaving a massive but empty area one mile long and just over half a mile wide, with heights varying from fifty to ninety feet. It stood deserted for almost a decade, and then the criminal element moved in and took it over.

The first to go underground were the whores, the pimps, and the drug merchants. They were soon followed by the fences, who built long, low warehouses in which furs, jewels, paintings, appliances, and the million and one collectible items that so fascinated the bored multitudes could age before going back on the market.

Then came the dealers in big-ticket contraband products. Robots had made a brief appearance in human society before people discovered that their presence created even more leisure time; they had been outlawed for years, but they could still be purchased in Darktown. Automobiles, either those that ran on fossil fuels or those requiring electric or solar power, were prohibited under most of the nation's domes, but the man who had the room to keep one in secret could buy it in Darktown. Weapon shops abounded, as did those stores specializing in the hardware of the burglar's trade.

The streets were usually empty, for Darktown was not a place for window-shoppers. If a man had business there, he knew where to go; if he didn't have business to conduct, he didn't come to Darktown.

There were no streetlights as such, but a number of argon lamps had been set into the rocky walls of the cavern, giving Darktown a perpetual dull-blue glow.

Jeremiah, all his worldly possessions in his backpack, and his entire bankroll—such as it was—folded in one of his pockets, slunk into Darktown as silently as one of the rats that prowled its alleys. He went straight to a dingy flophouse and, using an assumed name, rented a small room.

This done, he walked down the dank, foul-smelling street to the Bar Sinister, a drug saloon which, despite its relative inaccessibility, had acquired a reputation that extended far beyond the Chicago complex. Here a man could order up a glass of Venusian joyjuice—which did not come from Venus and was not a juice—and go instantly into a hallucinogenic trance that lasted anywhere from ten minutes to two hours. Some of the more notorious concoctions—the Big Bang, the Pulsar, and the ever-popular Dust Whore—were potent enough to burn out every neural circuit of a habitual user's brain in a matter of days; beginners had been known to die from two drinks. Jeremiah was no beginner.

He sat down at a small table and waited for one of the seminude waitresses to come over and take his order. Nobody seemed to notice him for the better part of five minutes. Then a well-dressed man approached him.

"Hello, Karl," said Jeremiah.

"What the hell are *you* doing here?" snapped Karl Russo, who was both the owner and bartender of the Bar Sinister.

"Waiting to order a drink," said Jeremiah.

"What are you using for brains?" demanded Russo. "Don't you know Moore's put out a hit on you?"

"His men will be looking for me at the Thrill Show," replied Jeremiah confidently. "It'll be days before they get down here."

"It will be, huh?" said Russo. "Then how do I know there's a price on your head?"

"What do you mean?"

"Who the hell do you think owns half the joints in Darktown? Moore, that's who! And you, like an idiot, let him get a description of you, right down to the color of your eyes! He's offered fifty thousand dollars to anyone who can finger you, and there's an artist's drawing of you plastered up in every joint down here."

"He works fast, doesn't he?" remarked Jeremiah, obviously unperturbed.

"He sure as hell does," answered Russo. "You'd better leave the city for a while, if you know what's good for you."

"Oh, I don't know. I kind of like it here."

"Then at least get out of Darktown."

"I especially like Darktown," said Jeremiah.

"Have you got rocks in your head?" said Russo. "How many people have you seen since you got here? Five? Ten? Half of them have probably already told Moore's goons where you are!"

"I suppose they have," said Jeremiah. "Now, how about that drink?"

Russo slammed a fist down on the table. "Goddamnit! You're acting like you *want* him to find you!"

"No. But I sure as hell want him to try."

"You're out of your mind! Whatever you think your angle is, forget it. You stay in Darktown two more hours and you're a dead man. Hell, you're probably one already."

"I'll have a Dust Whore, I think," said Jeremiah with a grin.

"You think you've got something Moore wants?" demanded Russo. "Some skill, some information? Forget it! All he wants is your scalp. I don't know why he's after you, but if he's mad enough to put out a hit and a reward, he's too damned mad to deal with."

"Not for a smart young feller like me," said Jeremiah, still smiling. He felt elated. If the whole of Moore's attention was focused on him, that would just make his bargaining position that much stronger later on.

"If you had half as much brains as guts, you'd be scared shitless," said Russo disgustedly. "Now get the hell out of here. They ain't going to shoot up my place just to get you."

"What are you talking about?"

"Get out. I'll give you a five-minute start, and then I'm letting Moore know you were here."

"I thought we were supposed to be friends," said Jeremiah.

"Only when it's good for business. And right now, being your friend is about the worst thing in the world for my business, to say nothing of my health." Russo pointed to a clock on the wall. "Four and a half minutes left."

Jeremiah shrugged, then stood up and walked to the door, giving one of the waitresses a salacious wink as he passed her.

"I'll be back next month," he said to Russo. "I figure you owe me a couple of freebies for this." He turned to the waitress. "I'll see *you* then, too."

He went to three more boardinghouses, rented a room at each of them, and was heading toward a fourth when he saw a number of men clambering down the stone stairs that were carved into the side of the wall behind the Bar Sinister. He ducked behind a small warehouse and scrutinized them carefully. They were dressed neither like wealthy slummers nor like the usual inhabitants of Darktown, and coming in quantity like this, they could only be Moore's men.

He was surprised that they had arrived so quickly, but not dismayed. It had been said, back before deer became extinct, that one such animal could easily hide from two armed hunters on a mere acre of forested ground; he was a hell of a lot smarter than a deer, and Darktown was a hell of a lot larger than an acre.

He removed his shoes and shoved them into his backpack, then donned a pair of rubber-soled sneakers and ran silently at right angles to the gunmen. He continued at top speed past a lengthy stretch of brothels and drug parlors, then ducked in between a pair of buildings to see if he was being followed.

So far, so good. He clambered up the side of one of the buildings and soon reached the roof, some twelve feet above the ground. Then, removing his backpack, he laid it down and stretched out, using it as a pillow. It would take them hours to check out the dozens of flophouses, and he'd be as safe here as anywhere. Food would be no problem, either; after he'd gone to Dream Come True, he had placed a number of small retort pouches of concentrated soya products in his backpack, enough to last him for more than two weeks, three if he was careful.

Some time later he awoke with a start. There was no way of measuring the passage of time in the subterranean chamber, but he was sure he couldn't have been dozing for more than a couple of hours, for he felt neither stiff nor refreshed. One of Moore's men was walking slowly down the street just in front of the building, and the hollow clicking of his feet on the damp pavement had awakened Jeremiah.

He arose and walked silently over to the edge of the roof. It would be an easy matter to jump down on top of the man; the force of the fall alone would probably be enough to kill him. But he rejected the idea; he wasn't out to fight a war, but rather to impress Moore with his ability to survive. Besides, if he killed the man, Moore would just send more.

He observed Moore's man for a few more minutes, then decided to go back to sleep. He turned and began walking back toward the middle of the roof. Suddenly his foot crashed through a weak section of rotting boards.

The man in the street turned and fired four quick shots in his general direction. Jeremiah raced to his backpack, picked it up on the run, and hurled himself off the back of the building. He landed on his feet and raced into the alleyway, zigzagging in and out of the long, eerie shadows.

He ran until he reached the end of the alley, then turned to his right past the nondescript building that constituted the unofficial headquarters of the city's unofficial murderers' guild. Nobody shot at him, which meant that they were either unaware of his identity or—far more likely—had no intention of helping a man who kept gunmen on salary. He ducked into a small abandoned firearms factory, raced to the back of it, and eased himself out through a broken window. He stopped for a moment, listening for footsteps, but couldn't detect any. Slowly, cautiously, he peeked out around the corner of the factory, trying to see what he could of the street. It seemed deserted.

Then, after stepping back out of sight, he turned and headed off in the opposite direction. He stopped when he came to the corner, and barely avoided bumping into another of Moore's men, who was advancing down the street, gun in hand.

He waited until the man was more than two hundred yards past him, then crossed the intersection. He had almost made it back into the dim shadows when he heard the sharp report of a gun, and little pieces of stone sprayed his face, ripped off from the edge of a building by the bullet.

He started running again, darting in and out of warehouses, changing directions every half-block or so, slowing to a walk whenever he dared. In less than an hour he had made an almost complete circle of Darktown, and now he could see the Bar Sinister glittering just ahead of him.

He got to within three hundred yards of it, panting heavily, then saw two of the gunmen standing in front of the entrance. Turning once more, he ducked into an alley that led him behind a row of drug parlors. When he came to an open back door he stepped through it, leaning against a wall and gasping for air. He could hear strange, gurgling moans ahead of him, and decided not to risk cutting through to the front. Chances were that the sounds were coming from someone who was too far gone in a featherheaded trance to be much of a threat, but he couldn't be sure that the person was alone, and it wasn't worth the risk.

He eased himself out through the back door, then saw a man coming down the alley toward him. He began running in the opposite direction, heard a number of shots, and felt a burning sensation just above his left elbow. He cursed, increased his speed, and ducked into the first building he came to that had a door in the back.

Without hesitating, he ran to the front of the building, out the front door, and across the street. Two more shots rang out from a new direction, and he darted into another structure.

It was large and well-appointed, with a circular staircase ascending to some upper level that was lost in shadows. He raced up the stairs, taking them three at a time, and burst through a door at the top. It closed automatically behind him, and he found himself in a sumptuously furnished drawing room. The rug was plush and deep, the wallpaper was flocked velvet, a number of tufted loveseats lined the walls, and soft, recorded music was being piped in through a hidden speaker system.

"Welcome," said a deep, resonant voice.

He jumped and looked behind him. The room was empty.

"You have just entered the Plaza Gomorrah, the ultimate experience in bordellos."

He ran to the door through which he had entered, but it was locked.

"We commend you on your selection of the Plaza Gomorrah, where sensual experiences undreamed-of await even the most jaded hedonist. Except for your fellow seekers after fulfillment and gratification, not a living soul is in attendance. Even the voice you are now hearing is a recording. You need fear no embarrassment here, no humiliation, no threat of public disapproval. Be wild, be wicked, be inventive, be uninhibited, be yourself! We ask only that you allow us to demonstrate our unique ability to serve you and cater to your every desire." There was a momentary pause. "Rooms four, fifteen, eighteen, and twenty-four are currently available. All can be found down the corridor to your left. Payment will be made on your way out. We accept every form of currency and credit card currently in use in Europe and the Western Hemisphere, as well as any properly endorsed corporate bonds rated double-A or better. Alternative forms of payment can be made by special arrangement."

A door on the left side of the room swung open, and Jeremiah shot through it. He tried the first room he came to, found that it was locked, and raced to the end of the long, dimly lit hallway, where he found a door with the number 24 affixed to it in blinking diodes.

He opened it, stepped through a dressing area, heard the door close and lock behind him, and walked swiftly toward a window on the far wall.

"Hi, good-looking," said a soft, sultry voice.

Jeremiah stopped in his tracks and saw a voluptuous redhead, totally naked, standing by the foot of a king-size brass bed.

"Not today, sister," he said. "I'm in one hell of a hurry."

"I'm glad you could make it tonight," said the redhead in level tones, reaching out and taking his arm.

"Look!" he snapped. "I told you—I've got no time for this now!"

He tried to pull his arm loose, and was astonished to discover that he couldn't.

"I've been waiting all week for someone like you," said the redhead, pulling him over to the bed.

He heard a door crash down in the distance.

"Damn it, they're here already!" he snarled. "Let me go, you stupid bitch!"

"If there is anything special you'd like me to do, you have only to ask," said the redhead, lying back on the bed. "I am programmed to perform any act in *The Kama Sutra*, *The Perfumed Garden*, or the works of Krafft-Ebing."

"*Programmed?*" shrieked Jeremiah, as two more doors caved in. "Oh God, let go of me, you damned machine!"

He began smashing his fists into the robot's face. She smiled and nibbled gently on his ear.

"Let me go!" he begged. "They're coming to kill me!"

She drew him down on top of her, wrapping her arms and legs around his body, moving her hips and torso rhythmically.

He drove a knee into her inner thigh, bit her neck, and poked his thumb into her left eye.

"Oh, you're going to be good, baby," she whispered mechanically. "Better than all the others."

He heard the door to his room cave in, heard the footsteps as five of Moore's men walked over to the bed.

"LET ME GO!" he screamed.

"Oh, baby, you're the greatest," droned the robot, as five guns went off in unison.

5

The roar of the shot was deafening.

"Where's the bullet?" asked Moore, lowering the gun to his side.

Pryor walked across the room. "Flattened out against the safe," he answered.

Moore turned to the eight security men who were standing uncomfortably in front of his desk.

"Gentlemen," he said, trying to control his temper, "using one of your own weapons I managed to hit a small wall safe at a distance of about twenty feet—and I am not a professional gunman. Now, has anyone got a reasonable explanation for what happened?"

There was no reply, and he stared directly at his chief of security.

"Montoya, you were the one who chased him into the Gomorrah. How did he get out?"

Montoya, a small, wiry man with dark, sunken eyes, just shook his head and shrugged.

"All right," said Moore, pacing up and down in front of the eight men. "Let me see if I've got this straight. Jeremiah raced up the stairs and went into one of the rooms, while Montoya waited for reinforcements. By the time four more men arrived, a robot was holding him totally helpless. The five of you walked in, surrounded the bed, leisurely took aim, and fired a total of forty-three bullets. Am I correct so far?"

"Yes, sir," said Montoya.

"You fired from no more than ten feet away?"

Montoya nodded.

"And five of the best-trained gunmen in the city, shooting at pointblank range, failed to kill or even maim a man who was right in front of them," continued Moore in a cold fury. "Not only that, but you blew the robot's head off, thus allowing Jeremiah to jump free, leap out the window, and completely evade you. To which I repeat: has anyone got a reasonable explanation?"

"I would be happy to undergo a session with the Neverlie Machine, Mr. Moore, if you feel that anything we've told you is false or incomplete," said Montoya.

"It's already been arranged," said Moore. "Each of you, when you leave here, will report to the Neverlie room. I might add that the voltage will be very close to lethal. Something funny is going on here, and I mean to get to the bottom of it." He turned to Pryor. "Ben, I want that room at the whorehouse examined. See how many slugs you can find in the walls, the robot, everywhere."

"I've already ordered it," replied Pryor. "We ought to be getting in the results shortly."

"I also want to know how the hell he got out of Darktown after the shooting."

"Right," said Pryor, nodding.

Moore turned back to the eight men. "All right—get out of here," he said disgustedly.

As they filed out, Pryor's pocket computer came to life.

"Got it already," he announced.

"Got what?" asked Moore.

"A report from the Gomorrah. They found thirty-two bullets in the head, arms, and legs of the robot, and four others in the mattress."

"And the other seven?"

"No trace. But we know Jeremiah was wearing a backpack. It was probably filled with retort pouches and maybe even a weapon or two. It's not inconceivable that four or five of the bullets got lodged in the pack."

"Why just four or five?" asked Moore. "Why not all seven?"

"Because there were traces of blood on the floor and the windowsill. He had to be hit at least once, maybe a few times."

"But not enough to slow him down," said Moore. "Damn it, Ben, the whole thing is unbelievable!"

"I agree," said Pryor. "But since he made a clean getaway, maybe we'd better start believing it unless you want to believe that a penniless beggar could somehow buy off five men who have been loyal to us for years." He paused to light a cigarette. "As nearly as I can reconstruct it, our other three men must have headed over to the Gomorrah as soon as they heard the gunfire, and Jeremiah evidently managed to slip by them and get out of Darktown while they were all still trying to figure out what had happened." He shrugged. "It's crazy, but that's the only way everything fits."

"It doesn't make any sense!" repeated Moore. "How could five crack shots fire forty-three bullets from less than ten feet away and not even slow him down? Hell, you'd think the noise alone would be enough to scare him to death."

"From what our men say, he was damned near out of his mind with fear even before they started shooting," said Pryor.

"I just can't find any rational explanation for it!" growled Moore. "I mean, it's not as if he has a surplus of brains. Look at what's happened. First, he sent a hundred-and-ten-pound woman to try to kill me with a weapon that required her to get within reach of me. That was just plain dumb. Second, he tried to camouflage the Bizarre Bazaar while I still had a business card with the address on it. Dumber still. Third, he used a maimed man and a Dartboard as his confederates—not the hardest people in the world to identify and track down. Fourth, he filled out the Dream Come True application form, which told us exactly what he looked like. Fifth, he walked into Russo's joint and let himself be seen. Sixth, while trying to hide from our muscle he climbed on top of the most dilapidated warehouse in Darktown and had the roof cave in under him. Seventh, he walked into a room with a robot whore and let it hold him helpless while our men came in and shot at him. Hell, a bona fide imbecile would have behaved more intelligently! And yet, he's still at large, and our entire organization looks like a bunch of incompetents."

"You do make it sound like something more than luck," remarked Pryor wryly.

"Do you call it luck that three-quarters of the bullets hit the robot?" retorted Moore. "These guys are specialists, Ben. They *couldn't* have missed!"

But the Neverlie Machine soon verified that the men had indeed told the truth, and Moore had no alternative but to order the manhunt to continue.

"Also, turn Lisa Walpole loose," he ordered Pryor, "and put a tail on her."

"If she knew where to find Jeremiah, she'd have told you while she was under the truth serum," said Pryor.

"I know," replied Moore. "But *he* might have some reason to see *her,* and if and when he does, I want to know about it." He paused. "Also, there must have been some fingerprints in the whorehouse. Check them out, and see if we can't find out just who the hell this guy is. Does he have a last name? Where does he live? And why is he after me? He can't be as dumb as he seems, or he wouldn't be able to dress himself in the morning without help. I want to find out everything we can about him."

Pryor nodded, then left the office to carry out his orders.

Moore punched a button on his intercom. "Send in Montoya."

The security man entered a moment later, and stood uncomfortably before Moore's desk.

"Sit down," said Moore, gesturing toward a wooden chair. "Difficult as I find it to believe, it appears that you were telling the truth, so we're back where we started. I still want to know why Jeremiah isn't dead."

"I honestly don't know, sir."

"Did you notice anything unusual, either about Jeremiah or about the room in general?"

"Not a thing," replied Montoya, shaking his head. "Hell, sir, he *couldn't* have known where he was going! I was hot on his tail, and he ducked into the first place he came to."

"Are you sure he didn't plan it to look that way?" suggested Moore.

"Absolutely."

"All right. Off the record, what would you say went wrong?"

Montoya shrugged eloquently. "I wish I knew."

"Could it have been the robot? Could it have been treated to attract bullets in some manner?"

"Not a chance. I *know* some of those bullets never touched the robot."

Moore grimaced. "Eleven of them." He paused. "How badly wounded was he?"

"Not so bad that he couldn't jump out of a window and hit the ground running." Montoya shook his head. "I still can't believe it, sir."

Moore dismissed him, toyed with questioning the other seven men, and decided against it. After all, they couldn't tell him anything more than they'd told the Neverlie Machine. Finally he summoned Pryor back into his office.

"Ben, we can't just sit here and wait for Jeremiah to make the next move. I want you to hunt up an actor who looks like me, dress him in my clothes, and send him around to all my usual places: restaurants, gymnasiums, bookstores, anywhere that I might be expected to go."

Pryor looked dubious. "I don't think he'll bite, but we can try it if you like."

"I like. And find out why the hell we're having so much trouble coming up with Krebbs. God knows he shouldn't be hard to spot."

"It would help if we had a picture."

"Hell, he's missing an eye and some fingers! Isn't that enough to go on?"

Pryor shrugged. "I'll pass the word that we're still interested in him."

"Also," added Moore, "from what little we know about Jeremiah, I'd say he can't seem to pass up anything that twitches. Check around and see if we can come up with a couple of girls who know him."

"Can I offer an inducement?"

"Five thousand dollars for any information." Moore paused. "No, make that ten. He's like an itch I can't scratch. The sooner we get something concrete on him, the better."

Pryor nodded and left.

Next on Moore's agenda was the girl from Dream Come True who had taken Jeremiah's application, but she couldn't add anything to the small body of knowledge they possessed about him.

Nobody at the Thrill Show remembered him, either. He had no
police record. Karl Russo knew him as a customer, but could
provide no useful information. Even Moore's contact inside the
murderers' guild couldn't help.

The first break came in midafternoon, when his private telephone began flashing. He picked up the receiver.

"Mr. Moore?" said a feminine voice.

"Who are you?" demanded Moore. "How did you get this number?"

"An employee of yours named Visconti gave it to me," she
replied. "He told me you might have something for me."

"Such as?"

"Such as fifty thousand dollars."

"You know Jeremiah?"

"Yes."

"Why didn't you give the information to Visconti?"

"Because he didn't have the money," she replied.

"Come on over and I'll have it waiting for you."

"No, thank you. If Solomon Moody Moore is willing to shell out
that much money just for information, then Jeremiah must be a
pretty dangerous man. I don't want to be seen anywhere near your
office."

"You name the time and place," said Moore. "I'll be there."

"Alone?"

"Absolutely not," said Moore. "I'm not going to be suckered
twice in one week."

"I'll have to think about it."

"Sixty thousand," said Moore instantly.

There was a momentary silence. "All right," she said at last.

"Fine. Where do we meet?"

"The Museum of Death."

"Never heard of it. Is it far?"

"It's in Evanston. You can find the address in the phone book."

"When?"

"Ten o'clock tonight."

"What if the museum's closed then?" he asked.

"It will be."

"Then how—?"

"Just be there at ten, Mr. Moore," said the voice. "I'll take care of
the rest. And Mr. Moore?"

"Yes?"

"Don't be late. I don't like to be kept waiting."

She hung up the phone.

Moore pressed another intercom button. "Get Visconti on the phone."

A few moments later his agent called in.

"Who is this woman who contacted you about Jeremiah?" demanded Moore.

"I don't know. She wore sunglasses, and the brightest red wig you ever saw. She wore real heavy makeup, but I have a feeling that she was pretty pale underneath it."

"Did you try to follow her?"

"No," answered Visconti. "I figured that if she really knew anything, I didn't want to scare her off."

"How did she know to contact you in the first place?"

"We sent the word out through the usual channels. It wouldn't have been too hard. After all, we're looking for Jeremiah, not hiding from him."

"True," said Moore. "Okay. I want you and Montoya in my office at eight this evening."

"Anything special?"

"I'm meeting the girl tonight, and I want you to confirm her identity, if you can."

He broke off the connection, and kept busy with his legitimate interests for the remainder of the day. He was just getting ready to leave with Montoya and Visconti when Pryor buzzed him on the intercom.

"What's up?" asked Moore.

"We just found Maria Delamond."

"Who the hell is she?"

"The old lady from the religious shop," replied Pryor.

"Good! Where is she?"

"Lying in an alley behind the third level of Monroe Street, with her throat slit from ear to ear."

6

Moore and his two security men walked up to the large, darkened building.

"Jesus, it's cold!" muttered Visconti, turning up his collar as the December wind blew in off Lake Michigan.

"It's been a long time since I was outside the dome during the winter," agreed Montoya, blowing on his hands. "I'd forgotten what it was like."

"Both of you are getting soft from too much city living," said Moore.

"Doesn't the cold bother you, sir?" asked Visconti.

"Not enough to complain about it."

"Look at those spires and turrets!" exclaimed Montoya. "The damned place looks like a gothic castle."

"More likely a reconditioned mansion, or perhaps a school building from the old Northwestern University," replied Moore. "I count at least six different doors. Visconti, pull your gun out and start trying them, one by one. Montoya, stick with me and keep your eyes open."

As Visconti, a huge, muscular man with close-cropped blond hair, strode up to the main entrance, Montoya turned to Moore.

"I haven't had a chance to ask you since the problem in Darktown," said the security chief in low tones. "What do you want us to do about Mr. Pryor, sir—keep up our surveillance, or concentrate everything we've got on Jeremiah?"

Moore considered the question for a moment. "Leave two men on Ben," he said at last. "Put everyone else to work on Jeremiah."

"Are you sure that's wise, sir?"

"Ben doesn't present an immediate problem," replied Moore. "Jeremiah's after me right now."

Visconti rejoined them a moment later.

"No luck," he announced. "The building's got six doors; I tried them all." He paused thoughtfully. "She knows you've got the money with you. Do you suppose this could be a setup?"

"You're the one who put her on to me," responded Moore. "Do you think we're being suckered?"

"I doubt it," answered Visconti after some consideration. "What's to stop us from walking away right now?" He shook his head decisively. "No, if she wanted to set you up, I think she'd do it inside the museum, not here."

"It makes sense," agreed Moore. "However, all the logic in the world won't make the slightest bit of difference if we're wrong." He glanced at his wristwatch. "It's five minutes to ten. I think we'll check the doors again at ten sharp."

Five minutes later Visconti walked up to the building and returned shortly thereafter to report that one of the side doors was now unlocked.

The three men walked up to it and paused. Moore looked inside, but could see only a darkened corridor.

"All right," he announced after a moment. "Montoya first. Visconti, you bring up the rear. And remember—your job is to protect me, not avenge me."

They entered the building and had taken a few tentative steps forward when a feminine voice spoke out: "Close the door behind you and walk straight ahead."

Moore nodded to Visconti, who did as the voice directed. The corridor turned sharply to the right after about forty feet, opening into a small room that was totally devoid of furniture. Standing in the middle of it was a woman with the whitest skin Moore had ever seen. She had short, black hair, very dark eyes, high prominent cheekbones, and a figure Jeremiah couldn't have ignored. Moore guessed that she was in her late twenties, but wouldn't have been surprised to discover that she was pushing forty.

"Have your men put their guns away," said the woman. "Weapons make me nervous."

"Clandestine meetings make *me* nervous," replied Moore. "The guns stay out." He turned to Visconti. "Is this the woman?"

"The hair and makeup are different, sir," said Visconti, "but it sure sounds like the same voice."

"Did you bring the money?" asked the woman.

Moore withdrew it and held it up for her to see.

"Good. Let's go to my office. We can sit down there and speak in comfort."

"Lead the way," said Moore, as he and his men followed her through a door at the back of the room. It led into a large hall that was filled with glass cases, each illustrating a scene of doom and destruction.

"This is our most popular exhibition room," said the girl, slowing her pace to allow Moore to study the displays more closely.

Case after case displayed life-sized figures in varying states of suffering and death. Here was Mussolini hanging by his heels, there was John Kennedy getting the top of his head blown off, over there was Lincoln a microsecond after John Wilkes Booth had fired his pistol.

"Very realistic," said Moore, pausing to examine Julius Caesar's death throes.

"We're especially proud of this one," said the woman, pointing to Marie Antoinette's head, which dripped a trail of blood and ganglia as it hung, suspended in time and space, midway between the guillotine blade and the small basket that awaited it.

"Not bad," commented Moore. "Have you got Braden anywhere?"

"In the next section," she replied, leading him through another doorway and stopping before a representation of James Wilcox Braden III, the forty-eighth President of the United States, and the only one ever to commit suicide in office.

"He doesn't look quite the way I remember him," remarked Moore. "Still," he added, staring at the blood that seemed to be flowing continuously from his wrist into a bowl of warm water, "it's impressive."

They walked on past the other exhibits. De Sade was again trying to find the ultimate breaking point of the human soul and body, Martin Luther King was staring in disbelief as the blood spread over his shirt, Nikolai Badeliovitch still had an uncomprehending expression on his face as a failing life-support system ended the first manned expedition to Venus.

Another room. Here there were plagues, famine, leprosy. The Andersonville prison. Auschwitz. Vlad the Impaler busy earning his sobriquet.

Still another room, and they came to the Christians falling beneath the fangs and talons of the lions, the huge dogs ripping children to shreds during the Calcutta riots of 2038, heroes and martyrs and star-crossed lovers—and, in a tall display case that took up fully a quarter of the room, Jesus writhed once again on his cross, his eyes asking in mute agony why God had forsaken him.

"What do you think of it?" she asked, when they had passed through the last of the displays.

"I find it fascinating," he answered. "Whoever created it certainly had a morbid preoccupation with death." He looked around. "How long has this place been here?"

"The building itself is almost two hundred years old," she said. "As for the Museum of Death, it's been in business just under five years."

"Who frequents it?" asked Moore. "I wouldn't have thought you could draw enough people to warrant the expenditure."

"We manage to make ends meet," she replied. "We draw a goodly number of tourists and sightseers. And of course we've also got a pretty steady clientele: historians, artists, costumers, and a fair share of freaks." She led the three men through a small doorway and up a flight of stairs to a row of offices. The first four doors, which seemed to lead to the same oversized chamber, were labeled stockroom.

"What do you keep in there?" asked Moore.

"Future exhibits. Would you like to see some of them?"

"Very much."

She unlocked one of the doors, and a rush of cold air hit them. Moore stepped inside and found himself staring at perhaps fifty corpses, all neatly labeled and lying on slabs.

"We keep them refrigerated until we need them," explained the woman.

"Then those *weren't* wax or plastic figures I saw."

"I should say not."

"Where do you get your bodies?" he asked.

"Originally the morgue supplied all our needs, but most of the specimens were too badly damaged to use. Recently we've been obtaining them elsewhere."

"For instance?"

"Trade secret," she said with a smile, ushering the three men out of the chamber. "My office is the last one on the left."

"I take it that you're something more than just a tour guide," remarked Moore dryly.

"Oh, I'm a little of everything," she replied, walking up to her office and inserting a computerized card in the lock. Moore got a brief glimpse of the gold lettering on the door before he followed her inside:

> MOIRA RALLINGS
> TAXIDERMIST

The woman turned to Moore. "Have your men inspect the office and then wait outside for us."

Moore nodded to Montoya and Visconti, who gave the room a thorough going-over and then reported that it seemed secure. Moore motioned them into the hall and closed the door behind them.

"Sit down, Mr. Moore," said Moira Rallings, seating herself on a wooden rocking chair in a darkened corner of the small, cozy office. Moore walked past a large bookcase that was filled to overflowing with anatomy and taxidermy texts and an occasional illustrated history book, then sat down on the edge of her cluttered desk.

"Shall we get down to business?" he asked.

"That's what we're here for."

"Fine." He leaned forward. "Who is Jeremiah the B? What's his real name?"

"I don't know."

"Where does he live?"

"He used to have an apartment in Skokie, but it's empty now."

"Why does he want to kill me?"

She looked surprised. "I didn't know he wanted to."

"Perhaps we're going about this the wrong way," suggested Moore. "Suppose you tell me what you do know about him."

"I know that I'd like to see him dead fully as much as you would," said Moira with obvious sincerity. "And I know that you can't trace him through the normal channels. He has no criminal record, and he once told me that he'd never been fingerprinted or voiceprinted."

"How about retina identification?"

"If you get close enough to him to take it, I don't imagine you'll need it," she replied with a smile. "Besides, they've only been doing it for eight or ten years. My guess is that he's not on record."

"You said you wanted to see him dead. Why?"

"He stole my life savings."

"How?"

She sighed deeply. "I'd better start at the beginning. One day, about three months ago, I saw him picking pockets right here in the museum and threatened to report him. He offered to split the money with me if I kept quiet about it."

"Did you?"

"I kept quiet," said Moira, "but I didn't take any of the money. He moved in with me a couple of days later."

"Into your apartment, not his?" asked Moore.

"That's right."

"Then for all you know, the Skokie address might not exist at all."

"It exists," she replied bitterly. "I went there five weeks later, right after he cleared out with my savings and my jewelry."

"I assume you didn't find him?"

She shook her head.

"How was the apartment registered?"

"In the name of Joseph L. Smith."

"*Joe Smith!*" said Moore incredulously. "How can an amateur like that still be on the loose? *Joe Smith*, for Christ's sake!" He shook his head in disbelief. "Well, let's get on with it. What did you learn about him while you were living with him?"

"He was born in Tel Aviv."

"I thought he was an American citizen," interrupted Moore.

"He is. His mother was an American archaeologist. They stayed in Israel until he was ten or eleven, then went to Egypt."

"Is she still alive?"

"No. Both of his parents died in an accident when he was fourteen, and he was sent back to the States to live with an aunt. I don't know her name. He left her house after a couple of months and has been on his own ever since."

"Where?"

"Let me think for a minute," she said, lowering her head. Finally she looked up at him. "Manhattan, the Denver complex, Seattle, and then here. He used to work in a library, but I don't know which city it was in. I got the impression that his duties were pretty menial."

"How long has he been in Chicago?"

"A little over a year," replied Moira.

"What did he do before he latched onto you?" persisted Moore.

"Begged, hustled, robbed. A little of everything—except work."

"Where is he likely to hang out?"

"I don't know."

"What are his interests?"

"He hasn't any," said Moira. "He knows a lot about archaeology, but that's probably just from his upbringing. He once told me that he speaks Hebrew and Arabic as fluently as English, but he may have been lying." She smiled ruefully. "He lies a lot."

"Has he got any aliases?"

"I only know of one—Manny the B. But I got the feeling that he had a lot of others."

"Does he gamble?"

She shook her head. "He didn't during the time I knew him. I gather he once lost his bankroll on a fight that he thought was fixed, and he hasn't made a bet since."

"How big a bankroll?" Moore asked sharply.

"I don't know, but from the way he talked about it, it must have been pretty substantial."

"What fight?"

"I don't know anything about boxing. He mentioned the names of the fighters as if everyone should know them, though. It would have been, oh, nine or ten months ago."

"That would probably have been the Tchana-Makki heavy-weight title fight," said Moore. "We'll be able to check with our bookmaking agencies, and see if we can get a lead from them. As for his parents, we'll just have to do it the hard way and check out every American archaeologist who was in Israel twenty years ago and died in Egypt during the past decade."

"Can an organization like yours *do* something like that?" she asked curiously.

"You'd be surprised what we can do when we set our minds to it," he replied with a grim smile. "Or, rather, when *I* set *my* mind to it." He paused. "Do you know if he's ever been married?"

"He never mentioned it," she said with a shrug.

"Any kids, legitimate or otherwise?"

"None that I know of."

Moore stared at her for a long minute. "You seem like a reasonably bright, reasonably attractive, reasonably selective woman," he said at last. "Why the hell did you ever shack up with a dumb hustler like Jeremiah?"

"I really don't know," she said uncomfortably. "It just happened."

"He must be an attractive man."

"Not especially," said Moira, her expression puzzled. "That's the funny part of it. He's not even very good in bed. Looking back on it, I'm even more surprised at myself than you are."

Moore stood up, stretched, and walked to a window that overlooked the darkened suburb. "From what you know of him, why do you think he might want to kill me?"

"I don't think he wants to," she replied thoughtfully. "If he did, you'd be dead by now."

"Who are you kidding?" said Moore with a contemptuous laugh. "He couldn't shoot a fish in a barrel without blowing off half his foot."

"He's a very unusual man," said Moira. "I don't know why or how, but he always seems to get his way. Call it luck if you want, but if he truly tried to kill you I think he'd succeed."

"I don't believe in luck," said Moore, trying not to think of the episode in the Plaza Gomorrah.

"That's up to you," she said. "But whether it's luck or something else, things have a way of working out for him."

"Then why is he still a small-timer?" asked Moore.

"I don't know."

"What are his ambitions? What is he after?"

"I don't think even Jeremiah could answer that. He just seems to live from one minute to the next. I've never seen him worried or upset. If he needed money, he just went out and got it."

"Why did he need money?" asked Moore quickly. "Was he feeding some kind of habit?"

"I know he used to go to Karl Russo's place down in Darktown, but I wouldn't say that he was addicted to anything."

"Then you think if I checked out all the local pushers I'd come up empty?"

She paused to consider the question. "Probably," she said at last.

"If you're right about his not wanting to kill me, just what *does* he want?"

"Knowing the way his mind works, I'd say he's trying to impress you enough so that you'll give him a top job in your organization."

"Do you really believe that?" asked Moore skeptically.

"It's an educated guess, nothing more," said Moira.

"How the hell did they ever let him out of kindergarten?" said Moore, shaking his head in amazement. He walked back to the desk. "If I told you he was wounded, where do you think he'd go to get patched up?"

"I don't know that he'd bother," replied Moira. "If he was healthy enough to elude whoever shot him, he's probably healthy enough not to risk visiting a doctor."

"Has he got any friends that you know about?"

She shook her head.

"Does the name Krebbs mean anything to you—an old man missing an eye and a couple of fingers?"

"No."

"How about Maria Delamond?"

"No."

"Lisa Walpole?"

"I've never heard of any of them."

"From what you know of Jeremiah, would you say that he's capable of slitting an old woman's throat?"

She considered the question for a minute. "I don't know if he'd do it himself, but he certainly wouldn't have any moral compunctions about getting someone to do it for him."

"You know," said Moore, "somehow I don't feel I'm getting my money's worth from you."

"You know more about Jeremiah now than you did twenty minutes ago," replied Moira. "And if you want him as badly as I think you do, you've gotten your money's worth and then some. After all, Solomon Moody Moore isn't exactly hurting for money."

"True," agreed Moore. "However, I figure you've only given me a thousand dollars' worth. Now you're going to earn the other fifty-nine."

She eyed him suspiciously. "How?"

"You're coming to work for me."

"The hell I am!"

"Let me make my offer before you refuse it," said Moore. "I'll pay you the sixty thousand now, and two thousand a day until I catch him."

"What do I have to do for it?"

"Just hang around and look pretty."

"As a decoy?" She laughed sarcastically. "Do you really think Jeremiah will swoop down and try to rescue me from your dastardly clutches?"

"Not at all," replied Moore. "I very much doubt that Jeremiah gives a tinker's damn whether you live or die. But on the other hand, I think he'll care quite a lot about what you may have to say to me."

"But I've told you everything I know about him."

"Perhaps," said Moore, "though we have a painless psychoprobing device at my office that will make sure of it. However, what you know and what Jeremiah thinks you *may* know are two different things."

"It won't work," said Moira adamantly.

"If it doesn't, you've got a guaranteed income for the rest of your life."

"All I would have to do is be seen in public with you?" she asked suspiciously.

"That's right."

"I won't have to sleep with you?"

"Absolutely not," Moore assured her. "I never mix pleasure and business. You'll be provided with your own private quarters in my office building."

"That's a lot of money," she said thoughtfully. "And I want to see Jeremiah dead as much as you do. But I'd have to leave the museum and give up my work until he was caught, wouldn't I?"

"Yes, you would."

"Couldn't I spend a few hours a day here?"

He shook his head. "For two thousand dollars a day, you'll stay where I want you to stay."

"There's a special exhibit I've been working on for the past two years," said Moira. "You'd have to let me take it along so I can continue working on it."

"Which one was it?" asked Moore. "The Crucifixion?"

"It's not on public display. Would you like to see it?"

Moore shrugged a semi-assent, and she led him out of the office. Montoya and Visconti fell into step behind them as they walked down the corridor to a large metal door.

"Just you," she said, and Moore nodded to his men, who returned to their places outside Moira's office.

She unlocked the door, then pushed it open and stepped into the darkened room. Moore followed her, and she immediately closed the door behind them.

"Are you ready?" she whispered.

"I'm ready," he replied in bored tones.

She switched on the colored overhead lights, and there, mounted on various platforms and podiums, were forty lifelike corpses. Grouped in twos, threes, and fours, nude or clad in kink, all were frozen into positions of almost unbearable ecstasy. Fellatio, cunnilingus, homosexuality, lesbianism, sodomy, bondage, flagellation, all were meticulously displayed, as were some aspects of the sex act that made even the raunchier performances at the Thrill Show look mundane by comparison.

"Do you like it?" asked Moira at last, her face suddenly alive with excitement.

"It's . . . ah . . . impressive," said Moore, mildly surprised that he could still feel shocked about anything sexual, and idly wondering what kind of mind could conceive and create such a display.

"It's my own project," she said proudly. "No one else has been allowed to work on it, and only a handful of people have even seen it." She lovingly stroked a nude male of Homeric proportions. "It's all mine, and I won't leave without it."

"You could only work on it when I didn't need you," said Moore.

She lowered her head in thought for a long moment. "I don't think I'm interested," she said at last. "My work is more important to me than your money."

"Then let me offer one final inducement," said Moore, who had been observing her carefully. "After I'm through with Jeremiah, you can have what's left of him for your project."

"Do you really mean that?"

Moore nodded.

A look of exaltation spread slowly across her chalk-white face, and her dark eyes widened with an unfathomable expression that almost scared him.

"Mr. Moore, you've got yourself a deal," said Moira Rallings.

7

Neptune's Palace was crowded, as usual. Big-time gamblers and top-dollar prostitutes rubbed shoulders (and other things) with Chicago's leading social gadflies, most of whom were looking for one last thrill on the way to senility or a first thrill on the road to adulthood. Painted transvestites, leather-clad exhibitionists of both sexes, the newly wealthy who now disdained their prior association with the proletariat, all spread money through the ranks of the Palace staff to secure prominent tables at which they could preen and be seen.

Ben Pryor and Abe Bernstein sat in a small, unobtrusive booth at the back of the huge room, sipping a pair of Water Witches and watching the unpaid clowns outdraw the professional ones. There were half a dozen empty glasses on the table in front of Pryor, and his ashtray was filled to overflowing with half-smoked cigarettes.

"So what do you think?" Pryor was saying.

"About this place?" replied Bernstein with a smile. "Give me a chance to make up my mind, Ben. I've only been here for five minutes. But off the record, I suspect my wife would kill me if she knew I was enjoying myself at Neptune's Palace while she was baby-sitting for two of our grandchildren." He paused for a moment. "And while we're on the subject of this place, exactly why *am* I here?"

"It's easier to talk in comfortable surroundings."

"You call *this* comfortable?" repeated Bernstein. "Unusual and exciting, maybe, but . . ."

"Well, *I'm* comfortable, anyway," said Pryor defensively. He dumped his ashtray into an empty glass and lit another cigarette.

"As long as you're paying the bill," said Bernstein with a shrug. He forced himself to stop staring at the patrons and turned to Pryor. "I don't imagine you invited me here to talk about this Jeremiah person that Moira used to live with, so what's on your mind?"

Pryor chuckled. "I'm sick to death of Jeremiah. He's just a god-damned beggar with delusions of grandeur." He suddenly became intent. "Tell me about Moira."

"About Moira? What's to tell?"

"You had her under the psycho-probe," persisted Pryor. "What makes her tick? I've met a lot of strange people in my life, Abe, but she's as weird as they come!"

"We probed her for information, nothing more," replied Bernstein. "She did tell me about her—what would you call it?—her *collection*, if that's what you're interested in." He took another sip of her drink. "Did Solomon really empty a four-room office suite so she could move it in?"

"It makes her feel at home," said Pryor, signaling a nude prepubescent boy in a turban to bring him another drink. "I wonder why Moore agreed to it, though. It's not like him to go around doing people favors."

"Who knows?" shrugged Bernstein. "I'm sure he had his reasons."

"I just wish I knew what they were," muttered Pryor.

"What difference does it make?"

"You've got to know your enemy before you can take him on."

Bernstein frowned. "Enemy?" he repeated. "What kind of talk is that?"

Pryor downed his drink and stared directly into Bernstein's eyes. "I'm going to take the organization away from him some day." Bernstein opened his mouth to protest, and Pryor held out his hand. "Don't act so surprised, Abe. Moore knows it and you know it, so let's just lay our cards on the table."

"I don't want to hear this," said Bernstein.

"Of course you don't," said Pryor with a smile. "You're Moore's man, Abe."

"Funny," replied Bernstein, startled. "That's the way I always felt about *you*."

Pryor shook his head. "Uh-uh. The organization is your only client, and you're as high up the ladder as you planned to go. You're fat, overpaid, and underworked—meaning no offense. You belong to a temple and a country club, you've put your kids through college, you own a big house out in Lake Forest. You've got what you want out of life, Abe. But I'm in a different position: *Moore's* got what I want."

"Even if that's so," said Bernstein, "what makes you think he'll give it to you?"

"He won't. That's why I'm going to have to take it away from him."

"That's dangerous talk," said Bernstein uncomfortably.

"Nonsense. It's business talk. I've put nine years of my life into this organization, Abe. I've worked more eighty-hour weeks than you can count and had three marriages fold out from under me." He paused. "I didn't do it so I could take orders from Moore for the rest of my life."

"If I'm Solomon's man, why are you telling me all this?"

Pryor smiled. "Like I said, I'm not telling you anything he doesn't know. And don't look so damned suspicious: I don't plan to preside over a pile of rubble, so I'll do the best job I can until I get rid of him." The nude boy returned with his drink. "And in the meantime, I've put a couple of things together on the side."

"Such as?"

"Who the hell do you think owns Neptune Palace?"

"Does Solomon know?" asked Bernstein.

"Of course."

"Then it would seem that you're doing all right on your own," noted Bernstein, waving a hand at the crowded room.

"Moore goes for the common man's dollar; as another guy named Abe once pointed out, there are so many of them. I wanted to show him we could go after the rich man's money, too. It spends just as well."

"And you've obviously become successful," noted Bernstein, taking another sip of his drink.

"Only because Moore isn't interested," said Pryor. "Otherwise, he'd buy Naomi off in a minute."

"Who's Naomi?"

"Naomi Riordan. Her professional name is Poseidon's Daughter."

"I've heard about her," said Bernstein, displaying some interest. "She's something of a sensation, according to the people I've talked to."

"You can decide for yourself," said Pryor. "Her act's due to start very soon now."

In less than a minute the house lights dimmed, and a huge aquarium tank, housing hundreds of exotic fish and a pair of large, jeweled sea castles, rose up out of the center of the floor.

"Watch," said Pryor.

Music from an unseen harp soon permeated the room. Then a spotlight hit the aquarium, the door to one of the castles opened, and Poseidon's Daughter made her entrance, wearing only a pale-blue mermaid's tail, which she soon removed. She began swimming around the tank, her movements taking on the fluid grace of some long-lost Lorelei of the sea, her muscles rippling exotically beneath her unblemished skin. Her long, flaming red hair trailed out behind her, undulating sensuously through the water as her body arched and banked and circled in intricate interlaced patterns. Soon the fish, attracted by her hair, fell into a synchronous choreopattern, and suddenly the girl, the hair, the fish, and even the air bubbles had formed a hypnotically whirling, swirling unity that transcended Grace and achieved Art.

And then, before the stunned audience could rise in thunderous applause, Poseidon's Daughter had disappeared beneath the second sand castle and all that remained of the performance was a small school of fish. Oblivious to the screaming, cheering spectators, they clustered just above the sand in a far corner of the aquarium and pursued their fruitless quest for algae.

"What did you think of her?" asked Pryor, when the applause had subsided and the tank had sunk back into the floor.

"Absolutely fantastic!" enthused Bernstein. "I've never seen anything like it!" He turned to Pryor. "Could I possibly meet her? I'd like to tell her how much I admired her performance."

"Perhaps some other time," replied Pryor ruefully. "We had a little disagreement last night."

"Oh?"

He nodded. "Yeah. We've been living together ever since I hired her, and I lost track of the time and didn't get home until sunrise."

"What could keep you away from something like that?"

"As a matter of fact, I was with Moira Rallings," said Pryor with no trace of embarrassment.

"I never thought of you as a man of poor taste before," said Bernstein. "But if you prefer that bloodless lunatic to—"

"It was strictly business," interrupted Pryor.

"If it was strictly business," replied Bernstein firmly, "Solomon would have been there first."

"There are certain problems I'm better equipped to handle than he is," said Pryor, not without a touch of pride. "I wanted to find out what she had on Jeremiah."

"To help Solomon or harm him?"

"To help him. Give me credit for a little intelligence, Abe. Being Number Two with Moore is better than being out on the street with Jeremiah. Anyway, nothing happened."

"Nothing?" said Bernstein dubiously.

"Nothing that I was personally involved in," amended Pryor slowly. "She's a pretty strange woman."

"*How* strange?"

Pryor stared at him for a moment, as if debating whether or not to answer the question. Finally he shrugged. "Abe, she's a goddamned necrophile!"

"I find that a little difficult to believe."

"So did I, until last night."

"I find it even harder to envision," continued Bernstein. "Making love to a dead woman may have its drawbacks, but at least it's possible, however disgusting the thought. But for a woman to have sex with a male corpse . . ."

"She's a taxidermist, remember?"

"Just the same . . ."

"Damn it, Abe!" snapped Pryor. "I was there! I watched her!"

"And you say *she's* weird!" laughed Bernstein contemptuously.

"It's the way she gets her kicks. She wouldn't talk to me *unless* I watched."

"Well?"

"It was fascinating. And I've got to admit it was exciting as all hell. If we could get some films or tapes of her, we'd sell five million copies."

"That's not what I meant," said Bernstein. "What does she have on Jeremiah? I put her through the psycho-probe and couldn't find a damned thing that Solomon hadn't already gotten from her."

"Nothing."

"I take it back," said Bernstein after a moment's consideration. "She did tell me one item of importance."

"Oh?" said Pryor quickly. "What was it?"

"She told me why Solomon runs this organization and you don't."

"Yeah?" said Pryor suspiciously. "Why?"

"Because she made a similar offer to him yesterday, and he turned her down flat. He went home to work in an empty apartment, while you left Naomi Riordan to spend the night with her."

"What does that prove?"

"Ben, whether you did it for kicks or you did it for Solomon, it comes to the same thing. All he wants is power; if you're interested in anything besides power, whether it's pleasure or perversion or money, you're going to stay in second place because you haven't got the single-minded intensity that he has."

"I *told* you why I was there," said Pryor defensively. "It's hardly my fault if I enjoyed it."

Bernstein shook his head. "That's a lousy answer, Ben. If

Solomon knew going there wouldn't help, then so did you—and if you say otherwise, you're just lying to yourself." He stared severely at Pryor. "Solomon lies to a lot of people, but he's never yet lied to himself. *That's* why you're never going to be able to take this organization away from him."

"We'll see about that!" said Pryor hotly.

"So we shall," agreed Bernstein.

"But in the meantime," continued Pryor, his attention suddenly captured by a top-heavy blonde who had just walked into the club unescorted, "we're all teammates. It's Jeremiah who's the enemy. We'll talk more about it tomorrow."

He signed for the tab, nodded pleasantly to Bernstein, and set off on an arduous and ultimately successful pursuit of the blonde.

And, as Pryor's thoughts turned once again to sexual conquest, Moore sat alone in his apartment, considering various ways to bring Jeremiah out into the open. A few minutes later one of his agents called to tell him where Pryor would be spending the night. He smiled, shook his head in wonderment, and returned to his planning.

8

Moore spent the next four weeks being visible.

With Moira Rallings in constant attendance at his side, he spent the bulk of the first week touring the legion of underworld dives and drug dens that flourished beneath Chicago's shining exterior, simultaneously shutting down the security—or at least that portion of it that was obvious—around his office building and his apartment.

There was no sign of Jeremiah.

The following week he began a systematic tour of the local retreats, those incredibly valuable pieces of real estate that extended from the westernmost portions of the Chicago megalopolis halfway to the Mississippi River. He went to the health farms, where the truly sick died in luxury and the hypochondriacs were soon convinced that they were truly sick. He went to the diet farms, where the results of years of boredom and inactivity could be starved and sweated off at a rate of five thousand dollars a pound (or ten thousand dollars a week, which usually came to the same thing). He went to the dryout farms, where the aromas of fruit juice and coffee assailed his nostrils from hundreds of yards away, and where repentant alcoholics and unrepentant but dying alcoholics were never more than a short walk from the church and all-purpose temperance lecture of their choice. He went to the R&R farms for tired businessmen, which were dedicated to letting their patrons win at rigged sporting games all day and score with rigged sporting women all night, and he went to the R&R farms for tired businesswomen, which were, if anything, even more wildly enthusiastic about providing for their patronesses. He went to the religious camps, the nature camps, and all the multitude of country estates that had been set aside, not to eradicate mankind's boredom, but merely to channel it in new directions.

Jeremiah remained in hiding.

Next came a series of visits to the sites of the city's most expensive diversions. He went to the Obsidian Square, the huge, almost legendary casino where everything from the chairs and tables to the very walls was made of shiny black volcanic glass, and which stood, with only a mild attempt at camouflage, at the very center of the old Loop. He went to the Sky Links, the most exclusive nine-hole golf course in the world, located a half-mile above the ground (and covered by an immense net, lest stray shots kill unfortunate passersby on the lower levels). He went to the Little K, the miniature nondenominational Kremlin that could be rented, at great expense, for weddings, funerals, baptisms, festivals of the arts, or just about any other function desired, including an occasional orgy.

Jeremiah was nowhere to be seen.

He went to Veldtland, that extremely costly and exclusive ranch in the northwestern portion of the state, which possessed fifty of the last three hundred lions left on Earth, all roaming at large over a thirty-mile tract. For the modest stipend of two million dollars, a man could shoot one of them; or, for one-tenth of that amount, he could strip himself naked and go armed with only a spear. He even promoted a welterweight championship fight, and used himself as bait by taking over the ring announcer's duties.

But as the month drew to a close there was still no sign of Jeremiah.

"Maybe those gunshot wounds really did kill him after all," mused Moore, sprawling on an overstuffed leather chair in his temporary living quarters down the hall from his office.

"Not a chance," said Moira firmly. "If he was dead, the body would have turned up."

"Lots of people die every day in this town," said Moore dubiously.

"You have your sources for hunting down the living," replied Moira, "and I have mine for finding the dead. If Jeremiah dies, I'll know of it the same day."

"Well, alive or dead, I wish to hell he'd become a little more visible," said Moore. "I'm running out of ideas." He shrugged. "Getting hungry?"

"Yes."

Under the watchful eyes of his well-hidden security men, Moore and Moira took a monorail to Randolph Street, then transferred to an escalator that took them to the upper levels.

"Where are we going this time?" asked Moira, who during the past month had grown increasingly used to splendid food splendidly served.

"A little place that specializes in French cuisine," replied Moore. "Have you ever had Oysters Bienville?"

"I've never even heard of them," said Moira. "What do they taste like?"

"You'll see," said Moore with a smile. "We're only a block away, and—"

Suddenly he froze.

"What is it?" asked Moira. "Is something wrong?"

"That man!" said Moore, pointing toward an elderly man walking toward them on the opposite side of the street. "It's *him!*"

"It's *who?*"

"Krebs—the old guy from the Bizarre Bazaar. Come on!"

Moore broke into a run, and instantly three large, well-dressed men emerged from the throng of shoppers to join him. They reached the old man in a matter of seconds. Moore's quarry made no attempt to evade him, but merely stared blankly ahead with dull, lusterless eyes.

"All right!" snapped Moore, unmindful of the crowd that was gathering around them. "Where is he?"

The old man gazed off into space.

"Where is Jeremiah?" demanded Moore.

The old man smiled vacantly. His face displayed no sign of intelligence or recognition.

"Just a minute," said Moira, finally catching up to Moore. "Isn't Krebs supposed to be missing an eye?"

Moore stared at the old man's two eyes in surprise.

"Maybe the eyepatch was a disguise," he said.

"How about his hand?"

Moore reached out and grabbed the old man's right hand. It possessed a thumb and four fingers.

"You've made a mistake," said Moira.

He shook his head savagely. "This is Krebbs, all right. I can't explain his hand or his eye, but this is the man."

"You must be wrong," persisted Moira. "The eyepatch may have been a disguise, but people don't grow fingers upon request."

"I'm telling you this man is Krebbs! Call Ben and tell him to have Abe Bernstein in my office in twenty minutes."

"Okay—but I think you're crazy."

"Then humor me!" he snarled, leading the old man to the nearest monorail as his security men made sure he wasn't interfered with.

He reached his office in fifteen minutes and gestured to the old man to sit down. The old man remained on his feet, staring expressionlessly at a wall.

Bernstein arrived a few minutes later.

"I'm glad you're here, Abe," said Moore. "We've got a little problem on our hands."

Bernstein took an ophthalmoscope from his bag and shone the light into the old man's eyes. Finally he looked up at Moore.

"Correction: you've got a *big* problem here. What happened to this man, Solomon?"

"I was hoping you'd be able to help me find out."

"Who is he?"

"Krebbs," said Moore.

"The old man who tried to set you up?" asked Bernstein. "I was told he was—"

"Missing an eye and some fingers. I know."

"Have you any reason to believe that you might have been mistaken about that?" asked Bernstein.

"None whatsoever."

"Then this man can't be Krebbs."

"He's Krebbs," said Moore firmly.

"What makes you think so, Solomon?"

"I don't think so. I *know* so. Hell, I'm not likely to forget what he looked like."

"A lot of old men look alike," suggested Bernstein.

"This isn't a lot of old men," snapped Moore. "This is one particular old man—an old man named Krebbs, who happens to be my only link to Jeremiah!"

"Why don't you pick up the phone, call the nearest hospital, and ask them when was the last time they had a case of digital regeneration in a human being?" said Bernstein in exasperation.

"A little less patronizing and a little more medicine," said Moore. "I say he's Krebbs, you say he isn't. Fine. We'll let it pass for the moment. Can you tell me what's wrong with him?"

"On the spur of the moment?"

"If not sooner."

Bernstein examined the old man again, checking pulse, heartbeat, respiration, and reflexes. Finally he stepped back and sighed deeply.

"You've come to the wrong kind of doctor, Solomon. For a man of his age, he's in excellent health. I'd say you need a good psychiatrist, and I emphasize the word 'good.' "

"Why?"

"Dr. Freud, may he rest in peace, would say that this is a classic case of hysteria. Since the word has come to mean screaming and ranting, I would amend it to say that he is suffering from extreme shock."

"How extreme?"

"Bluntly, it seems to have blown every neural circuit in his brain. This, of course, is only my own semiskilled opinion. Possibly a man versed in the field would totally disagree and bring him out of it in five minutes' time."

"How long will it take *you?*" asked Moore.

"I don't think you understand," said Bernstein. "Curing, or even diagnosing, mental cases isn't my field."

"You didn't answer my question," said Moore. "Look—this man is no use to me like this. You've got to find a way to make him rational. A couple of minutes is all I need."

"First, I am not a psychiatrist. And second, this man is not Krebbs." Bernstein paused. "I don't know how you can be so sure about something that is so obviously wrong."

"Either you believe in your instincts and your judgment, or you don't. I do."

"But—"

"You're still not helping me," said Moore impatiently. "I know a psychiatrist would be better, but I don't happen to have any on my payroll, and I don't have any time to waste. Now, what's the best way to bring him out of this trance?"

"You're asking me to do something very unethical, Solomon."

"Wrong," said Moore. "I'm *telling* you to."

Bernstein looked back at the old man, grimaced, and shook his head. "I'm just not well versed enough in the field. Let me call in someone who is."

"All right," Moore assented. "Get him here with everything he'll need in thirty minutes."

Bernstein walked to the phone, made a quick call, and hung up the receiver.

"All right," he announced. "I've called in Neil Procyon. He's on the staff of the Elgin Mental Hospital, and from what I hear he's pretty good with shock therapy."

"Do you know him personally?" asked Moore.

"Socially," answered Bernstein. "He and my son go skiing together up in Michigan."

"Well," said Moore ominously, "let's hope he knows his stuff."

Procyon showed up some twenty-five minutes later, carrying a small plastic case under his arm. He was a young man, intense and unsmiling, with the body of an athlete and the drawn face of a man who didn't know when to stop working. He greeted Bernstein formally, allowed himself to be introduced to Moore, and walked briskly to the old man. He conducted a brief but thorough examination, and then turned to Moore.

"What caused this man's condition?" he asked.

"I don't know—but there's a blank check waiting for you if you can snap him out of it."

"I'll send a team from the hospital out here to pick him up later this afternoon," said Procyon.

"Now," said Moore coldly.

"I beg your pardon?"

"Don't send any teams, Doctor. Cure him now."

"What makes you think you can give orders to me?" demanded Procyon hotly.

Moore made no reply, but pressed a button on his intercom console. Two armed security guards immediately entered the office and stationed themselves by the doorway, their weapons drawn.

"Dr. Bernstein, what the devil is going on here?" demanded Procyon.

Bernstein shrugged. "I'd suggest that you attempt to bring the old man out of his daze here and now, Neil. Mr. Moore is not known for playing practical jokes."

"And, knowing that, you called me in?"

"*I* would surely have killed the patient," said Bernstein. "*You* might not."

"I intend to make a full report of this as soon as I get back to Elgin."

"As you like," said Moore. "But in the meantime . . ." He gestured toward the old man.

"All right," said Procyon. "I just want it clearly understood that I am doing this under threat of death, and for no other reason."

Moore turned to one of the security men. "Get Moira and Ben in here. I want them to hear anything Krebbs might say."

"If he says anything at all," commented Bernstein, "it'll probably be that his name isn't Krebbs, and that he's been a wino or a junkie for the past five years."

"We'll see," said Moore.

"I'll need some help," announced Procyon.

"Anything you wish," said Moore, as Moira and Pryor entered the office.

"I want this man tied securely—and I mean *securely*—to his chair."

The security men, at a signal from Moore, holstered their weapons and carried out Procyon's instructions. The young doctor then unlocked the small case he had brought along and withdrew four transistorized devices, each about the size of a penny. He affixed one on each of the old man's temples, one over the heart, and the fourth on the roof of the man's mouth. He then withdrew a tiny control panel from the case.

"Stand away from him," he ordered. Then he turned to Moira. "You may want to avert your eyes."

"Fat chance," muttered Pryor.

Procyon pressed a button on the panel, and the old man's body began jerking spasmodically. A few seconds later the doctor removed his finger from the button, and the old man sagged limply in his bonds.

Bernstein walked over to the old man, lifted an eyelid, took his pulse, and measured his respiration.

"Well, he's still alive," he announced at last. "But that's about all I can say for him."

"Do it again," said Moore.

"But Mr. Moore . . ." protested Procyon.

"Again."

Procyon pressed the button, and the old man's body almost flew out of the chair.

"No reaction," said Bernstein, after examining him again.

"Once more," said Moore.

"Solomon, it'll kill him!" said Bernstein.

"You heard me," said Moore to Procyon.

The young doctor started to object, then took another look at the security men, sighed, and pressed the button again.

This time, after twitching furiously, the old man opened his eyes and glanced about the room, the total absence of expression giving way to a look of bewilderment.

"Krebbs, can you hear me?" said Moore, kneeling down beside the chair.

"Krebbs? Krebbs?" repeated the old man, mouthing the word uncomprehendingly.

"Where is Jeremiah?"

"Jeremiah?" said the old man, his face puzzled.

"Yes, Jeremiah!" snapped Moore. "Where is he?"

"Krebbs? Jeremiah?"

"You're Krebbs, and you tried to set me up for Jeremiah," said Moore. "I'll let you off the hook, but you've got to tell me where Jeremiah is!"

"Hook? Hook?" The old man repeated the word as if it were a name he couldn't quite recall.

"Give him a little time to recover," urged Bernstein. "He's awfully weak right now."

"Five minutes, no more," said Moore. "Unstrap him."

Bernstein untied the old man, then helped him to sit up more comfortably. A shock of white hair, wet with perspiration, fell onto the old man's forehead, and he reached up with his right hand to brush the hair back. As the hand came within his field of vision he stared at it with growing confusion, wiggling each finger in succession.

"Oh my God," he muttered.

"What is it, old man?" asked Bernstein.

"Oh my God!" he repeated, staring at his fingers.

"Where is he, Krebbs?" persisted Moore.

The old man gingerly raised his left hand and touched first one eye and then the other.

"Oh my God!" he shouted. *"JEREMIAH!"*

With a shriek of pure terror, he toppled off the chair and fell heavily to the floor. As quick as Moore and Bernstein were, Moira was even quicker, and was instantly kneeling over him.

"Is he alive?" asked Moore.

"No," answered Moira, her face flushed with excitement.

"Damn!" said Moore. "Just when he was getting cogent enough to tell us something!"

"I wouldn't say he was cogent," interjected Bernstein. "I'd say he was scared out of his wits, and I mean that quite literally. I think he died of fear."

"What scared him?" asked Moira, lovingly stroking the dead man's face and hair.

"I'm almost afraid to think about it," said Bernstein. He bent over and examined the old man's right hand closely. "There are no scars of any kind."

"What does that imply?" asked Moore.

"Let's allow Dr. Procyon to take his leave first," suggested Bernstein. "Then we can all speak a little more freely."

Moore signaled the security men to escort Procyon out of the office.

"I'll need the body for my report," said the young doctor, visibly shaken.

"No!" said Moira suddenly. "*I* want it."

"What on earth for?" asked Procyon, curious in spite of himself.

"She's kind of a collector," said Pryor with a grin.

"Very funny," muttered Procyon. "Now will you please have someone help me transport it back to the hospital?"

"That wasn't a joke," said Moore. "The lady is keeping the body."

Procyon took two steps toward the corpse, found his way blocked by the security men, then turned on his heel and left.

"He's going to get you in a hell of a lot of trouble, Solomon," said Bernstein.

"It's nothing we can't handle," said Moore, dismissing the subject. "What were you saying about his hand?"

"There are no signs of any skin grafting," said Bernstein. He lifted each eyelid in turn. "Neither eyeball is artificial, either. Let me ask you once more: could you possibly have been mistaken about his eye or his hand?"

"Absolutely not," replied Moore. "Ben, have this man's fingerprints checked out and see what we can dig up on him—and when you're through, have Moira show you where she wants you to stash the body."

Pryor nodded and summoned two more men to help with the fingerprinting, while Moore seated himself behind the desk.

"Well, Abe," he said, "are you finally willing to admit he was Krebbs?"

"I lean in that direction," replied Bernstein. "Tell me a little more about this Jeremiah. Moira made him sound like just another grifter, and not very bright at that."

"A little more is all that I *can* tell you. He's a normal-looking young man in his early twenties, or so I'm told. He's a con artist and a ladies' man. He's been known to frequent Karl Russo's place down in Darktown, but he's probably not an addict. He did his damnedest to set me up for a mugging, he's dumb as all get-out, and he's the luckiest son of a bitch I've ever come across."

"How so?"

"Five of my men cornered him in a room and fired at him at point-blank range. He not only came out of it alive, but managed to escape as well."

"Why does he want to kill you?"

"I don't know. In fact, Moira is of the opinion that he's just trying to scare me."

"And why do you say he's stupid?"

Moore launched into his explanation, and by the time he was done Pryor was back in the room with a computer readout clutched in his hand.

"That was fast," remarked Moore.

"Ex-cons are a little easier to identify than most," replied Pryor.

"What do you have on him?"

"Plenty," said Pryor, looking at the readout. "His name is Willis Comstock Krebbs, Caucasian male, age sixty-three, born in Tucson, Arizona. He served time for rape, arson, extortion, blackmail, bigamy, and second-degree murder."

"Nice fellow," commented Moore dryly.

"I'm not finished," said Pryor. "His identifying marks are as follows: he lost his left eye during a prison brawl in 2027, and lost the thumb and portions of two fingers of his right hand in a monorail accident in 2031."

"That's all?" asked Moore.

"So far."

"Okay, Abe, you're the expert—just what the hell are we dealing with here?"

"I'm not at all sure I want to know," said Bernstein.

"Could Krebbs have been a mutant?"

"Not a chance," replied Bernstein.

"You're sure?"

Bernstein nodded. "First of all, most mutations—well over ninety-nine percent of them—are so small and meaningless as to go completely unnoticed. And the remainder, almost without exception, don't make the mutant any more viable. They might consist of an extra finger, or one less vertebra in the spine, or a hair color that wasn't in the gene pool. Only writers dream up mutants who can control minds or breathe underwater; Nature hasn't gotten that far yet. Furthermore, if Krebbs had the power of regeneration, why did he go twenty years without an eye and sixteen without a couple of fingers before he decided to grow them back?"

"How about Jeremiah?" asked Moira, finally looking up from the body. "Could *he* be the mutant?"

Bernstein shook his head. "Once and for all, forget about mutants. The two of you keep assuming that a mutant would have the power to regrow lost organs and limbs, and I assure you that it just isn't so. And certainly no mutant, even if he possessed that power, could will regeneration upon someone else."

"Could Jeremiah be an alien?" suggested Moira.

"You've been watching too many bad television shows," said Bernstein. "I very much doubt that an alien would bear such a resemblance to us, and I find it just a little difficult to believe that an alien would spend all his time swindling our men and fornicating with our women." He paused and smiled. "I can also give you half a hundred sound scientific reasons to support my position, if you would care to hear them."

"Could a mutant—or a man, if you prefer—be able to control random chance, to make his own luck?" asked Moore.

"No more than you can," said Bernstein. "Whatever the reason for Jeremiah's escape from your men, it wasn't because he consciously or unconsciously willed them to miss him."

"Have you got a better explanation?"

"Not yet," admitted Bernstein. "At the moment, I'm much more concerned with how Krebbs regrew his missing parts than with Jeremiah."

"Don't be so sure that the two aren't related," said Moore. "After all, he screamed Jeremiah's name after he saw that he was whole again."

"That doesn't mean there's a connection," said Bernstein doggedly.

"It doesn't mean there's *not*, either," responded Moore.

"Jeremiah once told me that the ancient Egyptians had all kinds of magical healing arts," offered Moira. "Maybe he found out what they did and did it to Krebbs."

"Horseshit!" snapped Bernstein. "There's never been a case of regeneration in the history of humanity. What does a carnival grifter know about Egypt, anyway?"

"He lived there," said Moira.

"He's been to Egypt?" asked Bernstein, suddenly interested.

She nodded.

"And Israel too?"

"He grew up in the Middle East," said Moore. "How did you know that?"

"I didn't," said Bernstein thoughtfully. "Let's call it a lucky guess."

"Have you got any more guesses?" asked Moore.

"None that I care to put on the record."

"You look very disturbed, Abe."

"I am."

"If you know something, I think you'd better share it with us."

"I don't *know* anything. For just a second I had a crazy notion. Let's forget it."

"It's probably not any crazier than a man regrowing an eye and some fingers," said Moore. "Let's hear it."

Bernstein shook his head firmly.

"All right," said Moore with a shrug. "In that case, we'll operate under the assumption that Jeremiah is either a mutant of as yet unknown powers, or an incredibly skilled surgeon, which seems like the least likely explanation of all. I'll have Ben dig us up a scientist or two who knows something about mutation."

"It won't help," said Bernstein.

"Besides, Jeremiah hasn't been seen since Darktown," added Moira. "Why don't we just assume he's left the city? Then you can get back to work, and I can go home to the museum."

"Because if I let one guy get away with trying to kill me," explained Moore, "how long do you think it will be before others start lining up to take a crack at it?"

"Well, I don't like it," said Moira.

"You don't have to like it; you just have to do it," retorted Moore.

Suddenly Bernstein walked to the door.

"Where the hell do you think you're going?" demanded Moore.

"I've got a lot of thinking to do," replied Bernstein uncomfortably.

"You look like you're scared shitless."

"If truth be known, I am."

"You didn't answer my question. Where can I find you if I need you?"

"I'll be at my temple," said Bernstein.

Moore uttered a sarcastic laugh. "What kind of crap are you handing out here? I know you: every time you get scared you threaten to quit and move to Florida."

"I don't think quitting will help this time."

"And going to temple will?" asked Moore with a smile.

"Yes," answered Bernstein seriously. "I think it will."

9

"We've got him surrounded, sir!"

"Where?"

"Lakeport."

"I'm on my way."

Moore slammed the phone down, summoned Moira, Pryor, and half a dozen security men, and headed for Lakeport, the huge airport complex that floated atop Lake Michigan, some ten miles off Chicago's shoreline.

When they arrived they found that Jeremiah was trapped inside an empty hangar. As far as Moore could tell, there was no possible means of escape. Thirty armed men encircled the building, their weapons trained on every door and window. Still more men were backing up the first group, and the remainder of his security force was carefully checking the passengers on all incoming and outgoing boats and planes. Furthermore, the city—or those members of its government who were personally obligated to Moore—had blocked off all other means of ingress and egress: the ramps, the tunnels, the monorails.

"How did you spot him?" Moore asked the man in charge.

"He tried to buy a ticket to Cairo."

"Egypt or Illinois?"

"Egypt. A couple of our agents identified him."

"You're sure it's Jeremiah?"

"Him or his twin brother," came the reply. "He fits the description we've got to a T, and he raced off like a bat out of hell when we called him by name."

"And he's still in the hangar?"

"Right."

"Moira, you come with me," said Moore. "I want to be absolutely certain we've got the right man."

"I don't think you should go in," she said. "He could be more dangerous than you think."

"I want to make sure that what happened last time doesn't happen again," said Moore. "Or if it does, I want to see it with my own eyes."

He took a handgun from one of the guards and, gesturing to his own security team to accompany him, entered the hangar.

It was quite large, almost four hundred feet long by two hundred wide and eighty high, and displayed no sign of life. Moore directed one of the men to turn on the lights, but found that the additional illumination didn't make much difference. He looked up at a number of ramps that ran along the inside wall of the hangar at a height of about fifty feet, trying to locate a likely place of concealment. There was none.

"All right," he announced at last. "It's obvious that he can't get out past our men, so we can take our time about this. We'll proceed as a unit and go over every inch of the damned building."

They began following the wall to the left, moving slowly and carefully, looking under, behind, and inside every object large enough to hide a man. They had gone about two hundred feet when they heard a shuffling sound from the far wall of the hangar.

"Over there!" shouted Moore, racing in the direction of the noise.

He and his men got to within fifty feet of a large baggage carrier when a young man stepped out from behind it, his hands above his head.

"Is that him?" Moore asked Moira.

"Yes," she replied.

"You're sure?"

"Absolutely."

Moore stared at the young man for a long moment. Finally he shrugged.

"Kill him," he ordered.

"No!" screamed Jeremiah. "I'm unarmed! You can't do this! I'm—"

Seven guns exploded in unison, Moore's included, and Jeremiah was flung some thirty feet away by the impact of the bullets. As soon as he stopped rolling over he got groggily to his feet and began running.

"What the hell is going on here?" muttered Moore. He fired again at Jeremiah, who was limping painfully but rapidly toward a door at the far end of the hangar as a hail of bullets struck the walls around him.

Moore took up the chase, shooting as he went. Jeremiah fell twice more, but each time managed to regain his feet and continue running toward the door. He reached it mere seconds ahead of Moore and raced out into the sunlight.

Moore stepped through the doorway just in time to see an airplane skid off a runway and head directly toward the hangar. He took in the situation at a glance, then ducked back inside the hangar and threw himself to the floor. There was a loud explosion an instant later, followed by two smaller ones and a burst of heat and smoke.

The hangar caught fire instantly, and beams and girders began falling to the floor. Moore got to his feet and began running to the undamaged end of the building. Moira and two of the security men followed him, but the others had disappeared under the rapidly accumulating rubble.

When he reached the door through which he had entered, he stepped outside, checked himself for injuries, found nothing but some superficial bruises and abrasions, and circled around the hangar to view the carnage. The air stank of burning flesh, and fifty of his men lay dead or severely mangled near the wreckage of the plane. A rescue crew was already on the scene, and half a dozen more were speeding toward the scene.

"Where is he?" demanded Moore, trying to spot Jeremiah's corpse in among the other bodies.

"He couldn't have survived that," replied one of the security men firmly. "He was right in the middle of it. You'll be lucky if you can find the fillings from his teeth."

"I hope you're right," said Moore, "but I want the entire area checked anyway. And I want somebody to find out what happened to the plane—what made it skid and crash." He turned to Moira, who was bleeding from her mouth. "Are you all right?"

"I will be, after I see a dentist," she said. "I have a couple of teeth loose." She looked down at her torn, grime-covered suit. "I think I could probably use a change of clothes, too. How about you, Mr. Moore? You look dreadful."

"I'm okay. Just shaken up a little," he said. "Let's get back to the office. There's nothing much we can do here."

They arrived, patched up most of their wounds, and changed into fresh clothes just in time to receive Pryor's first report from Lakeport: the plane's landing gear had failed to function. A brief preliminary investigation hadn't turned up any signs of sabotage.

Ten minutes later there was a second call from Pryor. A horribly mangled young man who matched Jeremiah's description had managed to board an airliner at gunpoint, and was, according to the pilot's radio message, preparing to parachute down somewhere over the Pocono Mountains.

"I wish I knew what the hell is happening!" snapped Moore after hanging up the receiver.

"I don't understand," said Moira.

"Your boyfriend has more lives than a goddamned cat."

"You don't mean to say that Jeremiah is alive?"

"Alive and free," said Moore. "The son of a bitch not only lived through that holocaust, but he managed to hijack a plane."

"But that's impossible!" exclaimed Moira.

"Evidently not," replied Moore. "I seem to remember Sherlock Holmes telling Dr. Watson that when you eliminate the impossible, whatever remains must be the truth. If we apply that to Jeremiah, the one thing that remains is that there's no way in hell that he can be a normal man with normal abilities—if he's a man at all."

"I don't care if he's a man, a mutant, or an alien," persisted Moira. "No one could have survived that!"

"Someone did," said Moore. "*Him.*"

"There must be some mistake," she insisted. "Probably they identified the wrong man as Jeremiah."

"I don't believe that, and neither do you," said Moore soberly.

"But there's no other rational explanation!"

"You've noticed," he said wryly.

"He's *got* to be dead!"

Moore stared at her as if to argue, then shrugged. "I've been letting too damned many subordinates check up on Jeremiah. I think it's time that I did a little homework myself."

"Beginning where?" asked Moira.

"At the beginning," said Moore. "We've had people working around the clock trying to find out something about this guy. I want to go over every last shred of information they've put together. And I want *you* to submit to the psycho-probe again, once you get your teeth fixed. Maybe it can drag something out of you that it missed the first time around."

Moira left the office, and Moore waited until all the material, sparse as it was, had been assembled on his desk. Then he locked the door and began going over it slowly and methodically.

There still wasn't much.

To those few tidbits of information he already possessed were added the following:

- Jeremiah's parents were agnostic Jews, and he himself was an atheist.
- Jeremiah had had a vasectomy two years ago while living in Seattle.
- Jeremiah had not only had the normal childhood diseases, but had actually contracted typhoid and an unknown sleeping sickness. In both cases he was near death, but miraculously recovered.
- Jeremiah's mother had published two small monographs concerning some obscure theories about the ancient Mesopotamians.
- Neither had received any coverage whatsoever from the academic community.
- Jeremiah's full name was Immanuel Jeremiah Branch, and he was the son of Marvin H. Branch and Linda Branch.

And that, in a nutshell, was that. The sum total of his knowledge of Jeremiah wouldn't fill two sheets of typing paper. In fact, the only thing Moore had learned—or, rather, deduced—was the genesis of the names Jeremiah the B and Manny the B.

He heard nothing further from Pryor, and Moira was still undergoing the psycho-probe, so he decided to return to his apartment for the first time in days, hoping that in the comfort of his library he might be able to sort out the day's events and perhaps make a little sense out of them.

When he arrived home, he took a hot shower and tended to his wounds once again. Then he prepared a quick dinner consisting primarily of non-soya vegetable products, and spent two hours sitting on his old leather chair, pondering over the few notes he had scribbled and wondering what they had in common with a man who could survive gunfire and plane crashes with equal facility. It wasn't as if he had done it with style, either; Moore was certain that Jeremiah was fully as surprised at his ability to cheat death as everyone else was.

Moore stared at the notes for a few more minutes, and finally three words caught his attention: Immanuel Jeremiah Branch.

Somewhere, deep in the forgotten recesses of his mind, that name rang a bell, or perhaps a series of them. It seemed familiar, though he was sure he had never come across it before.

Curious, he walked over to a long-unopened copy of *Burke's Peerage*, and was not surprised to find that there was no such name listed there.

He then pulled down a couple of books devoted to coats of arms, with the same results. He even tried the Chicago and Manhattan phone directories, still with no luck.

And then, on a hunch, he picked up a copy of the Bible.

As far as the name Immanuel went, he knew of only one place where he could recall seeing it, and he turned to the Book of Isaiah, thumbing through it until he came to Chapter 8:

"Behold, a virgin shall conceive, and bear a son, and shall call his name Immanuel."

"Well," he muttered, "so much for Immanuel."

The hoped-for Immanuel, Isaiah went on to say, would eat butter and honey and learn to refuse evil and choose the good—which certainly didn't sound like the Immanuel that Moore was after.

He was about to put the book back when he riffled through the pages once with his thumb to shake the dust loose.

That was when he saw it, flashing briefly before his eyes.

He bent back the leather cover and let the pages race by again, but couldn't pick it out, so he began turning them one at a time until it reached out and hit him right between the eyes, capital letters and all:

"Here now, O Joshua the high priest, thou, and thy fellows that sit before thee: for they are men wondered at: for behold, I will bring forth my servant THE BRANCH."

It was the Book of Zechariah, and he read on, searching for some other reference to The Branch.

He found it.

". . . Thus speaketh the Lord of Hosts, saying, behold the man whose name is THE BRANCH; and he shall grow up out of his place, and he shall build the temple of the Lord; and he shall bear the glory, and shall sit and rule upon his throne. . . ."

Two minutes later he was on the phone to Bernstein.

"Abe, I'm sorry to bother you, but I've got to ask you a couple of questions."

"Did Moira give us something new?" asked Bernstein.

"I don't care what the hell she gave us. How conversant are you with the Bible?"

"I knew you'd ask sooner or later," sighed Bernstein, "but I never thought it would be this quick."

"You didn't answer my question."

"I grew up with the Old Testament. I'm not as well acquainted with the other one."

"That's okay. The Old Testament is what I'm interested in. What can you tell me about The Branch? All capital letters. It's in Zechariah."

"Hold on while I get my copy," said Bernstein.

Moore waited impatiently while Bernstein, with a great deal of noise and a muffled curse as he bumped into a chair, walked across his room, picked up a Bible, and limped back to the phone.

"I'm back," he announced painfully.

"Have you got the place?" asked Moore.

"Zechariah. Right."

"Fine. Who is The Branch, and why is he called that?"

"It's a guarded reference to the Messiah," said Bernstein, after reading the chapter half aloud, half to himself. "The Branch refers to his being a fresh branch from the withered Davidic family tree."

"Why the Davidic tree?"

"Because one of the few things the Messianic prophets agreed upon was that the Messiah—which is simply Aramaic for Anointed One—would come from the line of David."

"Ready for another question?"

"Go ahead," said Bernstein.

"How many present-day Jews can trace their ancestry back to David?"

"None."

"Then it's a dead line?" asked Moore.

"I have no idea. But I know that no one can trace his lineage back that far. You're talking three thousand years or more."

There was a long, uncomfortable pause.

"Are you thinking what I'm thinking?" asked Moore at last.

"It's crazy, Solomon."

"I know. So is everything else that's been happening lately."

"It's so farfetched that I'm embarrassed to even admit that the thought had crossed my mind," said Bernstein.

"Me too."

"He's more likely to be a man from Mars."

"I agree," said Moore. "But I want you to do me a favor anyway."

"If it's within my power."

"Meet me at my office tomorrow morning at eight o'clock sharp."

"That's all?"

"Not quite."

"What else?" asked Bernstein.

"Bring your rabbi."

10

"Solomon, allow me to introduce you to Rabbi Milton Greene," said Bernstein.

Moore arose and stared at the young man who stood before him in a striped, floor-length robe.

"Call me Milt," said Greene, extending his hand.

"That's quite an outfit you've got there," commented Moore, taking his hand.

"My coat of many colors?" replied Greene with a smile. He turned around once. "I wove it on my own loom."

"It must wake them up during your sermons," said Moore.

"Oh, I dress a little more formally for work," said Greene. "Actually, I'm going over to the Sky Links when I leave here."

"Surely you can't swing a golf club in *that*," offered Bernstein.

"I keep a sweater and a set of knickers in my locker," replied Greene, sitting down on one of the wooden chairs that were lined up in front of Moore's desk. "Well, Mr. Moore, what can I do for you? Abe told me to bone up on the Messiah before I came, but as yet I have no idea what for, since I'm probably the last person you'd want to see about converting to Christianity."

"I've got some questions to ask you," said Moore. He paused, staring at Greene again. "I don't mean to hurt your feelings, but you seem awfully young to be a rabbi."

Greene shrugged and smiled. "Well, if it comes to that, you seem awfully young to be a criminal kingpin."

"I'm just a businessman."

"That's not what the media thinks."

"Then why did you agree to see me?"

"Why not?" Greene smiled again. "Somehow, I have a hard time envisioning your organization muscling in on the God racket."

Moore turned to Bernstein. "I like him," he said approvingly.

"That's why I left my old temple and joined his," agreed Bernstein.

"Tell me, Rabbi—" began Moore.

"Milt," interrupted Greene.

"Tell me, Milt, what kind of advice does a guy like you give to an old-timer like Abe?"

"That's what you got me down here to ask?"

Moore shook his head. "Just curious."

"I tell him the usual crap about living a good life and worshiping the Lord," replied Greene. "Then, whenever I think his guard's down, I tell him to throw his son out of the house before he turns into a full-time deadbeat."

"Now, just a minute!" said Bernstein hotly.

"Abe, the kid is twenty-four years old and he's never done an honest day's work. All he does is go skiing on your money. You've really got to put a stop to it," said Greene, and Moore found himself agreeing silently.

A secretary entered the office just then and handed Moore a sealed report telling him where Pryor had spent the night and estimating when he could be expected at the office. Moore opened it, read it over, and put it in a desk drawer. As the secretary left the room, he told her to make sure he wasn't interrupted until his meeting with the rabbi was over.

"Well," he said, turning back to Greene, "shall we get down to business?"

"Fine," replied Greene. He pulled out a huge cigar. "Mind if I smoke?"

"Be my guest," said Moore. "Abe told you that I needed some information, right?"

"That's correct."

"Good," said Moore. "Let's start with an easy one: are you still waiting for the Messiah?"

Greene laughed. "You mean, right this minute?"

"It's pretty unlikely that he's going to walk in through the door while we're speaking," said Moore, resisting the urge to knock on wood. "I mean generally."

"Do you want a personal answer or an official one?" asked Greene.

"Take your choice."

"Personally, no. Officially, yes."

"Okay, let's keep it official for a while," said Moore. "Assuming that in your official capacity as a rabbi you believe in the Messiah and the Messianic prophecies, why don't you believe that Jesus was the Messiah?"

"There have been about ten thousand books that address that very subject," replied Greene. "Maybe I should just loan you a couple of the better ones."

"Could you condense them into a couple paragraphs for me?"

"I'll do better than that: I'll give it to you in a single sentence. Jesus didn't fulfill the Messianic prophecies."

"Almost four billion people think that he did," said Moore. "Why?"

"Some people are stupider than others," replied Greene easily. "Look, the first thing you've got to understand is that the Messianic prophecies aren't anywhere near as simple as the King James Version of the Bible would lead you to believe. Even before the discovery of the Dead Sea Scrolls, we know of three separate and distinct Messiahs that were expected by the ancient Jews."

"Three?" said Moore, surprised.

"At least. Probably there were more. The word 'Messiah'—which comes out as 'Kristos' in Greek, if you want to know how Jesus got his name—merely means 'anointed,' and anointed is what a king was supposed to be. The Messiah of the Jews was to be a king who would restore the race to its former glory, and of course Jesus failed to do this. In fact, the Jews were driven from Jerusalem in 70 A.D., only forty years after his death, and didn't reestablish themselves there for almost two thousand years."

"What else was expected of him?" asked Moore.

"Not a goddamned thing," interjected Bernstein.

"Abe's quite right," said Greene. "The only thing the Messiah had to do was establish an all-powerful kingdom in Jerusalem."

"Just a minute," said Moore. "I've been going over the Bible all night, and I've found a lot of other things he was supposed to do."

"No you didn't," said Greene, puffing on his cigar. "I told you that things aren't as simple as the New Testament makes them sound. What you're referring to are a number of signs by which the Messiah could be identified, but these were all preliminary. His only purpose was to establish a kingdom in Jerusalem." He shook his head sadly. "I never could understand how so many people could worship a man who delivered the preliminaries and blew the big event—meaning no disrespect if you happen to be one of them."

"Then why is he worshiped as the son of God?"

Greene shrugged. "Beats me. The Messiah's only got supernatural powers in the New Testament; in the prophecies he was just a man. A very special man, to be sure, since he had to possess even greater wisdom than Abraham and David, but a man, nonetheless."

"Let's get back to the signs for a minute. I was under the impression that Jesus had fulfilled them—riding into town on a white ass, being resurrected, and so forth."

"More smokescreen," said Greene firmly. "There were hundreds of signs predicted in the books of the prophets and other ancient Hebraic literature. The white ass was mentioned exactly once—and even that was probably added a century or two after the Crucifixion to agree with prior events."

"What are you talking about?"

"There hasn't been an awful lot written in stone since the Ten Commandments," explained Greene in amused tones. "The Bible was rewritten every generation or two, and usually changed to agree with the dominant beliefs of the period. As for the signs, his resurrection was never once prophesied. Don't forget—his kingdom was to be here on Earth. Heaven was, so to speak, God's domain."

"Then what signs would the Jews have accepted as proof of his Messiahship?" asked Moore in frustration.

"The most telling sign would have been the establishment of his kingdom. I know it's becoming repetitive, but setting up shop in Jerusalem is what being the Messiah is all about."

"Let me rephrase the question," said Moore. "If the Messiah were to show up during your lifetime, by what signs—short of the establishment of his kingdom—would you know him?"

Greene continued puffing on his cigar as he considered the question for a moment. Finally he looked up. "I think there are probably four signs that would be agreed upon by most Jewish scholars," he answered at last. "First, he'd have to come from the line of David; second, his name would have to be Immanuel; third, he would have to come out of Egypt before establishing his kingdom; and fourth, he'd have to resurrect the dead."

"Didn't Jesus fulfill those signs?"

Greene laughed aloud. "He's lucky if he's batting .250. Jesus is Greek for Joshua, not Immanuel. Nowhere is there any historic proof that he raised the dead. Nowhere is there any proof that he set foot in Egypt. And—"

"Just a minute," interrupted Moore. "The Gospels clearly state that he went to Egypt as a boy to avoid one of Herod's bloodlettings."

Greene turned to Bernstein. "Do you want to tell him, Abe?"

"Solomon," said Bernstein, "read your history books. There were *no* bloodlettings under King Herod!"

"Right," chimed in Greene. "And if this mythical slaughter didn't take place, I can't see any reason to believe that Jesus had to escape from it."

"What about his descent from David?" continued Moore. "Matthew documents it, generation by generation."

"Pure bullshit," said Greene. "Mathew made so many genealogical blunders that even the writers who codified it in his Gospel couldn't tidy it up."

"For instance?"

"For instance, he claims that Joram begat Ozias. But recorded history shows that there were four generations between Joram and Ozias, and that Ozias was actually the son of Amaziah. You know," he added, "when you write a Holy Book, the very first thing you should do is make sure that it can't be contradicted by the record. Matthew blew it." He paused to relight his cigar, which had gone out. "His biggest blunder was trying to place Joseph, and hence Jesus, into the Davidic line. I know of no Biblical scholar, Jewish or otherwise, who can substantiate that little tidbit."

"So you're saying that Mathew lied."

"Not necessarily. The damned thing was probably rewritten twenty or thirty times before the end of the Dark Ages. I'm saying that *somebody* lied. Which," he added, "is perfectly understandable. They had to twist certain facts and fabricate other ones if the Gospels were to establish Jesus as the Messiah."

"And what is the Jewish view of Jesus?" asked Moore.

"Mine, or the official one?"

"Let's keep it official."

"The prevailing view is that he was a good and intelligent man, one of many children of Joseph the carpenter and his wife, whose real name was Miriam, not Mary. It is assumed that he grew up somewhere in Galilee and—"

"Why do you put him in such a broad area as Galilee?" asked Moore. "Why not Nazareth?"

"Because there probably wasn't a Nazareth," replied Greene. "More likely the Nazarenes were a Jewish sect not unlike the Essenes. There were a lot of such sects around at the time, and his later career would certainly imply that he had taken his training with one of them. He was strongly influenced by John the Baptist, and took John's cause for his own. He must have had some basic knowledge of herbal medicine, since he cured a number of illnesses—though of course we don't believe that he cured leprosy or made blind men see."

"You also don't believe that he brought Lazarus back from the dead?"

"Of course not. Do you?"

Moore shook his head. "No."

"Good for you," said Greene. "Moving right along, we believe that Jesus chose his disciples from the lower classes because he himself came from that particular social stratum, that he led them to Jerusalem just prior to Passover, that he was outraged to see moneychanging going on in the Temple, and that his subsequent actions caused such a disturbance that both Pilate and the Pharisees felt he must either be discredited or run out of town." He paused. "And of course you know the rest. He was found guilty of treason and executed."

"And the resurrection?"

"A fairy tale. But even if it were true, it wouldn't signify his Messiahship in any way."

"And the Jews have been waiting for more than two thousand years since his death?"

"Some of them have."

"What does *that* mean?" asked Moore.

Greene grinned and leaned back. "I was hoping we'd get around to this subject, since I boned up on it before coming here. Did you think Jesus was the only man who claimed to be the Messiah and picked up a bunch of believers along the way?"

"I had assumed so," admitted Moore.

"Well, assume again, Mr. Moore," said Greene. "There were hundreds before him, and a hell of a lot after him as well. Back in the thirteenth century, a descendant of a noble Spanish-Jewish family named Abraham Abulafia convinced tens of thousands of people that he was the Messiah. In the early 1500s a dark, gnomelike dwarf named David Reuveni had so many followers convinced that he was the true Messiah that he was even granted an audience with Pope Clement VII."

"Really?" said Moore, surprised.

"Wait," said Greene. "It gets better. The most widely accepted would-be Messiah—including Jesus—was Sabbatai Levi, a seventeenth-century Turk. He heard voices exhorting him to redeem

Israel, and to fulfill the Messianic prophecies he went to Egypt, where he astounded half a million disciples by promptly marrying an internationally known prostitute."

Moore chuckled. "And that was the end of him?"

"Not quite," replied Greene. "He returned to Turkey amid rumors that he had a huge Jewish army hidden away in Arabia just awaiting his commands, and announced that he planned to depose the sultan."

"So what happened?"

"The sultan offered him a choice: he could publicly convert to Islam, or he could be chopped to pieces—testicles and head first. He converted, and another Messianic hope bit the dust."

"Were there any more recent ones?" asked Moore.

"There was Jacob Frank, a Russian, who declared that anyone could find redemption through purity, but that the true path was through *impurity*. He proceeded to enliven his pseudoreligious séances with sexual orgies, and was later excommunicated by the Turkish and Russian rabbis. He died in—when was it?—1791, I think. The last of the major pretenders to the Messiahship was Bal Shem Tov, who was born in the Ukraine at about the same time as Jacob Frank. He supposedly had a halo and performed miraculous cures, and by the time of his death in 1780 about half the Jews in Europe believed he was truly the Messiah." He paused and stretched his arms above his head, then relaxed. "So you see, Mr. Moore, while having a Messiah one believes in is a unique experience to Christians, having one who doesn't fulfill the prophecies is nothing new to Jews."

"So I gather."

"And now, Mr. Moore, I feel that I am entitled to ask you a question."

"Go right ahead."

"Who is *your* candidate for Messiahship?"

"I don't believe in Messiahs," said Moore.

"*That's* a relief," said Greene with a smile.

"Why?" asked Moore. "Wouldn't you like to see the Messiah before you die?"

"Not really," answered Greene. "The Lord, my God, is a jealous God, and not at all above flooding the Earth or totally destroying Sodom and Gomorrah. If he's got a Messiah in mind for us, I rather suspect that it will be a Messiah who rejects the power of love in favor of the might of the sword, and will burn the old kingdom down before erecting a new one on its ashes." He paused thoughtfully. "No, if the Messiah ever appears, I for one hope that I'm peacefully dead and settled in my grave before that happy moment occurs."

"One last question," said Moore. "Tell me about The Branch."

"Ah, yes—Abe mentioned that I should read Zechariah. It appears that Zechariah swiped Isaiah's metaphor about a fresh branch coming forth from the withered Davidic line, although later it appears that he's naming Zerubbable as the Messiah."

"Did Zerubabbel fulfill any of Zechariah's or Isaiah's prophecies?" asked Moore.

"Not a one." He paused. "Is that it?"

"Yes."

"Good! Then I can still get in nine holes before lunch. There's a great little Hungarian eateasy two levels down from the Sky Links. Someday if you get a chance, you might—"

"I already have," said Moore. He got to his feet and escorted Greene to the door. "Does your temple have any objections to receiving a donation from me?"

"Probably," said Greene. "If you feel that you must, why not give it to Abe and let him contribute it?"

"I'll do that," promised Moore.

Greene stopped in the doorway and turned to Moore once more. "Is your candidate batting better than .500?"

"I don't know," said Moore. "But I sure as hell doubt it."

Greene left the office, and Moore walked back to his desk.

"Well?" said Bernstein.

"I was hoping he would shoot a few hundred holes in the idea," said Moore, frowning. "Abe, what would you say if I told you that Jeremiah's full name is Immanuel Jeremiah Branch?"

"I wouldn't be surprised."

"Still, it's just too farfetched to believe," said Moore. "I like the mutant theory better."

"I was sure you would," said Bernstein.

"Just what the hell is *that* supposed to mean?"

"Solomon, when people come across something that is contradictory to their training and their experience, they tend to either ignore it or misinterpret it."

"Well, if *you* believe this Messiah crap, why aren't you leading a bandwagon for Jeremiah instead of helping me plot to kill him?" demanded Moore.

"There'll be time for that later," said Bernstein seriously. "Besides, it ought to be apparent to you by this time that no one is going to kill him."

"We'll see about that," said Moore. "In the meantime, he's only batting .500—his name's Immanuel and he's been to Egypt."

"By the way, I do have one little tidbit of information for you," said Bernstein.

"About Jeremiah?"

"Yes."

"Why didn't you tell me as soon as you got here?" demanded Moore.

"I wanted to wait until Milt Greene left."

"Okay. Let's have it."

"I checked the results of Moira's psycho-probe before Milt showed up this morning," began Bernstein.

"And?"

"Jeremiah once told her that when he was seventeen years old he was swimming with a friend, and the friend drowned after suffering a stomach cramp."

"So what?"

"Jeremiah revived him."

"And you call that resurrecting the dead?" scoffed Moore. "Hell, any Boy Scout can perform artificial respiration!"

"There's nothing in the prophecies that says he has to dig up a moldering corpse and magically return it to life," replied Bernstein. "His companion was dead. He revived him. Q.E.D.—and he's batting at least .750."

"It's a crock of shit, and you know it."

"I *don't* know it and neither do you, or you wouldn't have had me bring Milt over," said Bernstein stubbornly.

"Oh, come on, Abe! Jeremiah's a beggar and a thief, he's as dumb as people get to be, and he's not exactly on the road to establishing a kingdom in Jerusalem or anywhere else. I'd say he's as unlikely a candidate for Messiah as you're ever going to find."

"At the risk of sounding religious," replied Bernstein, "he won't be the Messiah because he's a likely candidate, but because he *is* the Messiah, plain and simple."

"Horseshit. He's no more a Messiah than you or me. If there was a Messiah at all, it was Jesus."

"You don't believe that any more than I do."

"No, I don't," said Moore. "But almost half the people in the world think Jesus was the Messiah. Maybe they know something we don't know."

"To quote my employer: horseshit."

"Then look at it another way. The Jews have been established in Israel for a century, and they've been trouncing the Arabs every decade or so. Maybe the Messiah showed up when no one was looking. Maybe he was David Ben-Gurion."

"An interesting notion," admitted Bernstein. "But unfortunately, it doesn't explain Jeremiah away."

"I don't want to explain him away," said Moore. "I just want to kill him. Hell, your rabbi did a beautiful job of explaining Jesus away, and billions of people still believe in him."

"It doesn't make them right."

"It doesn't make them wrong, either."

"Why should an avowed atheist suddenly defend Jesus' divinity?" asked Bernstein. "Could it be that if you can force yourself to believe in the Christians' Messiah you won't have to face the grim reality of the true one?"

"Perhaps," admitted Moore uncomfortably. He sighed. "I suppose the next order of business is finding out whether or not Jesus was really the Messiah."

Bernstein laughed sarcastically. "Hundreds of thousands of scholars have devoted their lives to finding that out. What makes you think you'll succeed where they failed?"

"They didn't know who to ask," said Moore. "I do."

11

It had achieved a measure of fame out of all proportion to its appearance. It was structurally unimpressive, just a little building divided into a foyer, a file room, and twenty cubicles. It was a branch of the Reality Library, known by reputation to tens of millions of people, and misunderstood by almost all of them.

Moore left his bodyguards at the door, entered the building, and walked up to the sole attendant, a portly, middle-aged man who sat behind a cluttered counter.

"Yes?"

"My name is Moore. Solomon Moody Moore, I made an appointment."

The man typed the name into his computer terminal. "Ah. Yes, Mr. Moore. I've reserved cubicle number seven for you."

"Do I pay you now or later?"

"Our fee is twenty thousand dollars an hour, and we require at least two hours' payment in advance."

"Fine," said Moore, scribbling down the identification number of his personal account.

"Thank you," said the attendant. "You can begin in a few moments, just as soon as our computer transfers the funds. Your bank has been notified that this transaction will take place, hasn't it?"

"Yes."

"Have you ever used the Library before?"

"No," said Moore.

"Do you know how it works?"

"Only what I've heard."

"Then perhaps you might appreciate a little backgrounding," said the attendant, producing a pamphlet from behind the counter. "Here. You might want to read through this. If you have any questions after you've finished with it, I'll be happy to answer them."

Moore thanked him, then walked over to a chair, sat down, and began reading.

The Reality Library, said the pamphlet, despite the incredible complexity of its techniques, was basically a form of entertainment, the logical culmination of all that had gone before. Phonograph records and audio tapes appealed to only a single sense, theater and the cinema to only two—but even if one found a medium that appealed to all five senses, as the short-lived feelies had attempted to do back in the 2020s, one would still be only a spectator, a voyeur whose experience would remain totally vicarious.

But the Reality Library had changed all that. When a user (the pamphlet disliked the word *"customer"*) sat down in his cubicle, he would find two nodules that he would attach to his temples, as per the carefully rendered illustration. He then flicked a switch on the right arm of the chair, and contact with the main bank of the Library in Houston was immediately established.

The Library had more than a quarter million works of literature recorded. The user had merely to select any character, no matter how great or small, from any book in the tape catalog, and he would for all practical purposes become that character for the duration of the tape. He would feel exactly what the character was feeling, know what he knew, see what he saw. The user would be unable to act independently or change the prerecorded pattern of what occurred in the chosen work of literature; rather, he would seem to find himself in a secret section of the character's mind, sharing every thought and experience, and following him through to the conclusion of his saga.

The pamphlet went on to explain how actors had originally been tied in to vast banks of machines that sorted and stored their reactions, which were then temporarily transferred to the brains of the Library's patrons. The results were less than satisfactory, since what the patron was then receiving was an actor's interpretation of an author's work, and of course wars and death scenes were almost impossible to manage. Over the years, though, the Library's technology had grown increasingly more sophisticated, to the point where a user could now live a book without having it filtered through actors, directors, adapters, or any other middlemen. A single tape usually took a team of four technicians between two and three years to complete; and with half a million technicians under contract and more being trained each day, the Library's catalog was growing geometrically.

Moore read a little further, found nothing except an inordinate amount of self-congratulatory hyperbole, and finally returned to the counter.

"Any questions?" asked the attendant, taking the pamphlet back and putting it out of sight behind the counter.

"Does it hurt—attaching these things to my head?"

"Goodness, no!" laughed the attendant. "Who would come back a second time if there were any pain involved?"

"You'd be surprised," said Moore, thinking of some of the more notorious exhibits at the Thrill Show.

"I assure you that you won't feel the slightest discomfort, Mr. Moore."

"I'll take your word for it," said Moore with a shrug.

The attendant's computer terminal beeped twice.

"Ah! Your money has been transferred."

"Your prices must scare away a lot of customers," commented Moore.

"Not as many as you might suppose," replied the attendant. "We offer you experiences that nobody else can duplicate. Have you ever wondered what the female orgasm feels like? You can become Fanny Hill, live her life, feel her sensations. Do you dream of empire? You can be Caesar, Elizabeth, Bonaparte—not just observe them, mind you, but *become* them. Do you fantasize about your physical abilities? Then be Tarzan, locked in mortal combat with Numa the Lion."

"How long does it take to run through a tape?"

"It varies, but by and large you can live a tape in about forty minutes. Of course, if you wish to be Natasha in *War and Peace*, it will take a little longer. And, conversely, if you wish to be a character who appears in only a single chapter of *War and Peace*, it might run only two or three minutes."

"What if I want to be a character at only one point of a story?" asked Moore. "How can I do that?"

"You must signify which portion of the story you want, in advance," answered the attendant. "You will be totally powerless to act independently once it begins. In fact, you won't even be aware that you are living a tape rather than a life. Therefore, all limitations must be decided beforehand."

"Where can I find a list of your tapes?"

The attendant gestured toward a door. "Go through there, and you'll find yourself in our Catalog Room. Write down the titles and code numbers of the tapes you want, as well as those portions of the tapes that you wish to live. Then bring the list to me and I'll feed it into the master computer while you arrange yourself in your cubicle."

Moore went into the Catalog Room and returned with his list half an hour later.

"Ah," smiled the attendant, looking at the titles. "I see you are a religious man."

"Not especially," replied Moore.

"Then you wish to become one?"

"Not especially."

"You'll feel differently after you have died for our sins and risen again."

"I doubt it."

"Then why should you wish to be Jesus?" asked the attendant, curious.

"I don't," said Moore, scribbling down the character whose life he wanted to live. "Let's begin with the Gospel of John."

He went to his cubicle, attached the nodules to his temples as directed, felt a pleasant drowsiness come over him, and . . .

He was Judas Iscariot, and he was furious. Jesus had entrusted him with the bag that contained the disciples' money, solely so that he would be held accountable if anything was missing, and he resented it. He was a thief, and now there was nobody to steal from except himself.

Why had he ever fallen in with this gentle, white-robed man in the first place? Surely this was no Messiah, but merely a teacher, a rabbi with strange, revolutionary ideas. He should leave, should be out trying to make or steal a living . . . and yet, there was always that chance, that minute possibility.

How long, how many times, had his people implored the God of Israel to unleash His Messiah and reclaim the former glory of the race? Claimant after claimant to the Messiahship had come forth, tried to rally the masses, and been stoned to death or crucified for his trouble. And although he would bide his time before deciding if this man Jesus was the One his people had been awaiting, he felt certain that in the end he would prove no more of a Messiah than any of the others.

Still, while he watched and waited, he had to do his master's bidding, and it enraged him to play the part of a holy man of peace. He sat now in the house of Lazarus, watching while Mary, the sister of Lazarus, took out a pound or more of very costly ointment, placed it on Jesus' feet, and rubbed it in with her hair. Finally Judas could stand it no longer.

"Why was not this ointment sold for three hundred pence, and given to the poor?" he demanded.

He cared no more for the poor than for the Romans, of course; but the profit from the sale would have helped fill out the money pouch—and if Jesus turned out to be nothing but a man, there would have been that much more of a stake for Judas in whatever new life he chose for himself.

"Let her alone," answered Jesus firmly. "Against the day of my burying hath she kept this, for the poor always ye have with you, but me ye have not always."

The other disciples all stared at him in mute disapproval, and for perhaps the hundredth time he cringed in humiliation before his master. He nurtured his hatred, let it grow and blossom within him. Soon they would go to Jerusalem for the Passover. Then he would act. The money he would receive for betraying his master would make three hundred pence seem like so many grains of sand on the desert.

Soon the moment would come. Soon . . .

And suddenly he was thrust into the hot, barbaric world of Kazantzakis' *The Last Temptation of Christ*. He was huge, raw-boned, virile, with the strength of a bull, and a great red beard that was the envy of every man. . . .

He was Judas, and he was impatient. Once, months ago, he had loathed the sight of Jesus, had even gone to a desert monastery to kill him. But the strange, pale-skinned young man with the haunted eyes, the ascetic who seemed always to be running not toward the Messiahship but away from it, had convinced Judas without even convincing himself that he was indeed the One.

And now Judas grew increasingly impatient. Why did Jesus not wield the sword? Why did he not bring the Romans and the Pharisees to their knees? Why did he dance and drink, and rub shoulders with the scum of the earth? This was no way for the Messiah to act! The Messiah must carry the terrible sword of the Lord's wrath and vengeance. They were wasting time, Jesus and his scrawny, flea-ridden, cowardly band of followers, and it was up to Judas to show him the way, to convince him that the time had come to strike the blow that would set his people free once and for all.

But that night Jesus took Judas aside and spoke to him of a vision he had had while lying all alone atop Golgotha. The prophet Isaiah rose up in his mind, holding aloft a black goatskin covered with letters. Suddenly Isaiah and the goatskin vanished, leaving only the letters, which writhed like living beasts in the air.

Sweating and trembling, Jesus had read them aloud: " 'He has borne our faults; he was wounded for our transgressions; our iniquities bruised him. He was afflicted, yet he opened not his mouth. Despised and rejected by all, he went forward without resisting, like a lamb that is led to the slaughter.' "

Jesus stopped speaking. He had turned a deathly pale.

"I don't understand," said Judas. "Who is the lamb being led to slaughter? Who is going to die?"

"Judas, brother," said Jesus, trying to control his terror, "*I* am the one who is going to die."

"You? Then aren't you the Messiah?"

"I am."

"I don't understand," growled the redbeard, torn between rage and grief.

"You must help me do what must be done," pleaded Jesus. "You must go into Jerusalem."

"Why do you choose *me?*" demanded Judas.

"Because you are the strongest," replied Jesus. "The others don't bear up."

And because he was the strongest, and the most devoted, he slunk out into the night toward Jerusalem to do his master's bidding. . . .

And suddenly, instead of the hot, arid streets of Jerusalem, he was catapulted down, down, down, to the depths of the *Inferno* of Dante. . . .

He was Judas Iscariot, and he was in such agony as no man had ever known before.
Above him, beyond him, souls were suffering all the torments of the eternally damned. They endured rivers of fire, hideous mutilations, transformations into serpents, living burials, every monstrous indignity and torture that Hell could provide.
He would gladly have traded places with any of them.
At the very epicenter of Hell squatted Lucifer, the archfiend of all Creation. He had three faces and three mouths. In the mouth on the left was Brutus; in the mouth on the right was Cassius; and in the largest of the three mouths, the one in the center, was Judas.
He had been in that mouth, chewed and mangled by Lucifer and made unthinkably unclean by his very nearness, for all eternity. He would remain there for all eternity. The agony was unendurable, and yet he endured it. He tried to direct his mind away from the pain, but whenever he did so he saw the face of his master looking down at him from the cross, and even the agony of Lucifer's black, jagged teeth was preferable to that.
He screamed.
He had screamed an infinite number of times in the past. He would scream an infinite number of times in the future. He was Judas Iscariot, and he had betrayed his God. . . .

Free from the nethermost regions of Hell, he found himself back in the suffering, oft-raped body of Palestine, the land of Asch's *The Nazarene*. . . .

He was Judah Ish-Kiriot, and he was troubled. The Temple was to be destroyed, and Jerusalem was to be leveled with the earth and trodden underfoot by the gentiles.
"Who has said these dreadful things, man of Kiriot?" demanded Nicodemon.
"My rabbi!" wailed Judah. "He who I believed would bring salvation to Israel!"
Nicodemon shook his head sadly. "Your rabbi has said that he

who will not be born again shall not see the kingdom of God. I did not understand this, so I asked him: 'How can a man be born when he is grown old? Can he enter into his mother's body again?' And your rabbi replied, 'He that is born of the flesh, is flesh; but he that is born of the spirit, is spirit.' This is true, but are we born of the flesh alone? Is not the Torah our mother, and are not Abraham, Isaac, and Jacob our fathers? So I said to myself, this rabbi's doctrine is good and great for those who are born without the spirit, or for such as would deny the spirit. And on that day I withdrew from your rabbi."

Judah stared at him uncomprehendingly.

"Is it not possible," continued Nicodemon softly, "that your rabbi has come for the gentiles?"

The more he thought about it, the more likely it seemed to his anguished brain. And yet, to redeem those millions of souls who had been born without the spirit, he would play his part in the tapestry of pain and death that was yet to come. . . .

And from the house of Nicodemon he journeyed to a Jerusalem suspended in time and space, in Dunn's epic poem, *Satan Chained*. He seemed insubstantial, shadowy, ethereal. . . .

He was Judas, and yet he was not. He was a toy, a pawn in an eternal chess game that had begun when Satan and his demoniac generals had led the revolt. Scenes shifted, time progressed, and yet the battle-game went on, unchanging.

But God had decided to bring a new piece onto the board: His Son. And so Satan had countered with Judas Iscariot. The Son would try to save the human race; Judas would try to nail Him to the cross.

Judas won, yet in winning he lost, and the setting moved elsewhere. . . .

And finally, back from Somewhere, he was once again in Jerusalem, living the Gospel of Matthew. . . .

He was Judas Iscariot, and he was tortured. He had sold his master for thirty pieces of silver, and he still didn't know why.

Was Jesus really the Messiah? He didn't know that, either. All he knew was that he could no longer tolerate the possession of the money for which he had made his betrayal. Whether Jesus was man or Messiah didn't matter anymore; whether Jesus lived or died did, and so he determined to sacrifice his own life to save that of his master.

He raced to the Temple and sought out the elders and priests.

"I have sinned!" he cried, hurling the money to the floor in front of them. "I have betrayed the innocent blood!"

"What is that to us?" asked the high priest sardonically.

He knew then that Jesus was indeed doomed, and he left the blood money on the floor and raced out into the night.

He tried once again to examine his motives. Was he trying to force Jesus into some sort of Messianic action? Was he trying to punish him for not being the kind of Messiah he wanted him to be? Or was he merely trying to save the people of Israel from another dashed hope when their new Messiah turned out to be only a man after all? He didn't know. All he knew was that Jesus of Nazareth would die because of thirty pieces of silver.

He found a length of rope on the ground and picked it up, making a slipknot noose at one end of it. Then he went off to find a tree with a sturdy, low-hanging limb. . . .

Moore was back in his cubicle. The tapes were over, though it took him a few minutes to acclimatize himself to his surroundings. Finally he emitted a sigh, replaced the nodules, and walked out to the foyer.

"How long was I at it?" he asked.

"Just about ninety minutes," replied the attendant. "A refund of ten thousand dollars will be transferred to your personal account." He paused. "If you don't mind my saying so, you look a little shaken, Mr. Moore."

"I am."

"It's not every day that one gets to betray the Messiah so many times," said the attendant wryly.

"*Was* he the Messiah?" asked Moore.

"I have no idea. I should have thought Judas would know."

"Judas didn't know any more about it than you do."

"Odd," mused the attendant. "I wonder why."

"Maybe he didn't have all the facts before him."

"What fact was missing?"

"A man named Jeremiah," replied Moore.

12

The Golden Lobster, like most other eateasies, was well camouflaged. It was on the fourth level of State Street, and was fronted by a rather plain dry-cleaning shop, which seemed to do a considerable amount of business in its own right.

Once inside, though, the decor delivered on the restaurant's promise. The walls were totally covered by gold and yellow Japanese screens and tapestries dating back many centuries, and the chairs and tables were all hand-wrought and gilded. Even the tiles and carpeting glistened like gold, and the dishes and serving carts were gold-plated. Crustaceans of every imaginable size and variety resided in carefully tended triangular golden tanks in the four corners of the room, and the waiters and waitresses were covered with metallic gold body paint and very little else, though each did possess a crown made of glitter-covered seashells.

Moore and Pryor were ushered to a table in the back of the restaurant, where Moore ordered for both of them.

"It's fabulous!" exclaimed Pryor, looking around the room. "I've been meaning to get here for a year now, ever since it opened, but I just never got around to it."

"The food's even better than the surroundings," replied Moore. He waited until a waitress brought Pryor a drink—he himself abstained, as always—and then turned to his assistant.

"You heard where I went this afternoon?"

Pryor nodded. "The Reality Library. Learn anything?"

Moore shook his head. "A waste of time and money. We seem to be running into one dead end after another."

"So we're back to where we started?"

"It's starting to look that way," said Moore grimly. He turned to Pryor. "Ben, what's *your* thinking on Jeremiah?"

"I think he's a hard man to kill."

"Thanks a lot."

"You want a stronger statement?" said Pryor. "Okay. I think that, for some reason we haven't put our fingers on yet, he's literally *impossible* to kill. Personally, I lean toward the mutant theory. It may be weird, but it's a hell of a lot easier to swallow than Abe's Messiah crap."

"I'm open to suggestions," said Moore. "Got any?"

"I'm no scientist," said Pryor. "But then, neither is Abe. I think I'd find a few people, maybe down at the University of Chicago, who know something about mutation and see what they have to say."

"We might as well," agreed Moore. "Take care of it when you get to the office tomorrow morning."

"You look dubious."

"I'm not a betting man, Ben," said Moore. "But if I was, I'd lay plenty at twelve-to-one that they support what Abe says about mutation. Mutants aren't supposed to be able to do what Jeremiah does, and I imagine scientists are pretty much like everyone else—they don't like to come face to face with anything that goes contrary to their beliefs."

"Just like Christians," chuckled Pryor. "Wouldn't it be funny if he was the Messiah?"

"Hilarious," said Moore dryly.

The waitress reappeared with their dinner—lobster tails for Moore and a variety of shellfish in a wine sauce for Pryor—and they spent the next half hour enjoying the delicious and highly illegal meal. After a flaming dessert was brought to the table, Moore turned to Pryor again.

"Even if he can't be killed, I want to keep up the pressure. Put out a contract on him."

"It's already been done."

"A bigger one," said Moore, stirring some sugar into his coffee. "A million dollars. So far we've kept this thing in our organization. Let's pass the word to the freelancers too. Maybe it'll buy us a little more time."

Pryor pulled out a pair of cigars and offered one to Moore.

"No, thanks," replied Moore. "I only use them for props when I'm trying to convince people that I'm a real tough customer."

"I've seen you let them go out just so the muscle can re-light them," said Pryor, returning one of the cigars to his lapel pocket. "It's amazing how much a show of deference from a bunch of three-hundred-pound bruisers can impress people."

"Speaking very calmly helps, too," said Moore. "Most people expect to be yelled at."

"Nothing like keeping them off-balance," agreed Pryor, lighting his cigar. "By the way, you said that you wanted to buy us a little time. What for?"

"Because we've all been overlooking one very important fact."

"Oh? What's that?"

"Jeremiah thinks he can be killed. Once he figures out that he can't, he's going to stop running away from us and start running *toward* us."

Pryor frowned. "I hadn't thought of that." He paused for a moment, then shrugged again. "Still, what the hell can he do?"

"I don't know—and I sure as hell don't intend to sit around and find out."

"So far the only talent he's demonstrated is strictly a defensive one. I think if he had any offensive capabilities he would have demonstrated them by now."

"Maybe he doesn't know what they are," replied Moore. "Remember, we're not dealing with any mental giant here. Whatever else he's got going for him, brainpower isn't a part of his arsenal."

"You hope," said Pryor.

"I *know*," said Moore.

The waitress brought the check, and Moore left seven hundred dollars on the table. He picked up his bodyguards at the door, said goodnight to Pryor, and went back to his apartment, where he spent most of the night reading what he could find on mutation. By the time he arrived at the office in the morning, he knew more about mutants than he had ever cared to know—but he still couldn't decide what Jeremiah was.

He spent most of the morning attending to routine business. Then, just before noon, he summoned Moira, Pryor, and Bernstein into his office.

"What's up, Solomon?" asked Bernstein.

"Abe, could luck be a mutant talent?" asked Moore.

"You mean precognition?"

Moore shook his head. "No. If he had precognition, he wouldn't keep blundering into traps. I'm talking about luck—or, to put it in your terms, an involuntary reaction that enables him to overcome the statistical averages."

"Such as evading forty-three bullets at point-blank range?" asked Bernstein with a smile. "Do you know how silly that sounds?"

"All right," said Moore. "Could he conceivably have developed a skin that is practically impervious to bullets?"

"No," interjected Moira, shaking her head decisively. "I've seen him cut himself shaving."

"Besides," added Bernstein, "that wouldn't explain what happened at the Gomorrah. Those bullets didn't bounce off him, Solomon—they *missed* him."

"Ben," said Moore, "have you got anything from the biologists yet?"

"Too soon," answered Pryor. "They probably won't get back to me for a day or two."

"You're seeking outside council?" asked Bernstein. "What will you do after they agree with me, Solomon?"

"Ask me when it happens," replied Moore.

"I'll be happy to," said Bernstein. "May I make a suggestion in the meantime?"

"Be my guest."

"Since you have to wait a couple of days to evaluate the mutant theory, perhaps you should consider the alternative in the meantime?"

"Damn it, Abe—he doesn't *act* like a Messiah! Even when he's done something that was predicted, he's blundered into it. It's just crazy!"

"Solomon, there is more evidence that he's the Messiah than that he's a mutant, whether you care to admit it or not."

"Messiahs just don't pull the kind of boneheaded stunts that Jeremiah pulls," said Moore. "You've got religion on the brain, Abe."

"Have you ever considered that you might be attacking the problem ass-backwards?" suggested Bernstein.

"What are you talking about?"

"You've been hell-bent on proving that Jeremiah isn't the Messiah. You've talked with Milt Greene, you've been to the Reality Library, you've seen what Jeremiah did to Krebbs, you've matched his performance against the accepted Messianic signs, and no matter how much you protest, you haven't been able to prove a damned thing. I suggest that instead of trying to prove that he isn't the Messiah, you try to prove that he is, and see what you come up with."

"I don't see the difference," said Moore.

"It's a matter of approach," explained Bernstein. "Take a cataleptic. Without a stethoscope or a fogging glass it can be pretty hard to prove that he's alive. But stick him with a pin and watch the blood flow out of the wound, and it's easy to prove that he's not dead."

"That's a pretty weak example."

"I'm not selling examples; I'm selling approaches. You have a certain amount of evidence before you, and you have been unable to prove that Jeremiah isn't the Messiah—and believe me, your experts are going to confirm everything I've told you about mutation. Therefore, why not see if trying to prove that he *is* the Messiah works a little better?"

"That's asinine," said Moore.

"Have you got anything better to do with your time?"

"Lots," said Moore. "But if it will finally shut you up about this Messiah crap, we'll give it a try."

He pressed an intercom button and told his secretary to have lunch for four sent into the office. Then he turned back to Bernstein.

"All right, Abe—what do we know about Jeremiah that leads us to think he's the Messiah?"

"His name is Immanuel, he went to Egypt as a child, and he has resurrected the dead. That's three-quarters of the signs right there."

"Some resurrection," snorted Moore. "What about his being from the Davidic line?"

"Who knows?" said Bernstein. "It's possible."

"Do you even know for a fact that David really lived?"

"There seems to be some historical evidence. But even if a man named David did not exist, that doesn't alter anything."

"Oh?" said Moore. "Why not?"

"Because we're interested in the king that the Bible refers to as David, and personally, I don't much give a damn whether his name was David or George or anything else. It's just a symbol for the man. I'll keep calling it the Davidic line because it's a handy term, but when I use it I am referring to the bloodline that traces back to the man the Bible rightly or wrongly calls David."

"Which doesn't solve anything," said Moore. "Your own rabbi said there would be four signs by which we'd recognize the Messiah. Even stretching the facts, we can only confirm three of them. And, as I recall it, he was supposed to establish a kingdom in Jerusalem. He hasn't quite gotten around to that, has he, Abe?"

"Not yet," said Bernstein.

"Then until he does, I guess the subject is closed."

"I disagree," said Moira.

"Another quarter heard from," commented Moore wryly. "Okay, let's get it all out now, and then maybe we can go back to doing something a little more practical."

"All I did," began Moira, "was follow Dr. Bernstein's advice: I asked myself if I could disprove the assumption that Jeremiah was the Messiah. To do this, I had to prove that he hadn't fulfilled what you claim are the vital prophecies. I know for a fact that the first three are true, so that left only the prophecy about the Davidic line." She paused. "Now, obviously it can't be proved either way, since no records go back more than a few hundred years—but that doesn't mean that there isn't another way to tackle the problem."

"Such as?"

"If I am assuming that Jeremiah is the Messiah, I must therefore assume that he's of the Davidic line, and then ask myself what logically follows."

"And what does?" asked Moore.

"Well, if the Messiah is from the line of David, it seems logical to assume that the line has been kept alive all this time in order to produce him. This would mean that he is the only male in the world who traces directly to David. Now, what does this imply to you?"

"That you're as crazy as Abe is," said Moore.

"No, Mr. Moore," said Moira. "It implies that if the Messiah is ever to be produced in accordance with the prophecies, Jeremiah cannot be killed. He almost died a few times of childhood diseases, but he always recovered—and your own men were also unable to destroy him."

"Then you're saying that he'll manage to keep alive until he sires a male to succeed him in the line?" asked Moore.

"No, Mr. Moore. I'm saying that Jeremiah himself is the Messiah."

"Why?"

"Because Jeremiah had a vasectomy two years ago. The line ends with him."

"By God, she's right, Solomon!" exclaimed Bernstein.

"Not so fast," said Moore. He turned back to Moira. "What if Jeremiah isn't the only direct descendant of David? What if there are fifty of them?"

"Then why couldn't you kill him?" responded Moira. "If he defies all the laws of chance and nature, there must be a reason. I've offered mine, Mr. Moore; do you have a better one?"

"Not at the moment," admitted Moore grudgingly, as a cart with four meals was wheeled into the office.

And, thirty hours later, when every biologist had confirmed what Bernstein had told him, he still didn't have a better answer.

13

Moore gradually became aware of a persistent buzzing on his nightstand. Finally he threw the covers off and groped blindly for the phone.

"Yeah?" he muttered at last.

"I'm at the office. You'd better get down here right away."

"Who is this?"

"Ben."

"What's up?"

"Moira's flown the coop."

"I'm on my way," said Moore.

It took him five minutes to get dressed. Then, accompanied by his bodyguards, he left his apartment and headed to the office, arriving just before sunrise.

Pryor was waiting for him, a note in his hand.

"From her?" asked Moore, taking the folded piece of paper.

Pryor nodded, and he opened it up and read it.

Dear Mr. Moore:

Facts are facts. If you don't want to recognize them, that's your problem. Mine is surviving, so I'm joining the side that seems to afford me the best opportunity of so doing.

Moira Rallings

PS: If you kill him, which I personally consider impossible, you still owe me his body.

"That's what I like," said Moore dryly. "Loyalty in an employee. How long ago did you find this thing?"

"About two minutes before I called you," said Pryor. "Naomi and I are . . . ah . . . no longer roommates, and I've spent the last couple of nights here."

"I know where you've been spending them," replied Moore curtly. He tossed the note onto his desk. "We'd better move fast on this thing. I want that girl dead or alive, but mainly I want her before she can contact Jeremiah."

"We can't find him. What makes you think she can?"

"Things have a way of working out for that bastard," said Moore. "I think we'd better always assume the worst when dealing with him." He turned to Pryor. "Which reminds me: how's *your* loyalty holding up these days?"

"If I turn on you, it won't be to go over to Jeremiah's side," answered Pryor.

"Why not?" asked Moore curiously.

"Because if he as the Messiah, he doesn't need me. I wouldn't be doing myself any good by joining him."

"And if he's not?"

"Then sooner or later we're going to find a way to kill him."

"Reasonable," commented Moore. "The underdog will always have a bigger reward for you than the favorite."

"You think we're the underdog?" said Pryor with a disbelieving smile.

"It's sure starting to look like it," replied Moore seriously.

Nothing that transpired during the next three weeks changed that assumption. Moore increased his payroll and broadened his search, but Moira Rallings was nowhere to be found. She had not used public transportation to leave the Chicago complex, but within ten days Moore was forced to conclude that she was no longer in the state of Illinois, and by the time twenty days had passed he was certain that she wasn't within five hundred miles of him.

Business was still booming, of course. The Thrill Show was doing better than anticipated, and even Dream Come True was starting to turn a profit. The city officially declared that Mr. Nightspore and Mr. Thrush had died of natural causes, and there was no coroner's inquiry into the untimely death of Willis Comstock Krebs. Two more congressmen were in the bag, and one of Moore's royally bred three-year-olds had won a stakes race in Florida.

And yet, as the weeks turned into months, the tension among the members of Moore's hierarchy became almost unbearable. It was broken forever on the morning of June 23, 2048, when a uniformed woman, clad in maroon, entered Moore's private office.

"Yes?" said Moore, looking up from a stack of computer readouts.

"CPS, sir," she said briskly.

"Continental Parcel Service can damned well leave its goods in the outer office with one of the secretaries," said Moore, turning back to his paperwork.

"I'm sorry, sir," said the woman, "but this parcel has been shipped under the FYEO code."

"What the hell does *that* mean?" asked Moore irritably.

"For Your Eyes Only," came the reply. "I have been instructed to wait until you open it before leaving."

"All right," said Moore. "Let's have it."

The woman walked over to his desk and handed him a flat manila envelope. He opened it and withdrew a photograph of Jeremiah and Moira standing beside the wall of a nondescript brick building.

"Who gave this to you?" demanded Moore.

"My supervisor, sir."

"Where was it sent from?"

"I don't know. I can check on it and get back to you this afternoon."

"Do that," said Moore, dismissing her with a wave of his hand, and knowing full well that it wouldn't have been shipped from within a thousand miles of wherever Jeremiah and Moira were hiding.

Pryor walked into the office. "I saw CPS in here a moment ago," he said. "Anything up?"

"You might say so," replied Moore. He held up the picture for Pryor to see — and as he did so, his eyes fell on a two-word message scrawled on the back:

I know.

PART 2

14

The movement began so slowly that Moore, insulated in his Chicago offices, wasn't even aware of it for a number of months — but finally the reports began to trickle in.

Jeremiah had miraculously — and with no cameras to record the feat — restored sight to a blind child in Newark.

Jeremiah had been adopted as the true Messiah by four minor Protestant sects, then by a major one.

Some two hundred American Reformed rabbis were proclaiming that Isaiah's prophecy was now being fulfilled.

Twice more Moore's men had Jeremiah seemingly at their mercy, and twice more he escaped, not unscathed but alive. If he had any headquarters, they were unknown. If his new religion had a name, it too was unknown. Indeed, his motives, his religious philosophy, his whereabouts, and his eventual goals all remained mysteries.

The press and the networks started the game of counting his followers. What was once a laughably small sect soon numbered almost a million. It was still no threat to the established order, but those in power began doing a little mathematics of their own and decided to investigate the phenomenon of Jeremiah the B.

And as the notion of a Messiah — even one it didn't believe in — began to permeate the public consciousness, dissatisfaction set in for the first time in half a century. Social mobility and innovation had remained static for decades, as apathy and boredom buried the dream of a better life and a better world more efficiently than a thousand wars had done. But now people began to understand that even if Jeremiah was a fraud, there might nonetheless be a better way; that although they didn't yet know how to manipulate the machinery of change and progress, it could indeed be manipulated.

Despite tapping this responsive chord, Jeremiah made no promises, no predictions, no prophecies. It was Moore's firm conviction that, Messiah or not, Jeremiah didn't have the brains to figure out what to do with his mass of followers, how or where to lead them.

And still the wave of belief grew. It crossed the Atlantic first, then spread through Europe and Asia and snaked its tentacles into Africa. Israel alone openly condemned him as a fraud—but Israel knew better than anyone else where his kingdom would be, if indeed he had the inclination and the power to establish it.

Soon requests began pouring in for Jeremiah to appear on television, before committees, and in private audiences with religious and political leaders. He made a few video appearances to replenish his coffers, but rejected all other public and private confrontations, stating curtly that the Messiah had no need for any such dealings.

And then, still in need of money, Jeremiah entered the only business he knew anything about: sin. With his followers nearing the three million mark, he had enough clout and enough connections to enter the pornography and prostitution business, and to make his initial purchases of some lower-echelon politicians.

Moore felt the pinch slowly at first. Pornography was down three percent, prostitution seven percent, the domestic drug traffic six percent. But within a handful of months all of his major business enterprises were down by thirty percent or more, and Dream Come True, which had been burgeoning into a healthy money-maker with offices in eleven states, was virtually bankrupt, since the populace preferred buying their dreams from a Messiah rather than an underworld kingpin.

When his gross had been cut in half, Moore tripled the reward and sent out the kill order once again—and many of the employees who would normally have been laid off because of the disastrous slump in business were kept on salary and ordered to help destroy the financial empire Jeremiah was building at Moore's expense. Moore closed his distributional outlets to Jeremiah's products—and Jeremiah established new ones. Moore had his own politicians and policemen crack down on Jeremiah's prostitution ring—and found that Jeremiah had enough politicos and cops on his own payroll to keep his girls working. Moore plugged up every narcotics route — and Jeremiah created new routes just as quickly.

Finally Moore decided that if he couldn't get at Jeremiah's businesses directly, he would do the next best thing and try to discredit him in the eyes of his millions of followers. To this end, he hired a number of research and media teams.

It wasn't difficult to make Jeremiah appear to be an uneducated, ill-mannered, and womanizing fool, for he was all of those. It wasn't even hard to dig up his financial records and show the world that he had already accumulated almost two hundred million dollars. Jeremiah not only admitted it, but stated that he planned to double that amount every six months for the next two years. His scheming, panhandling youth was made public — and far from denying it, Jeremiah took a certain measure of pride in supplying Moore's reportorial teams with some of the more salacious details they had overlooked.

But when it came to proving that Jeremiah was a fraud, the going became more difficult. He had laid his hands on a crippled girl's legs — after receiving a substantial donation from the child's grandfather — and made her walk again. In a most un-Messiahlike ploy, he had jumped, sans parachute, from a helicopter flying at a height of two thousand feet in front of a paying audience numbering in the hundreds of thousands — and though he had to be rushed to the nearest hospital with broken legs, multiple fractures of the spine, and severe internal hemorrhaging, he walked out on his own power nine days later, perfectly healthy. He visited a dying village in Baja California, and while he was there the impoverished farmers experienced rain for the first time in more than a year.

Every Sunday ministers and priests took to their pulpits to proclaim that Jesus was the only Messiah, and every Sunday there were a few less people in their congregations. A thousand authors and biographers tackled the enigma of Jeremiah, and came up with a thousand different conclusions.

Jeremiah reveled in the publicity. The only thing he wouldn't do was codify his philosophy. It was enough, he stated time and again, that he was the Messiah; all else, including his personal beliefs, faded into insignificance beside that fact.

Within another year his followers numbered more than twelve million, and his finances grew apace. Then came the revelation that Jeremiah was building a military machine, and the governments of the world, which had largely been ignoring him in the hope that he would go away, sat up and took notice. Spies of all nationalities and religious persuasions infiltrated his organization. Up to a point they were successful: he had so many men and so many weapons and such and such a military capacity. But as to why he needed an army and where he intended to deploy it, no answers were forthcoming.

Since Moore had done more research on Jeremiah than anyone else, he found himself granted amnesty for all past crimes—and, the implication went, all *future* ones as well—in exchange for his cooperation with the various agencies that had committed themselves to Jeremiah's destruction. There were a lot of them, too, since almost every religious institution found its own existence threatened by the possibility of a living, breathing Messiah.

Now, with the financial and intelligence resources of virtually the entire world at his fingertips, Moore went after Jeremiah with a vengeance. His priests and lieutenants were assassinated, his speeches and broadcasts were disrupted, much of his money was impounded—and *still* his following increased.

And then came the incident that turned the tide of events in Jeremiah's favor for the first time. It came from a totally unexpected source, but its effect was both enormous and immediate.

It was *The Gospel of Moira*, penned by Moira Rallings, and it sold forty million copies during its first two months of publication.

15

And he made a blind child see and a legless girl walk, and when the people saw him and knew him for who and what he was, then in truth did the Word spread across the bleak, unhappy land.
—from *The Gospel of Moira*

Pryor's office was as cluttered as Moore's was barren. It was far larger, and every inch of wall space was covered with computer screens, punctuated only occasionally by television monitors. The office housed a large conference table, a wet bar, a pair of leather couches, and a huge, mahogany desk with a leather judge's chair.

Moore entered the room, walked directly to Pryor's desk, and tossed a copy of *The Gospel of Moira* onto it.

"Well, what do you think of it?" he asked.

"She's not about to win a Nobel Prize for Literature," replied

Pryor. "It's some of the worst dreck I've ever read." He opened his desk drawer and withdrew his own copy.

"It's also some of the most *dangerous* dreck you've ever read," said Moore. "Check the copyright page."

"Mine is the fifty-third printing," said Pryor without opening the book. "What's yours?"

"The fifty-seventh," replied Moore. "They must be defoliating whole forests to keep up with the demand for this thing." He sat down on one of the couches. "And in the meantime, our gross is off forty-two percent this month; and we finished the last quarter deeper in the red than ever. I think we're going to have to pull out of Kentucky and Tennessee altogether."

"I know," said Pryor grimly. "Even the legitimate enterprises are dropping through the floor."

"You wouldn't think it would be that goddamned hard to kill him," said Moore with a heavy sigh. "After all, they killed the last Messiah without any trouble."

"You know the answer to that: if they killed him, then he wasn't the Messiah." Pryor picked up the new Gospel and began thumbing through it. "*And Moira Rallings became his concubine, and thus was she blessed above all other women,*" he intoned.

"It sounds like some no-talent producer's idea of a Biblical epic," snorted Moore.

Pryor kept thumbing through the book, reading occasional snippets. "*And he went into Egypt, as the prophets foretold. . . . And he began his ministry sullied and abused, an outcast among men. . . . And in the sin-ridden city of Chicago dwelt a servant of the Devil named Moore. . . .*" Pryor looked up. "It's all here—everything but the Sermon on the Mount." He smiled. "I guess she's saving that for the sequel."

"It's not that funny, Ben. If half the people who buy this book throw it out, and half of those who keep it think it's hogwash, she'll still have gained him ten million converts in six weeks—and every last one of them is going to think Judas wasn't all that bad a guy compared to me."

"We can't keep the books out of their hands," replied Pryor. "They're not going through our agencies—and from what I've been able to find out, almost half of them are being sold by computer or through the mail."

"I know," said Moore. "Besides, with that many copies in print, I'd say it's a little late in the game to get a restraining order or an injunction to prohibit distribution. I don't see how we could make one stick, anyway." He paused for a moment, drumming his fingers on the arm of the couch. "What's the last word we have on him?"

Pryor shrugged. "As of yesterday, we have sworn statements that he's in Albuquerque, Buenos Aires, the Manhattan complex, and Iceland. Take your choice."

"Damn MacIntosh, anyway!" snapped Moore suddenly.

Xavier MacIntosh was the only agent of Moore's to successfully infiltrate Jeremiah's expanding organization and gain a position of authority. There was absolutely no question that he would have access to Jeremiah's schedule, and would probably be privy to his future plans as well. But Xavier MacIntosh had wired his resignation to Moore four days ago, explaining that he had seen the light and had elected to become one of Jeremiah's disciples.

"It's not unheard of," said Pryor. "I've been in touch with some of our new . . . ah . . . associates, and they've had pretty much the same problem. As soon as they've got a plant in a position to do then some good, he—well, he *converts*. I don't suppose there's any other term for it."

"And just how *are* our new associates doing?"

"Not very well. If Jeremiah ever commits his forces to some military objective, they may prove useful—but as things stand now, they're no better at infiltrating his organization than we are. We'd probably be better off with industrial spies and saboteurs."

"True," agreed Moore. "Except that industrial cartels don't offer amnesty; governments do. Besides, look at what's happened to our finances in the past year. No business organization is going to lock horns with Jeremiah. There may be easier ways to go broke, but there aren't any quicker ones." He paused. "Anyway, our immediate problem is that damned book Moira's written. It pinpoints me as the greatest arch-villain in human history, and it's gaining Jeremiah more support than anything he himself ever did." He shrugged. "You know, it's always possible that she's right—that I am the Devil incarnate for trying to kill Jeremiah."

"I doubt it," replied Pryor seriously. "After all, lots of people have tried to kill him. The only reason you're being singled out is that you're the one who drew Moira into this thing to begin with."

"By that same token, I ought to be canonized instead of condemned," said Moore wryly. "Neither of them had any idea what he was before I got involved."

"They'd have figured it out sooner or later," said Pryor. "After all, if he really is the Messiah, it's not just because you pointed it out to him."

"I know, Ben. It's just so frustrating! Sometimes I feel like we're all walking around underwater, we react so slowly. I thought Moira would prove to be a weak spot, and she's done him more good than the rest of his group put together."

"It's just a book."

"Yeah, and Adolf Hitler was just a painter."

Pryor's intercom buzzed, and he pressed a button. "What is it?"

"Ben, is Solomon in there with you?" asked Bernstein's voice.

"Yes, Abe. Do you want to see him?"

"No. Just tell him to turn on a TV to Channel 9 if he wants to see an old friend."

Moore walked to a monitor and activated it.

Moira Rallings, her skin whiter than ever, sat on a love seat, a copy of her Gospel in her hand. She had added about ten pounds and displayed a hitherto unknown fondness for see-through clothing, but seemed otherwise unchanged.

She was being interviewed by Stormin' Norman Gorman (formerly Herbert Russell), a twenty-year-old entertainer who had been a pop music star during a recent revival of acid rock until continued exposure to the high decibel level had caused him to go deaf. His millions of fans wouldn't let him retire from the limelight at seventeen, so he had learned how to read lips and now hosted the nation's third-ranked syndicated noontime talk show.

". . . figures must be immensely gratifying to you," Gorman was saying.

"Oh, they are," replied Moira with more enthusiasm than Moore had ever seen her display for anything except a corpse. "The money all goes into Jeremiah's treasury, of course. I'm just pleased and happy to know how many wonderful people have now seen the light."

"Check out that transmission and see if it's live," Moore instructed Pryor.

"And will there be a further Gospel in the years to come?" asked Gorman.

"Certainly," said Moira. "If not by me, then by someone else. Jeremiah's ministry is just beginning, Norman. He still has most of his work ahead of him."

"What, exactly, *does* lie ahead of him?" asked Gorman. "He's been very vague on that point, and I'm sure all our viewers would like to know."

"He reveals the details to no one, not even myself," replied Moira. "But it's common knowledge that he will ultimately fulfill all the Messianic prophecies."

"Does that include the establishment of a kingdom in what is now the nation of Israel?"

"It's possible."

"You're begging the question," said Gorman. "The Hebrew prophets expressly state that the Messiah must establish his kingdom in Jerusalem."

Moira smiled. "Which Hebrew prophets?"

"Isaiah, for one."

"Did he?" she said, still smiling.

"Absolutely," said Gorman. "Would you like me to quote chapter and verse?"

"Of what?" asked Moira. "Of the prophet Isaiah himself, or of the ten generations of Jews who repeated his prophecies around campfires, or of the Hebrew scholars who finally wrote it into the Torah, or the Greeks who rewrote it, or the monks of the Dark Ages and Middle Ages who rewrote it again, or of the men who rewrote it for the King James Version?"

"Then you're saying that Jerusalem is not his goal?"

"I'm not saying anything about his goals," replied Moira. "I'm sure he'll reveal them in his own good time. I'm simply saying that fulfilling a prophecy and fulfilling what people *think* is a prophecy may not be the same thing."

Pryor, who had been speaking quietly on the phone, hung up the receiver and walked over to Moore.

"Pre-recorded yesterday in Philadelphia," he said softly. "Moira showed up, spent the day doing about twenty interviews for talk shows, and vanished. Six agencies put tails on her, and she managed to lose all of them within ten minutes."

Moore nodded, never taking his eyes off the screen.

"I see that our time is almost up," said Gorman. "Have you any last words for our viewers?"

"Yes," said Moira. "I have a message from Jeremiah."

"I'm sure we'd all like to hear that."

"*Solomon Moody Moore!*" she intoned, staring into the camera with dark, wild eyes. "Judas! Embodiment of Satan! If you're watching or listening, I implore you: cease your persecution of the One True Messiah!" She turned toward another camera. "Members of the New Faith, believers of the New Truth: a man who would be the Christ-killer is in your midst! His name is Moore, and he would strike down the Messiah! Band together! Do not let him do this dreadful thing!"

The camera zoomed in on her until her eyes filled the screen. Moore felt they were looking straight at him.

"Repent, Judas Moore, before it is too late!"

The picture faded out, to be replaced by a commercial.

"Charming girl," said Moore, turning off the set.

"We'd better tighten the security around the building," added Pryor.

"Right. It'll give the impression that I'm still here."

"Won't you be?"

"Ben, you've been spending too much time messing around with your girlfriends," said Moore. "Don't you understand what you just heard? He's getting ready to march on Jerusalem, or at least to begin his military campaign."

"How do you come up with that?" asked Pryor, genuinely puzzled.

"Why else would Moira throw up a smokescreen like that? I bet if you get tapes from the other nineteen shows, you'll find that she gave them all the same cock-and-bull story about how the Messianic prophecies didn't necessarily refer to Jerusalem."

"I don't follow you."

"Ben, a lot of the Old and New Testaments got rewritten, and a lot of stuff was edited out for political reasons, and a lot of stuff was invented to make it seem like Jesus was the Messiah—but there is one thing you're forgetting."

"And what is that?"

"The concept itself. Abe's rabbi told me that the literal meaning of 'Messiah' is 'Anointed One,' or 'king.' By definition, a Messiah is the king of the Jews—and by definition, the king of the Jews rules from Jerusalem. If she's trying to convince anyone that it isn't true, it's because Jeremiah's getting ready to move and he wants as many people as possible looking in some other direction."

"What about the love and kisses she directed at you?" asked Pryor.

"It makes it a hell of a lot harder for me to get around," admitted Moore, "and it probably encourages a few thousand fanatics to go hunting for my scalp. We'll increase our security here for show, but I think it's time I got out of Chicago for a while."

"Where to?"

Moore shrugged. "It doesn't make much difference—but I'm going to have a little meeting with some of our associates, so fix me up something a little more luxurious than usual."

"Right," said Pryor.

"And Ben?"

"Yes?"

"Put out a contract on Moira Rallings."

16

Jeremiah bellowed like a bull moose as his body jerked through the inevitable contortions of the sex act. Then, panting and sweating, he slid off the motionless figure of Moira Rallings and rolled onto his back.

"Christ!" he spat. "It's getting so I have a hard time telling the difference between you and one of your goddamned corpses!"

"Learn to be a little more skillful, then," she said, pulling the covers up over her breasts.

"I'm the goddamned Messiah!" he shouted. "I'll learn what I want to learn and screw the way I want to screw!"

"Then don't complain when there's no reaction," she replied calmly.

She started to get out of bed, and he grabbed her arm, pulling her back.

"Where are you going now?" he demanded. "Off to fuck a statue?"

"One gets satisfaction where one can," she answered with no show of embarrassment.

"Which one is it tonight—the general, or the one done up like the Emperor Augustus?"

"Whichever strikes my fancy."

"That's a well-traveled fancy you've got there," he said disgustedly. "Why do you dress all those corpses up if you're just going to strip them down for action every night?"

"So as not to shock you."

"I'm pretty hard to shock," he replied with a harsh laugh. "Someday I'll tell you what I did this morning with three female members of my flock."

"Well, then," said Moira, "maybe I find them more attractive in uniform. Maybe *they* feel better about it."

"It makes small difference to the dead if they are buried in tokens of luxury," said Jeremiah in amused tones.

"Since when did you start quoting Euripides?"

"Since I read his fucking poems," he answered, reaching over to his bedtable and picking up two pills of indeterminate properties. "What the hell difference does it make to you, you damned necrophile? I read them, that's all." He put the pills into his mouth and swallowed them.

"Recently?"

"Yes, recently."

"And when did you learn what *necrophile* means?"

"Maybe I'm a little smarter than you think!" snapped Jeremiah.

"Maybe you are," she said, frowning.

"And getting smarter all the time!" he added. "Things that were incomprehensible to me a few months ago are suddenly becoming very clear."

"Like the word 'incomprehensible'?"

"What the hell are you talking about?"

"That you really *are* getting smarter every day," she replied, sitting up. "You're using words you never knew before, you're reading books you'd never heard of and wouldn't have understood, and when you take the obscenities out of your speech even your sentence construction is more complex."

"Everyone gets smarter, just like they get older," he said. "Otherwise there'd be even more stagnation than you see now. So what? Leave it to a frigid pervert to start changing the subject."

"The subject was intelligence."

He ripped the covers from her and pulled her unprotesting legs apart, "The subject is what I'm looking at, and nothing else! God and Messianic destiny are half horseshit and half hokum, cooked up for a bunch of sheep. The secret of the universe is right between your legs, and I'm getting fucking sick and tired of your clogging it up with a bunch of corpses!" He glared at her. "God! If it wasn't for that book of yours and the sequel you're writing, I'd have your ass out of here so fast you'd never know what hit you!"

She listened to him as he continued castigating her—*really* listened, for the first time in many months. She listened to the choice of words, to the concepts couched in vulgarisms, and she knew he was *changing*. It wasn't complete yet, and he wouldn't rank with Shakespeare or Einstein for a long, long time, if ever; but the signs of a growing intellect were unmistakably there.

And, being a survivor by nature, she opened her body to him when he threw himself onto her, wrapped her legs tightly around his torso, shrieked in splendidly false ecstasy, made sure she dug her fingernails into his neck and back so hard that she drew blood, performed acts that even she had never attempted before, and forced herself to beg for more when at last he lay exhausted beside her.

Long after he was asleep she rose quietly from the bed, tiptoed out of the room, and found her own special form of satisfaction. The knowledge that she was indeed on the winning side, and that that side was growing in power almost by the minute, made the experience even more exhilarating and satisfying than usual.

Jeremiah awoke the next morning to find himself in bed with the sexual tigress of his dreams. What she may have lacked in sincerity, she more than made up for in motivation and enthusiasm, as she made certain, in ways he had previously only fantasized about, that no one would soon be supplanting her at the side of the Messiah.

17

Officially it was known as the North Central Caribbean Undersea Dome, but its inhabitants called it the Jamaica Bubble.

It was a large, totally submerged structure, residing on the ocean floor some three miles southeast of Kingston and well out beyond the coral reef. The Bubble was almost a mile in diameter at its base, and the top of it came to within forty feet of the ocean's surface, where a series of elevators connected it to a floating airport.

The Bubble possessed a trio of water desalinization plants that turned out more than ten billion gallons of fresh water every twenty-four hours, barely enough to satisfy the ever-increasing needs of Mexico, the islands, and the eastern seaboard of the United States. Sharing the limited space were four compact seaweed-processing laboratories and two research institutes.

Also inside the Bubble was the New Atlantis, a luxury hotel that offered a truly impressive array of food, drink, drugs, entertainment, gambling, and sin. Solomon Moody Moore, hidden behind an impenetrable corporate veil, was its owner.

The New Atlantis was twelve stories high. On the top floor, above the bars and the nightclubs and the casinos, Moore kept a suite of rooms. Unlike the Spartan surroundings of his headquarters, these apartments were used solely for entertaining and reeked of luxury, from the spun gold draperies and fur-covered couches to the platinum bathroom fixtures. Van Goghs and Picassos and Chagalls and Frazettas were displayed haphazardly on the walls, as were a pair of century-old original Pogo and Li'l Abner strips. In addition to the many windows that overlooked the activities of the Bubble was a huge "porthole," a circular view screen tied in to a high-resolution video camera that was perpetually trained on the sea life outside the dome.

Moore hated the place. He felt uncomfortable, as he always did when surrounded by the luxuries that blurred the dividing line between himself and the masses. He had spent most of the day sitting morosely in a whirlpool tub of Homeric proportions, got out in late afternoon for a meal of filet of sole almandine, and finally dressed himself in the style of a Tombstone gambler, complete with black sombrero and silver spurs. Then he walked into the lush parlor and waited.

Soon they began to arrive:

Caesar DeJesus, an Argentine cardinal in the Catholic Church, a surprisingly blond, fair-skinned man swathed in velvet robes; Felix Lewis, purportedly the richest investor on Wall Street and activist head of the Jewish Defense League, a small, dapper, graying man carrying his own hashish pipe; Naomi Wizner, Israel's Defense Minister, whose shaven head and slit skirt belied her fifty-six years; and Piper Black, head of the Black and Noir Conglomerate, a seven-foot-tall mulatto wrapped in gold and purple silks and wearing a jeweled turban.

Moore greeted each in turn, opened a bottle of century-old sparkling burgundy, and filled crystal glasses for everyone except himself. Then he chatted idly about sports and the weather and the wonderful results of the Bubble's technology, allowing each of them a chance to admire the artwork and the decor, and to make sure that there were no secret microphones or cameras planted about the apartment.

Finally, after some twenty minutes had passed, all four visitors were sitting comfortably in the drawing room, sipping contentedly from their glasses and staring at the viewscreen, and Moore decided that it was time to get down to business.

"I'm very glad all four of you could make it here," he announced, turning off the screen and focusing their attention upon himself. "If anyone is hungry, I can have some food sent in, and once we're through all of the attractions of the New Atlantis are at your disposal. But we've got a lot of ground to cover tonight, so if there are no objections, I think we'd better get started."

"All right, Solomon," said Black, lighting up an oversized cigar. "Just why *are* we here?"

Moore leaned forward slightly in his wingback chair. "I have reason to believe that Jeremiah is getting ready to mobilize his troops."

"What makes you think he *has* any troops?" asked Lewis.

"What makes you think he hasn't?" Moore shot back. "Look— you know the stock market; that's your field of expertise. Well, my field of expertise is Jeremiah, and I'm telling you that even if he doesn't have enough troops, he can afford to go out and buy some more." He turned to the huge mulatto. "How much are you down this year, Piper?"

"What makes you think we're down?" demanded Black.

"We're not going to get anywhere if we don't put our cards on the table," said Moore. "My own gross is off almost seven hundred million dollars in the past nine months."

"Half a billion," said Black emotionlessly.

"No one is saving any more money than they used to, so it's not unreasonable to assume that almost a billion and a quarter of our dollars, or dollars that should have been ours, have gone straight to Jeremiah this year."

"Why only Jeremiah?" asked Lewis. "Why not others as well?"

"I'm not particularly inclined to tell you all the details of my business operation, and I'm sure Mr. Black feels much the same way—but I think we can both assure you that the nature of our business is such that it doesn't encourage competitors. No one except Jeremiah could take a single dollar from us without our consent. Am I right, Piper?"

Black nodded.

"So money for mercenaries is not exactly his biggest problem," concluded Moore.

"If he's got any problems at all, I sure as hell haven't spotted them," said Black.

"That's why I've called this little meeting," said Moore. "To see if we can't create a few for him."

"You've seen him, talked to him," said Naomi Wizner. "That's more than any of us has done. What's his secret?"

"No secret at all," responded Moore. "He's got the brainpower and emotional stability of a hyperthyroid twelve-year-old. I've asked Piper to join us because his interest in Jeremiah is similar to mine: we're both getting hit in the pocketbook. But you others have been financing me and encouraging me and supporting my private little war, and the time has come to put the question to you: are you ready to come out of the closet and wage a *public* battle against Jeremiah?"

"We've been doing that!" said Lewis hotly.

"No!" replied Moore. "You've been making pious statements while my people have been in the trenches! I'm telling you that this man is going to stop being merely a religious threat and is about to become a military one. He's got more money than he needs, and he has no reason to wait. Before I commit what remains of my holdings, I want to know where you stand on this."

"He's got to be stopped," said Naomi Wizner.

"Killed," added DeJesus.

"All right, Cardinal," said Moore. "Let me put the question to you. You say he's got to be killed?"

"Absolutely."

"Isn't that just a little inconsistent with your religious principles?"

"My religious principles are the veneration and worship of the Holy Trinity," replied DeJesus. "My fealty is to the Church and the Pope."

"Even if they're wrong?" asked Moore.

"That's unthinkable!"

"Well, you'd better start thinking about it pretty seriously," said Moore. "Because every piece of evidence we have points to Jeremiah's being the Messiah."

"You could pick a better Messiah out of the phone book," interjected Black sarcastically.

"How can you claim this . . . this *animal* is the Prince of Peace?" added DeJesus.

Moore shook his head. "Will the pair of you try to get it through your heads that if he is the Messiah, then he's the Messiah of the Old Testament? He is *not* the Prince of Peace or the Son of God. He is simply the person God—or *some*one—has chosen to establish a kingdom in Jerusalem—and for what it's worth to you, once you get rid of all the rotten poetry in *The Gospel of Moira*, the facts are correct. They ought to be; she got them from me. Jeremiah *did* bring a drowning victim back to life; he *did* spend some time in Egypt; his name *is* Immanuel; and he may very well be from the Davidic line. At least, no one can prove that he isn't."

"I oppose him because I know Jesus to be the Messiah," said DeJesus. "But if in your opinion Jeremiah is the Messiah, why do *you* oppose him?"

"He's not *my* Messiah, Cardinal," said Moore. "My interest in the future of Jerusalem and the Jewish race is minimal. Besides, if he's the best that God could come up with, I don't know that I care to have anything to do with either of them."

"That's a very glib answer," said DeJesus.

"You want a better one?" asked Moore. "All right. If he's the Messiah of the Old Testament, he's just a man, nothing more. I don't give a damn what he plans to do in Jerusalem. I care about what he's doing now—and what he's doing now is trying to kill me and take over my organization. That's my motivation, plain and simple—and I'll stack its staying power up against yours anytime." He turned to Lewis. "As long as the Cardinal brought the subject up, let me ask it of you: if he's the Messiah, why shouldn't the Jewish Defense League accept him?"

"You haven't spoken to a hell of a lot of American Jews, have you?" said Lewis, taking a puff on his hashish pipe. "I don't care if he is the Messiah. He's a disruptive influence." He paused thoughtfully. "Judaism isn't so much a religion as a way of life. Our culture means more to us than the details of our religion, and this man threatens to destroy that culture. I don't care if he sets up a kingdom in Jerusalem or not; after all, there are less than five million Jews in all of Israel, and there are twelve million in the Manhattan complex alone. But if he succeeds in taking over Jerusalem, he can't help but change what being Jewish means, and we cannot allow this."

"Let me repeat this, just to make sure I've got it right," said Moore. "Neither the Jewish Defense League nor the Catholic Church—or at least those portions that are represented here tonight—will back down even if Jeremiah is what he claims to be. Is that correct?"

Lewis nodded.

"He is not," said DeJesus firmly.

"But *if* he is?" persisted Moore.

"If it seems that he is, then he is the Devil, the Prince of Liars, and we must destroy him."

Moore decided that he wasn't going to get a better answer from the Cardinal, shrugged, and turned to Naomi Wizner.

"How about you? Do you speak for your government?"

"Absolutely. For all practical purposes, if it comes to an attack on Jerusalem, I *am* the government."

"And what is Israel's feeling?"

"Israel feels like it's under attack."

"Israel always feels like it's under attack from someone," said Black with a chuckle.

"And Israel *always* defends itself!" she replied hotly. "This time is no different from all the others!"

"But it is," Moore pointed out. "If Jeremiah is the Messiah, it means Christianity has been dead wrong for two thousand years—but why won't Israeli citizens accept him with open arms? After all, you never accepted Jesus, so why shouldn't Jeremiah seem like the fulfillment of the prophecies?"

"He'll come with the sword and the fire," replied Naomi. "I'm sure God won't mind if we protect ourselves."

"That's not an adequate answer," said Moore.

"It's the best you're going to get, Mr. Moore," she said. "What do you expect my government to do—turn the country over to him on a silver platter?"

"What if he convinces your government that he's the Messiah?"

"And just how do you think he's going to do that?" she scoffed.

"By taking Jerusalem."

"Mr. Moore, do you have any idea how many times Jerusalem was conquered between the time of the prophets and the establishment of the State of Israel in 1948?"

"No."

"Well, take my word for it: it happened more often than you can imagine. We never accepted any previous conquerors as the Messiah. Why should this man be any different?"

"Because he *is* different," said Moore. "When Moira Rallings writes of the some of the things he's done, she's not exaggerating. I'm not saying that he is necessarily the Messiah—but he sure as hell is different."

"You sound like you're more convinced than any of the rest of us, Solomon," said Black.

"That's irrelevant," said Moore. "Messiah or not, he's a man, and he's got to have a weakness. He's been trying to ruin me, and I'm not going down without a fight."

"Bully for you," said Lewis, clapping his hands slowly. "Now, do you have any plan in mind, or do you just like making speeches?"

"I've got a number of plans," replied Moore, turning to him. "I've come to the reluctant conclusion that whatever he is, we're not going to be able to kill him. This means that we've got to consider alternatives."

"Such as?" asked Lewis.

"Here's the simplest one," said Moore. "Let him take Jerusalem. That's all he's supposed to do, isn't it?"

"What?" cried Lewis and Naomi in unison.

"Let him have it. It's just a city. Your government can always relocate."

"It took the Jews two millennia to regain Jerusalem!" snapped Lewis. "Giving it up without a fight is out of the question!"

"Is it?" asked Moore. "He's got something like thirty million people who'll buy guns and pay their own passage over there to fight in his Holy War. Why not just turn it over to him?"

"It's unthinkable!" said Naomi. "Why not just turn Czechoslovakia over to Hitler? That's all he wants! Except that it wasn't all he wanted, and Jerusalem isn't all that Jeremiah wants. Once he's got his army, he's got to keep them fed and active. How do you think he'll do that, Mr. Moore? He'll march into Egypt and Syria and Jordan and Lebanon, and then he'll cross the Mediterranean into Europe."

"With what?" scoffed Black. "He hasn't got any planes or tanks, or even any ammunition."

"He'll get them," said Naomi. "Do you know how many churches would be happy to unload their treasuries on him in exchange for lenient treatment? How many officers would turn over military equipment to him in exchange for favored positions in his army?"

"Not that many," said Black. "He's still small potatoes."

"Is he?" she said. "This man was a penniless beggar less than three years ago. Today he's worth about four billion dollars, he's got more than thirty million followers and is picking up half a million a week, and one church out of every ten has decided he's divine. What, in your opinion, would it take to make him a *big* potato, Mr. Black?"

Black seemed about to reply, then changed his mind and kept silent.

"All right," said Moore. "Since no one wants to take the easy way out, we fight him. But you have to understand that military action is out of the question."

"Why?" demanded Naomi. "We're prepared to do battle with him down to the last man, woman, and child."

"More power to you," said Moore dryly. "But Jeremiah doesn't have a standing army yet. Where will you launch your attack? How can you cut a supply line that doesn't exist? Even if you didn't mind slaughtering civilians, you couldn't attack his home base; no one knows where it is."

"The man is right," said Black with a grin. "Until he mounts a legitimate army, there's nothing to fight."

"Right," said Moore. "So what I propose is a concerted and coordinated media attack on his credibility. We've done it in bits and pieces, but we've been working at cross-purposes. Naomi fears a military attack, the Cardinal fears that Jeremiah is the Antichrist, Piper fears a further loss of money, Mr. Lewis fears for his cultural values, Lord knows the Chinese and Indians and Africans have things to fear—but we've been speaking out as individuals, or at least as single interest groups. Jeremiah has to be discredited not just in the eyes of the Jews or the Christians or the Moslems, but everywhere at once."

"I'll commit every cent I've got," said Black. "But first there's got to be an understanding."

"What kind of understanding?" asked Lewis suspiciously.

"If we're successful, there's going to be a very healthy piece of change up for grabs," continued Black. "Don't go looking so superior, Mr. Lewis. You've still got all of your money. Do you really think I give a damn about Jews or Christians, or about who rules Jerusalem? And if Solomon cares one whit more than I do, it's because he's lost his objectivity. We're businessmen, and whether the business is sex or drugs or stopping a would-be Messiah, we expect to turn a profit."

"Are those *your* sentiments?" Lewis asked, turning to Moore.

"I have my own reasons for wanting to destroy Jeremiah," said Moore, measuring each word carefully. "He's the closest thing to a blood enemy that I've ever had, and I'm in this to the finish, with or without your help." He paused. "But, as my friend Piper has pointed out, I'm a businessman, and I certainly intend to share in the spoils if we're successful. However, I don't think we need to go into the details right now," he added. "You have my pledge that we won't take anything that anyone else wants."

He stared directly at Black, who decided to let the subject drop.

"Now," continued Moore, "if we're all in agreement, we'd better start talking about just what kind of media campaign we're going to be mounting. Cardinal, how many television stations does the Church control in South America?"

"We *own* stations, Mr. Moore," said DeJesus defensively. "We don't *control* them."

"No one's keeping notes," said Moore. "None of this will ever leave this room. In exchange for that, I feel I have the right to expect straightforward answers. Now, how many stations do you control?"

DeJesus glared at him for a long moment, then shrugged. "Between six and seven hundred," he said at last.

"And the Jewish Defense League?" asked Moore.

"Personally, I own or control five," replied Lewis. "The League doesn't control any, and that's the truth."

"Newspapers and newstapes?"

"Me, ten; the League, maybe two dozen."

"How long will it take you to raise enough money to blanket the papers and networks with a hate campaign?"

"Three months, maybe four," said Lewis promptly.

"Too long," replied Moore. "You'll have to dip into your own capital and do it in six weeks."

"Why so quickly?"

"Because if Jeremiah's getting ready to move, it's not going to take him four months to get his act together. These are religious fanatics we're talking about. If he puts out the call tomorrow, they'll start buying tickets to Jerusalem before the weekend."

"I'll see what I can do," said Lewis.

"I can't commit any funds," said Naomi Wizner. "Every penny is going to strengthen Jerusalem's defenses."

"I wasn't going to ask you for any," replied Moore. "I just wanted to make sure that you weren't planning on throwing in the towel after we've committed everything we've got. As for Mr. Black and myself, between us we control a third of the press time on the North American continent. I'm sure we can gear up to print a few billion anti-Jeremiah tracts in a matter of weeks."

"So *that's* why you pulled me in and didn't invite Quintaro!" exclaimed Black. "He's strictly drugs and whores, but I've got printing presses!"

Moore nodded. "Our contributions will be press time and distributional channels."

"Makes sense at that," agreed Black.

"You're in?" asked Moore.

Black nodded.

"Good," said Moore. "Then may I suggest that we meet here again in two weeks?"

"Fine by me," said Lewis, He stared at Moore for a moment. "Do you really think much good can come out of this meeting?"

"It's usefulness is extremely limited," replied Moore.

"Then why are we here?"

"Because I had to start somewhere," said Moore wryly. "Tomorrow I'll be meeting with a Greek Orthodox leader, the Foreign Minister of Egypt, and Henri Piscard."

"Who is this Piscard?" asked Lewis.

"Another businessman," replied Moore. "He provides pretty much the same services in France and Belgium that Mr. Black and I offer to the United States."

"And I assume you've got still more meetings lined up?"

"Six of them. I think by the time I see you again we'll have put together a pretty useful organization." He got to his feet and walked to the door. "And now, let me suggest that you partake of some of the pleasures of New Atlantis before returning home."

DeJesus, Lewis, and Naomi Wizner filed out, and Moore closed the door behind them. Then he turned to Black, who hadn't moved from where he was sitting.

"Hi, Solomon," grinned the mulatto. "We've come a long way, haven't we?"

"Hello, Piper," said Moore, sitting down and returning his smile. "Yes, we have."

"Not bad for a couple of small-time hoods."

"Speak for yourself," said Moore. "I was never small time."

Black laughed. "And here we are, fighting for Right, Justice, and the Christian Way."

"Or for Judas' seat in Hell."

"Oh, well," said Black. "I never did want to go to Heaven anyway. I *like* heat."

"I never really thought you were in much danger of freezing in the next life," said Moore.

"Which brings up an interesting point, Solomon."

"And what is that?"

"I've been an atheist all my life—but if Jeremiah is the Messiah, that sure as hell seems to imply the existence of God, doesn't it?"

"You can't have the first without the second."

"Well," said Black, "if there is a God, do you suppose He wants us messing around with His Messiah? I'm going straight to Hell anyway, and I aim to go in style, but what about *you*—you never enjoy your money anyway, so why fight God for it?"

"Don't think I haven't given it a lot of thought," Moore said slowly. "I think there's a good chance Jeremiah is the Messiah, with all that implies."

"Then why *aren't* you keeping your hands off?" asked Black.

"And remember that this isn't Cardinal What's-his-name asking you."

Moore picked up an ornate platinum cigarette lighter and toyed with it.

"I could take the easy way out and say that you and I had paid our entry fees to Hell long before Jeremiah appeared on the scene," he said ironically. "But I won't. If there's a God, and Jeremiah is His handiwork, then I'm acting contrary to His wishes by trying to kill him. But, damn it, Piper—look at the other side of the coin!"

"What other side?" asked Black.

"Why now, and why Jeremiah?"

"I don't think I follow you."

"Where was God when the Jews got thrown out of Jerusalem two thousand years ago? Why did He let us blow up Hiroshima and run an Inquisition and starve eighty million African babies?"

"You expect God to take a day-to-day interest in what's going on down here?" said Black with a smile.

"If Jeremiah's the Messiah, then that's just what He's finally done!" said Moore, his rage, held so long in check, finally boiling over. "Not when we needed Him, but now! And not with a healer or a peacemaker or even a reasonably wise ruler, but with Jeremiah!"

"You know what they say: He works in mysterious ways."

"If Jeremiah is the best He could come up with, His ways are more than mysterious—they're out-and-out irresponsible!"

"Son of a bitch!" laughed Black.

"What's so funny?" demanded Moore.

"I just figured it out," said Black. "Jeremiah is just the god-damned battlefield. You've declared a Holy War on God!"

"Look around you," said Moore grimly. "There are nine billion people out there, each of them going a little crazier every day, and what does He do? He sends down a selfish, womanizing, slow-witted moron. If He truly exists He may be *your* God, but He sure as hell isn't *mine!*"

"I didn't know you had a choice," said Black. "I mean, either He's God or He isn't. And if He is, then maybe we both ought to reconsider what we're doing and start praying to Him."

"Never!" roared Moore. "If there's a God, He gave me a brain, and then saw to it that the only way I could keep it active was to break every goddamned Commandment He created. He set up the rules for a Messiah close to three thousand years ago, and we wound up with Jeremiah. He waited two thousand years for the Jews to kick and claw their way back to Jerusalem without His help, and now He's sent Jeremiah to burn it to the ground and build a new kingdom. I'd sooner worship the Devil!"

"My, you *are* one troubled criminal mastermind, aren't you?" said Black, amused.

"Not any more," said Moore, willing his emotions back into the tortured recesses of his mind. "I know what I have to do."

"Maybe you ought to see a good shrink, Solomon," said Black, his smile gone. "Being angry is one thing, but you're *driven.*"

"Then I'm just going to have to get back in the driver's seat," replied Moore.

"God's a pretty sharp customer," said Black. "Maybe He wants you to make all this fuss about getting back in the driver's seat so Jeremiah can hang on to center stage. Maybe you're being manipulated."

"No one manipulates me," said Moore with more certainty than he felt, "Not Jeremiah, not God, not anyone." He paused. "Besides, when I'm being rational, I don't believe in any of this shit."

"Okay, but I think—"

"The subject is closed," said Moore, and now the emotionless mask was completely back in place.

Black puffed silently on his cigar for a few minutes, while Moore reactivated the viewing screen. Finally the huge mulatto stretched, placed the cigar in an ashtray, and turned to Moore.

"Ready to talk a little business, Solomon?"

"That's what you're here for."

"So how do we split it up?"

"I think we play it very, very safe," said Moore. "If we stop Jeremiah, it's going to be because we have a lot of help. I figure his weapons are up for grabs; probably Israel will wind up with them."

"And his billions of dollars?"

"We don't touch them."

"I think this artificial air has softened your brain, Solomon," said Black. "You're talking about three, maybe four billion dollars."

"Try to understand, Piper: we're being tolerated. We're a couple of pretty big operators in our own ballpark, but look at who we're dealing with now—ambassadors, statesmen, cardinals, people who could land on us so heavy that we never get up again. Let them keep the money."

"Then what's in it for us?" demanded Black. "I never knew Solomon Moody Moore not to have an angle."

"There's an angle," said Moore with a smile. "Who's the biggest drug dealer in the world?"

"Piscard, or maybe me."

"The biggest pornographer?"

"You, unless Davenport in Britain has caught up."

"The biggest fence?"

"Quintaro," said Black. "What's all this getting at?"

"Nothing—except that your answers were wrong. Jeremiah is the biggest."

"I wasn't counting him," said Black. "I figure he won't be around that long and . . ." He stopped, and a huge grin spread across his face. "So we split up his sources and outlets and equipment!"

"And double whatever we were making four years ago," concluded Moore. "And we're not taking anything that could be of any possible use to any of our associates, so who's to tell us not to?"

"What about Piscard and the rest?" asked Black. "We'll have to let them in."

"We will," agreed Moore. "I get thirty-five percent, you get twenty-five, and they can fight over what's left."

"I thought we were going to be equal partners, Solomon."

"I don't take on equal partners," replied Moore, his smile vanishing. "That's my offer: take it or leave it."

"And if I leave it?"

"If you leave it, Piper, we'll just have to make do without your services as best we can—and I might add that your life expectancy will be, not to be too pessimistic about it, perhaps twenty minutes."

"What the hell," shrugged the huge mulatto. "Twenty-five's better than nothing, and that's just what I'm making with Jeremiah around—a big, fat zero."

He rose, walked over to Moore, and extended his hand. Moore took it.

"Tell me, Solomon—would you really have killed me?"

"I never joke about business or about Jeremiah," said Moore.

"I'm a pretty big guy, Solomon," said Black.

"I know," replied Moore. "That's why there are three pretty big guns trained on you right now, behind two of the paintings and that one-way mirror in the foyer."

Black threw his head back and laughed.

"Same old Solomon! You've always got every angle covered. I wouldn't want to be in Jeremiah's shoes, not with you after him!"

"He seems to be doing pretty well so far," noted Moore.

"Then he'll fall that much harder when we bring him down," said Black. "And they always fall, Solomon, no matter how big they grow. Even Messiahs."

"Let's hope you're right," said Moore. He found himself tiring of the conversation, so he walked Black to the door and gave him the number of a room that was reserved for Moore's special guests. Black grinned again and walked out into the corridor.

Moore closed the door, went into the bedroom, and began undressing, trying to decide whether to go straight to bed or stop by the whirlpool first. Then a flashing light told him that he was wanted on the phone, and he picked up the receiver.

"Moore here."

"This is Ben. Are you sitting down?"

"What's up?"

"We've got him!" said Pryor excitedly.

"Who's got who?" asked Moore, not daring to hope.

"We've got Jeremiah! Do you want us to bring him to the Bubble?"

"No!" said Moore emphatically. "The damned plane would probably explode. Where are you calling from?"

"Cincinnati. You can figure out where."

"Hold him right where he is, and don't take your eyes off him. I'm on my way."

Moore was half dressed and halfway out the door before Pryor realized that the connection had been broken.

18

In the third decade of the twentieth century, the people of Cincinnati, anticipating their city's continued rapid growth, passed a bond issue to build a subway system beneath the downtown area. Work began immediately, and continued for a few years until it became apparent that far from increasing, the population of the river city had become absolutely constant. It neither rose nor fell during the next century, and the construction of the subway was completely abandoned.

Until Moore's organization decided to open up the Cincinnati market, that is. At that time the ownership of two miles of subterranean tunnels changed hands privately, and Moore's people set up shop in the deserted and almost forgotten subway.

Moore arrived in Cincinnati two hours after receiving Pryor's call, went directly to a run-down Tudor home that was owned by a nonexistent Chicago realtor, climbed down the rickety basement stairs, opened a hidden door, and found Pryor waiting for him.

"Where is he?" demanded Moore as the two of them walked through the long, empty tunnel, their footsteps echoing off the damp stone walls.

"Relax," said Pryor. "He's sedated and under heavy guard. It'll be awhile before he wakes up."

"Has anyone tried to kill him?"

"Yes."

"It didn't work, of course."

Prior shook his head. "Visconti put a gun to his temple and pulled the trigger—and the damned thing backfired and blew his hand off. I have a feeling that if we tried to electrocute him, the whole blasted city would go dark first."

"I agree," said Moore. "How did we get our hands on him?"

"It was crazy. He called a press conference up in Dayton to push Moira's book, and we simply put the snatch on him."

"I see he hasn't gotten any brighter," remarked Moore. "But I'm surprised that he wasn't able to get away."

"That is the surprising part," agreed Pryor. "We got to him while he was putting on makeup in his dressing room, and he just raised his hands and surrendered. There were two other doors and a first-floor window, and based on our previous experience with him you'd have thought he would make a break for it. The bullets would collide in midair or some such thing, and he'd be on the loose again."

"It's more than surprising," said Moore thoughtfully. "It's very disturbing. He must have known that we were going to try to kill him. Maybe he doesn't die, but he sure as hell feels pain. Why put himself through it? In fact, why choose to speak in Dayton when he knows we've still got muscle in Ohio?"

"All we did was capture him," said Pryor thoughtfully. "Maybe whatever protects him is only concerned that he stays alive."

"It's a possibility," said Moore, considering the notion. "Maybe we can do anything we want to him except kill him. Lord knows he hasn't led a painless life up to now." He paused. "By the way, is Abe around? This seems like a good time to try to get some straight answers from Jeremiah."

Pryor shook his head. "He's wavering. He says he's still on our side, but just to hedge his bets he's not going to get involved with this."

"Damn it!" snapped Moore. "He's involved up to his god-damned neck! What does he think Jeremiah is going to do—absolve him?"

"He says he'll quit if you order him to work on Jeremiah."

"We'll take care of Abe later," said Moore after a moment's thought. "Right now our problem is Jeremiah. Just how tight is our security?"

"Come see for yourself," said Pryor, leading him down the corridor to a door that was guarded by a dozen armed men. The structure they entered had originally been a bomb shelter built well beneath a luxurious center-hall Colonial home that was now registered in Montoya's name, but sometime during the past century it had been transformed into a truly elaborate room. It housed an ornate Spanish four-poster bed, a number of chairs, a built-in wet bar, and a functional marble fireplace that was somehow tied in to the house's chimney. Six more armed men, including Montoya, stood within the room, while Jeremiah, naked and unconscious, lay spread-eagled on the bed, each of his limbs tied to a corner post. His right arm bore numerous puncture marks of recent vintage.

"Either you loaded him up enough to kill him," observed Moore, "or he's on the needle himself."

"Only two of those holes came from us," answered Pryor. "The rest are his own project."

"How much longer should he be out?" asked Moore.

"Maybe half an hour or so—if he's a normal human being. Otherwise, he could wake up any second."

"It's cold in here," said Moore, turning to Montoya. "Start a fire."

"But Mr. Moore," replied the security chief, "it's got to be eighty degrees."

"I don't recall asking you the temperature," said Moore. He turned to another of the men as Montoya shrugged and started passing the order for firewood. "I haven't eaten in a few hours. I'd like a sandwich."

"Any particular kind, sir?"

"Whatever's handy."

"I'll have one sent in right away, sir."

"The bread might be hard," added Moore. "I'll need a very sharp knife."

The man nodded and departed.

Moore sat silently in a corner while Montoya built a fire, and set his sandwich aside without touching it.

"Stir that up a little with the poker," he said to Montoya once the firewood was ablaze. "No, leave the poker in it. Why get ashes on the floor?"

Finally he turned back to Pryor.

"Ben, do you think there's any chance that we can kill him?"

Prior shook his head. "I don't think it can be done."

"I don't think so either," said Moore. "I don't even see much sense trying."

"Then what do you plan to do?" asked Pryor.

"Whatever I have to," said Moore grimly. "Take the men out with you."

"Leave you *alone* with him?"

"I'll be all right. And even if I'm not, the room is still secure. Then call the press and get them upstairs in the Colonial with their cameras in about three hours' time."

"But—"

"That was an order, Ben, not a request."

Pryor nodded curtly and ushered the men out, after which Moore bolted the door from the inside. He picked up a rocking chair, placed it next to the bed, sat down on it, took a bite of his sandwich, and stared thoughtfully at Jeremiah.

He hadn't changed much. There wasn't a scar on his body, except for the needle marks, and they'd doubtless vanish in a few days. As for bullet wounds, knife scars, or any of the rest, his flesh was as clean and unmarked as the day he'd been born. He had put on some weight, perhaps fifteen pounds, none of it muscle, but he still didn't appear overweight, though he was far from athletic.

Moore finished the sandwich, walked over and stoked the fire, then returned to the chair. In a few minutes Jeremiah began moaning and twitching. Finally he tried to sit up, found that he couldn't, shook his head vigorously, and focused his eyes.

"Have a nice nap?" asked Moore.

"*You!*" whispered Jeremiah.

"Who were you expecting?"

"Where am I?" demanded Jeremiah, his speech slightly slurred.

"Where nobody can find you," said Moore. "What difference does it make?"

"What are you going to do with me?"

"A much better question," said Moore. "To tell you the truth, I haven't really decided. I thought we might discuss it."

"Fuck you!" snapped Jeremiah.

Moore picked the knife up, touched the point of it to Jeremiah's foot, pressed, and cut a deep gash the length of the arch.

Jeremiah howled in pain.

"Stupid," commented Moore calmly. "Very stupid, Jeremiah. If our positions were reversed, I sure as hell wouldn't speak to *you* like that."

Jeremiah spat at Moore, who applied the knife to his other foot with similar results.

"Just like training a puppy," he said. "Repetition is the key."

Jeremiah bit his lip and glared at Moore.

"As I was saying," Moore continued, "we've got a number of things to discuss. Let me know when you're ready to start."

"All right," muttered Jeremiah.

Moore pressed the point of the knife next to one of the gashes. "I didn't hear you."

"*ALL RIGHT!*"

"Better," remarked Moore dryly. "I have to admit that you're something of a problem. I've got a feeling that nothing I do to you can kill you."

"Nothing can kill the Messiah!" Jeremiah shouted.

"You're possibly right," said Moore calmly. "However, I don't know of any reason why I shouldn't be able to keep you tied to this bed for the next twenty or thirty years. What would you say to that?"

"It'll never work!" hissed Jeremiah.

"Oh yes it will," said Moore. "I think that if we try to starve you to death it won't work; something or someone doesn't want you to die just yet. But I have a feeling that as long as your life isn't directly threatened, you're as powerless in that position as anyone else."

Jeremiah made no reply, but Moore could tell that he was considering the idea.

"And, after all," continued Moore, "why should I want to kill you? I'm considerably older than you are, I have no wife or children, and to be perfectly honest, I don't care if the whole world goes to hell in a handcart five minutes after I'm dead. Can you come up with any reason why I shouldn't follow this course of action?"

"My followers will find me," said Jeremiah. "And when they do, I won't leave enough of you to burn or bury!"

Moore pressed the knife into his foot again.

"You keep forgetting who's in control here," he said, raising his voice to be heard over Jeremiah's screams. "I find this procedure every bit as distasteful as you do, but on the other hand, you probably find it more painful. I think you'd be well advised to keep that in mind and stop making threats, or else you'd better be prepared to suffer the consequences. Look at the discomfort you're suffering, and then consider that we haven't even begun talking about alternatives yet."

"What alternatives?" grated Jeremiah.

"Oh, there are always alternatives," said Moore. "I think I can keep you here as long as I want, but I could be wrong. You think no one can hold you prisoner for any length of time, but *you* could be wrong. It seems to me that the logical thing to do is search for some common meeting ground."

"For instance?"

"Well, for starters, you're worth a great deal of money, a lot of it mine. I'm not a greedy man; I think I'd settle for half."

"You go to hell!" snapped Jeremiah.

Moore reached out with the knife and put another gash on Jeremiah.

He waited until the young man stopped cursing, then continued speaking in a conversational tone. "This is a time for negotiation, not for threats. I'm a little rusty at this kind of thing; there's always a chance I might lose my temper and turn the world's greatest lover into a eunuch. If I were you, I'd really try to avoid making me mad." He paused. "Shall we get back to the subject at hand?"

Jeremiah glared at him and nodded.

"Very reasonable," commented Moore. "I think I should tell you, Jeremiah, that even though I'm a dedicated businessman, there are a lot of things that I care about more than money. One of them, for instance, is my life. I think that as a gesture of good faith you might pass the word to your rather fanatical disciples to take my name off their hit list. Certainly a man of your particular qualities isn't afraid to show a little Christian charity."

He placed the point of the knife just below the young man's left ear.

"I agree!" yelled Jeremiah.

"Excellent," said Moore. "Now we're making some progress." He paused. "Still, I can't help wondering just how this message will be passed to the ranks of your followers."

"I don't know what you mean."

"Well, I can't just let you walk out without it having been done," said Moore. "After all, what guarantee do I have that you'll keep your word—your honest face? Your past history of generosity to me and my organization?"

"What guarantee do you want?" rasped the young man.

"Oh, I'm sure if we put our heads together we'll think of something," said Moore pleasantly. Suddenly he snapped his fingers. "I think I've got the solution to our problem!"

"What?" asked the young man, eying him fearfully.

"Why do all these wild-eyed fools follow your orders in the first place? You're a beggar and a thief, a gambler and a dope addict, you seem intent on bedding every woman on the face of the Earth, and to be perfectly candid about it, you haven't the intellectual capacity of a retarded barn swallow. So why should your word have any weight with the masses?"

"You know why!" snapped Jeremiah.

"Yes I do," admitted Moore. "They seem to think that you're the Messiah."

"I am!"

Moore jabbed him gently with the point of the knife.

"Please don't interrupt me. Now, it seems to me that if they didn't think you were the Messiah, they wouldn't be so all-fired anxious to do your bidding. Does that make sense to you, Jeremiah?"

"What are you getting at?"

"Simply this: if the people decided that you weren't the Messiah, they'd stop listening to you. They wouldn't want to kill me, they wouldn't try to drive me out of business, they might even consider throwing down their weapons and going about their normal daily business. Do you agree?"

Jeremiah glared silently at him.

"Well, at least you don't disagree. So while I appreciate the fact that you're going to sign over half your treasury to me and order your people to leave me alone, the crux of the matter still comes down to this misconception the masses have about what you are." He paused. "Now, who do you suppose can set the record straight? Certainly not me. If I tried to tell them you weren't the Messiah, they'd probably shoot me down in cold blood before I got the first sentence out. Moira? No, I have a feeling that they wouldn't believe her either." He paused again. "Who can we get to do it, Jeremiah? Who is the one person they might believe?"

"Never!" screamed Jeremiah. "I don't give a damn what you do to me! Rip my eyes out of my head, it won't make any difference!"

"Who said anything about your eyes?" asked Moore. "For one thing, you'll need them to sign half of your money over to me. For another, we wouldn't want you looking anything less than your best, since you're going to be making a television address in a couple of hours."

"That's what you think!" snarled Jeremiah.

"Wrong," said Moore, walking over to the fireplace and withdrawing the poker. "That's what I *know.*"

The hideous screams that followed continued for almost forty minutes. At last Moore, his face ashen, unlocked the door, walked out into the tunnel, and slammed it shut behind him. The security men backed away from him, and even Montoya seemed to regard him with a mixture of awe, disapproval, and terror.

"Give him about twenty minutes," he told Pryor. "Then get him dressed and carry him upstairs to the house's living room. How soon do the newsmen get here?"

"An hour or two."

Moore nodded, walked to a makeshift bathroom, and vomited. He rinsed his face off and emerged a few minutes later.

"One of you men," he said to the security team, "get a thin piece of wire about five feet long. Picture-hanging wire will do just fine. Then bring it to the living room."

Pryor came out of the room, looking sick.

"My God, Solomon—what did you do to him?" he said shakily.

"Nothing he won't recover from."

"It's awful!"

"Sometimes people have to do awful things."

"But his body—it's all . . ."

"It won't be for long," said Moore grimly. "When he gets upstairs, sit him in a stiff-backed chair so that he doesn't slump, and use the wire you'll find there to tie his legs to the chair so he can't make a run for it."

"*Run?*" repeated Pryor. "I don't even know what's keeping him alive."

"Just do it, Ben."

Pryor nodded numbly and went off to attend to Jeremiah. Moore rinsed his face again, waited a few more minutes to regain his color, then climbed up the basement stairs and walked into the living room, where Jeremiah sat motionless on a ladder back chair. The young man's face was still unmarked, and a loose robe covered all traces of his recent ordeal.

Moore walked up to Jeremiah and placed a hand under his chin. "Can you hear me?"

Jeremiah nodded.

"Good," said Moore. "Now, in a few minutes the press will be here. Do you remember what you're going to tell them?"

"Yes," whispered Jeremiah.

"Have you tried to walk?"

Jeremiah shook his head.

"Take my word for it: you can't. I'm sure the thought has also crossed your mind to say something other than what we agreed upon. Let me assure you that if you do the story will never leave this building, and what I do to you afterward will make the last couple of hours seem like a Sunday-school picnic."

Jeremiah nodded.

"Ben, have someone get him a little water to drink."

Within a few minutes the color began returning to Jeremiah's face, and ten minutes after that Moore was convinced that he was coherent enough to make the brief statement.

The press finally arrived, late as usual, and Moore waited upstairs while Pryor led them into the living room. There were two cameramen, who immediately went to work setting up their lights, and a reporter who kept dabbing powder onto his face.

"No questions tonight, please," said Pryor. "Jeremiah has a brief announcement to make."

The reporter looked disappointed, but stood back while the cameras were trained on Jeremiah. Finally one of the cameraman nodded his head.

"My name is Jeremiah the B," said the young man, "and I want the world to know that I am making this statement freely and under no coercion from any quarter." He stared directly into the nearer of the two cameras. "I am a fraud. I am not the Messiah. I was never the Messiah. I never believed I was the Messiah. I can no longer live with my conscience. I can no longer look at the worshipful faces of my followers without feeling guilt and remorse beyond measure. I apologize for what I have done. Such monies as I have accumulated will be distributed to those I have robbed and misled. Believe me, I meant no harm—but also believe me when I tell you that I am not the Messiah."

He fell silent, and pandemonium broke loose.

"My God, what a story!" exclaimed one of the cameramen.

"Who's forcing you to make this statement?" demanded the reporter.

"No one," said Jeremiah.

"Why did you come to Cincinnati to make it?" persisted the reporter.

No answer.

"How are you dividing the money?"

Before Jeremiah could respond, Pryor had the security guards clear the room over the outraged protestations of the reporter, and then signaled Moore to come downstairs.

"Very good, Jeremiah," said Moore. "I'm quite proud of you."

Jeremiah, groggy from the effort of addressing the cameras, merely glared at him.

"We're going to keep you under lock and key for about a week," continued Moore. "Long enough for every television station, every radio station, and every newspaper to run that story over and over. After that you're a free man."

He walked out the front door, followed by Pryor.

"I'm going back to Chicago. Keep him on ice until the story gets out."

"And then?" asked Pryor. "Do you really intend to let him go?"

"Why not? Who believes discredited Messiahs?" Moore smiled. "Someday I'll have Abe's rabbi tell you the story of Sabbatai Levi."

"You're the boss," said Pryor, a troubled expression on his face.

"Relax, Ben," said Moore confidently. "It's all over now."

But, of course, it wasn't.

19

From WHTB (Hartford):

"So you now recant your recantation and claim that you are the Messiah? Is that correct?" The interviewer had a condescending smile on his face.

"That's correct," said Jeremiah, looking soulfully into the camera. "I was tortured into making a false denial."

"You're telling me that God allowed His Messiah to be tortured?" scoffed the interviewer.

"If you're a Christian, you believe that God allowed His Messiah to be crucified," said Jeremiah with a smile.

"But really . . ."

"What the hell do you know about Messiahs?" demanded Jeremiah impatiently. He raised his hands above his head and intoned: *"LET THERE BE RAIN!"*

And, instantly, the rain came.

Jeremiah looked wildly at the camera. "How do you like them apples, Moore?" he bellowed.

From KPTO-TV (Denver):

"This is Jeremiah the B. You know who I am and what I am. Senator Caldwall Burke would deny me. He runs for reelection the day after tomorrow. He has publicly stated that I am not the one true Messiah. Can you guess what I want you to do?"

Burke lost by half a million votes.

From BBC-3 (London):

"And you've been blind from birth?" asked Jeremiah, standing at center stage of the New Palladium.

"Yes, Lord," said the old woman.

"And you will pledge your everlasting fealty to me and turn all your worldly goods over to me for the gift of sight?"

"Yes, Lord."

He laid his hands on her eyes. "Then so be it."

He removed his hands and the woman slowly, fearfully, opened her eyes. She blinked a few times, and then a torrent of tears burst forth.

"My God, I can see!"

"Take that and stick it in your ear, Moore!" shrieked Jeremiah, his face flushed with triumph.

From WQRQ-TV (New York):

"Who am I?" he cried to the wildly cheering throng of people who had gathered in Times Square.

"JEREMIAH!"

"And *what* am I?"

"THE MESSIAH!"

"The day is fast approaching when the Messiah must lay claim to his throne. Will you help me?"

The answer was so loud that it blew every circuit in WQRQ's sound system.

From WLKJ-TV (Miami):

Jeremiah looked up from the burn victim, whose skin was already starting to heal.

"Who am I, Moore?" he gloated, grinning into the camera.

From UBS Radio (Network):

"Do you hear me, Moore?" he screamed into the microphone. "Calling a sheep's tail a leg doesn't make it one, and torturing the Messiah into renouncing doesn't make him any the less a Messiah! I am the Expected One, and nothing else counts! Blow it out your ass, Moore!"

From KFD-TV (Seattle):

"I don't need your support, but I do want it! The Messiah is a law unto himself, but those who support me will be remembered and rewarded—and those who oppose me will be remembered even better! Start saying your prayers, Moore—I'll be listening!"

20

"Take a look," said Moore, tossing the handwritten letter onto Pryor's desk.

Dear Solomon:

I am not ungrateful for all the years I have worked for you, but it seems to me that the handwriting is on the wall. I am a Jew, and I can no longer oppose the man who seems to be the living culmination of my religious beliefs.

I have been in constant contact with Moira Rallings for the past week, and have been granted an amnesty of sorts in exchange for my pledge of allegiance to their cause. This I have freely given.

I shall divulge none of your plans to which I am privy, nor will I give them any details of your past actions in reference to Jeremiah.

I wish you well, but urge you to call off your vendetta before it is too late. I know you are a resourceful man, but face facts, Solomon— he is the Messiah!

Abraham Bernstein

"Not exactly a surprise," commented Pryor, putting the letter down.

"I suppose not," admitted Moore. "But damn it, Ben, I hate to lose another of our insiders to Jeremiah!"

"I know. How long do you think he'll keep his word about playing dumb?"

"Twenty minutes, tops," said Moore. "It doesn't matter. He can't do us any harm. Get Piper Black on the phone for me."

Moore returned to his office, pacing the floor restlessly until the light atop his telephone flashed.

"Hello, Piper," he said.

"Solomon."

"How are things coming along at your end?"

"You've got to be kidding, right?"

"I'm quite serious," responded Moore. "We've got a PR campaign to begin."

"Come off it, Solomon," said Black. "You had that son of a bitch in your hands and you turned him loose. Not only that, but he's saying that you tortured him until he signed over half his money to you."

"It'll never stand up in court," said Moore. "I just did it to tie up his funds while we're fighting him."

"Sure you did, Solomon," said Black. "Listen to me, you bastard! We had an agreement, and you broke it by trying to cut me out. Fight him yourself!"

"All right, Piper," said Moore. "I tried to cut you out. So what?"

"What do you mean, so what?"

"What's changed?" asked Moore. "Is your business any better? Is Jeremiah any less of a threat? We've still got to work together, unless you expect him to just up and vanish."

"Oh, we can still work together, Solomon," said Black. "But this time I make the bargain."

"Name your terms," said Moore.

"Forty for me, twenty for you, and forty for the rest of them."

"Done."

"What did you say?"

"I agree."

"Too fast, Solomon. What's the catch?"

"No catch," answered Moore. "Maybe I just want to break him more than I want to break you."

There was a long pause.

"Okay. I can accept that," said Black at last. "But you tell that little bloodsucker Pryor what we agreed to. I'll have my brother get in touch with him tomorrow and take care of the details. It's all going to be recorded and put under lock and key—and God help you if you try to pull anything fancy."

"God isn't exactly who I'm worried about," said Moore, breaking the connection.

21

Moore sat in a leather wingback chair in his apartment atop the New Atlantis. He stared at the fish in the viewscreen for a long moment, marveling at how they seemed to preen for the camera, then turned back to his associates. Naomi Wizner had been here before, but it was his first meeting with General Josef Yitzak of the Israeli Army.

"So he's definitely on the move," said Moore at last.

"There's no question about it," replied Naomi Wizner. "He's got about a quarter of a million volunteers in Egypt and Lebanon, and probably five times that many just across the Mediterranean."

"They're not very well organized," added Yitzak. He paused thoughtfully. "Of course, there is no reason for us to have supposed that they would be. Nothing we've been able to learn about Jeremiah indicates that he possesses any knowledge of the techniques of modern warfare."

"It doesn't make any difference," said Moore. "What's harder to fight, General—five trained soldiers who want to live to fight another day, or one untrained fanatic who wants to die for his cause?"

Yitzak nodded. "This has been our most serious problem—the knowledge that they're going to be vying with one another for the privilege of throwing themselves in our line of fire."

"What kind of firepower has he got?"

"Strictly conventional," replied Yitzak. "But we're not here to discuss military strategy with you. The Israeli Army is quite capable of taking care of itself."

"If the Israeli Army was capable of taking care of itself, you wouldn't be here," Moore pointed out. "Now, what can I do to help you?"

"I must know more about him," answered Yitzak, electing to ignore Moore's comment. "You know him better than anyone else who opposes him. You may have some knowledge of how his mind works that could prove useful to us. Who knows—you may even be able to suggest a weakness."

Moore laughed. "He was my prisoner six weeks ago. Does it appear to you that I've discovered any weaknesses in the man?"

"Why did you let him go?" asked Naomi.

"Why not? Since I couldn't kill him, I thought that I could at least discredit him. As it turned out," he concluded dourly, "I was mistaken."

"Then you can suggest nothing?" said Yitzak.

"Not at the moment," admitted Moore. "I keep coming back to the notion that if you can't stop him—and it looks like you can't—then you ought to concentrate on unconverting his followers."

"How do you unconvert an army of religious fanatics that is massing on your border?" asked Yitzak ironically.

Moore shrugged. "I wish I knew."

"Can you give us any other information that might help us prepare for Jeremiah's attack?" asked Naomi.

"Not a thing," said Moore. "You probably know more about the disposition of his army than he does."

"This is no time for levity," said Yitzak sternly.

"I'll let you know when I'm joking," replied Moore. "Jeremiah has no interest in learning how to deploy his forces, nor will he especially give a damn if ten million of his followers must die to get him what he wants."

"I find that difficult to believe."

"I don't doubt it," said Moore. "But if Jeremiah thought and acted like a normal man, he wouldn't be knocking at the door to your city. By the way, exactly where is he now?"

"We aren't sure," admitted Yitzak. "We know he's not in Egypt or Lebanon, but we haven't been able to pinpoint him yet."

"You probably won't, until he decides to attack," replied Moore. "He can stay hidden better than any man I've ever known."

"Then in your opinion he's just going to magically appear at the proper psychological moment to lead his troops to victory?"

Moore shook his head. "You still don't understand him. My own guess is that he won't appear until *after* Jerusalem has fallen. Why should he be a target if he doesn't have to be?"

"Your advice, then, would be to make Jerusalem all but impregnable?" persisted Yitzak.

"Eliminate the words 'all but,' and you've got it," said Moore. "Leave him an opening and he'll have his foot in the door before you can slam it shut. Look at what he's done in less than four years." He grimaced. "Give him another four and he could probably pass a constitutional amendment proclaiming his divinity."

"What will he do if we fight him to a standstill?"

"If you fight him to a standstill, he's already won," answered Moore. "How many new citizens emigrate to Israel in a year? Less than Jeremiah picks up in a day. If you fight to a draw it's all over, because he'll be back twice as strong six months later. You've got two choices: beat him decisively the first time you meet him, or sue for peace. There's no third alternative."

"And not a government in the world has offered to stand with us," said Naomi Wizner bitterly.

"We have always stood alone against our enemies," said Yitzak. "Why should this time be any different?"

"That's the wrong attitude," said Moore. "They're not giving out

prizes for bravery this season. He's already got twice as many followers as you have citizens. You're going to have to get help."
"From where?" asked Yitzak with a bitter laugh.
"How the hell should I know? Arm the Catholics and the
Moslems. Get ITT to finance an army. Tell the Chinese they're next
on his hit list. But do *something!*"
"You're right, of course," interjected Naomi hastily. "And I won't
be revealing any secrets if I tell you that we have been actively
trying to rally support to our cause—thus far without noticeable success." She paused. "However, these are definitely not your problems, Mr. Moore. What we would like you to do is come to Jerusalem in an advisory capacity."
"I don't know anything about fighting a war."
"We are aware of that," said Yitzak.
"Then what do you need me for?"
"Of those people committed to the defense of Jerusalem, you are
the only one who has ever met Jeremiah face to face. I realize you
think you have told us everything you know about the way his mind
works, but there is always a chance you have overlooked something—or, more likely still, that you will be able to improve some
section of our defense based on facts and insights that we do not possess. To this end, we are prepared to offer you a temporary commission in the Israeli Army if you will come to Jerusalem and let us pick
your mind as best we can."
Moore considered the offer for a moment, then turned to Yitzak.
"And what if you become convinced that he's the Messiah?"
"Then I shall do his bidding," replied Yitzak promptly. He held
up his hand as Moore began to speak. "But let me add that the only
way he can convince me is by defeating our army in battle, at which
point the entire matter becomes academic."
Moore walked over to the viewscreen and studied the fish for a
few minutes. Finally he turned back to the two Israelis.
"All right," he said. "I'll go. And you can keep your commission;
I'm no soldier."
"It will get you preferential treatment and quarters of your own,"
said Yitzak.
"I don't know any protocol," protested Moore. "And I have a
feeling that I won't like saluting fellow officers."
"Israeli soldiers don't salute—they *fight*," said Yitzak, not without
a trace of pride. "From this moment on, you are Colonel Solomon
Moore. You are responsible to no one but myself, and your sole duty

will be to analyze Jeremiah's actions and advise me on how best to respond to them." He smiled wryly. "I cannot promise to take any of your advice, but I *do* promise to listen."

"Fair enough," said Moore.

Yitzak stood up. "How soon can you be ready to leave?"

"I've got some business affairs to put in order," replied Moore. "It'll take about a day. I don't think I'll be returning to Chicago, so I'll catch the next flight to London from Kingston, and make connections there."

"Nonsense," said Yitzak. "I'll have my own plane ready and waiting for you twenty-four hours from now. We are about to become inseparable companions."

"Whatever you say."

Moore led them to the door, then picked up the phone and began putting his affairs in order.

First he instructed his lawyers to place what remained of his personal holdings into a blind trust. While he was waiting for them to fly out to the Bubble for his signature, he called Pryor on his vidphone.

"What's up?" asked Pryor, adjusting the picture he was receiving. "The last time you bothered with video contact was the day you bought out the Portofilio Family."

"We've got a lot to talk about, Ben," said Moore. "I thought it might be more comfortable to do it this way."

"Fine by me," said Pryor, pouring himself a drink.

"I'm leaving for Jerusalem tomorrow."

"Good! Either you'll kill him, or I'll wind up in charge of things. Either way I'm happy."

"How touching," remarked Moore dryly.

"You don't really want me to lie to you, do you?" asked Pryor easily. "How long before Jeremiah attacks?"

"Soon. A week or two at most, based on what our associates have told me. However, that's neither here nor there. I called to give you some information you're going to need if I don't come back."

Pryor turned on a tape machine. "Shoot."

For the next two hours Moore listed the politicians, criminals, businessmen, newsmen, and religious leaders who were either owned outright by the organization or at least beholden to it. He spent another hour laying out the details of those enterprises that he had never committed to paper, and noted with some satisfaction that even Pryor was surprised by the extent of them. All were hurting at the moment, but few of them were so moribund that Jeremiah's demise couldn't bring them back to glowing health and solvency in a year's time.

"And Ben," he concluded, "I want you to understand that until you have proof of my death, nothing has changed."

"I'm not sure I understand."

"Don't play stupid, Ben; it's unbecoming. I want you to think very carefully before letting your reach exceed your grasp. I'm still in charge."

"Absolutely, Solomon."

"I don't expect to be gone more than a couple of weeks, a month at the most. You haven't time to consolidate power during that period, and I strongly suggest that you allow discretion to remain the better part of valor."

"If I were the type to move prematurely, I'd have grabbed for the brass ring before now," replied Pryor frankly. "Besides, the odds are that you'll be dead in two more weeks. I've waited nine years; I can wait half a month more."

Moore smiled. "That sounds more like the Ben Pryor we all know and love. And now let me give you a final order: take the hit off Jeremiah and Moira, and bring our operatives back into the business. It's strictly a military matter now, and our people are out of their depth. Let the Israeli Army handle Jeremiah from here on out; we'll concentrate on making money."

His call completed, he phoned Chicago on a private line that Pryor knew nothing about, and instructed a couple of spies to make sure that Pryor didn't try to jump the gun. This done, he lay down for what he anticipated would be his last comfortable night's sleep for quite some time, awoke nine hours later, conferred with his lawyers, concluded a couple of business arrangements that he had decided to withhold from Pryor, and had an order of eggs Benedict sent up to the room. He ate, showered, and donned the rather bedraggled uniform that Yitzak had sent up to his room at midmorning.

Then, at the appointed time, he took an elevator to the ocean's surface, took his private helicopter to Kingston's airport, and found Yitzak waiting for him. The Israeli general led him to a small plane, they walked up a mobile stairway, the door closed behind them, and a moment later they were airborne.

"Any change in the situation?" asked Moore, sitting down on a swivel chair that was bolted to the floor.

"We still don't know where Jeremiah is, if that's what you mean," replied Yitzak. "As for his army, they're practically knocking at the door. They're in Gaza, they're on the Golan Heights, they're at various positions in Sinai. And, of course, they're almost impossible to identify: no uniforms, no similarity of weapons, no common language. Someone is obviously giving them orders, telling them when and where to move, but we haven't been able to penetrate their chain of command."

"Any skirmishes yet?"

"No," answered Yitzak. "It's my own guess that Egypt and Jordan have made some accommodation with them which includes confining the battle to Israeli soil."

"Why play by their ground rules?" asked Moore.

"I don't believe I understand you."

"What's to stop you from attacking them now, before they reach Israel?"

"Because, as I mentioned, they are indistinguishable from the natives of the surrounding countries. The only way to wipe them out at this time would be to unleash our thermonuclear arsenal, and literally tens of millions of innocent people would die." He paused. "We, of all people, are just a little sensitive about committing genocide."

"Can't you move your army across the border and attack with conventional weapons?" persisted Moore.

"Genocide on *any* scale is unacceptable to us," replied Yitzak. "Our best hope is to capture or kill Jeremiah before it comes to that."

"It's going to come to that sooner or later," said Moore. "You're not going to kill him, and he's not going to chance being captured. So why not fight on Syrian or Egyptian or Jordanian soil? Slice them down quick enough and you might give the rest of his followers second thoughts."

"It is not my decision to make. The order has already been given. For the moment, there is to be no bloodbath."

"Stupid," commented Moore.

"Now that I've given you the official line," said Yitzak, suddenly looking very tired, "let me personally agree with you. While we have made no military alliances, we cannot be sure that the same is true of Jeremiah. The sooner we join this battle, the better."

They discussed the situation further as the plane raced toward Yitzak's beleaguered country. Finally, when they were through speaking, Moore dined on knishes and kreplach, washed them down with a red wine, positioned himself as comfortably as he could on his chair, and fell asleep.

He was awakened some time later when the plane started bucking like an untamed horse. "What the hell is going on?" he demanded, sitting up abruptly.

"Ground fire," said Yitzak. "We're over Sinai." He tossed a parachute to Moore. "Here. Slip this on, just in case."

Moore watched Yitzak, copied his movements, and soon had his own parachute on.

Yitzak looked out a window. "We should be out of range in another minute or—"

There was a thunderous explosion, the plane shuddered convulsively, and Moore looked out just in time to see a wing catch fire. They went into a spinning nose dive, trailing flames and black smoke, and Yitzak helped Moore to a hatch.

"I'll go first," he announced. "When you see my parachute open, pull the rip cord on your own."

"Where is it?" asked Moore, surprised that he didn't feel more panic-stricken.

Yitzak pointed it out to him, opened the door, and jumped. Moore followed him a second later. It took him a couple of seconds to get his bearings, but finally he figured out where up and down were. Then he looked ahead and saw the flaming plane plunging toward the earth.

After a time he became aware that Yitzak had already opened his parachute, and he pulled the ripcord on his own. He thought for an instant that the sudden jerk on the harness would rip him in half, but it didn't, and suddenly the parachute blossomed like a giant flower and his rate of descent slowed somewhat, though he was still certain that he would be crushed the moment he hit the ground.

When he was about two thousand feet from the ground he looked once again for Yitzak's chute, and saw it about half a mile northeast of him. He became disoriented again, then forced himself to stare at the ground until he once again regained his bearings. A gust of wind hit him at fifty feet and carried him toward Yitzak. It stopped as quickly as it had begun, and he had to decide whether to attempt to land on his feet or hit the ground rolling. He opted for the latter, watched the sandy loam racing up to meet him, tried to remember how he had been taught to fall during his brief interest in judo, realized at the last second that he was positioning his body wrong, and lost consciousness the instant he landed.

22

Moore slowly became aware of the fact that Yitzak was trying to help him to his feet.

"Is anything broken?" asked the Israeli.

"I don't know," mumbled Moore. "How do you tell if something's broken?"

"If you can move your arms and legs, nothing's broken," replied Yitzak with a smile. "Nothing important, anyway."

Moore spit out a tooth and a mouthful of blood. "I must have landed on my face," he grunted.

"It's possible," said Yitzak. "Difficult, but possible. And of course you'll have a minor concussion. You can't be knocked unconscious without concussing. But on the whole, I'd say that you made an exemplary first jump under hazardous conditions. We lost the pilot and the crew."

Moore took a step, wobbled slightly, and had to hold on to Yitzak's shoulder to keep from falling. "I'm too old for this kind of thing," he said painfully.

"It could be worse," said Yitzak, supporting him. "At least we landed in our own territory."

"It's all desert," said Moore, trying to focus his eyes. "How can you tell the difference?"

"No one is shooting at us," replied Yitzak. "Besides, Israel is a tiny country. It's not too difficult to spot a landmark or two, such as that tel over there near that grove of trees."

"What do we do now?" asked Moore, rubbing his jaw and spitting out another tooth.

"We wait. The way that plane was blazing, I imagine everyone within fifty miles must have seen us. They'll be sending out search parties."

Moore began feeling dizzy, and decided to sit down and await his rescuers. They arrived about twenty minutes later in a pair of sixty-year-old Land Rovers. Yitzak issued a few terse commands, and one of the drivers helped Moore into a Land Rover and drove him straight to a hospital at the northern end of Jerusalem.

He was examined, medicated, and sent down the street to a dentist, who took one look at his mouth, shook his head dismally, shot Moore full of painkillers, and began repairing the damage. Moore leaned back, his mouth propped open, and spent the next twenty minutes concentrating on not falling off the chair. Finally the drugs they had given him at the hospital began to take effect, and he surveyed his surroundings.

The room itself was quite small. There were three certificates on the wall, all in Spanish, and that in turn led him to scrutinize the dentist, whom he had originally taken to be a Semite but now, in light of the certificates, could just as easily be Hispanic. It was then that he saw the golden crucifix suspended from the dentist's neck.

"What the hell are you doing in an Israeli dental clinic?" he managed to mutter.

"Fixing your teeth," replied the dentist with a smile.

"But you're a Catholic!"

"And Catholics can't repair teeth?" asked the dentist.

"But why here? This is a battle zone."

"I know who you are, Mr. Moore," was the reply. "And you are no more Jewish than I am. Why are *you* here?"

"To fight Jeremiah."

"I, too. The false Messiah must be destroyed, and if by being here I can free another Israeli to do battle against him, then I am content."

"What makes you think that he's *false?*"

"He must be!"

"Don't bet every last penny you've got on it."

"But we must totally discredit him!"

"I'll settle for just stopping him," said Moore.

"That is not enough," said the dentist. "There must be no shred of doubt remaining that he is a fraud."

"What difference does it make, as long as we beat him?" asked Moore.

"I am a practicing Catholic, and yet I freely acknowledge that my Church has done many wicked things, Mr. Moore. The Papacy itself has been sold numerous times, and more than one Pope has littered Europe with his bastard children and the bodies of his enemies. We slaughtered millions of Moslems during the Crusades, tortured thousands of intellectuals during the Inquisition, crushed the skulls of Incan and Aztec babies immediately after baptizing them to make sure their souls would go directly to Heaven, and fought far too many Holy Wars. And yet it is precisely because of these evils that I will defend Jesus as the true Christ to my dying breath."

"I don't think I see the logic of that," commented Moore.

"My God, Mr. Moore!" whispered the dentist. "Think of how many millions of people have died for no reason at all if He is *not* the Christ! Jeremiah must be killed if for no other reason than that!"

"Well, it's a novel approach," remarked Moore. Then the dentist leaned forward and began working on his mouth again, and he could make no further comment.

The repair job took about two hours, with instructions to return a week later for still more work, and when Moore finally got up to leave he found Yitzak waiting for him in the outer office.

"I understand that you have nothing more than a few bad bruises and some broken teeth," said the Israeli vigorously. "You should be feeling just fine by tomorrow morning."

Moore grunted. "We are not amused."

"I expect you'll want to see your quarters. They aren't as luxurious as the New Atlantis, but I trust you will find them sufficient."

"I'm sure I will," replied Moore. "The New Atlantis isn't exactly to my taste."

They walked to an ancient but well-kept apartment building, where Moore followed Yitzak up two flights of stairs. The general unlocked a door and turned the key over to Moore.

"There's a staff phone beside your bed," he said. "Feel free to use it whenever you wish. Your refrigerator is well stocked, and if you wish, a roommate can be supplied."

"That won't be necessary," said Moore. "What are my duties, and who do I report to?"

"Your duties are simply to evaluate the situation, and you'll report directly to me. Any suggestions I find useful will be transmitted to Prime Minister Weitzel. You have free run of the city, and on your nightstand you'll find a pass that will get you into all but a handful of our military installations." He paused. "Try to get some rest now, and I'll be back tomorrow morning to show you around."

Moore thanked him, locked the door, and began inspecting his apartment. Except for the lack of books, it was very similar to his Chicago dwelling: small, comfortable, and unpretentious. He found the pass, pinned it to his lapel, and walked to the bathroom, where he undressed and took a long, hot shower.

When he emerged he went to the kitchen and checked out the refrigerator, and discovered that someone had gone to great lengths to learn his taste in food. He warmed up a frozen dinner of veal parmesan, but found that his mouth was too sore to chew, so he settled for drinking a quart of ice water. Then, suddenly very tired, he took a couple of pills the hospital had given him and collapsed on the bed while the medication went to work.

23

Jeremiah suddenly sat up in bed.

"He's there!" he announced.

Moira stirred sleepily and opened one eye. "Who's where?"

"Moore!" said Jeremiah excitedly. "He's in Jerusalem!"

"What makes you think so?"

"I don't *think* so. I *know* it!"

"Big deal. You're just going to kill him anyway."

"Poor little necrophile!" said Jeremiah with an amused laugh. "You don't even begin to understand what's happening, do you? Moore is the last person in the world I want to kill just now. Our fates have become linked to one another."

"What are you talking about?" asked Moira, rubbing her eyes.

"You think you and that fucking book of yours are important?" said Jeremiah sarcastically. "Well, let me tell you: it makes no difference to me whether or not you ever sell another copy or write another word. It's all clear to me now. Moore is my most important ally, not you."

"Be sure to tell him that just before he blows your brains out," said Moira disgustedly.

"Oh, I will," chuckled Jeremiah. "I will!"

24

Moore awoke feeling very stiff, but in considerably less pain. He was in the process of cooking some soft-boiled eggs for himself when Yitzak arrived.

"How is our wounded warrior feeling today?" asked the Israeli.

"A little the worse for wear," replied Moore. "I'm too old to take up parachute jumping." He poured himself a cup of tea. "What's on the agenda for this morning?"

"A tour of the city. You can't spot our weak points if you haven't examined our defenses."

"You're wasting your time," said Moore. "I wouldn't begin to know what to look for. If you tell me the city's secure, I have to take your word for it. If you tell me there are weak spots, you'll have to point them out to me before I know they're there. I think it's a waste of time."

"I'm fully aware of this," said Yitzak. "But I've got a lot of time to spend. As you have doubtless guessed by now, my sole responsibility is to shepherd you around while listening to you and evaluating your observations."

"We're going about it all wrong," said Moore. "Finding weak spots isn't the way Jeremiah works. He's more likely to walk right up to fifty riflemen—and twenty of them will miss him while the other thirty rifles will explode."

"So you keep telling me," said Yitzak patiently. "Nonetheless, I would appreciate it if we could do this my way."

"You're the boss," said Moore. He finished his eggs and tea, and then accompanied Yitzak out into the street.

They climbed into a Land Rover and began driving around the city on the Jaffa and Gaza roads. Jerusalem, more than most cities, was a mixture of the old and the new, with fifty-story steel-and-glass office buildings towering over the Mandelbaum Gate, fast-food stands lining Jericho Road, and a rugby field buttressed up against the Lion's Gate.

Only the Wailing Wall was not surrounded by new structures; it stood alone, untouched by any recent century, guarded by twenty crack Israeli soldiers.

"We've created a rectangle, the corners of which are the four Gates—Lion's, Jaffa, Zion, and Mandelbaum," explained Yitzak, pointing out the various fortifications to Moore as they drove by. "For all practical purposes, the city of Jerusalem is within that perimeter. Of course, this doesn't mean we will allow Jeremiah's army to march over the Israeli border without a fight, but Jerusalem is his ultimate target, so this has become our final line of defense. We don't know what part of the city he'll hit first, but this perimeter encompasses all of the Old City, including the Moslem and Christian shrines, plus the Knesset, the Prime Minister's palace, and the various other governmental buildings. If it's secure, Jerusalem's secure."

"Where do you expect the attack to originate?" asked Moore, gazing off in the distance.

"Not in the direction you're looking," replied Yitzak with a smile. "They'll most likely approach from Abu Tur to the south, Tel Arza to the north, and the Golan Heights to the northeast. You're looking almost due west, which is the one direction we're not too worried about, since we've got about half a million troops stationed there, halfway between Jerusalem and Tel Aviv."

They continued driving around the Old City, which an army of almost eight hundred thousand Israelis was poised to defend to the last man, woman, and child. There was sufficient ammunition for a four-month pitched battle, and the air force, geared for action, was ready to take off at an instant's notice. Radar and sonar blanketed the area, laser weapons were revved up for the conflict to come, and tanks guarded the perimeter at regular intervals.

"A mosquito couldn't get through all that," said Moore when they had arrived at Yitzak's headquarters, the nerve center of the communications network.

"You're quite sure?" asked Yitzak, escorting Moore into a nondescript office and offering him a beer, which he refused.

"I can't imagine any army launching a successful attack—at least, not on the ground. Just how good are your air defenses?"

"Excellent," replied Yitzak. "Furthermore, according to our information, Jeremiah hasn't got more than half a dozen planes."

"Fifth columnists?" asked Moore.

"I tend to doubt it," said Yitzak. "This is not the Messiah of Christianity we're dealing with here. Whether our people believe in him or not, we all know that he's not exactly coming as a Prince of Peace."

"Do they believe in him?" asked Moore.

"Who knows?" replied Yitzak with a shrug. "It makes no difference. This is the only homeland we have, and we don't plan to turn it over to him without a fight."

"As far as fighting goes, I'm no expert—but I don't think you've got much to worry about from Jeremiah's army. Jerusalem seems about as well fortified as cities get to be."

"Good. Tomorrow we'll tour it on foot, and see if you still feel that way." Yitzak paused thoughtfully. "Possibly we'll go well beyond the perimeter. You can put yourself in Jeremiah's shoes, so to speak, and try to foresee how he might lead the attack."

"I keep telling you—he won't be leading anyone into battle. It's not his style."

"If his army is expected to overrun Jerusalem without availing itself of his special talents, he's going to have to wait until it's larger and better-trained," said Yitzak. He turned to Moore. "I find it difficult to believe that having come this far, he'll be willing to wait any appreciable length of time."

"Could this be a feint?" asked Moore.

"What do you mean?"

"What's to stop him from attacking every other square foot of

Israel first? All he has to do is keep clear of Jerusalem and Tel Aviv and assume you won't leave them unguarded."

Yitzak shook his head. "You still don't comprehend just how *small* Israel is. We could cross it in ninety minutes in that beat-up Land Rover we used this morning. Believe me, there is no place he can attack where we can't retaliate instantly, and without appreciably decreasing our security around Jerusalem."

"Then I'm out of ideas," said Moore. "I don't know what the hell he'll do next." He shrugged. "I guess we just sit back and wait."

"For the moment," agreed Yitzak.

And so they waited. For two weeks there was no change in the disposition of Jeremiah's forces. Yitzak and Moore toured the perimeter of the city daily, looking for weak spots, for anything that might give Moore an idea as to when and where Jeremiah would strike.

They found nothing.

It was late on the night of his sixteenth day in Jerusalem that Moore decided to call Pryor in Chicago to see how the business was going. He quickly discovered that the phone in his room could only make contact with headquarters, so he wandered over to Yitzak's office to place the call from there. He nodded to the various members of the night staff, which consisted primarily of lower-echelon officers and orderlies, then let himself into the office and closed the door behind him.

He put through the call, was informed that Pryor was in Boston on business, and hung up. Since he didn't feel like going right back out into the oppressive heat of the Israeli night, he walked over to the refrigerator and poured himself a glass of orange juice that the general had started keeping for him. He carried it over to Yitzak's desk, sat down on a swivel chair, stretched his legs out, took a long sip from the glass, and closed his eyes.

"That drink sure looks good," said a familiar voice from behind him. "Mind if I join you?"

Moore spun his chair around and leaped to his feet.

"Hello, Solomon," said Jeremiah. "Long time no see."

25

"How did you get in here?" demanded Moore.

"Relax, Solomon," laughed Jeremiah. "You'll have a stroke. Now, how about that drink?"

As Jeremiah strolled over to the refrigerator, Moore quickly walked to the door and found that it was locked.

"There's nothing to see in the outer office anyway, except for a bunch of sleeping soldiers," said Jeremiah. He pulled out a can of beer. "Hope you don't mind," he said, popping the top open, "but I gave up fruit juice when I was four years old." He took a long swig of it, wiped his mouth on a shirtsleeve, and then finished it. "Good stuff. Mind if I have another?"

Moore sat back down at the desk and stared at him while he opened a second can.

"Thanks, Solomon. It's hot as hell out there. I'm not used to the climate anymore." He chuckled. "I'd forgotten just how uncomfortable the Middle East can be at this time of year."

"You still haven't answered my question," said Moore. "How did you get in here?"

"I just walked in."

"Don't give me that shit!" snapped Moore. "There are a million armed men and women out there!"

"Nevertheless," said Jeremiah, breaking out into a huge smile. "I didn't hear a single shot."

"There weren't any. I walked straight from my camp to this office. Nobody saw me, nobody heard me, nobody tried to stop me. It was really amazing, Solomon—I simply walked right by them and they acted like I wasn't there. Then, when I got here, I just told everyone in the outer office to go to sleep, and they did." He grinned again. "I *like* being the Messiah!"

Moore slid a desk drawer out, found a letter opener, and withdrew it.

"Then I guess I'll have to kill you myself," he said ominously.

"No you won't, Solomon," replied Jeremiah, making no move to defend himself. "But *your* job is done. I can finally kill *you*—and if you annoy me, I will."

"What are you talking about?"

"Up until this moment, you've been as impossible to kill as I have, Solomon," said Jeremiah, pulling up a chair and facing him. "But you've been so concerned about killing me that you never realized it." He paused, obviously enjoying himself enormously. "Remember that day in Chicago when the plane crashed into the hangar? I got away, but you survived too. Lisa Walpole couldn't kill you, either. And while you've been trying to kill me for four years, I've had a hit out on you, too. Even shooting down your plane didn't do the trick."

"What are you driving at?" asked Moore, laying down the letter opener and staring at him.

"I thought you were supposed to be the one with all the brains," said Jeremiah. "And yet you still don't see it, do you?"

"Keep talking."

"Take a look at the record, Solomon. You've spent the past four years alerting millions of people to my presence; indeed, you've been the best advance man anyone could want. And now you've even helped to make Jerusalem totally impregnable. You did your job well, Solomon."

"*My* job?"

"Yes, Solomon," said Jeremiah. "You see, you're the Forerunner. You are Elijah, come to pave the way for the Messiah."

"You're crazy!" snapped Moore.

"No, Solomon. I'm right, and I can tell from the expression on your face that you're beginning to realize it." He paused. "How was Elijah to come to Jerusalem?"

"You tell me."

"He was to streak across the skies in a flaming chariot," replied Jeremiah. "We don't have chariots anymore, but I'd say that you chose the closest thing. *'Behold, I will send you Elijah the prophet before the coming of the great and dreadful day of the Lord!'* That's Malachi 4:5, Solomon."

"Bullshit!"

"I got a million of 'em," grinned Jeremiah. "Do you want me to start quoting them?"

Moore shook his head, lost in thought.

"I would have attacked much sooner," Jeremiah continued, "but when I figured it all out, I thought I'd wait and see just how much of the way you would prepare for me. I'm glad I did, too. I knew you'd make me a household name, but I never dreamed that you'd also present me with an impregnable Jerusalem. As I said, Forerunner, you did your job well—but your job is over now. You live or die at my whim. You're simply not needed any longer."

Moore remained silent for a few minutes while Jeremiah opened a third can of beer. Finally he looked up, a rueful smile on his face.

"In other words, if I had just ignored you . . ."

"You couldn't have, Solomon. The Messiah must have his Forerunner. It was written in the Book of Fate eons ago that you and I should play out these roles at this time and place."

"Such eloquence," said Moore sardonically.

"Oh, I know I was a pretty dumb little bastard when all this started," admitted Jeremiah. "But the Messiah must rule with the wisdom of David and Solomon. I see things more clearly these days."

"So what's next?" said Moore. "Do you establish a poverty-free utopian state?"

"Oh, no, Forerunner," said Jeremiah with a nasty smile. "First I raze civilization to the ground. I burn out the evil and put mine enemies to the sword—figuratively, of course. After all, I've got an army to do that kind of stuff for me. Then and only then do I set about rebuilding the world the way I want it."

"And what kind of a world will it be?" asked Moore.

"I really don't know," answered Jeremiah. "But I'm sure it will come to me in time. Most things do, you know."

Moore nodded. "I know." He paused. "Will your army march into Jerusalem the same way you did?"

"I haven't the slightest idea," said Jeremiah. "But I rather suspect that I won't need them any longer. After all, you've presented me with a ready-made army."

"And what makes you think they'll accept orders from you?"

"Historic inevitability. If they don't take orders from me, then I can't establish my kingdom, can I? Unless we're to have a military bloodbath, that is—and I don't think God would want that. When all is said and done, I'm the Messiah of the *Old* Testament, and the Israeli Army represents a healthy chunk of God's chosen people."

"The wholesale slaughter of His chosen people never seemed to deter Him in the past," noted Moore dryly. "Forty days and forty nights of flooding wasn't exactly the act of a compassionate deity."

"True," responded Jeremiah. He shrugged. "Well, whatever I have to do, I'm sure the solution will dawn on me when the time is right. But right now I'm afraid I have a more immediate problem, Solomon."

"Oh?"

"What am I to do with a Forerunner who has outlived his usefulness?"

"What did you have in mind?" asked Moore warily.

"I'm not sure," admitted Jeremiah. "On the one hand, I'm certainly grateful that you accomplished your purpose so effectively. But on the other hand, you *have* been trying to kill me for four years. I realize that this was predestined, and that of course I can't be killed—but you did cause me an enormous amount of pain, Solomon. I certainly have to take that into consideration." He paused. "Have *you* any suggestions?"

"You're holding all the cards."

"True," agreed Jeremiah. "Well, I'll figure it out eventually. In the meantime, I suppose I'll let you hang around for a while. After all, you *are* my Forerunner. I owe you something for that, even if it's just another few days of existence. Just see to it that you don't leave the city."

"Thanks," said Moore ironically. "Well, who do you kill first? What city goes up in flames tomorrow—Jerusalem, or something inhabited by the infidels?"

"I think I'll play it by ear, Solomon. But this much I know: the ground will turn red with blood before I'm done. So it is written; so it must be." He finished his beer. "Now why don't you show me how the communications system works?"

He unlocked the door, and the two of them walked into the main office, where almost two dozen soldiers lay in a trancelike sleep.

"Ah!" said Jeremiah, his face lighting up with interest as he walked over to a bank of radios. "Look at all this lovely machinery. I've never understood computers and electrical systems, Solomon, but they have always impressed the hell out of me."

"What do you intend to do?" asked Moore.

"Address my people."

"They're forty miles away."

"You still don't understand," said Jeremiah. "*All* people are my people." He looked around the room. "Is there some public address system here?"

"Who do you want to reach?"

"The whole city."

"I suppose you'd have to rig the air-raid sirens to a microphone."

"And where is the control panel for the sirens?"

Moore pointed it out.

Jeremiah found the massive line that powered the sirens, ripped it out of the panel, and wrapped the exposed ends around a portable microphone that he appropriated from one of the radios.

"You'll electrocute yourself," said Moore.

Jeremiah merely laughed.

"At any rate, you'll never be able to turn *that* into a PA system."

"The Lord works in mysterious ways," said Jeremiah. "Turn the power on."

Moore flipped the appropriate switch.

"*MY PEOPLE!*" said Jeremiah, and Moore felt the building

vibrate as the earsplitting sound permeated the still night air of the city. *"I AM JEREMIAH, COME TO LAY CLAIM TO THAT WHICH IS MINE. PREPARE YOURSELVES! THE EARTH WILL CATCH FIRE, AND THE RIVERS WILL FLOW RED, AND NOT A BLADE OF GRASS WILL REMAIN STANDING! THE DAY OF THE LORD IS AT HAND!"*

26

The next morning—October 4, 2051—Jeremiah set up temporary headquarters in the penthouse of a luxury hotel on the outskirts of the Old City. He ordered a general amnesty for all Israeli citizens and soldiers who had opposed him.

Moore, who had spent the remainder of the night trying to assimilate what he had learned, made a pair of long-distance calls to Rabbi Milton Greene, bought a copy of the Talmud, and vanished from sight.

On October 5, Jeremiah issued orders that Moore was to be shot if he attempted to leave the city.

Moore remained in hiding.

On October 6, Jeremiah paid a visit to Prime Minister Weitzel and accompanied him to a closed cabinet meeting and an emergency session of the Knesset.

Moore remained in hiding, and waited.

On October 7, Jeremiah called a press conference and announced that he was abolishing the Knesset.

Moore remained in hiding, and waited.

On October 8, Jeremiah summoned two hundred of his own officers from the plains and hills beyond the city and put them in charge of the Israeli Army. The remainder of his followers were instructed to return to their homelands and await the further biddings of their Messiah.

Moore remained in hiding, and waited.

On October 9, Moira Rallings showed up. Ashen as ever, she remained at Jeremiah's side as he went about the business of consolidating the various branches of the government, making them more immediately responsive to his needs.

Moore remained in hiding, and waited.

On October 10, Jeremiah held another press conference and announced that he intended to make Moira his Queen. She looked as surprised as the reporters, but offered no objection.

Moore remained in hiding, and waited.

On October 11, Jeremiah executed some seven thousand Israeli men and women who still opposed him and offered an ultimatum to Syria, Jordan, Lebanon, and Egypt: accept his divinity and his authority, or suffer the consequences.

Moore remained in hiding, and waited.

On October 12, Jeremiah offered the same ultimatum to all other Middle East nations, and suggested that dissenters would do well to read the prophets of the Old Testament.

Moore remained in hiding, and waited.

On October 13 (which shunned historical tidiness by falling on a Wednesday rather than a Friday), Jeremiah presided at his own coronation in the ceremony that gave official sanction to the already acknowledged fact that Israel had crossed over the line from democracy to monarchy.

And Moore was all through waiting.

27

Jeremiah's penthouse, situated at the eastern edge of the Old City, overlooked the broad expanse of Dayan Boulevard. Moore took a cab to the front door of the building, walked across the tiled lobby, and was approaching an elevator when two soldiers barred his way.

"What's your business here?" demanded one of them.

"I'm here to see Jeremiah."

"I'm sorry, sir," said the soldier, "but Jeremiah is not seeing visitors."

"He'll see *me*," said Moore.

"No one is allowed upstairs without a priority pass."

"Why not phone him and tell him that Solomon Moody Moore is in the lobby?"

"Moore," repeated the soldier, frowning. "I know that name. There was some order concerning you."

"The phone?" repeated Moore.

The soldier stared at him for a moment, ordered his companion to keep an eye on him, and walked to a house phone. He returned less than a minute later.

"I'm sorry for the inconvenience, Mr. Moore. He'll see you immediately. Take the last elevator on the left; it goes directly to the penthouse."

Moore thanked him, entered the elevator, and emerged a few

seconds later on the top floor of the building, at the edge of a large, luxurious sitting room. Jeremiah was nowhere to be seen, but Moira Rallings was seated on a plush velvet sofa, reading a magazine.

"Hello, Moira," said Moore. "It's been a long time."

"Hello, Mr. Moore," she replied. "Have you read my book yet?"

"Hasn't everyone?" he responded with a smile.

"I want to apologize for some of the less flattering references to you," she said. "I had no idea who and what you were when I was writing it. Everything will be corrected in the revised edition."

"Your apology is accepted," said Moore, as Jeremiah, wearing a white silk robe, entered the room.

"Have a seat, Solomon," he said pleasantly. "I've been wondering what happened to you." He opened a bottle of wine and filled three glasses. "Care for a drink?"

Moore shook his head. "Why in the world would I want to drink with you?"

"To help me celebrate," answered Jeremiah. "After all, I couldn't have done it without you and my oversexed little Boswell here."

"And now that you've done it, have you decided what you're going to do with *me*?" asked Moore.

"I've been giving the matter considerable thought, Solomon," replied Jeremiah. "You seem to be a little different from the rest of the sheep. They all love me these days, but I get the distinct impression that you still nurture hostile feelings."

"Maybe they don't know how many people you intend to kill," said Moore.

"It's got to be done, Solomon," said Jeremiah easily. "Millions upon millions must die. But that's beside the point, said point being what I intend to do with you. I must confess that you are turning into an embarrassment to me. I mean, after all these years of futility, you still harbor thoughts of killing me. Don't bother to deny it; the bulge under your coat is unmistakable."

"You mean this?" asked Moore, withdrawing a wicked-looking revolver.

"What good would it do, Solomon?" laughed Jeremiah. "I can't be killed. Hell, I don't even have my soldiers inspect visitors for concealed weapons."

"I know. I made sure of that before I came."

"If you shoot me," continued Jeremiah, totally ignoring the revolver, "I'll lie near death for a day or two, and by the end of the week I'll be as good as new. And my retribution will be considerably harsher than what you did to me back in Cincinnati."

Moore shook his head and sighed. "When Moira writes of your last days on Earth, she's going to point out the basic tragedy of your nature: that your intelligence, despite its admittedly rapid gains, never quite caught up with the rest of you." He pulled a silencer out of his pocket and screwed it onto the muzzle of the gun.

"You're crazy!" snapped Jeremiah. "Nothing can kill me! You know that!"

"I've spent a lot of time thinking about that," said Moore. "That's why I've been avoiding you until today—because I didn't want you to force me to act before I was ready."

"What the hell are you talking about?" demanded Jeremiah.

"*Why* can't you be killed?" asked Moore, cocking the hammer.

"Because *nothing*—not you, not anyone, not anything—can stop me from establishing my kingdom in Jerusalem!"

"Very good, Jeremiah," said Moore, pointing the pistol at him. "And what particular event took place today?"

Jeremiah merely stared at him, wild-eyed, for a long moment. Then a look of dawning comprehension and terror slowly spread across his face.

"That's right, Jeremiah," said Moore softly. "And that's why I didn't want to see you before now. But as of this afternoon you are the King of Jerusalem, indeed of all Israel. You've done what you were destined to do, you've served your purpose and fulfilled the prophecies—and now you're fair game."

"No!" screamed Jeremiah. "It can't end like this! First the sword, then the fire, then—"

"An interesting theory," said Moore. "Let's put it to the test."

He fired the pistol.

Jeremiah staggered backward into a wall, clutched at the rapidly spreading red stain on his chest, and collapsed to the floor. He moaned twice, convulsed, and then lay still.

Moore walked over to him, picked up his hand, and felt for a pulse. There wasn't any. He put four more bullets into Jeremiah's temple, then turned to Moira.

"I made you a promise a long time ago," he said quietly. "Do you remember?"

Moira nodded, her eyes aglow with excitement.

"I'm keeping it now," said Moore. "He's all yours."

Moira scurried across the room, no trace of sorrow or remorse on her face, and knelt down beside Jeremiah's body. She lifted his bloody head to her lap and began stroking it passionately, murmuring words that Moore couldn't quite make out.

He watched her for a moment, grimaced, and then looked around for a telephone. He found one, and placed a call to Chicago.

"Pryor here," said a familiar voice a few minutes later.

"Hello, Ben."

"Solomon!" exclaimed Pryor. "How are things out there?"

"Everything's under control. I killed Jeremiah not five minutes ago."

"How?"

"I'll tell you all about it when I get home."

"Uh . . . Solomon?"

"Yes?"

"Maybe you'd better tell me about it on the phone."

"Trouble?"

"Not exactly . . . not for me. But I've waited a long time to sit in this chair, and I don't think I want to give it up."

"I see," said Moore softly.

"You always encouraged ambition, Solomon."

"I know I did, Ben."

"It's nothing personal," continued Pryor. "But as soon as I hang up the phone, I'm putting out a hit on you. It's *business*, Solomon."

"No hard feelings, Ben," replied Moore. "But you've just signed your own death warrant."

"We'll see, Solomon," said Pryor. "But for your own good, stay away. I've uncovered your spies and taken care of them, and I just entered into a partnership with Piper Black. He'll be putting out a hit, too."

"Fair enough, Ben," said Moore. "But you've got something that's mine, and I'm going to get it back."

"You're welcome to try."

"No quarter asked or given?"

"None," agreed Pryor, sounding just a little less sure of himself.

"I'll be seeing you soon, Ben," promised Moore.

He hung up the phone and walked to a window. Hundreds of soldiers and civilians were scurrying about their business, completely unaware of what had happened three hundred feet above their heads.

"Moira?"

"Yes, Mr. Moore," she said, wiping some of Jeremiah's blood from her face.

"I kept my promise to you. Now I want you to do me a favor."

"What favor, Mr. Moore?"

"Give me a six-hour head start before you tell anyone what happened in here. Will you do that?"

She looked down at Jeremiah's body for a moment, then met Moore's eyes. "Six hours," she said, nodding her head.

He took one last look at them, the corpse-lover and the corpse, and then, tucking the pistol into the back of his belt, he entered the elevator.

28

He stole a Land Rover that was parked near the building and drove to the southwest, passing into Egypt and continuing on for another four hours before he ran out of gas. Then he got out, pushed the vehicle into a small gorge, and started walking.

By midday the heat had become oppressive, and, slightly dehydrated, he climbed into the foothills of a nearby mountain, seeking out the slowly shifting shade. When darkness fell he decided to spend the night there rather than chance meeting his pursuers on foot in the desert. The temperature fell sharply, and he gathered some shrubbery and built a small fire, huddling over it to keep warm.

Finally he lay down, pillowing his head on his right arm, and went to sleep.

Sometime later he awoke with a start. The moon was directly overhead, the stars shone down brightly, and there was no trace of wind. Yet *something* had awakened him, and he got to his feet, prepared to search for intruders.

Then he noticed that one of the bushes he had set fire to some hours earlier was still burning, and he walked over to it. It shimmered with a cold glow and seemed to pulsate with energy.

And suddenly, within his head, he heard a voice speak out in stentorian tones.

WHY HAST THOU KILLED MY MESSIAH?

"Who are you?" demanded Moore.

I AM THAT I AM.

"I must be dreaming," he muttered to himself, looking into the shadows beyond the fire for a sign of life.

SOLOMON MOORE, WHY HAST THOU SPILLED THE BLOOD OF HIM THAT I SENT? The bush became brighter with each word.

"Where are you?"

I AM HERE, WHERE I HAVE ALWAYS BEEN, FOR BEFORE THIS WAS MOUNT SINAI IT WAS MOUNT HOREB,

AND IT WAS HERE THAT I SPAKE TO MOSHEH.

"Then why didn't you send someone like Moses?" said Moore bitterly. "Why a bloodthirsty fool like Jeremiah?"

I OWE YOU NO EXPLANATION. IT WAS ENOUGH THAT HE WAS THE ONE, AND YOU SLEW HIM.

"And I'd do it again!" snapped Moore. "Where were you when we needed you? Why didn't you send a little help during the Inquisition, or save your chosen people from the Nazis? What kept you?"

THOU HAST KILLED HIM.

The unspoken words grew louder, and the light of the fire became so bright that Moore couldn't look at it.

"Yes, I killed him!" yelled Moore in a cold fury. "But *you* chose him. Which of us is guiltier?"

I HEREBY ANNUL MY COVENANT WITH MAN! NEVER AGAIN SHALL I CONCERN MYSELF WITH YOUR AFFAIRS.

"We'll get by!" Moore shouted at the skies. "We got along just fine when you were too busy to bother with us, and we'll get along now!"

There was no answer, and, unable to sleep, he wandered through the foothills for the remainder of the night. Then, as the sun began rising, he stepped out into the desert.

The coming days and months and years weren't going to be easy ones. Pryor controlled what was left of his organization, and probably had fifty hired killers out after him already. Black would have fifty more. Behind him an entire nation would be mobilizing its army for the sole purpose of finding and executing him. Thirty million people across the face of the planet would be screaming for his blood.

But, regardless of their numbers, they were just people, and he had made his fortune by his ability to manipulate them. He thought of the events of the past two days, of what he had done and what company he had kept, then raised his eyes and sought out the horizon.

Somewhere out there, beyond the vast expanse of desert, was the Gulf of Aqaba. Beyond that was the Red Sea, and the Suez Canal, and a way home. Along the way he would have to evade tens of thousands of enemies and reclaim a financial empire. But at least he wouldn't die of boredom—and in this day and age, on this world that he had inadvertently helped to shape, that was sufficient.

He took a deep breath, released it slowly, and began walking.

He looked forward to the challenge.

Interview With the Almighty

*R*ESNICK: I'M SITTING HERE WITH GOD IN SID & Sylvia's 5-Star Deli. The tape recorder's on, and we're ready to go.

GOD: Relax. Have a knosh. They tell me the chopped liver is outstanding.

RESNICK: Can you tell me why you've agreed to this interview, after being silent for so long?

GOD: I hadn't realized that no one knew how to write the last time I gave one.

RESNICK: Can you tell us a little about your background?

GOD: Sure. In the beginning, I created the heavens and the earth.

RESNICK: Speaking of creation, Bertrand Russell once remarked that telling a child that "God made you" implied another question, which is "Who made God?"

GOD: That Bertie! What a card!

RESNICK: Then you don't mind if I ask it?

GOD: Ask what?

RESNICK: Who made you?

GOD: I just *hate* questions like that. And by the way, how come your name is all in caps, just like mine?

RESNICK: I'm tape-recording this. How did you know my name would be in caps?

GOD: I'm God, remember?

Resnick: No offense intended.

GOD: That's better.

Resnick: So tell me about the Big Bang.

GOD: It happened very fast. If you blinked, you'd have missed it.

Resnick: That's *it*? That's all you've got to say about it?

GOD: What do you want? No one invented the Polaroid camera for another fifteen billion years.

Resnick: If you're God, you could have invented it any time.

GOD: And if you're so smart, you could have bought Polaroid at eight and a quarter.

Resnick: What was here before the Big Bang?

GOD: Everything. But it was all kind of scrunched up. You know how it takes you a pair of nine-hour plane trips to get to Kenya? Back then you could have made it in a nanosecond. Well, maybe two nanoseconds.

Resnick: Why did you create the universe?

GOD: Beats the hell out of me.

Resnick: How can you forget? After all, you're *God*!

GOD: That's me — mysterious, unfathomable, unknowable. It can be quite a strain at times.

Resnick: By the way, is there something else I should be calling you?

GOD: Like what?

Resnick: Isn't your name YHWH?

GOD: You're kidding, right? How do you pronounce a name with no vowels (unless you're light-heavyweight champion Bobby Czyz, and there have been nights even *he* couldn't pronounce it after getting punched in the head for ten or twelve rounds).

Resnick: Well, they say it's pronounced Yahweh — but they also say that anyone who utters it will be destroyed.

GOD: Silliest thing I ever heard.

Resnick: Then it's not true?

GOD: Not a bit of it. I see what happened: they screwed it up translating it from Aramaic to Greek to Latin and then into English.

Resnick: So people can call you Yahweh without being destroyed?

GOD: Of course. Yahweh I don't mind at all. Call me *Chubby* and I'll destroy you.

Resnick: Like you destroyed Sodom and Gomorrah?

GOD: That's right—blame *me* because they had substandard building codes.

Resnick: What about the flood?

GOD: I give up. What *about* the flood?

Resnick: Why did you cause it?

GOD: How do I know? It was a long time ago. Maybe I was having a bad hair day.

Resnick: You're not being very responsive.

GOD: You're asking too many negative questions. Ask something positive.

Resnick: Okay. What are Man's three greatest accomplishments?

GOD: Let me see . . . Well, the discovery of fire has to be one. And I think I'd have to say the Renaissance—I mean, Leonardo and Michelangelo and that whole crowd. And the third would be the Designated Hitter rule.

Resnick: You're kidding!

GOD: I never joke. But okay, you don't like my answer, I'm not gonna argue. Substitute the flush toilet for the Renaissance.

Resnick: Moving right along, I've got a question that I think is on many of our readers' minds these days.

GOD: One of the usual, I suppose?

Resnick: The usual?

GOD: Why do all the elevators arrive at once? Why can't any adults open a childproof bottle? How come there was an Upper Volta but there was never a Lower Volta? One of those.

Resnick: No, as a matter of fact, it wasn't any of those. But now that you mention it, why *wasn't* there a Lower Volta?

GOD: You know, I got so tired of hearing that one, I changed Upper Volta's name to Burkina Faso. Now, what was your question?

Resnick: You're God, right? Perfection personified. So how did you manage to create both Richard Nixon and Bill Clinton?

GOD: Give me a break. Do *you* win a Hugo for every story you write?

Resnick: No, but . . .

GOD: Besides, do you think it was just Nixon and Clinton? Everyone's flawed.

Resnick: Everyone?

GOD: Name one that isn't.

Resnick: How about Albert Einstein?

GOD: Einstein couldn't make a free throw to save his life.

Resnick: Madam Curie.

GOD: Do you know how many times she trumped her partner's ace?

Resnick: Sophia Loren.

GOD: Okay, you got me. But *most* of my creations are flawed.

Resnick: Why, if you're God?

GOD: If you wrote the perfect book, would you ever write another?

Resnick: I don't know.

GOD: Neither do I. But I have a feeling I wouldn't. After all, I made five Marx Brothers and all those damned Kennedys, but I only made one Sophia Loren. What a dish!

Resnick: That hardly sounds godly.

GOD: I can't admire a pretty girl? Hell, I created every pretty girl you ever saw.

Resnick: Well, as long as you brought up the subject, what was Mary like?

GOD: I had an inappropriate relationship with her, and that's all I'm going to say.

Resnick: An inappropriate relationship?

GOD: Yeah, that's a legally accurate description.

Resnick: People have been arguing for two thousand years about whether Jesus was your son or not. Maybe you can clear that up?

GOD: They didn't have DNA testing back then, did they?

Resnick: No.

GOD: Then go talk to my lawyer. I have nothing further to say on the subject. Now, have you got any more questions before I leave?

Resnick: Have you any words of wisdom for our readers?

GOD: Of course I do. I'm God.

Resnick: So what's your advice?

GOD: Never draw to an inside straight. Never bet a front-runner who's moving up in class on a muddy track. Watch out for overly aggressive redheads name Thelma. And always go to your basement during a tornado watch.

Resnick: That's *it*? God comes down for the first time in thousands of years, and that's all you've got to tell your people?

GOD: Okay, what the hell, I'll give you one more: buy low, sell high, and stay out of commodities unless you can afford to take some heavy losses.

Resnick: Thanks. I guess.

GOD: You're welcome.
Resnick: I'll see you around.
GOD: Fat chance.
Resnick: I didn't mean in this life.
GOD: Neither did I.

✤ ✤ ✤

A Few Blasphemous Words

UPON PICKING UP THIS MIKE RESNICK COLLEC-tion, some of you might have simply assumed this book was filled with blasphemous stories about religion based on reading the title. Well, the fact that they make you question what you believe and what you are told means that, yes, they are. But by the time you have reached my afterword you will have also discovered that this collection comprises so much more than that; it showcases Mike's diverse writing talents and his ability to connect to his readers on topics that effect us all.

Within this book you will have journeyed through the humorous, serious, and thought-provoking, and even confronted pieces that all use the element of religion in some way to make the readers ask themselves: to what degree do our spiritual beliefs define who we are on a fundamental level, or how we react to pivotal situations in our life? Mike questions this through science fiction or fantasy settings that open our minds to all the possible permutations in life, showing us it is all simply a matter of perspective.

After working with Mike on our collaborations and getting to know the man behind the writing, I've discovered some insights into his own religious beliefs. I know that he's a lifelong atheist. I also know that he has enormous respect for religion for the good it can do (although he also acknowledges the not-so-good), and he would love to believe that there is forgiveness for his sins or an afterlife with a benevolent god—but he doesn't. It does mean however that he had no problem writing *The Branch*, because he believes all religion to be just as fictitious as the story, and so to him, writing it wasn't blasphemous.

In *The Branch* we are not even asked to question if the Messiah actually exists (which would be blasphemous to a lot of people), but rather to explore the consequences of blind faith. What if we did discover a man who unequivocally fits all the parameters of the prophesized Messiah, but whose actions make him more of a danger to the human race than the Savior he was believed to be? *Should* he be the Messiah simply because the religious texts decree he fulfilled a prophecy?

Mike explores this by his inclusion of another character in the book who would clearly benefit from atoning for his multitude of sins. Evident from the murderous way he created his financial and business empire, he will stop at nothing to prevent this Messiah from taking power and money away from him. However, although he is overtly acknowledged as the "bad guy" in the book, it's through his eyes we grow to see that the Messiah is not a model leader himself. Mike could have shown us this by having a counterpart character who was inherently good, to show us through comparison how the Messiah didn't deserve his title. But the realization of how dangerous the Messiah truly is is all the more striking through witnessing his battle with a man who is equally as callous and deadly. And we ultimately realize that the Messiah is *more* dangerous, because of the blind faith of so many religious followers supporting him.

Walpurgis III also shows us how blind faith (not necessarily religion) can hinder our survival as a race. In this piece Mike created a Satanist world whose people have formed religious covens that worship the devil or some other Satanic icon, their lives revolving around rituals and superstitions. But when someone truly evil comes to their world and sets up shop—a serial killer who massacres entire cities under the guise of their religious icons—how can they say they didn't really want a Satanic aspirant spilling blood within their temples and towns without going against all their beliefs? Their government can't physically remove him because doing so would be considered blasphemous and go against everything the world has worked centuries to create.

So what do they do? They hire an assassin to kill him, enabling

Mike to juxtapose two characters whose perceptions of success and moral ethics are completely different based on their life experiences and beliefs, subtly asking us who is more evil: a compulsive killer who murders *en masse* under the guise of religion, loving to torture his victims brutally before they die, or the assassin hired by the "Good Guys" to rid the world of the mass murderer, who wouldn't hesitate to kill anyone—even a colleague—if it got him closer to obtaining his goal. At the start of the book we are rooting for the assassin, seeing his victim as a "just" kill, but by the end Mike has subtly shown us that there is no difference between the man who kills because he loves to see others suffer, or the one who will kill cleanly without malice, simply because it is the easiest way to aid him in reaching his target. Both are murderers. Both could justify committing murders because of their personal beliefs.

It didn't make either of them right.

This was subtly shown to us in two very different ways. One was through the inclusion of a secondary character who worked for the law, who desperately wanted a brutal serial killer neutralized but was then confronted by the actions of the assassin who was meant to be helping him. Through the evolution of his thought processes in the story Mike was able to talk directly to us, and like the character we start to question the actions of both killers and start weighing up whether committing a lesser evil to combat a greater evil can be justified as any less wrong.

The second, even more subtle way Mike got us to question who was the more evil—or indeed, the more dangerous—was through the quotes he inserted at the start of each chapter. He quoted from both of the killers, showing how very different their approach was to life (or as often was the case, their approach to death). The serial killer appeared deranged, malicious and thus unpredictable, the assassin more measured and methodical, thus seeming less dangerous from the onset. However, as each chapter passed and we discovered more about each man, their quotes started to echo each other, to eventually become exactly the same by the closing of the book. This showed us that even if their motivations were different, their individual actions held no less malevolent intent for their victims; absolute power in anyone's hands can be dangerous.

Which brings me to "The Pale Thin God", my favorite story in this collection and also one of the shortest. Jesus is known by two billion people as being the One True God. But how would other Gods see his reign over mankind? Mike explores that in this poignant short piece by judging the consequences of Jesus' divinity. The fact that the other Gods ultimately bow to him at the end of the piece is quite disturbing (and very thought-provoking). Not because Mike wrote something that disagreed with what's laid out in the Bible, but because of the equally plausible, but completely different way the African Gods perceived his reign.

This story and the other ones mentioned above have the ability to make us look deeper into ourselves and consider the effect our perceptions have on the decisions we make. And if questioning our individual beliefs and their ramifications is considered blasphemous, then I think that everyone could to with a little more blasphemy in their lives.

I'm having blasphemous thoughts right now. How about you?

Lezli Robyn
October 2009

Three thousand copies of this book have been printed by the Maple-Vail Book Manufacturing Group, York, PA, for Golden Gryphon Press, Urbana, IL. The typeset is Electra with Diskus Medium display, printed on 55# Sebago. Typesetting by The Composing Room, Inc, Kimberly, WI.